FAST, CLEAN, DEADLY

Tonto's gorge rose as he felt the death spasms of the youthful enemy under his knee. The kid thrashed and shuddered, then went still. Tonto pulled his knife from the wound and wiped it on the black jacket worn by the VC. Only then did he break his total concentration to look around.

Four more VC in various positions of repose stared at him. The kill had taken less than thirty seconds. Now they seemed galvanized by the death of their comrade. Everyone made a dive for a weapon.

All around Tonto the jungle erupted in a roar of gunfire. Reflexes flung bodies of the dying VC in every direction. Over the fusillade, Tonto heard the voice of Zoro Agilar. *Viva Zapata! Viva Pancho Villa! Arribaarriba!*

Jesus! The kid had gone nuts. It had the desired effect on the surviving VC, though. They froze in position long enough to die at the hands of the SEALs.

The firefight, one-sided as it had been, lasted only another half minute. Even the howl of disturbed monkeys and the screech of rudely awakened birds died out, to leave an eerie silence.

AVON BOOKS, INC.
1350 Avenue of the Americas
New York, New York 10019

Copyright © 1998 by Bill Fawcett & Associates
Published by arrangement with Bill Fawcett & Associates
Visit our website at **http://www.AvonBooks.com**
Library of Congress Catalog Card Number: 97-94763
ISBN: 0-380-78713-X

First Avon Books Printing: June 1998

AVON TRADEMARK REG. U.S. PAT. OFF. AND IN OTHER COUNTRIES, MARCA REGISTRADA, HECHO EN U.S.A.

Printed in the U.S.A.

WCD   10 9 8 7 6 5 4 3 2 1

Acknowledgments

The authors would like to acknowledge and thank the following for their unstinting assistance given to make the court-martial scenes accurate in detail. In particular, the officers and enlisted of the Trial Office of the Staff Judge Advocate, Fort Riley, Kansas, and especially to Janice Scales of that office. Particular thanks and gratitude go to Colonel Jim Mogridge, military Trial Judge from Fort Carson, Colorado, and Dr. Tom Tomes, of Chicago, Illinois. Any errors or omissions contained in this work are the fault of the authors alone.

Mark K. Roberts
Chief James Watson
Fort Pierce, Florida

SEALS
TOP SECRET #2
Operation: Shoot and Scoot

CHAPTER 1 ⸻

NOW THIS is what he called duty! A cool breeze off the South China Sea kept the sun warm on his bare chest as he lay back against a mound of pale amber sand and sipped from an icy can of Miller. The beer tasted great, not like that local swill, *Bahmibah*, the Vietnamese imitation of the notoriously lousy French brew, "45," which the sandy-haired Yeoman First Class Kent Welby had never tasted. Down the beach a ways, music came from a battery-powered radio.

A Beatles song. Seated by it, a Riverine sailor, also on R&R liberty, chorded a guitar along with Paul McCartney, while Ringo Starr did his usual on the drums. Doc Welby liked the Beatles. Their songs were about things he had experienced in the world. At least the world before he came to Vietnam. Lately, though, they had gotten into that protest shit. Maybe he would have to find another band to listen to. Doc Welby raised his head to reveal handsome, youthful features, and took another swig. He cast his gray-eyed gaze along the beach, filled to capacity by the newlies among the River Tigers. The Riverine Force had rotated two boat companies and some technicians.

They were the lucky ones, Doc thought to himself. Not here a week and already soaking up the rays and hitting the water. Doc had gotten to know one of them: Jorge

Rodriguez. From New Mexico of all places. Who had ever heard of a sailor from the desert? Rodriguez was down the beach about a hundred yards with a couple of his buddies. He raised a red-and-white can of Budweiser and waved to Doc. Welby gestured back. Usually on liberty, guys stuck with their own. As a SEAL, Kent Welby hung around with other SEALs.

The elite Sea, Air, and Land special warfare units of the Navy had been in existence for only six years under that designation. In that time, they had racked up some impressive history. Even without Vietnam, enough hot spots existed around the world that required the special talents of the former Underwater Demolition Team members who had become SEALs. Kent Welby had always felt enormous pride in being a SEAL. He even stood up for the Team when his membership caused a frightful rift between himself and his wife, Betty. The SEALs and the Team came first, Kent had insisted. The best of the best, with far more training in underwater operations than the Force Recon Marines, or the Blanketheads of Army Special Forces.

SEALs operated under or on the surface, could come at the enemy by helicopter or parachute, and fought on land like any combat troops. It had given them their name, and the acronym; SEAL. Jorge Rodriguez had confided to Doc Welby that he had applied for the UDT/R school, but had to make his rating first, a bitter disappointment to many who had listened to the honeyed words of a recruiter, instead of learning what the regulations required. Silently, Doc Welby wished his new friend the best of luck in his quest.

Jorge Rodriguez lay back in the warm sand and watched big, puffy clouds laze by in an azure sky. The feeling he had been shafted by the recruiter had diminished considerably by the time he had been accepted for Boathandlers

School. As a coxswain, he knew he had a rating. All he need do is make some rank, and he would reapply for BUDS training. Rank came fast in a combat zone. That much he had learned the first day at the Riverine base at Tre Noc, in the Mekong Delta.

God! Fighting in a jungle. Jorge envied the SEALs their easy attitude, and stood in awe of the flat, far-off, killer look in their eyes. Or did he just imagine that? New Mexico was never like this. Rodriguez loved the seashore. As a child, his father had taken him, along with his six brothers and sisters, to Padre Island, Texas, in the Gulf of Mexico. A week of absolute paradise, far from the desert rocks and sand of his home. The image of those waves never left him. Three days after graduating high school, Jorge Rodriguez joined the United States Navy. Jorge flashed a white smile in his dark brown, strongly Indian face and drank deeply of his Budweiser, grateful for the ample supply, iced down in fifty-five-gallon drums strewn along the beach. None of that sour-tasting *Bahmibah*, the local brew. Even if they could not have booze aboard its ships, the Navy looked out for its men on shore. Could war get any better than this? Jorge Rodriguez doubted it.

Jorge Rodriguez suddenly lost his confidence in this peaceful vista, ruined by a fluttery sound that warbled down through the azure sky. Belatedly, came a cry from one of the old hands on sentry duty. "In-n-n co-o-o-m-m-i-i-ngggg!"

The finned bombs began to explode, ruining his brief taste of paradise.

Pandemonium erupted on the beach as huge gouts of sand, black now from the exploding powder in the mortar bombs, were flung skyward. The dull crump of bursting shells all but drowned out the screams of the wounded. Men and body parts flew in a hail of shrapnel. Doc Welby

had experience enough to run in the direction from which
the mortar rounds had been fired. Many of the others did
likewise. The new men, particularly among the Riverine
Force, crisscrossed the paths of one another in their anx-
iety to escape from the deluge of deadly ordnance.

Doc Welby angled toward the Shore Patrol jeep used
by the security force that policed the beach recreation
area. A helmeted SP in the rear seat yelled into the handset of a radio. As Welby neared, he could hear the man
clearly.

"Watchdog, this is Beach Blanket. We are under mortar attack. Over."

Crisply, the reply came through a scratchy speaker
from the USS *Burton Daniels*, a destroyer cruising offshore in the South China Sea. "Roger, Beach Blanket. I
copy a mortar attack. Gunfire Support is on it now. We
should have them ranged in a short. Over."

"Better make it goddamned short, Watchdog, or there
ain't gonna be any of us left out here. Beach Blanket,
out." He turned to the SEAL. "Whadda you make of
that? Sparks there sits on his fat ass, miles from Charlie
Cong, and tells us to hang in there."

Doc Welby still grasped his 9mm, MP-43 *Schmeisser*
submachine gun. He nodded to it as he spoke. "There's
a squad of SEALs on the beach, Chief. We could go find
Charlie for you."

"Don't bother. There's gonna be some five-inchers
coming over anytime now," the Chief Master at Arms
responded.

That jerked Doc's attention toward the sea. In the distance, hidden by a low layer of mist, he saw some flashes,
followed shortly by the muted rumble of muzzle blasts
over the water. *Write paid for the friggin' VC*, he thought
darkly.

*   *   *

On board the USS *Burton Daniels*, DD-271, the call for help arrived during a routine hosing and scraping session for the Deck Division. Counterbattery radar quickly targeted the flight path of the mortar rounds, and calculated their point of origin. Simultaneously, the call went over the speaker system for the forward turret personnel to man their battle stations. General Quarters rang out a second later. Every sailor on board dropped what he was doing and hauled ass.

Within a frenzied two minutes of the first mortar shell exploding on the R&R beach, the guns in the forward turret were manned and ready. The solution came down from the counterbattery plot room, the turret swiveled, the barrels elevated. After a tense moment, the heart-stopping blast of the twin five-inch naval rifles filled the air. Wobbly smoke rings formed around lances of flame from each muzzle. The heavy shells sped on their way.

With twin packages of relief on the way, men still scrambled frantically on the beach to escape the deluge of mortar shells that continued to fall on them. Jorge Rodriguez saw the SEALs he recognized dashing into the tree line, headed toward what must be the direction from which the mortar rounds came. It had to be. Only then did Jorge realize that he was still holding his rifle, an M-16.

A good enough popgun for open-country fighting, he had heard it described by many. But not so hot in thick jungle. Its only advantage lay in its weight, or rather the lack of it. Not like his father's M-1 Gerrand. Now, that snortin' old .30-06 could punch right through a coconut tree. Some of the guys, Jorge knew, did a brisk business in swapping their M-16s with the pint-sized Vietnamese in ARVN (Army of the Republic of Vietnam), who still carried M-1s. But, what the hell, Jorge thought. He'd been issued the M-16, so he had better stick with it. It might earn him some points if he went along and helped wipe out the Cong with the mortars, he reasoned. Behind him a shell burst, and he heard screams from two unlucky sailors. Something hot stung the back of his left thigh.

Jorge ignored it. He pushed on into the jungle. It was all he could do to keep the bare back of Kent Welby in sight. The Yeoman First Class moved quietly as a snake through the trailing vines and low cabbage palms. Jorge sensed his own clumsy advance and tried to quiet his thrashing through the bush. He was getting damned thirsty, Jorge noted. The odor of beer oozed from his pores. His mouth went dry, and his vision blurred for a second.

Next thing Jorge knew, he was down on one knee. What the hell had happened? Looking around, Jorge noted how dark it got under the shade of the three-tiered jungle growth above. Darker than he thought it should. Then the scenery began to spin around him and he fell heavily onto one shoulder. Head turned so he could see behind him, Jorge Rodriguez saw a trail of red splotches. He'd been bleeding like a stuck hog. That was Jorge's last thought in the fleeting moment before he blacked out.

"Hold it here," Chief Tom Waters called out softly to the men of First Squad, First Platoon, of Team 2 SEALs. "Let those shells get over us first."

Over his last word came the railroad roar of two five-inch shells ripping a path through the air. They had reached the apex of their arc and now plummeted earthward. Tonto Waters estimated they would impact some six hundred meters ahead of them. Moments later they did, creating a turmoil of their own.

Chad Ditto, who had only recently been replaced as the official "kid" SEAL of the platoon, and Archie Golden started to head off as the sound of the explosion rumbled around them. "Hold it. They'll lob at least a couple more for a safety."

No sooner had he cautioned the others than Tonto heard the faint onrush of more shells. A tremendous uproar came from ahead when they crashed down onto the target. Almost on top of the second pair, came a third salvo. Huge gouts of dirt and tree trunks rose in the air. Clods still rained down when Tonto said with a grin:

"Let's move out."

"There's someone back there, Tonto," Kent Welby spoke up, pointing.

Without replying, Tonto retraced his steps to where Jorge Rodriguez lay on the matted vegetation of the jungle. Tonto bent and examined his pale, green-tinged face. "It's that River Tiger newlie friend of yours, Doc. He's out cold."

Doc quickly scanned the bush while joining Tonto. "I don't see Fil Nicholson anywhere. What are we gonna do about it?"

Tonto considered it a moment. "We can't leave him here. And we'll play hell taking him along. Take Chad and get him back to the beach. He's lost a lot of blood, so put a pressure bandage on him, then haul out of here."

"Yeah," responded Doc thoughtfully as he looked at the bloody hole in Jorge's leg. "Shrapnel fragment. That leaves three of you to go on."

"No sweat," Tonto answered cheerfully. "One of 'em's Archie, right?"

Doc Welby grinned. "You've got that right, Tonto."

When Doc had first come to Team 2, and to First Platoon, Archie Golden had already been a legend. The carroty-haired Archie, the oldest man in the squad, had a fixation on things that went *Boom!* When the naval-ordnance people failed to give him exactly what he wanted, Archie invented things to use as explosives. Married and the father of three, Archie was reputed to be the most faithful man in the SEALs, if not the whole Navy. Yet, he threw all restraint out the porthole when it came to demolitions.

Not caution, Doc Welby reminded himself. Archie always handled explosives with the respect they deserved. Although, Doc had to admit, Archie didn't shrink from popping off some of his jewels uncomfortably close to friendly bodies. *His* friendly body in particular, Kent recalled from their recent search and destroy mission.

Doc and Chad reached the beach to find it in a shambles. Fil Nicholson, their platoon medic, and two hospital corpsmen from the Riverine Force worked with incredible calm on the wounded. Chad Ditto swallowed hard, and his voice croaked when he spoke.

"I've seen my share of blood, but it always gets to me when it's from our own guys."

"I know what you mean, Repeat. Let's get Rodriguez taken care of and see what we can do to help."

They soon learned there wasn't much to do. After twenty minutes crawled by without any sound of gunfire in the jungle, Doc began to worry about his teammates. He needn't have. When the familiar, burly figure of Tonto Waters emerged from the line of trees and low brush, Doc trotted over to him.

"What did you find?"

Stocky, and built close to the ground, with thick shoulders and arms, Tom Waters was considered a SEAL's SEAL. A grim smile accompanied Tonto's gallows humor. "Bits and pieces. Those five-inch shells blew the hell outta those Cong. Good thing that tin can was out there."

"You got that right, Tonto. What now?"

Tonto Waters looked hard at Doc Welby and pulled an even grimmer smile. "One guess as to who gets the job of finding the VC who are doing this."

*   *   *

Captain Stuart Ackerage put down the handset of the secure line to Saigon. He looked across the short space between his desk and the chair occupied by his S-2, LCDR Barry Lailey. Ackerage found it hard to believe that Lailey had once been a SEAL. Several years of sailing a desk had made him soft, unlike other old SEALs, with a substantial gut pushing him away from his paperwork. He was slope-shouldered and balding, with a premature gray fringe around a growing bare pate. A lazy fan hummed above them, moving the humid air at Binh Thuy with casual indifference. Captain Ackerage licked his lips and spoke in a low tone.

"Barry, there's been another mortar attack on a recreational beach. Fortunately the *Burton Daniels* was offshore at the time. Damnit, Charlie has been getting entirely too excellent a quality of intel on the beaches where our personnel are taking in-country R and R."

"I'd say the time has come to put a stop to it. Three beaches hit in less than a week," Lailey growled.

"You're right. And the men best suited to the job are those of First Platoon, Team Two SEALs. Get with the S-Three and draw up an Op Advisory for Marino's men."

LCDR Lailey smiled inwardly. *Once more in harm's way for you, Marino,* he gloated. Outwardly, he made do with a nod and few words. "Right away. Vocal order be okay?"

"For now, yes. But get the work started on a written operations order," the captain responded.

Sunlight filtered through the tall trees in golden spears. Two dozen sailors lounged on the beach. The cooks had rigged up a split fifty-five-gallon drum as a grill and several broiled hamburgers over the flames, which they doused with beer from the ample supply when they became too rambunctious. The aroma of cooking meat and woodsmoke spurred appetites for everyone.

A burly Chief had come to his feet and began to amble toward the food when the first flutters of mortar rounds could be heard above. Four shells descended on the unsuspecting sailors. One landed so close it almost tore the Chief apart. Four more came in, then another deadly quartet. The beach security put in a hurried call for support. Men scattered everywhere in an attempt to evade the warbling destruction that rained down.

Within three minutes, the guns of a destroyer offshore had been sighted by counterbattery radar and opened fire. Within that time twenty mortar shells struck the beach. Then sudden silence reigned. Charlie had broken off.

"What the hell?" asked the Chief in charge of security. "They've never done that before. Not from the reports I've read, anyway."

"Charlie's getting smart. No way they want to get blown to bits," suggested a Marine gunnery sergeant assigned to the security detail.

"Whatever it is, it means trouble for our guys," the Chief opined. "If we can't nail 'em with Gunfire Support, we're gonna be in some deep shit."

Chief Waters's prediction proved only too accurate. The SEALs had been back at Tre Noc for only two days when Lt. Carl Marino called a platoon briefing. For once, the map displayed on the wall of the platoon bar—the most convenient location for a daytime briefing—was of "friendly" territory. Circled in red were three beach areas. Pope Marino wasted no time in getting to the point.

"You all know from personal experience that Charlie has been hitting our R and R beaches. Five, counting the one today. We've been given a verbal alert to undertake a mission of hunting down the VC responsible and taking at least a couple of prisoners for interrogation. We don't know how Charlie is learning what beach we use, but we have to assume that they will know which one will be next. The trouble is, on the hit today, the VC pulled a Bedouin. They folded their tents and boogied, before any Gunfire Support could be directed onto their positions," Marino explained.

"It's my guess," he went on, "that they have spotters, or they have acquired a radar of their own. So, it figures that this verbal alert is going to be followed by an operations order for a mission to find out what is going on and to stop it. You won't be restricted to the base until the actual op order comes down. But, don't plan any long trips anywhere. I'd say we can expect it tomorrow."

CHAPTER 2 ⎯⎯⎯⎯⎯⎯⎯⎯⎯⎯⎯⎯

THIS IMPENDING mission did not sit well with YO/1C Kent Welby. He had problems "big-time" and no way to solve them appeared to him. Still no word from Betty about the divorce. Which made his situation with Francie Song all the more doubtful. He spent the rest of his duty hours stewing over it. When they were told at last to stand down, he hurried off base and down to the Vietnamese village that had sprung up outside of Tre Noc. There he took the quickest route to Doc Tri Alley, and along the narrow, twisting street to the My Flower Laundry.

Operated by a congenial mammasan, Rose Throh, the establishment actually did do laundry. It also featured a small bar, with a dime-sized stage, a wind-up Victrola, and the inevitable boom box battery-powered radio. Here, the steady stream of customers could buy beer, rice wine, and occasionally some black-market scotch. Today, Doc Welby became the first SEAL in the place. He was to meet Francie Song here after she got off work in the Special Operations office of the Riverine Detachment. And he wanted to fortify himself for the ordeal he knew it would become when he told her of their impending mission.

Doc had lifted his second beer to drain the dregs when Francie entered My Flower. Although barely two inches over five feet, Francie commanded attention whenever she entered a room. She had a striking figure, that had taken away the breath of Kent Welby at first sight. She affected him the same way now. Her long, glossy black hair had been pulled back into a thick, luxurious ponytail that swung freely with each intriguing sway of her enticing hips. Her generous lips formed a broad smile that lighted her amber eyes. She crossed the floor directly to where Doc sat at a small table.

"You are early," she pouted. "How many beers have you drank—er—drinked?"

"Drunk," Doc corrected her English.

Francie gave him an accusatory look. "You are? Already?"

Doc laughed. "No. That's the proper verb form. Drink—drank—drunk."

Those luscious lips formed a small moue. "Oh, yes, I see now."

His mood sobered at once, Doc opened his mouth to tell her the news. An invisible hand clutched his throat and he make only a squawking sound. Francie sat and extended long, supple fingers to lightly touch his bare forearm. "I know. I saw it in the operations office. You are on alert for a mission."

"Yes . . . but . . . how did you . . . ?"

"I work there now, thanks to you, *mon cher*. You *do* remember that, don't you?"

"Of . . . course I do." Doc lapsed into a frowning silence, unable, or unwilling, to go on. Francie read him clearly.

"But that's not the only thing troubling you, is it?"

"No, Francie. No, it's not."

"Are you going to tell me?" she asked coyly.

"I meant to. Only it's so hard to start. It's . . . about my wife. She has yet to send the divorce papers. We— we're still married."

Pain in her heart and spirit brought a deep furrow to Francie's high, smooth brow. "But it is over between you two, isn't it, Kent?"

Francie, Doc knew, was determined that his marriage was over and his love for Betty dead. That was truer than she knew. But the reality was that he and Betty were still married, and that made his relationship with Francie adulterous. Which made what he intended to say all the more difficult. Another look at her lovely face, grooved with concern, obliterated his intentions.

"Yes—yes, of course it is," he blurted.

Francie brightened at once. "Then take me to dinner at Phon Bai and then we can go to my apartment. Thran is staying with the woman of the herbalist."

Thran was Francie's eighteen-month-old son. The herbalist was an herb doctor who ran the Chinese apothecary shop on the ground floor below Francie's apartment. For the first time, Doc Welby had to give this consideration. He relented quickly, though, with one look at the appeal in her features and the sound of her voice.

"All right. I have to go back, though. The alert and all."

"I will miss you. I had hoped we could spend the whole night together, to celebrate my first month of working in Special Operations."

"We can do that when this mission is over. It shouldn't take long."

Francie finished a glass of wine, brought to her by Rose Throh, and they left for the restaurant. Phon Bai had a disreputable appearance from the outside. The entrance was lighted by a single, twenty-five-watt bulb that put out a feeble, yellow glow. Three heavily worn steps led down to the doorway. Doc held the portal open for Francie and they entered.

Inside, the restaurant bore no resemblance to the exterior. Chains of bright Oriental lanterns hung along each wall and dipped in low arcs across the center of the room. Handmade tables, in a riot of pastel colors, sported real cloth accessories, the napkins peaked in the precise center of each place setting. Small dishes, like miniature Japanese headrests, supported pairs of chopsticks. Beside them were the ladle-shaped Oriental spoons and, as a concession to some of the Western items on the menu, knives.

Lithograph posters of peaceful countryside scenes further decorated the walls. A large, oval, bevel-edged mirror, cracked at one end, reflected the light of the lanterns. The head waiter led the way to their usual table and seated Francie with a flourish. He bowed low and produced a pad to take their drink order.

"Beer," Doc ordered. "Tiger or Saporo if you still have some."

"Oh, yes, *M'sieu* Welby."

"White wine, please," Francie ordered in Vietnamese.

They waited in silence until the drinks had been delivered and the head waiter whisked off to greet more new arrivals. After a first, satisfying swallow, Francie took up the question of Betty and the divorce. Doc dreaded what he knew he would have to say.

"Yes. It's true what I said at My Flower. Our marriage is over in my mind, and I'm sure in hers. She's . . . just someone I once knew. Yet, until she files for divorce we are still married. That makes what—you and I are doing . . ."

"Wait!" Francie ejected urgently. "Don't say it. Please don't use that word."

"Francie, it only makes it harder. Don't you see? Until Betty sends the divorce papers, we should not, we cannot go on as lovers. I love you dearly, but we should try to keep our relationship on a simple friendly note so's . . . Oh, damn, I'm so awkward at things like this."

By far the more practical of the pair, Francie offered her suggestion. "Then forget about it for now. Drink your beer, and we'll talk about our day at the office." She stifled a small giggle that tried to rise in her throat. "Funny that I should think of what you do as a 'day at the office.'" Francie frowned and her lips turned down. "Darling, it's all so dangerous, what you do. I worry about you every day. More so now that I see the reports that come into my office."

It wasn't a topic that Kent Welby wanted to talk about any more than his situation with Betty, but it was at least a change of subject. "What reports are those?"

"About the attacks on the recreation beaches. Someday you might be there, on one of those strands chosen for an attack."

Quietly, Doc told her. "We were, only three days ago," then he added, "You see? Didn't I tell you that you might find reason to regret working for the Riverine Force?"

"*Touché*. What is it one says in English? Hoist by my own . . . ?"

"Petard. It means to get blown up by your own bomb. Or run up the flagpole upside down."

Francie's laughter tinkled musically in the large dining room. "Oh! Oh, you delightful man. With a few words you have dispelled all my worries. What would you like to eat?"

"How about some of that Lemon Grass Chicken? And Imperial Rolls, of course. And some of those little back-ribs. Don't forget the prawns."

"You American men," Francie protested in mock disapproval. "You eat enough at one meal to feed a family of six."

"It's not because I am an American, Francie. It's because I am a SEAL. We easily burn five times the energy of an ordinary man every day. Some days, ten times."

Francie pulled a face. "You are not ordinary, true enough. But you do sound a little smug."

"I have a right to be. SEALs are the best there is at anything."

Francie leaned close to him, so that she was whispering into his ear. "Especially at making love."

Doc Welby left Francie Song's apartment shortly before curfew. Their ardent lovemaking had left him with a warm, satisfied glow. Twinges of guilt began to manifest in his mind halfway back to the main gate. By the time he reached it, and the Marine sentry, he saw himself as a total heel. The guard reminded him of the time.

"I can read a watch, Jarhead!" Doc snapped.

All the same, he increased his pace to an airborne shuffle, sort of a gait a slight bit short of full double time. He reached the concrete block building that housed his quarters a full minute before curfew. He had his shirt off and his boondockers in place at the foot of the bed when Midnight Charlie chose to serenade the base.

One after another, four fast mortar rounds dropped in. Then Charlie folded the legs of his mortar and drifted off to harass someone else. It was going to be a long fucking night, Kent Welby thought as he dropped his trousers.

The operations order had come down shortly after morning quarters. The gist of it was simple.

Tomorrow morning would be an R&R beach trip for personnel from the Binh Thuy base. They would be partying at Cau Cung Hua. During daylight hours today First and Second Squads of First Platoon would be transported to . . .

"An Initial Point that will place them two kilometers behind the indicated beach." Pope Marino read it off for the assembled SEALs. "See Appendix One for map coordinates. Paragraph three—Movement to designated units' AO will be overland. All personnel are to be in positions indicated on map, see Appendix Four, by 0330 hours on the morning of the sixth. Paragraph four—Rules of Engagement. Upon making contact with hostile forces, this will be considered a free-fire engagement. Designated units will suppress enemy fire and capture or destroy any mortars within the area.'' Pope Marino put the paper aside. ''Well, that's about it. Plain and simple. More humpin' our butts over jungle ridges and trying to find Charlie before he finds us. Then when we do find him, we kick ass and take names. We're supposed to take two or more prisoners. Also to look for anything that might serve as early warning for Charlie. Thing is, he's been foldin' up and haulin' out before counterbattery radar can provide a firing solution to our ships out there.''

''What'll that be, sir?'' BM/2C Andrew Holt, the replacement for True Blue Oakes who had been KIA on the big munitions raid, asked quietly.

''Tell you the truth, Holt, I don't know.'' Lieutenant Marino gestured to the open doorway of the platoon bar. ''Use your imagination. They could have some superpowerful light-accumulating glasses. Long-range and see through the sea mist. Or it could be their own radar. Anyway, Charlie is takin' a pass on any beach lately where there is a DD or frigate standing offshore for fire support. Once we waste the Cong on site, we will have plenty time to look for it.''

Richard ''Archie'' Golden raised a big, bristly-haired hand. ''How we going to know if Charlie is going to be there, Pope?''

Lieutenant Marino produced an enigmatic smile. On him, it looked menacing. ''Simple, Archie. There won't be any support vessels out there tomorrow. That was made clear in the R and R orders cut for the Binh Thuy people, I would suspect. So, whoever is getting word to the Cong will know about it. We're there to see that when they bite, they'll get hooked and reeled in.'' He rose from his grenade-box stool, satisfied that the casual atmosphere had been maintained, despite the new, very uptight, men.

All of the briefings they would have attended so far would have been as rigid as the steel rod up the briefer's ass. This quick and dirty little mission should shake them down well enough to see what kind of SEALs they were. The only kind, Pope's mind chided him. *The best!*

"Pope, why don't we run this as a parakeet operation?" Tonto Waters asked in his New Jersey–tinted accent.

"Can't this time. We're not going for a fixed location," Lieutenant Marino went on, sensing in Tonto's question an invitation to inform the newcomers. "We have to find Charlie on the ground first, then move on him."

"What's a parakeet?" Andy Holt asked Doc Welby in a loud whisper.

"For your edification, Holt," Pope Marino interrupted, his voice raised slightly, "a parakeet is a fast insertion by helicopter, often with a rappel down the ropes, and usually with gunship support. We hit 'em so damned fast and hard, they don't have time to form any resistance, then grab what we want and out fast the same way."

"It's a groove to see one in action, with everything going the right way," Doc Welby added.

"Do they ever *not* go the right way?" a wide-eyed Andy Holt asked.

"So far, I'm pleased to say, they have not. Every one we've pulled off has been letter-perfect," Pope Marino assured him. "Only had one slight wound on the first one we did. Since then, everyone goes in and comes out without a scratch."

Holt produced a sappy grin. "Then I agree with the Chief. We oughtta do this as a parakeet."

That brought a round of chuckles from the old hands. These new kids learned fast. Lieutenant Marino concluded the briefing and asked for questions. As usual, there were none. "All right, draw weapons. Think light, we've got a long way to walk. Also think small. We'll be goin' out by chopper, hopefully with a couple of prisoners." He looked directly at Andy Holt. "You're the exception to that, of course. Since you've come in to replace our SAW. Hope you like luggin' an M60 around all day."

"Funny thing is, sir, that I do. I love that machine gun. Squad Automatic Weapons man is just where I want to be."

Pope Marino had to turn away to hide the grin that spread on his face. The way he saw it, grateful as he was for its presence, hauling the heavy M60 and its belted ammunition around took a real headcase. Then he dismissed it, having many other worries to occupy his time.

Powerful engines throbbed in the PBRs that plowed through the thick, brown water of the Bassiac River, on the way to its juncture with the Mekong. The SEALs sat with their backs to the engine housing. Tonto Waters had been serious about wanting this to be a parakeet op. For all the risks of any firefight, this travel by patrol boat, river was the worst part for him. The unarmed Huey slicks didn't seem as vulnerable to Tonto as these small, speedy boats, with their open decks and close proximity to the enemy.

At first, Charlie had been unaware that the river patrol boats were being used to transport the SEALs to their operational areas. The big brouhaha that had resulted in destroying some thirty tons of enemy weapons, ammunition, and medical supplies had left no doubt. Charlie knew now that anytime they saw one of the swift little PBRs it could hold their hated opponents, the Men with Green Faces. As a result, the occupants of the PBRs had been taking fire of late. Not that they were unable to give back in kind.

From a stanchion mount on the aft deck, a big .50

caliber machine gun could lash at either side. The gun-
wales to port and starboard bristled with M60s and the
nasty 40mm Honeywell automatic grenade launchers. Add
to that all of the small arms of the SEALs, if some were
aboard, and the offending VC might as well try to stomp
a nest of cobras barefoot. For all of that, Tonto Waters
still didn't like the exposed, dangerous rides along any
river in the PBRs.

Part of that lay in his first experience with the river
patrol boats. They had been in Puerto Rico. Several of
the new patrol boats had been brought down for trial runs.
The trials had been held on the Rio Piedras. There had
been strict regulations regarding taking one of the craft
out of the river environment. There had also been a first
class boatswain's mate named Nestor, who commanded
the PBR on which Tonto and the rest of 1st Squad had
ridden during the performance tests. As coxswain, he not
only outranked Tonto, then a mere 2d class, but everyone
on board, by virtue of commanding the vessel.

It turned out he had a strong dislike of SEALs, based
on jealousy actually. He had wanted to become one and
had washed out. Nestor determined he would have two of
his wishes fulfilled at the end of the test run. He would
get to take the PBR into blue water, and put some smart-
ass SEALs in their place . . .

"Coxswain, you're headed away from the estuary,"
Chief Draper, who led 1st Squad at the time, observed.

"Yep. I know that, Chief," Nestor responded as he
eased the throttles to full.

The PBR already had a bone in her teeth. Now the
salt-tanged spray leaped up to fly over the thwarts in a
fine mist. A heavy chop cut across the starboard quarter,
lifting the bow and slamming it down violently as they
cut their way out of the river outflow and bore into the
sea. Ominously, the PBR began to pitch and roll.

Not in his entire career as a cruiser sailor had Tom

Waters ever been seasick. Now Tonto Waters found himself with a hot, swaying lump in his gut that threatened to turn into an acid geyser that would spew forth. A clammy sweat broke out on his brow, and his tongue turned to a furry stick. Although seated, dizziness washed over him with each gyration of the tiny vessel that viciously slammed across the blue surface of the southern part of the North Atlantic.

"This shit has got to stop!" his mind yammered at him.

Through eyes gone blurry with unshed tears, Tonto Waters caught sight of the coxswain, Nestor. The boat driver had one hand on the wheel, one on the throttle, his head thrown back as though in ecstasy. His features had twisted into a maniacal grimace. Sudden determination shot through Tonto Waters. His legs found new strength and his mind cleared to sharpness with renewed resolve.

No matter that this lunatic outranked him. He, Thomas James Waters, was going to personally end this maniac dash across open water. *After all, it is unauthorized, right?* he asked himself. *So I bust this little fucker in the chops, chances are he'll be the one to face a court, right?* Another violent lurch of the PBR launched Waters into action. He came up on his feet and lunged forward to the control console. In one swift, sure move, he fitted the muzzle of his M-16 under the chin of BM/1C Nestor.

Waters's voice held a low growl of menace as he spoke close in the coxswain's ear. "You're gonna shut this fuckin' thing down, turn back, and take us into the river like this boat's supposed to be, or I turn your brain into hamburger."

That's all it took. Meek as a little lamb, Nestor hauled back on the throttle, turned the wildly lunging PBR 180 degrees, and set course for the river mouth. Afterward, he said nothing about the insubordinate, mutinous if one split hairs, actions of one QM/3C Thomas Waters. Afterward,

Tonto saw it as a stroke of fortune that had allowed him to escape a general court-martial. He had spent the rest of his Navy career in a dedicated effort never to encounter that board of grim-faced men, intent on sending the one facing them to Portsmouth Naval Prison for a long, long time . . .

"End of the line," the boat commander announced, which jarred Tonto Waters out of his reflections.

A few feet from the muddy bank of the Mekong, the PBR idled with slowly turning screws to hold against the current. The SEALs went over the side into waist-deep water. At least they didn't have to swim. During training, Tonto Waters had learned that he really didn't like to swim. But that's what SEALs did, so he went at it with grim determination and never a complaint.

He accepted the condition as the price he must pay in order to pursue his boyhood dream. As a boy of fifteen, he and his friends had indulged in the Saturday afternoon ritual of going to the matinee at the local theater. One fine day the feature had been *The Frogmen*, starring Richard Widmark. The adventurous life portrayed in the film had indelibly impressed young Tom Waters, to the extent that he made it his career goal when he joined the Navy.

Well, here he was, he had sure gotten what he wanted. Ass deep in muddy, brown water, in the middle of a hostile jungle, filled with little men in black pajamas who sought to kill him at every opportunity could sure be called a career achievement. When the last man had reached the riverbank, Tonto took his place on point and the squad moved out. Birds and monkeys made their usual protests at this invasion of their domain, and the trees themselves seemed to conspire against the advance of the SEALs.

Tonto soon discovered that they hadn't far to go to encounter the VC. He took a turn to the left to follow the compass bearing that would take them to the area behind the recreation beach and came upon a dozen of the little brown men in black pajamas. They were seated around a small fire in a sand-filled gallon can, eating rice and shreds of fish with their fingers.

Not for long! Tonto, although several inches under six feet, bulked over the Viet Cong, his Ithaca shotgun held at high port. Before the Cong could react, he swung the muzzle and sprayed them with No. 4 buckshot from the duck-bill shot disperser at the muzzle of the 12 gauge.

Those not slashed with pellets dived for their weapons. A Matt-49 chattered, a stream of 9mm slugs ripped past Tonto's head and chewed wood from a mangrove tree behind him. Swiftly he silenced the submachine gun with another round of deadly pellets. Then the rest of the squad came on the scene and one hell of a firefight developed at the VC evening rest stop.

CHAPTER 3 ─────────────

BULLETS FROM the Type 56, 7.62×39mm rifles in the hands of the VC shredded a lot of vegetation. Doc Welby heard one crack by overhead, with a second past his ear a fraction later. He didn't even drop to the ground. The Stoner in his hands chattered and a five-round burst of 5.56mm rounds chopped down the Cong who had fired at him. To his right, Andy Holt's M60 roared out a deadly beat on full rock and roll.

Gouts of jungle floor spurted upward as the line of 7.62mm NATO slugs dug into the ground. Andy raised his point of aim and put away a slender Charlie who fired indiscriminately with a one-hand grip on his weapon, while he still clutched his bowl of rice. Hell paid a short visit to the Mekong Delta, as lives lost all value and mercy became a word without meaning. With a brief letup on the trigger of the light machine gun, Andy Holt searched for another target.

Three of Uncle Ho's heros sought to avoid their doom by running. Andy, with the M60, and Doc with the Stoner, tracked them. Leaf shreds exploded from a cabbage palm, and a trailing liana vine dropped to the ground as the converging streams of lead advanced on the targets. One VC screamed and threw his arms in the air before he toppled facefirst into the mulchlike floor of the jungle.

Then Doc fixed his Stoner on a spot between the shoulder blades of another Cong.

A light pressure took the slack out of the trigger. When Doc squeezed through, it was as though an invisible sledgehammer had smashed into the VC's back. He lurched forward, leaped clear of the ground, and came down with a crash. The third veered to the left. Doc swung the Stoner and let go a short burst that cut the legs from under the fleeing man. He went down with a shriek. Something tugged at the sleeve of his BDU jacket, and, right on top of it, he heard the crack of the bullet.

Awh, hell, someone's takin' this real personal, Doc thought, a faint twinge of his earlier precombat jitters tweaking him. Off to Doc's right a grenade crashed loudly, the shrapnel making slashing sounds in the underbrush. Silence, save for the groans and moans of the wounded VC, followed.

"They weren't the ones we're looking for," Pope Marino declared when Second Squad caught up to the shooting site. "Not a mortar to be found. We'll have to move overland until we run into Charlie again."

"Oh, joy. Oh, delight," Tonto Waters groaned in mock agony.

"Are we goin' to leave the bodies right here?" Archie Golden asked.

"Good thinking, Archie," Marino came back. "No sense advertising our presence in the event the mortar crews aren't in place as yet. We have a fifty-fifty chance they'll come in the morning." The SEAL lieutenant turned to the men of Second Squad. "Since Tonto and this crew did all the work so far, you people get the pleasure of cleaning up after them."

His face screwed up in a sham of pain, Chief Dan Sturgis launched a protest. "Cut us some slack, L-T.

Some of those guys are blown into chunks. It'll get *messy* cleaning up.''

"My heart is bleeding, Chief," Lieutenant Marino quipped back.

In half an hour the small clearing that straddled the trail the SEALs had been following had been swept clean of blood and the signs of a struggle. Second Squad policed up the brass after dragging the corpses deep into the brush. Then they scattered fresh dirt and unspattered leaves over the disturbed ground and used branches to smooth out the result. Unless someone knew for certain that a firefight had occurred here, what the crafty SEALs left behind would never alert them to the fact.

After the first night in the bush, Tonto Waters had enough mosquito bites to qualify as a lichee nut. Bumps rose, red and angry, all over. He felt put out about it because the bites came in profusion regardless of how much of the so-called "superior quality" insect repellent he had applied. He could use a beer, too. Damned if he couldn't! No beer here, though, except for what Charlie had. And Tonto had no desire to share a *Bahmibah* with a little brown man intent on killing him.

"You're thinkin' about a beer, aren't ya, Tonto?" Archie Golden asked in a low, quiet voice.

Tonto shot him a rueful glance. "How'd you figure that?"

Archie's eyes held a twinkle. "Whenever the subject of beer comes up and you can't latch on to one, you get this faraway look in your eyes."

"Awh, come on, you're bullin' me," Tonto protested.

"No, really. It's as though for you everything else took off for someplace else."

"Can the chatter," Marino interrupted. "Let's harness up and move out."

The way the SEAL lieutenant saw it, the odds were

the VC had made their move during the night and now were between them and the beach they had targeted. Provided, of course, the enemy had heard of the planned R&R and acted upon it. He mulled it over while they made good time through the jungle.

With Tonto Waters at point, the SEALs made it to their first checkpoint with time to spare. The headquarters types from Binh Thuy would not show up until around 1100 hours. Tonto stopped abruptly and signaled the others to go to ground. The hairs stood up on the back of his head. He could *smell* the VC. A blend of garlic, fish, and *Nuoc Mam*. Down on all fours, Tonto cautiously eeled his way through the clutter of brush, most of it thorny and unwelcoming. Fifty meters ahead, he came to a stop behind a mangrove knee and waited tensely. Gradually he raised his camo bandanna-wrapped head above the stout wood of the root system.

He saw nothing, but he heard a faint exchange of human voices. He made his way a little farther forward and caught sight of a conical woven rattan hat. Then another. The shape of a typical pith helmet stood out from the jungle background. A French paratroop kepi came into sight. He had found the Cong. A couple of rankers among them from the bits of foreign gear visible as the figures of the men came into view.

Tonto heard a heavy thud as though someone had dropped a coffin on the ground. Metallic clatter came a moment later. Some of them, he decided, were setting up a mortar. Tonto eased his way down and backward, his sneaker-covered feet making no sound in the detritus that littered the jungle floor. With speed governed by caution, he hastened back to where he could signal Enemy in Sight.

Pope Marino came forward when he received word. "What have you got?"

"Six of them up ahead. With a mortar."

"There's bound to be more."

"Yeah, I know."

Lieutenant Marino considered a moment. "I'll send Second Squad on an end run to find them." He spoke into a small handheld radio. "On their way." A grin brightened the green-and-black-daubed features of Pope Marino. "It's sure easy when you have the right commo gear."

"Say that again. Why don't I take a look-see for some more Charlies. What is it? They usually send out four mortar crews?"

"Right on, Tonto. Point out the crew you've spotted, and we'll deploy to take them out."

"Okey-dokey. See you in a short, Pope." Tonto gave the location of the mortar crew and ghosted off into the jungle.

Sergeant Gow Thon had the reputation of a brave man. He had fought with vigor against the hated Southern government's soldiers, the ARVN, and against the Americans since they first came. His courage was no more questioned than his loyalty to the Viet Cong. Only one thing truly frightened Sergeant Thon. He had never said anything to anyone about it. What turned Sergeant Thon's bowels to water were the Men with Green Faces.

Since being posted to the Delta, Gow Thon had fought against the dreaded SEALs twice. What made his experience miraculous was that he had lived through it, totally unscathed, both times. At least he had not been physically wounded. Thon's gaping, bleeding wounds lay in his mind. He had seen their ferocity during the first encounter and again the second time. And he had observed one of the green-painted barbarian faces, albeit briefly, up close and personal, a moment before a lateral buttstroke had laid him out cold at their second meeting. Now, at least, a way had been found to exact retribution on these monsters in green and black.

Sergeant Thon would have embarrassed himself in front of his troops with a wet spot in his crotch had he but known that one of the dreaded SEALs observed everything they did that morning from less than ten meters away. Confident, then, in his ignorance, Sergeant Thon saw to the installation of his squad's second mortar and called a rest stop to brew tea and eat a little rice. If all went well today, they would be safely in their home compound by time for the evening meal. Roast pork and sour vegetables the menu had read. The thought of it made Thon's mouth water.

Tonto Waters had found the second mortar crew within fifteen minutes of his departure from leading Lieutenant Marino to the first. He lay low, wrapped in silent study of the enemy, ignoring the incessant buzz and sting of a myriad of flying insects, and the steady trickle of perspiration down the sides of his neck and along his back. The little brown man in the pith helmet had moved on to this crew. *He must be good*, Tonto admitted to himself, *to have moved so quickly through the jungle without making a sound that could be heard.*

Half an hour passed and the honcho gook called a halt. The VC broke out small cans filled with gasoline-soaked sand and commenced to brew tea. At least that's what Tonto assumed they were doing. Some of them produced palm-leaf pouches and began to two-finger scoop rice into their mouths. Others came out with what looked like food bundles with edible wrappers. Tonto's sensitive nose soon told him they were a mixture of rice and dried fish, wrapped in seaweed, and heavily seasoned with garlic and hot peppers.

When first seen by one of the replacements, Zoro Agilar had dubbed them "gook tamales."

They had to taste as foul as they smelled, Tonto reasoned, yet sure enough, one of the Cong dudes bit off the end of one, then drowned the interior with *Nuoc Mam,* poured from a small tin flask. Tonto's stomach churned. Unlike Kent Welby, who consumed the ubiquitous Southeast Asian condiment with slurps and smacks, Tonto had seen too many Vietnamese making the stuff. A sight like that, he believed, was enough to gag a maggot.

He rudely jerked his mind back to the business at hand. Given the distance between mortar emplacements, and he had to assume the other pair to be equally spaced, it would require they split the squads to take them on. From the actions of the enemy, they sure didn't expect unpleasant company. To Tonto, the time seemed ripe to really spoil their day.

He returned to Lieutenant Marino and explained the situation. Pope considered only a moment and made the decision Tonto had anticipated. "You take Archie and one of the new men. Hit the second mortar. We'll clean out this one." The radio in Pope's hand vibrated silently. "Eagle One," he spoke into the mike. A squawking answered him. Then, to Tonto, "Sturgis and his guys found the other two mortars. Says it's a piece of cake."

Tonto pulled a face. "Don't hold your breath. It can get damn hairy, damn fast."

Sgt. Gow Thon had the peace of his midmorning repast irreparably shattered when a shotgun went off apparently right in his ear. The hot sting and painful impact of the specially hardened No. 4 buckshot pellets smashing through his right shoulder blade drove him forward off his feet. After a stunned moment, in which the world around erupted in a cacophony of gunfire, Sergeant Thon found it hard to believe he still had his head on his neck.

Others around him, Thon soon found out, had not fared so well. A Stoner on full rock and roll shredded the air.

Two of the mortar crew screamed and fell to thrash out their lives in the brush. A small, greenish black orb hurtled through a gap of blue sky and landed by the base plate of the elderly, but highly efficient, 82mm M-1943 Soviet mortar. A moment later, it went off and silenced forever the gunner and his assistant. The shotgun roared again, and Sergeant Thon risked a quick glance over his shoulder.

There, at the edge of the clearing, perfectly blended into the background of trees, he saw him. One of the Men with Green Faces. The shotgun he held had an odd appearance. Like the muzzle had been squashed flat and split down the sides. Its operator knew his business, though, Thon acknowledged to himself. Only too well. Thon wondered if he could lie still until the Americans had finished their grim work and gone on their way as his past experience told him they were wont to do. If so, he might escape.

From the distance he heard the rattle and thump of more gunfire. This was no casual encounter, then, he realized. These dreadful Green Faces had come hunting them. Anticipated them being there, in place some three thousand meters from their intended target. Thon's hopes to evade his enemy sank with this realization. Perhaps he could do something to get them to kill him, so he would not be captured and made to talk?

Knocked that first joker ass over a teakettle, Tonto Waters thought as he watched Sgt. Gow Thon bowled off his seat on a fallen log. He cycled the pump action of his Ithaca and chambered another round. Two more buck loads. That would make sausage out of whoever it hit. He'd have to reload quickly. He saw the sphere of the M-26 frag grenade Archie threw, and dropped behind the recently vacated tree trunk.

For good reason, Tonto reminded himself. When Archie got busy with his beloved explosives, he often forgot that anyone else was around. When the little hand bomb went off, Tonto came upright again and sent a horizontal spread of No. 4 buckshot slashing across the clearing. Five pellets doubled over a startled Cong, with his rice-sticky fingers still stuck in his mouth. Reflex to the sudden pain caused the VC to bite down and he got a mouthful of his own blood. Next to Tonto, Porfirio Agilar, Zoro to the Team 2 SEALs, chopped steadily away with his Stoner.

Funny, the 5.56mm choppers worked best for the SEALs here in the Delta. Tonto had heard that the Blanketheads of Army Special Forces held a strong dislike for the Stoner. A lot of complicated crap, they maintained, that could and would screw up in the bush. Yet, they had so far to cause problems for the SEALs. Maybe, Tonto reflected, SEALs were just less demanding, as some wag around General Belem's SPECWARV office had suggested. Which didn't seem would happen soon, Tonto observed as Zoro Agilar dumped another VC into the brush.

Three hot rounds from a Matt-49 cracked past Tonto's ear and reclaimed his undivided attention. These little fuckers could still kill him. For him, the intensity of the firefight drowned out any sound of other gunfire. Yet, Tonto felt certain that Second Squad would be mixing it up good with the other mortar positions. The last of the mortar crew fell without a sound, his head shattered by a three round burst from Zoro's Stoner.

Silence. Sweet, blessed silence. And the acrid odor of burned powder and sickly-sweet stench of spilled blood. Slowly, too, rose the vile fumes of voided bowels from where the dead lay. It never changed. Every close-in battle left behind the same mixture of scents. Over the months in Vietnam, Tonto Waters and the other SEALs had become inured, if not accustomed, to it. From the direction of the VC squad leader, the first man gunned down by Chief Tom Waters, came a soft moan.

Tonto turned on one heel in time to see Gow Thon force himself upright. He had a weapon in his hands. Before he could center it on the chest of Tonto Waters, Doc Welby's speedily drawn suppressed Smith & Wesson M-59 "hush-puppy" spat a silent round. The bullet shattered the right shoulder joint of Sgt. Gow Thon, who was flung back-ward to lay gasping, lips compressed, and white with sti-fled pain. Doc Welby and Filmore Nicholson reached the spot first. "This one's still alive, Tonto," Doc called out. "He's bleedin' a lot, but not badly hurt."

"Save him, Fil. We can ask him a few questions back at Tre Noc."

The VC noncom made only soft sounds of distress while the platoon medic, Fil Nicholson, worked on him. Fil cleaned and bound the broken shoulder first. Then he probed for and found the four buckshot pellets. Despite his best efforts to remain stoic throughout, Gow Thon cried out when the forceps entered his ravaged flesh, and he fell back unconscious.

Minutes later, Fil announced with satisfaction, "Got the last of 'em. Some of his uniform shirt, too. They'll have to do a neater job at the hospital."

Pope Marino showed up while Fil Nicholson bound the shotgun wound. "I see you got one, too. Second's bring-ing in a wounded survivor. Could be we can gain a good deal from them. Only thing I want to know first off is how they are aware of our CB fire and know to haul ass. Tonto, I'll leave it up to you, Archie, and Dusty to sweat our two prisoners and learn the answer. Now's a good time, I think, to call for the choppers and get out of here."

Starshii Lortyant (Sr. Lt.) Alexi Maximiovich Kovietski smiled pleasantly across the desk of his office of his headquarters in Cambodia. At his left hand, a chilled tulip glass of vodka smoked as the frost on the outer surface boiled off in the humid jungle air. He lifted the four-page report and gestured with it, to convey meaning in his words.

"Now, this is what I call acceptable cooperation. If we continue to receive such agreeable collaboration from your office, General Hoi, we will be able to foresee an early achievement of our mutual goal."

"Thank you, Senior Lieutenant Kovietski," his visitor responded, mouth twisted into what passed as a smile for the slightly built North Vietnamese general. "Actually I am quite proud of the accomplishments of our Viet Cong allies in this mission."

"When you first proposed we shell the recreational beaches used by the American Navy personnel I had my doubts. Your results have removed them all."

"You were most generous in providing us the means of nullifying their counterbattery fire."

Kovietski shrugged and sipped from his vodka. "A matter of timing, actually. We happened to have the equipment around here and no use for it. It's old, but your technicians mounted it on the little junk without difficulty?"

"Oh, yes. A rather large, motorized junk, actually. The requirements for the generator, you understand."

General Hoi had not come to Kovietski's headquarters to curry favor or to seek compliments. Rather, after the loud and acrimonious flare-up of Kovietski's temper following the destruction of so much ordnance and medical supplies and the necessity of postponing a planned offensive in the Delta, General Hoi had come to get the measure of this sinister-seeming Soviet soldier. With him had come his G-2, Colonel Nguyen Dak.

Dak had assured the general that Kovietski was older than he looked. That he carried himself as one endowed with greater rank than what showed on his shoulder-boards. Kovietski's nearly two-meter height, broad shoulders, and thick shock of blond hair could easily intimidate. Nguyen Dak was immune to that. He felt confident that Kovietski was KGB. His arrogance, and the way he had unhesitatingly upbraided a senior general officer of the NVA literally guaranteed that. Most likely a major or lieutenant colonel, he had advised his superior. Neither General Hoi nor Colonel Dak liked Senior Lieutenant Kovietski. Dak secretly envied him, though, and vowed to someday achieve the same exalted status for himself. Before that time came, however, he had a lot of similar meetings to attend with this and other haughty Soviets.

For his part, while Kovietski was acutely aware of his guests' scrutiny, he, too, used this time together to gain insight on them. Mouse takes cat, checkmate in one move, KGB Major Rudinov, in the Spetznaz lieutenant's uniform, told himself with silent amusement. And, perhaps out of all this newfound cooperation, a way might be found to deal with the troublesome American SEALs, one in particular, Lieutenant Carl Marino.

CHAPTER 4 _____

ON THE ride back to Tre Noc aboard PBR 233, Chief Tom Waters studied the faces of his squad. He recalled good times and bad he had shared with nearly all of them. All, except the replacements. Tonto Waters remembered the day they had arrived. Particularly Andrew Holt . . .

. . . Archie Golden took one look and blurted out exactly what Tonto had on his mind. "M'God, are they turning them out from a mold now?"

Tonto had to agree. Andrew Holt had the stocky build, straw blond hair, and cobalt eyes, that could have made him a twin to Chad Ditto. At the age of twenty-two, he had the fresh-faced good looks of a movie star. Tonto shrugged before responding.

"I don't know. But I hear that this one has already acquired a nickname. Back at Little Creek, they called him Randy Andy."

"No kiddin'? How do you think he got a moniker like that?"

Tonto gave him a long look. "I suppose, Archie, because he tried to boff everything in skirts over the age of sixteen."

An impish grin formed on Archie's face. "Weelll," he breathed out softly. "I reckon as how the legendary Tonto Waters may have a rival from now on, eh?"

Tonto had his mind on only one woman at the time. He shook his head. "Naw. Eloise is too old for him, Archie."

They had taken the newlies to My Flower to properly initiate them into the select company of in-country SEALs. There, they found that the replacement for Dave Kimball, Porfirio Agilar, had an enormous capacity for beer. So much so that he, too, rivaled the reputation of the suds champ of first Platoon, if not all of Team 2, Tonto Waters. In an attempt to reduce Agilar's consumption, and thus preserve his legendary status, Tonto began to quiz the young Mexican American on his background.

"Where do you hail from, Porfirio?" Tonto opened his salvo, although he knew from the kid's 201 jacket full well.

Agilar flashed a wide, white smile in an olive-brown face, as smoothly unlined as that of Holt/Ditto. "Chula Vista, Chief. That's in California."

"Yeah. I know. What'd you do before the Navy?"

Agilar puckered his brow in a frown. Tonto did not know what prompted it. "School, of course, and . . . And I trained."

"A boxer, huh?" Tonto opined.

"Uh—n-no. Not boxing. I was into *torear. La Fiesta Brava.*"

"Hey, ain't that what they call bullfighting in Spanish?" Archie Golden invaded the conversation.

For a fleeting moment, Agilar looked uncomfortable, then his indomitable pride in his first chosen profession overcame and shone through. "That's right. I trained at Rancho Santa Veronica, outside Tacate, Baja California. I wanted to become a *matador.*"

Totally uncharacteristic, Archie made a sour face. "That's disgusting. It's nothin' but a blood sport. One time we were out in D'ago and some of us took a day liberty to T-Town. Went to the bullfights there. I cheered for the bull."

Boyish eagerness to be understood and accepted by these men overcame any deference to rank or age Porfirio Agilar might have possessed. "But you shouldn't do that," he blurted. "You don't understand, Archie. From the beginning, the bull has it all his way. He is big and powerful, weighs around five–six hundred kilos, horns fifty to seventy centimeters long. He's fast, too. At a full charge across the arena, he can reach thirty-five miles an hour by mid-sand. And he can turn in half his body's length. What mere, puny man can stand against such sheer ferocity?" From where he sat, Tonto Waters could see the kid was enjoying himself. This was a spiel he had often recited, the Chief judged.

"What about brains?" Archie countered. "Bulls are dummies. Anybody who'd git in a rage over a red flag has got to be a quart low in the crankcase."

A smug smile, quickly stifled, lighted Porfirio's face. "Bulls, like many larger mammals, are color blind. To them, the bright red of the *muleta* is only a lighter shade of gray. No, *mi amigo*, that is a myth. The color could be anything, blue, chartreuse, anything, and the bull would still charge."

Archie scratched the balding spot on the top of his carroty-forested head and pulled a puzzled expression. "Why's that?"

"It's movement they attack. And for more than three thousand years, Iberian bulls have been selectively bread to charge ferociously anything that moves."

"I don't believe they've been fighting bulls for that long," Archie denied scornfully.

"Not in the present form," agreed Aguilar pleasantly. "But the Minoans used the Iberians—that's bulls from Spain—in their religious games as far back as that. Young boys and girls, naked of course, would vault through their horns and do flips on their backs.''

"Naked?'' That rang of a note of hope.

"Oh, yes, Andy.''

"How old were these naked girls, Agilar?'' probed Randy Andy.

"Some as young as ten. Most in their mid to late teens.''

A mischievous slyness shined in Archie Golden's eyes as he turned to Tonto Waters. "There you go, Tonto. Might be you'll want to take up bullfighting.''

"Get hosed, Archie,'' Tonto barked in mock anger.

"As I said, they don't do it that way now.''

Andy Holt worked his full lips into a moue of regret. "All the more reason to consider the sport to be barbaric.''

"That's the point I was trying to make,'' said Porfirio in exasperation. *"La Fiesta Brava* is not a sport. It's— it's more like a—a—ah—morality play. 'The bright, the graceful, the civilized triumphs over the dark forces of evil,' '' he quoted from Tom Ley. "And it's done in three acts. The first *tricera* is the testing, the discovery of the power of evil. The second is the punishing and taming of that evil. The last *tricera* is the atonement through the *auto-da-fé*—act of the faith—and freeing of the redeemed spirit through death. Good triumphs over Evil.''

"Yeah,'' Archie summed up glumly. "And Good gets rewarded with two ears and the tail.''

Drollness lighted the obsidian eyes of Porfirio Agilar. "Only if Good—the *matador*—had been sufficiently skillful and suitably spectacular in his performance.''

"Hey!'' Doc Welby spoke into the long silence that followed. "Don't give this guy a soapbox again soon, huh?''

"You got that right, Doc,'' Tonto Waters approved. . . .

. . . And he remembered only so well. Now looking at Agilar, after his first major firefight, an inspiration struck Tonto. The kid had handled himself well. Nearly as professional as the old hands. Kid like that needed a fitting handle, a name that suited his abilities and personality. He rose to a crouch from where he had been sitting against the hatch combing of the engine compartment and moved along to Agilar.

"Well, kid, I know what you're gonna be called from now on."

"What's that?" Agilar asked as he looked up with apprehension.

The throttles cut back then as the coxswain nudged the PBR up to the fenders attached to the dock. It allowed everyone in the squad to hear. Tonto Waters patted the youthful would-be bullfighter on one shoulder and spoke loudly.

"We're gonna call you Zoro. You know, after that guy on TV back in the fifties?"

Zoro Agilar produced a sage expression. "You mean back in Old California? We Mexican Americans know all about Zoro. He was a hero to us long before you *gringos* got ahold of him." Then the realization of what Tonto said struck him. His eyes went wide and he blushed deeply. "I will be deeply honored to be called Zoro by my SEAL *hermanos*. Thank you, Chief. *Muchísimas gracias.*"

First Squad found themselves at My Flower following the successful attack on the mortar crews. Intelligence at Binh Thuy would squeeze anything useful out of the prisoners. LCDR Barry Lailey, the S-2 for NAVSPECWARV, had been pleased with the capture of an NCO and another man.

"You boys do good work," he had complimented First Squad. Which, for Barry Lailey, could be considered lavish praise. Particularly to anyone under the command of Lt. Carl Marino.

A pyramid of beer cans had begun to form on one of the tables taken by the SEALs as they kicked around the unusual compliment. After the debriefing, and cleaning their weapons and gear, they had been given liberty until curfew. Tonto Waters, who had been first to be debriefed, and thus had a head start for the platoon bar, peered glassy-eyed at his squad mates and rendered his own opinion.

"I don't think ol' Barry-baby meant a gawdamn word of it. You know how he gets the ass at Pope. I figure he had to say something, what with all those Riverine guys standin' around. But, if he had his way, Pope would be doin' hard time at Portsmouth."

"Why's that?" Randy Andy asked, his kid face alight with curious innocence.

Tonto Waters took a long pull on his Sapporo and prepared to do his Team historian bit. "It goes back a ways, three or four years. Pope was a Jay-Gee then, runnin' a platoon in Lailey's team."

"Commander Lailey was a SEAL?" Zoro Agilar asked, dumbfounded. "I can't see that, man, no way."

"Well he was," Waters insisted. "Not that I am saying he was a *good* one, mind you, just that he was a SEAL. Something went wrong on an op in Central America. Couple of our guys got wasted. Lailey tried to hang it on Lieutenant Marino. Marino didn't say nothing, the way I heard it. The board of inquiry found the facts from the guys in the Team. It was bad enough to have cooked Lailey's goose, only he's such a brown-nose with the brass hats that he just got deep-sixed from SEALs an' put in a permanent desk job. At least, that's the way I heard it."

"What's he doin' here, then, *hombre*?" Zoro asked.

Tonto gave a big shrug. "You tell me. Those kind

usually shun combat zones like people used to treat lepers. Yet, there's Lailey, fat, dumb, and happy, sittin' in the middle of the Delta, lappin' up this wartime service.''

''That could be it,'' opined Archie Golden. ''Nothin' looks better on a career officer's record than combat duty. Maybe Lailey thinks he can wangle a command again if he does well and maybe earns a citation or two here in the 'Nam.''

''That'll be a cool day in hell. But we've gotta look out for our lieutenant.'' Tonto got a faraway look for a moment while he studied on an idea. ''Maybe one of you Yeoman types could get ahold of some of Lailey's personal forms, put Pope in for a commendation for the raid on the mortars?''

Archie liked the idea. ''Yeah. Sign Lailey's name to it and it wouldn't have to pass through his office again. It'd be a done deal before he even got wind of it.''

''Naw,'' Tonto ice-watered the scheme. ''If something, any little ol' thing, screwed up, they'd hang our asses out to dry. Not to mention what it would do to Pope's efficiency report. We'd best shitcan the whole idea,'' he concluded. None of the new men saw the judicious wink exchanged between Tonto and Archie.

Doc Welby knew all about LCDR Lailey being a SEAL. In fact, he was the first to hear Lailey's version of the incident in Central America. So, when Tonto Waters launched into the true version of what happened, he and Francie Song slipped away to the privacy of her apartment.

Once inside, Francie draped her arms around Doc's neck and gave him a long, moist kiss. The intensity of it startled him, although he had been expecting something of the sort. When she broke off, he held her at arm's length, not in rejection, but affectionately.

''Now, what's that all about?''

"A thank-you. Thank you, thank you, Kent Welby for getting me my job. It is wonderful, everyone is so nice, and so much money."

Her bubbly attitude infected Doc. "I didn't get you that job. You did it yourself. All I did was open the door for you."

"All the same, I owe you. What is it you Americans say? Big-time?"

Doc threw back his head and laughed. When his amusement ran its course, Francie kissed him again. Doc stiffened somewhat, this was not what he wanted. Guilt feelings still tormented him. His situation with Betty vexed him, as well as getting in the way of his feelings for Francie. He vowed to avoid anything more amorous than their previous kisses. At least until Francie plied him with a couple of glasses of a sweet liqueur that he had expressed pleasure over earlier.

The B&B warmed Kent Welby and spread a feeling of well-being through him. It also served to lower his inhibitions. Francie excused herself to check on her son, she told him. When she returned from the bedroom, she wore only a sheer, diaphanous peignoir. Doc could see every delightful curve and plane of her pale bronze body through the revealing cloth. His mouth gaped.

"My God, Francie, you are so beautiful. I—in the last few days I have forgotten how exquisite you are."

Francie affected a pout. "So quickly the memory fades? I thought I had made more of an impression than that."

Doc hastened to protest the innocence of his remarks. "It's not that, I never forgot *you*. I only forgot how perfect you are."

"That's better, Kent," Francie taunted. "Now prove it to me." She held open her arms, and it had the effect of a magnet on a steel bar.

Doc propelled himself off the edge of the small,

wooden chair and into her arms. He kissed the hollow of her neck, unable to resist the raw, yet silken desire she aroused in him. They embraced and Doc nibbled at one tiny earlobe. Francie cooed her appreciation. One big hand slid down the arch of her back to clasp her buttocks. Doc moaned softly as he put his mouth on hers.

She opened invitingly to let him enter. They probed and explored alternately. Francie squirmed against him, and Doc found himself quickly becoming breathless. He also had a rigid, pulsing erection. Francie felt it through their clothing and rotated her pelvis against it. Their kiss continued while she began to unbutton his shirt. Doc cupped one small, melon globe in his other hand. He didn't know how long they could sustain the intensity of their mingling.

When their embrace ended, both gasped for air, and Doc's shirt hung out of his trousers, open down the front. "We . . . can't do . . . anything here," he gasped out.

"The bedroom," Francie said practically.

"Your son," Doc offered in halfhearted protest.

"Thran is not here."

Doc pulled a rueful face. "You knew I could not resist you?"

Francie contrived to look contrite. "I hoped you could not."

They entered the bedroom hand in hand. Francie undressed Doc. He slid the filmy gown from her shoulders and let it fall. Doc dipped at the knees and lifted her off the floor. She stifled a soft giggle as he carried her to the bed.

"Oh, Kent, Kent, I have so missed these times with you. I have craved you so much it is sinful."

"Yes, it is. After all, I am still a married man."

He said it without much conviction as he slowly entered her. She received him eagerly, as his languorous penetration teased them both into flaming ardor.

*   *   *

"They squeezed those jokers dry," Lt. Carl Marino began the briefing for another mission. "There are six mortar crews on constant standby. Our resident spook called it right. They have somehow acquired a counterbattery radar. They stay in contact with the duty crews by radio. If they even spot an echo that looks like a destroyer or frigate, they fire a single salvo and haul butt. The radar is mounted on a junk. It always stays on the Mekong. What we're going to do is go in and waste it. And this time, Tonto, you get your druthers.

"That's right, we have a parakeet operation laid on. Air in—air out for this one. The goal is to pull someone with specialized knowledge off the junk. Small arms only. We suppress, neutralize, and take prisoners. Departure time is zero–eight hundred today. So it's a quick breakfast, draw weapons, and load on board the slicks. We'll be making the approach along the usual mail routes at twelve to fifteen hundred feet to avoid suspicion. That means the two slicks and four AH-One-Gs will link up less than a klick from the target." Lacking a specific location to indicate on the maps left Lieutenant Marino feeling handicapped. He worked out how to dispel similar apprehension in his men before he continued.

"This is a big-ticket operation. The target will be located for us by a high-altitude overflight by an ECM-equipped Air Force job. They'll detect any radar emissions and radio the position to our pilots.

"Final approach will be at a hundred meters. The gunships will make one pass, then we come in, rappel down free lines, and sweep the junk clean. It'll be swoop, shoot, and scoot. Time on the ground, or rather aboard, three minutes max." Pope Marino nodded to Archie Golden. "Just long enough for you to set satchel charges to blow the radar and the boat to hell."

"Can do, Skipper," Archie responded through a grin. Time to make a big bang again.

"Anchor Head," Pope Marino addressed to Dan Sturgis, Second Squad's leader. "You will take out the mortar crews. If possible, First Squad will swing over and back you up. Questions?" There were none. "All right, this will stand for morning quarters for your two squads. Dismissed. See you at the birds."

Like a vast, rippling green sea, the jungle passed by below. A brown ribbon ran sinuously through it, the Mekong River. After departure, at a standard altitude of fifteen hundred feet, the Huey slicks had sped along, with only blue sky and an occasional puffball of cloud to be seen through the open doors. Strapped in the sling seats around the outer bulkhead, the SEALs mostly stared straight ahead, in an attempt to keep their minds blank. For all their experience, the rational, logical parts of their minds too frequently reminded the SEALs that it was insanity to exit a perfectly good aircraft before it landed.

They zigged around the sky for a while, pretending to be mail choppers to any onlookers below. Unheard by the passengers, the pilots received coordinates to the target and altered course. At the IP (initial point), they began a steep descent that brought stomachs up tight against diaphragms and produced a queasiness akin to seasickness. When the altimeters had unwound to indicate a scant hundred feet AGL (above ground level), the Hueys crabbed insectlike across the terrain, the one containing First Squad and the Cobra gunships headed for the Mekong, while the second Slick sprinted toward the suspected location of the VC mortar crews.

A red light flashed on the bulkhead between the passenger bay and the flight deck. The crew chief gave the SEALs the thumbs-up alert signal. Tonto Waters unsnapped from his flight harness and attached the end of his rappeling rope to the pad eye set in the recess below the starboard door. He had time only to make a quick adjustment to the way the Ithaca 12 gauge hung around his neck before a cacophony of minigunfire drowned out even the deafening noise of the Huey engine. Two . . . three salvos, then a second later, the flight flashed green and the crew chief tapped him out the door.

Even through the special gloves, Tonto Waters could feel the heat of his rapid descent along the three-quarter-inch nylon line. He slithered along, seeing the swiftly approaching deck of a huge junk between the toes of his boots. He also saw the astonished faces of four Viet Cong. The bodies of two more lay sprawled on the deck. Then his boots thumped on coconut palm matting and he dropped to a crouch, the 9mm Browning Hi-Power pointed steadily at one of the surprised Cong.

He barely felt the jerk of recoil as the Browning exploded into life. A black hole appeared in the hollow at the bottom of Charlie's throat. No prisoner there, Tonto thought automatically, as the hole rapidly filled with bright red blood and the VC toppled over backward. Tonto pivoted to his right . . . clear, a one-eighty to his left . . . clear. The rest of the squad had already reached the deck and suppressed all resistance. A thin stream of smoke trickled from the muzzle of the Stoner in Randy Andy's hands.

"Gawdamn," the fair-faced kid said in a tone of awe, "they went down like tenpins."

"That was the easy part. There'll be more of those fuckers belowdecks and we have to clean them out," Tonto advised him from his three months' in-country experience.

In his usual spot on point, Tonto led the way to a companionway that gave access to the lower deck. Archie and Zoro, backed up by Chad Ditto, made their way to the deckhouse, where the radar set had to be located. The antenna on the roof had become a twisted, smoking heap of rubble under the onslaught of the Cobras. Archie flattened himself to the bulkhead at one side of the dogged-down hatch to the deckhouse. Zoro Agilar did the same at the other side. Chad braced himself as Archie took tentative hold of the locking wheel and gave it a tug.

Surprisingly it yielded. "Get ready, Repeat," he mouthed quietly to Chad Ditto.

Quickly, Archie spun it to the full-open position and flung it wide. Instantly, Chad filled the interior with a stream of 5.56mm death. Copper-jacketed slugs screamed off the metal walls that lined the interior of the wooden structure. When the long burst ended, Archie went through in a crouch, his CAR-15 leading the way. There was blood and piss everywhere. One burly Vietnamese had been literally sawed in half by the hosing given him by Repeat Ditto. Two more lay in a heap beside a chart table. A lone survivor cowered behind the radar console.

"C'mon in, guys," Archie called out as he eyed the squirrelly little VC with the Coke-bottle glasses. Had to be the radar operator, Archie surmised.

When Repeat entered, he asked eagerly, "How'd I do?"

"Made a mess," Archie told him. "We got a prisoner. You two watch him while I set the charge."

"*Por Dios!* It stinks in here," Zoro Agilar declared as he cast around the deckhouse.

"Small wonder. Your buddy there chopped this turkey in half. Everything emptied out."

"Do you . . . do you ever get used to it, Archie?" the young replacement asked in a choked tone.

Archie Golden eyed him with a scornful expression, then answered with more truth, "No fucking way."

Muffled shots sounded from belowdecks. Archie gave

the time-pencil detonator a twist to five minutes, then laid an affectionate pat on the forty-pound satchel charge. More shots sounded. Zoro and Repeat exchanged worried glances.

CHAPTER 5 _____

TONTO WATERS fired a round down into the lower deck, which sent a spray of buckshot that rebounded around the engine compartment. The immediate return chatter of an AK-47 informed him that some big tickets among the VC had to be aboard. So far, and particularly here in the Delta, the good-quality Soviet assault rifles had been scarce. More so, after the destruction of the stockpiles of arms and munitions the SEALs had carried out three weeks ago.

Quickly cycling the shotgun, while the Cobras circled overhead, Tonto responded with a second load of No. 4. A scream answered him. That brought a satisfied, albeit grim smile to Tonto's lips. He sensed someone at his side and cut his gaze to the left to see Archie Golden.

"We ain't got time for this, Tonto. Here, let me flush 'em for you." So saying, Archie pulled the pin on an M-26 frag grenade and slipped the spoon. He silently mouthed, "One . . . two . . ." and dropped the hand bomb down onto the lower deck.

Two seconds later it went off with a metal-ringing roar. Smoke gushed up through the open companionway. Tonto went first, before the clouds of greasy gray dissipated. The Ithaca barked once more, followed by ominous silence.

"Clear, Archie."

"Oh, boy, I'm gonna love this," chortled Archie as he dropped belowdecks.

It took him only twenty seconds to locate the optimum spot. He wedged the satchel charge in athwart the fuel tanks. With deft fingers he inserted the detonator in the primer hole of the charge, set it for four minutes, and they all scrambled out the hatch. Lieutenant Marino had organized the others in the squad to secure the deck. When he saw Archie's head emerge through the hatchway, he lifted the handy-talkie to his lips.

"Eagle One to Sky Jock. It's done. We've got an extra customer. Get us out of here."

"Rog-o on that, Eagle One. I copy an extra guest, over."

"Roger that, Sky Jock. We've got . . ." He looked at Archie, who showed three and a half fingers. "Three and a half minutes."

"Copy, Eagle One. I'll set it down so you can step aboard."

"Appreciate it, Sky Jock. Eagle One, out."

Their pickup went without a hitch. Marino accepted the headset offered by the crew chief and spoke on the intercom to the pilot. "Letter-perfect parakeet. Now link us up with Second Squad."

"Not quite perfect, Lieutenant," the pilot responded. "Your Second Squad ran into some heat. They're takin' fire real heavy. Two guys WIA, so far."

"Damn," Marino blurted. "Make it a quick one. Those Huey Cobras still around?"

"Two of them are over there now. Choppin' jungle to salad size. The other pair headed that way when we cleared the LZ."

"I like people who think for themselves," Pope Marino praised.

"Nothin' to it, Lieutenant. You order a banquet, you get everything from soup to nuts. That's our motto."

A moment later, the charge in the deckhouse, confined by the thin armor plate, went off with a tremendous roar.

Flames shot from the door and portholes. The belowdecks charge followed quickly, enveloping the trembling, shattered sampan in a roiling ball of orange flame.

They came in fast, hot, and low. Radio contact advised the gunship pilot of their approach and the vector. He swung in line to burn an opening for them. The AH-1G Huey Cobras each opened up with a pair of TOW missles from the portside pylons of the outboard hard points. The roar of their staged departure got drowned out by the bellow of three-barrel 30mm miniguns and automatic 40mm grenade launchers, all on full rock and roll. The slick carrying the SEALs came in right behind.

Their pilot skidded to a stop and the SEALs again rapelled to the ground, while the Cobras circled overhead. With Tonto at point, they spread out and sought to lock onto their buddies from Second Squad. The Cobra orbited to give them time to locate their beleaguered friends. In the silence of its wake, they heard the thin, tinny snap and rattle of small-arms fire. Tonto struck out to find the firefight.

He didn't have far to go. Anchor Head Sturgis popped his cammo green face out of the waving fronds of a low cabbage palm and grinned his welcome. With silent hand signals he laid out the enemy positions for Tonto, who nodded his thanks and ghosted off into the green maze of jungle. Unfortunately for Charlie, Tonto Waters had excellent pathfinding abilities.

Twenty minutes passed when he came upon the first mortar crew, sprawled in death, in a small clearing fifty meters from where Anchor Head hid himself. Tonto made a quick check to make certain none of the enemy played possum. Convinced, he moved on. First Squad followed him, silent and invisible. Another fifteen minutes burned away in tense silence.

A VC was relieving himself against a tree, his bladder

nervous from the intense firefight into which he had been suddenly thrust. Tonto saw him first.

A blast from the Ithaca ended the youthful communist's life. He went down with rag-doll limpness. Immediately return fire crashed into the ground around Tonto. He dodged and cut his way to a thick mahogany tree and took shelter behind it. For two minutes, bullets snapped by his position. Then it ceased. Tonto knew better than to believe the VC had given up. He waited in silence.

Vines rustled, and a cabbage palm leaf bent forward toward the hidden SEAL. Still, Tonto waited. A brown face, shadowed by a USMC boonie hat appeared above the low palms. Still, Tonto waited. Head and shoulders emerged. Tonto Waters could sense his mates around him. He waited.

Two more faces came into view. The bodies followed. Tonto slowly pointed his pistol-grip Ithaca and sighted in, one finger along the axis of the barrel in point-shoot style. A fourth VC materialized out of the jungle. Tonto took a deep breath and hoped his teammates were in position. Then he fired a round, which took out the Cong with the Marine hat, quickly recycled the action, and put another load of No. 4 downrange. Then he went for a third.

He needn't have worried. The moment he fired, gunfire erupted in a semicircle around Tonto Waters, and the dark sphere of a fragmentation grenade sailed through the air and landed at the feet of the pair immediately behind their point man. All three VC were cut down in the blast. When the SEALs ceased fire, an eerie silence replaced the uproar. Through it came a weak, feeble cry for aid. The language was Vietnamese.

"Son of a bitch!" Tonto blurted. "I can't believe it, I missed that dork on point."

"I got him, didn't I?" Archie Golden quipped, studiously ignoring the cry for help the same as Tonto Waters.

"Yeah," Tonto fired back. "And you fuckin' near blew my left hand off with the shrapnel."

"Show me. Show me one place where you're cut with a fragment from a grenade I threw," Archie challenged.

"Be nice now, Archie. I was only jerkin' you around."

"I know that," Golden grumbled. "We gonna check out that wounded gook?"

Tonto pulled a face. "That depends on whether he's willin' to die for Ho Chi Minh."

Archie grimaced as he recalled Riverine sea stories of wounded VC who had pulled the pin on a grenade and concealed it until turned over by an unwary grunt. An ugly business. "Only one way to find out."

"Yeah. Go there," Tonto agreed.

Anchor Head Sturgis and his men saved them the trouble. They came forward, cautious as always, and drifted through the SEALs of First Squad without exchanging a word. Twenty minutes went by and they returned with a wounded VC in custody.

"That makes a total of three, I think. You bagged that radar guy, Pope was tellin' me. Should warm the cockles of their hearts at the spook locker."

"You got that right, Anchor Head," Tonto Waters agreed. "Now let's mop up and boogie the hell outta here."

Their mood remained the same until the Huey slicks returned and lowered to a foot off the ground. The SEALs gratefully boarded, and the helicopters lifted out and away. No attempt to interrogate the prisoners was made during the middling run to Tre Noc. The SEALs completed the trip without incident.

"Let's have a go at those Cong before the spooks get here to relieve us of them," Pope Marino urged.

Ensign Wally Ott thought it a good idea, too. He and the men from Second Squad frog-marched the prisoners to a small, windowless, concrete-block building. There the intellectual type was slammed down in a chair. Pope Marino stood over him, menacing in his size. His steely, light blue eyes burned into the uncertainties the prisoner felt and fueled his fright.

"Now, then, considering that you are a technician, I assume you speak English," Pope fired his opening salvo.

"*Ni—ni.*" The man shook his head in resignation.

Pope Marino grabbed the captive's shirtfront and balled it, then yanked the slightly built Vietnamese out of his chair. "If you don't speak English, how the fuck did you know what I said to deny it? Come on, you little prick. Unload, and we just might let you go."

Haltingly, the radar technician revealed his knowledge of English. "You . . . mean, you would actually . . . release me for my co—cooperation?"

"Naw, just that we'd let you go without cutting your nuts off." The young man paled. "You've heard the stories about what the American running dogs of the capitalists do to prisoners, haven't you?"

He nodded. Pope released him and let the prisoner ease back onto the seat.

"Let's make it easy. Start with your name."

"I am Quai Nguyen."

"What is your unit name?"

"I am a member of the Glorious Sunrise People's Liberation Group."

"What's the strength of the unit?"

"We are a battalion," Nguyen answered proudly.

"Are you all technicians?"

"Yes, yes, we are. Of course there is the Guards Company. They provide security."

"Dandy. You're being most cooperative, Quai." Lieutenant Marino thought a little praise was called for. "How did you get on the junk with the radar?"

"We were sent for from the North. It was an honor and privilege to serve in the Delta."

"How did you get the information on which beaches we would be using?"

For the first time, Nguyen hesitated. "I do not know."

Lt. Carl Marino's eyes took on their thousand-mile "gunfighter's" stare. "Then it's a nutting you're headed for, *amigo*. We need to know that information. I figure from what you said, you know it. So give."

Tonto Waters and Archie Golden added their rather intimidating presence to the threat. Shaken again, images of emasculation alive and well in his head, Quai Nguyen lost the color in his cheeks. He weighed the statements for truth and found no cause to doubt the man who menaced him. He ducked his head, turtlelike, and peered upward with watery eyes.

"It would mean my life if I revealed any of this. We were sworn."

"It's simple, Quai. You tell us, and we see if we can get you into one of the Provincial Recon Units. You hold out, or lie to us, and we see you get a nice funeral."

"I—it sounds all so simple. What if . . . ? My superiors will never know?"

Pope allowed himself a small smile of satisfaction. "They will never think you are in the Phoenix Project. They'll believe you died heroically with the rest. Or that you were blown up with the junk."

"All right, then. There is an agent, one who works for the Soviet, Kovietski. He is a workman on your base at Binh Thuy. He removes trash from the offices."

All smiles now, Pope Marino reached out and gently patted the VC prisoner on one shoulder. "You have been most helpful. Thank you, Quai. Could you identify this spy?"

"Oh, yes. I have seen him many times. This is all you wanted?"

"For now, yes." Lieutenant Marino signaled the others, and they left the room together.

Outside, Pope nodded to the closed door. "We take our little canary to Binh Thuy to point out the traitor. Also, we'll let Jason Slater wring him out a bit more. I've a feeling we can gain a lot from Quai"

Slowly the main rotor of the Huey slick wound down from landing speed to a lazy revolution that in turn slacked off to the motionless droop of the long, slatlike blades. First Squad had the honor of delivering the prisoners to Binh Thuy. On hand to greet them was Jason Slater, station chief for the CIA. He smiled broadly and extended a hand for Marino to shake.

"I'll get a couple of Lailey's best men. We'll sweat these turkeys and that way you'll be first to know what they give up. Shouldn't take long. Might as well stick around and wait for the word."

"Have they opened that chief petty officers' mess that was touted so big last month?" Pope Marino asked.

Slater nodded. "Sure have. Opening night was last night. Grab some chow and a couple drinks and I'll meet you there when we finish with your contribution to the flow of information."

No one thought anything of seven men, faces daubed in camouflage and armed to the teeth, entering the CPO mess. It did startle a couple of female civilian types fresh over from the States. They took it in stride, though, with only one hesitant, backward glance to verify that the base had not come under attack. In the rest room, the SEALs removed their greasepaint and emerged looking considerably more civilized. They commandeered two large, round tables, slammed them together, and ordered pitchers of beer.

A grizzled Master Chief ambled over after the good bartender had brought the mugs and beer to the table. He had a badly bent, scarred nose and the start of a cauli-flower ear. A former fleet boxer, no doubt, Doc Welby judged. He was also obviously very drunk. He slammed down his own mug and grunted out the menu. "Dere's a buffet . . ." He pronounced it like being tossed by the wind. "at twelve hunnard hours. Ya also got the Polish sausages on a hard roll wit grilled onions and sauerkraut. Or . . ." He made a face of overwhelming disgust. "Tuna fish sandwich. I hate fuckin' tuna fish sandwiches."

"What? No hamhocks and beans?" Doc Welby asked, remembering his first meal at Tre Noc.

The old hand scratched a balding spot, alcohol fumes fogging his brain. "Fuck no, man. When you ever get navy beans in the Navy?"

"Three months ago at Tre Noc," Doc told him with a straight face.

Understanding dawned. "Aah, youse fuckin' Riverine Force sailors. Youse got it cushy as shit." He had no idea they were SEALs. "What'll it be, youse gobs? I'll call the gook to git yer order."

"I'll take three Polish," Repeat Ditto chimed in.

"Yeah, same for me," Randy Andy added.

"Two for me," Kent Welby ordered.

"Do they have anything without pork?" Archie Golden asked.

"They can have Cookie burn you a hamburg. Dat okay?"

"Sounds kosher to me," Archie punned at his own expense.

A fey light twinkled in the old salt's eyes. "Oh, yeah, I gitcha. Dis ain't the Ritz-Carlton, youse knows. But, they provide. Be right back."

"What for?" Lieutenant Marino asked.

"To get dem pi'chers an' refill 'em, of course. These are on me. Youse River Tigers got a rep for beer drinkin'."

"We're not Riverine Force," Tonto Waters informed him with all the dignity and restraint he could muster. "We're SEALs."

The inebriated Master Chief smacked his forehead with an open palm. "Oh, shit, then I don't think they *got* enough beer." Then he was gone.

"We oughta have a place like this at Tre Noc," Tonto opined.

Pope Marino gave him a level gaze. "If the base grows, we will. Though I don't know if I'll like it all that much. Place like this gives birth to too many hangovers."

"*Pope!*" Tonto and Archie chorused with wounded dignity. Then Archie concluded, "Are you implying that we can't hold our booze? Especially this sissy three-point-two beer they provide in-country?"

Marino waggled his head in surrender. "Present company excepted, naturally. Never let it be said a SEAL can't drink any fleet swab under the table anytime, anywhere."

They ate and drank, and drank some more. Tonto excused himself to wander around the new club. He found a quiet reading room and settled in to catch up on the rest of the world. The first magazine he picked up was an English language edition of *Le Monde*. In it was an article by Eloise Daladier. It covered their search and destroy mission against the hidden bunkers, which had prevented a major offensive in the Delta. Tonto skimmed the article, his mind filling with some of the hairy action they had encountered . . .

. . . Twenty heavily armed VC waited them on one island. First and Second Squads had been assigned the task of sweeping the enemy off their island arsenals. Then Third and Fourth would go in and blow up the caches of arms, ammunition, and medical supplies. Tonto watched them from a screen of leaves.

With infinite patience, he eased back and went to

where he had signaled the Squad to hunker down. Silently, Tonto indicated the number of enemy on hand. Lieutenant Marino, who traveled with First Squad, detailed men to positions along the riverbank. He gave them the usual time to reach the spot. Then the Grim Reaper visited the Bassiac River.

A storm of small-arms fire ripped open the night. Viet Cong fell in windrows. True Blue Oakes kept up a steady rhythm with five-round bursts from his M60 light machine gun, while the Stoners hummed steadily. Archie flung one grenade after another. Every third one was white phosphorous. They provided illumination as well as fiery death for several unwise Cong.

Exposed as the enemy was, the firefight lasted only two minutes. Chalk up another success. Then the chatter of several Chicom Type 50 submachine guns came from behind the SEALs. Unfazed by this unexpected encounter, the Squad made a quick turn about and laid down withering fire on their as-yet-unseen enemy.

"Jeez, where did they come from?" Doc Welby asked of no one in particular.

"Keep your head down and keep shooting," Marino advised.

"Oh, mutha, we in some deep shit now," True Blue declared for all to appreciate. He found a fallen mangrove trunk and hunkered down behind it. With the forestock of his M60 resting on the top surface, he could command a large expanse of open savannah before him. He licked thick, suddenly cold, lips with a pink arrow of tongue.

A Chinese Type 61 grenade crashed off to True Blue's left and he swung the muzzle of the M60 in that direction. Sure enough. It looked like half a hundred little brown men swarming out of the jungle in a determined charge. True took out the front rank in a long, sustained burst. Then he yanked open the cover of the feed tray and seated another belt of 7.62mm rounds. He seated the round in the feed tray and felt to see that the retaining pawl engaged the second round. Quickly he closed the cover and put the weapon on fire.

Three more Charlies went off to the big *politburo* in the sky. "Whooie! They's sure a lot of dem." True Blue never spoke street language unless he was badly scared. Suddenly, True Blue ducked low as bullets cracked over his head from the direction of the island . . .

. . . It had turned out to be friendly fire, from Third and Fourth Squads, Tonto Waters recalled. And, man, had that been welcome. There had been other, nastier surprises during the two-day, two-night operation. Like when that ancient Czech APC came lumbering out of the jungle during their extraction. They didn't even have one of those pip-squeak LAW rockets along. Tonto had sweat bullets and his balls crawled up inside. But they never broke, and they never asked for quarter. They were SEALs and they gave their 110 percent every time. The armored personnel carrier was eventually cracked by close air support, and the SEALs boarded their slicks for a quick trip home. All except True Blue Oakes, Tonto recalled.

Truman Oakes had taken serious hits from the 12.7mm machine gun mounted in the commander's cupola of the APC. He died in the arms of Kent Welby on the way back to Tre Noc. It was a bitter pill for every member of the squad and platoon. The tears that had burned the cheeks of Tonto Waters had been forgotten, but not the brave young black man, who had remained outside the slick to cover the life of their lieutenant, Pope Marino, and the platoon Chief, Tonto Waters. Damn, Tonto thought as he sat aside the magazine article, he sure hoped that Randy Andy Holt would prove half as good a squad mate as True.

Tonto returned to find a grinning Jason Slater helping himself to a foam-capped stein of beer. He greeted the spook with a small wave and poured more brew for himself. "What'd you get? I assume you got something or you wouldn't have that shit-eating grin, or be back yet."

"You're right, Chief. We got a whole lot. Most important to you is that there is someone among our people, in the Plans and Operations office of the Riverine Force that is providing quality product to the Cong. Your bug-eyed technician has no idea who is producing this information, it comes through a dead-letter drop. He has also indicated that there is some high-level dude coming into the Delta on a special mission. He is Vinh Toy Giap, a brigadier general in the NVA."

"You know this general?" Archie Golden asked.

"Oh, yes. Only too well. And I'll tell you right now, I'm gonna move the pyramids if I have to to get you SEALs to find out all you can for me on General Giap."

CHAPTER 6 ⸻

THEY MOVED across the water in small boats called STABs (Seal Team Assault Boats). Every man was heavily armed, their faces covered in smears of green, black, and brown camouflage paint. This was what they had been training for. Each SEAL knew that death waited for them on the distant shore. The lake waters burbled softly on the twin prows of the Zodiac-like vessels; the special-made silent-running engines did not disturb the serenity of the night.

None of the communist enemy would be alerted to their approach. If everything went all right, the attack would be over in less than five minutes and they would be on their way back across the lake to at least neutral, if not friendly, territory. They would bring with them an important prisoner. That was what this operation was all about. In the STAB on the right, Lt. (jg) Carl Marino waited tensely with a squad. He had been tasked with right flank security. In the center, lead position, was their platoon leader, Lieutenant Lailey . . .

. . . *Goddamned Barry Lailey!* Marino snapped awake and came rigidly upright in his bunk. He had been dreaming again. And, as always, the same old dream. He need not even think hard to recall the details in vivid exactitude.

Alpha and Bravo Squads (First and Second) of Second Platoon had been given the assignment of extracting a locally recruited, CIA-trained agent from among the communist guerrillas in a highly sensitive Central American country. To preserve his cover, he was to be taken as a prisoner, along with one of the key cadre within the guerrilla infrastructure, one Juan Domingo Gutierrez.

The *Viente y tres Septiembristas* would be "interrogated," Gutierrez for real, by the Americans, and then turned over to the local government authorities. They would be allowed to escape through the ineptitude of the corrupt officials. That would, it was believed at Langley, enhance the reputation of the agent inside the guerrilla force. It would also provide the only contact with him due to a monumental screwup in which he lost his means of communication and was then assigned by Comandante Espada (Sword) to a unit operating deep in the interior on Lake Orosco.

Everything went fine until Alpha and Bravo Squads began their exfiltration from the guerrilla base camp. Additional elements of the "Freedom Fighters," as they were so fondly called in the American media, happened upon their route of march and fell on the SEALs with terrible ferocity.

Although blessedly brief, the firelight proved costly. In the midst of it, Barry Lailey lost it for a few minutes and two SEALs died. They needn't have, Carl Marino believed at the time and knew for certain now. The simple fact was, for all the excellence of training, the program did not detect that Barry Lailey was totally unsuited for a combat command, though his personal courage could not be questioned.

He had made it through the UDT/R training, and all that followed: Airborne School, Ranger School, Jungle Warfare. Just like all the others. Only, when saddled with the stress of command, and the gut-wrenching fear of being shot at, Barry Lailey dropped the ball. Things might have gone different, Carl Marino thought now with grim resignation, had it not been for another trait of Lt. Barry Lailey.

The young SEAL officer had a propensity for kissing up to the Brass Hats. He enjoyed enough success at it that Lailey had been encouraged to attempt to shift blame for the deaths to his junior officer, Lt. (jg) Carl Marino. It nearly worked, except for the testimony of the squad members as to what actually went down out there in the Central American rain forest. As a result, Lailey had been quietly mustered out of the SEALs and transferred to an obscure posting as a deskbound officer for, it was anticipated, the remainder of his career.

Shortly before the arrival of first Platoon, Team 2 in Vietnam, Lailey had pulled strings and gotten assigned to a combat zone. This time the Ron Sat Special Zone, at Headquarters NAVSPECWARV, Vietnam. Which put him in a senior position above Lt. Carl Marino. It was, to say the least, a situation neither of them enjoyed. Recently, after nearly continuous missions in the most hazardous Areas of Operations (AOs), Marino had come to suspect that Lailey used his position as S-2 to see that First Platoon received the deadliest of all operations.

Damn that sounded paranoid, Pope Marino chided himself as he wiped icy sweat from his brow with the gnarled back of one big hand. But even paranoids had real enemies, he reminded his reasonable side. A glance at the diving watch strapped on his left wrist informed Marino that it was useless to try to stack any more zees. He swung his legs out of bed and shoved feet into rubber shower shoes, grabbed up a towel, and headed for the shower room recently added on to the cramped cinder-block head. He'd dump, shower, and shave and be ready to harass the troops at morning quarters.

*   *   *

Senior Lieutenant Kovietski awoke as usual at 0430 hours. He was in a foul mood. The KGB major was always in a foul mood. Unless he had the pleasant company of an energetic young Cambodian woman in his bed the previous night. Odd, but after three years in this assignment, he had forgotten exactly what the body of a Russian woman was like. From what he could recall, Kovietski judged that he was not missing much, if anything. The stereotypical Russian citizen-worker bore more of a resemblance to the national symbol than to a Hollywood movie starlet. And certainly was more ursine than an erotic and shapely Asian girl.

Tepid water drummed down on Kovietski's bare, hairless chest. He bore few signs of his thirty-four years, less of his arduous ascent of the KGB power ladder. Oh, he had scars enough. In the early days, while on internal duty, there had been that smuggler who had turned desperate. Instead of surrendering in abject resignation, as did so many offenders in the Soviet Union, he had drawn an illegal 9mm Tokarev service pistol and opened fire. Two slugs had pierced flesh and left Alexi Kovietski with a long, puckered gouge along his right ribs and a white, sunken circle near the point of his left shoulder.

A lousy shot, Kovietski later acknowledged. But then what could one expect from a populace long deprived the ownership and use of firearms, unless a member of the rural militia, the police, or the armed forces. It made for a peaceful, orderly society, an *obedient* one. If, of course, one overlooked the recent, rapid increase in alcoholism and its resultant violence. Yet, one must never criticize or question the *Rodina*. One *served* the Motherland, at the expense of all other things, Alexi Kovietski admonished himself as he liberally soaped his torso.

Over the years of such blind dedication, he had won the right to be a bit—as his superiors described it—eccentric. Once severely crew-cut, his curly, blond hair now grew long and covered the upper portion of his ears. It suited him for it to be so. His six-foot-one-inch height made him tower over the Orientals he dealt with daily. His light, Caucasian complexion, reddened rather than tanned by the harsh tropical sun, further added to his intimidating image.

He had heard that some of those on Gen. Hoi Pac's staff called him, behind his back, "The Crimson Dragon." Let them. Dealing daily with their plans and schemes often made him feel dragonish. This sinister renown had gotten afoot among the Cambodians he also advised. That amused Lt. Alexi Kovietski. He rather liked them, as opposed to how he felt about their devious and sinister Vietnamese counterparts.

The Cambodian military men he dealt with were direct men, brutal and violent, totally devoid of any compassion or respect for life. He considered the Vietnamese to be the sort to smile and nod to your face and stab you in the back. Rather like the Japanese, he was fond of saying to his station operatives, Feodor Dudov and Maxim Yoriko. As Kovietski was *Residentura*, Dudov and Yoriko felt constrained to refrain from reminding their boss that the Soviet Union was currently trying to improve relations with Japan, the better that way to spy on them.

Kovietski knew this and didn't mind a bit. After all, that was why he, rather than one of them, was resident chief of the KGB station in southern Cambodia and the Delta region of Vietnam. Only time would tell how much and how positive an effect this duty would have on the career of Major Pyotr Maximovich Rudinov/Alexi Maximiovich Kovietski.

He rinsed himself, turning slowly under the tingling, needle spray of the shower nozzle. His orderly would have heard the shower running and would have a glass of tea ready. For all the heat and humidity in this accursed jungle, Alexi, like most proper Russians, preferred a good, strong glass of hot tea to that insipid, capitalistic, American invention: *iced tea*. Toweling himself vigorously, he looked forward to the ubiquitous Russian beverage with anticipation.

Then his mood swung viciously to the major irritant of his past few weeks. Those *kotorohye solip'shim* US Navy SEALs had destroyed the radar unit he had provided to the Viet Cong in the Delta. In a swift, unexpected blow, they had descended from the sky, blasted the motorized junk with fire from a gunship, then landed men aboard and completed the job with explosives. There was no way he would be able to obtain another radar from either the Army or the KGB.

Worse luck, the attacks on the recreation areas of the Americans was beginning to have the desired effect. It was one of the more brilliant plans of General Hoi, charged with securing total area control over the Delta and expelling the American presence there. It had also reflected well on his efforts in the Delta. Now all of that was over. History, as the Americans were fond of saying. It did not amuse Lieutenant Kovietski.

Dressed in his usual uniform, the gray background, black-and-green-striped camouflage jumpsuit of the Spetznaz elite force, he stomped barefoot back into his quarters for his boots. He pulled them on, yanked at the laces in an effort to expel his anger at the SEALs, and strode into the orderly room.

Mladshiy Serzhant (Junior Sergeant) Boris Vukovo shot to his feet, his boots making a solid *klump!* as they hit the floor. His black beret canted at a rakish angle over one side of his forehead. A real member of the *Voiska Spetsialnovo Nazacheniya* (Spetznaz), he affected the usual swagger of his elite brothers in the presence of all whom they considered inferior. His rigid position of attention reflected his attitude toward superiors. Particularly one as intimidating as Senior Lieutenant Kovietski.

"Dobrahyee ootrah, Tovarish Starshii Lortyant."

"Good morning to you, Junior Sergeant."

"Pitkin has gone for your tea, Comrade Senior Lieutenant."

"I should hope so," Kovietski answered icily. He began a mental drafting of a report, and a request he would send to Moscow Central. One way or the other, he would have what he needed. So far he still had no idea what was going on in the Delta that had attracted so much activity among the Army of North Vietnam and General Hoi in particular. If it tied in with this increased activity by the SEALs, he would need every bit of help he could get from his superiors.

"Negative, Lone Pine," Lieutenant Marino barked into the handset of the AN/PRC 25. "You were three hundred meters short. All you did was piss them off. Over."

"I copy, Eagle One. Will adjust and make another pass. Over."

"We will mark with smoke," Pope Marino prompted. "Eagle One, out." He turned to Zoro Agilar. "Put a smoke round in that blooper, Zoro, and mark the target for that sky jockey."

"Aye, sir," the young replacement snapped. Still painfully new to the easygoing nature of the Teams and of men in a combat situation, Zoro maintained a degree of formality rarely seen around the SEALs of First Platoon.

He opened the breech of the M-79 grenade launcher he carried, selected a smoke round, and inserted the 40mm cartridge. He took aim and fired. The projectile whizzed through the air to its maximum range and detonated in a plume of white smoke. Pope Marino reached out for the handset, which Repeat Ditto, his RTO, handed him with alacrity.

"That, Lone Pine, is the leading edge of the enemy's

position. Use Anti-pam if you have any left. Eagle One, out.''

First Squad had enjoyed a brief moment of celebrity following the destruction of the VC radar and capture of an important Cong technician. Brief to the point of a single day. They had been sent out on a security sweep of a portion of the Bassiac and had come under fire almost at once. A large number of VC had them pinned down along a small tributary of the second largest river in the Delta. They had been under fire now for the better part of half an hour, an unusual situation considering Charlie's usual tactics. Relief was at least on the way.

It came in the form of the Marine A-6 now lining up to make another run at the enemy position, and from a pair of PBRs (patrol boat, river) speeding down the river toward them. Doc Welby crouched to the other side of Lieutenant Marino, his hands wet against the wood and metal of the Stoner he carried. A few feet to the left, Randy Andy Holt had found a place for his M60. He plied it with consummate skill, cutting off three- to five-round bursts that shattered vegetation and kept the heads of the enemy low.

So far the VC had not figured out how few they numbered. That suited the SEALs quite well. Going against an unknown force, in the unaccustomed daylight hours, had caused the Cong to refrain from a direct, frontal assault. Now it looked like they would not get the chance.

Overhead, the A-6 roared toward the target. It lined up with the unseen VC line and released an oblong, silvery object. Lacking fins, the Anti-pam canister flipped end over end on the way down. It disappeared into the lush green of the trees and then struck. Propelled by inertia, a long, roiling spew of black-edged, bright orange flame raced through the jungle. This time it hit dead on. Without the need of being told, the SEALs opened up.

An enormous volume of lead slashed into the inferno

of napalm that cooked the VC as it volatilized hungrily. The salvo of small-arms fire ended after thirty seconds. In the numb silence that followed, the soft rumble of PBR engines came as almost an anticlimax.

Pope Marino rose from his make-do firing position. "Saddle up, guys. Time to go home."

Back at Tre Noc, Jason Slater waited for First Squad when they returned. He produced a broad smile, tipped back his 4X Stetson, and clapped a big, ham hand on the shoulder of Lieutenant Marino. "I've gotta fess up, Marino. When I said I knew of General Giap, I didn't tell you every little thing I knew about him. Thing is, he's the NVA's crack expert on interrogations and brainwashing. And I've since learned something that tells me why he's comin' south."

Doc Welby stood close by and took in their exchange with considerable interest and not a little growing apprehension. Pope Marino cocked his head to one side and gave the CIA station chief a suspect look. "So, tell me. I'm all ears."

"That was the good news. Now, here's the really bad news. I've come down here to Tre Noc to call on help for a special mission. There are five big-ticket Company men being held captive somewhere in the Delta. No doubt they are the cause of Giap's visit."

Marino replaced distrust with a scowl. "Something tells me I'm not going to like the rest of this."

Dressed as usual, in a Western-cut suit, complete with M. L. Leddy handmade cowboy boots, Stetson, and frilly-front white shirt, Jason Slater did not look the least the highly skilled area director of the Central Intelligence Agency he in fact was. He wore his hair long and carried his regulation 9mm Browning at the small of his back, preferring to pack a .45 Colt Single Action in a buscadero holster strapped around his waist. He took a step back now and feigned an expression of hurt and disappointment.

"You wound me, Pope. Truly you do. All I'm asking is that you take First Platoon out to locate these captive Agency people."

"That can be better done by aerial recon, right?"

"We've tried that and got zip. So you have to go out and find them."

"And?" Pope Marino prompted.

"And then you lay on a rescue. It wouldn't be a bad idea," Slater added as a quick afterthought, "if you were to bring General Giap out with them."

At first, Marino thought Slater had gone around the bend. "Just like a friggin' spook," he muttered to himself.

"What's that? Did you say you'd be glad to oblige?"

"I said it was impossible. Even for us. Oh, we can find this camp if it exists, but it will take a larger force than we can muster to break anyone out. Count on it."

"You'd get all the support you need."

Pope Marino continued to protest. "It wouldn't make that much difference."

Jason Slater became conciliatory. "Think on it. What a hell of a coup it would be. Take your time and you'll come around, I'm sure. I'll give you twenty-four hours."

If a flamboyant dresser, Jason Slater was nothing if not determined and persistent. He would not be put off by Marino's assertion that the proposed mission was impossible for so small a unit to carry out. He left Tre Noc and went directly to Binh Thuy. Using a frequently employed spook tactic, he visited the office of the S-2, LCDR Barry Lailey. Well aware of the animosity between the lieutenant commander and Lieutenant Marino, Slater decided to take advantage of the situation to get what he wanted.

"Always have time for the Agency, Mr. Slater, do come in, come in," LCDR Lailey announced unctuously.

"What is the occasion of your call? I'm sure that, as important as you are, it is hardly social."

Jason Slater felt as though he had been dipped in the purest extra-virgin olive oil. If collaboration with this cloud merchant got him what he wanted, Jason promised himself, he would see to it that Lailey had to squat to piss for the rest of his life. He forced a smile he did not feel.

"You're right of course, Commander. It's a matter of a little task I have for you SEALs, and a combined ops force."

"Sounds interesting. Let me get our S-Three in here."

Slater raised a hand, palm forward, to halt the flow of insincere verbiage. "No need for that at this stage. Right now the matter is strictly between thee and me."

Lailey cocked a shaggy, graying eyebrow. "Oh? You have me thoroughly hooked. What is this about?"

Slater sighed heavily. "I hate to admit that anyone in the Company can screw up. The truth is, some have, bigtime."

"Some? Please go on, Mr. Slater."

"Five to be exact. At varying times and under differing circumstances, they have been captured by the Viet Cong. It is my understanding that there is a POW camp somewhere in the Delta, run by the NVA. Our men are supposed to have been taken there."

LCDR Lailey smiled a cat-and-canary smile. "I sense the dawn about to break."

"Yes, indeed. Needless to say, we want our people back. Now, this particular enemy does not believe in prisoner exchanges. That leaves us the sole option of a forcible repatriation."

Jesus, these spooks have one hell of a vocabulary, Lailey thought to himself. "What you're getting at," he said aloud, "is that you want our SEALs to extract your colleagues from this camp, if it indeed exists."

"Why do you doubt it does, Commander Lailey?"

"If you were certain, you'd offer a little quid pro quo."

"Precisely."

Slater's nonsequitur confused Lailey. He decided to be more direct. "To put it bluntly, what's in it for us?"

Slater knew that *us* meant *me* to the potbellied bureaucrat across the desk from him. "The satisfaction of a job well-done. And perhaps some first-class R and R in say ... Tokyo for those who make it happen."

LCDR Lailey produced a hungry shark smile. More than he had expected. Not on a par with a promotion, but definitely something to strive for. And, all considered, if this madcap mission fizzled, it would provide a wonderful opportunity to fix Carl Marino's wagon. Obviously something to aspire to. Lailey put on a face of decisiveness and nodded curtly.

"We'll do it, then. For that matter, I'll send the best. First Platoon will receive the assignment."

Jason Slater left the office cream-in-cat satisfied with himself. He'd played that buffoon perfectly.

CHAPTER 7 —————————————

WONDERFUL, KENT Welby thought when he got the word. He had a big party laid on for the birthday of Francie Song. Instead, they were being put on alert for an impending mission that would begin early the next morning. He would have to meet her immediately she got off work and explain.

When 1600 hours rolled around, Doc Welby waited outside the Riverine Force offices. A slight tic at the corner of his left eye betrayed his nervousness. What the hell, he chided himself. *It's not as if we were married*. That got him to thinking about Betty and her refusal to send the divorce papers. Damn her for leaving him to hang out and dry like this! Which saw him in a dandy mood when Francie Song came through the open doorway.

She brightened at the first sight of Welby. "How nice. You've come to walk me home?"

"Uh—n-no, Francie. That is, I can't leave the base. There's an operation tomorrow. So we're on alert. I'm afraid your—ah—dinner will be delayed a few days. I'm sorry."

Her light mood altered in an instant. "Is that all? You are sorry?"

"Well—uh—I'm disappointed, too. Of course I am. This damn war's getting to be a nuisance."

"Is that what I am, too? A nuisance?"

Doc could not understand her shift into a quarreling mode. He gaped and stammered and tried to untie his tongue. "Oh, no. N-no, you could nev—never be. It's not what I mean at all."

"If not for the war, we would have never met," Francie accused. "So, if it annoys you, then I must, too. You men!" she railed on as she stamped one small, sandal-clad foot. "You are all alike. I do not know why we tolerate you at all."

So saying, she turned on one heel and darted to the bicycle rack. There she retrieved her aged Schwinn and pedaled off toward the front gate without a backward look.

What the hell did I do? Kent wondered as he watched her ride away.

Twelve hours later, Kent Welby boarded a PBR in darkness with the rest of his squad. The plan was to reach their AO (Area of Operations) shortly after daylight. For all their effectiveness against the enemy, Charlie still ruled the night in the Delta. It had been that way when they arrived and continued to the present. The nightly mortar rounds still harassed Tre Noc.

Shortly after twilight faded to darkness, unless the VC were celebrating a victory or some Marxist holiday, mortar rounds rained down for five to ten minutes. Never the same number, or for the same duration twice in a row, it was Charlie's intention to create a "waiting for the other shoe" complex in the Americans. *Au contraire*—all it served to do was piss them off and harden the determination to break the backs of the Viet Cong infrastructure. Some, like Tonto Waters and Archie Golden, Doc Welby reflected, had come to ignore it entirely. Doc eased his back against the engine compartment hatch combing and shifted his thoughts to his primary problem.

Betty sat on the divorce to torment him, and Francie was mad at him. How had things gotten in such a state? For that matter, who was it he really loved? When with Francie, he profoundly believed that he loved her. Yet, was he truly ready to leave his wife for another woman? And a Vietnamese at that? Not that Kent Welby had been raised a bigot; in truth, he had not a prejudiced bone in his body. Francie's race had nothing to do with anything from his point of view. Yet, he could not ignore the effect his relationship with Francie Song had on certain others.

In particular, non-SEAL officers. Doc had his own theory about that. SEALs were single-minded. Dedicated as they were to the arts of Mars, they had no room in their minds for such frivolous things as bigotry. Desk sailors, on the other hand, seemed to thrive on it. It came out in a lot of ways. For one, in the contempt shown toward the informal relationship between SEAL officers and their enlisted men. The word PROTOCOL seemed to be emblazoned in bold-faced letters on the minds of the deskbound Navy.

Then there was their attitude toward marriage between American sailors and Asian women. Vietnam being a war zone, it was flatly prohibited. Doc could understand that for security reasons. Yet, the prejudice extended to encompass Philippine and Japanese women as well. At least, he had heard, the paperwork was mountainous and deliberately restrictive. The Brass Hats made it all but impossible. That had no immediate effect on Doc. The best he could expect for himself and Francie was to continue as in the present. They would cohabit and hope for a change in policy.

What about children? There would be a lot of half-American children without fathers when this mess finally ended in Vietnam. Doc knew that only too well. Did he want to contribute to it because of Navy policy on marrying Vietnamese women? Not likely, he told himself. A sudden shift in the revolutions of the water-jet propulsion unit took Doc's mind off all that.

"There's always a Cong outpost around this bend," the coxswain informed his passengers.

Without being asked, Doc eased himself upright and stepped to the starboard rail. There he put one hand on the operating handle of a Honeywell 40 mike-mike grenade launcher. A quick visual check showed the belted rounds to be in position and ready to feed. The PBR slewed farther outward into the mainstream, and Doc canted the weapon to compensate. A cocoa-colored bone rose from the bow of the powerful boat as the coxswain again increased speed.

"We'll try to run past them before they can react," the boat driver explained.

"Chatty feller ain't he?" Tonto Waters muttered to Archie Golden.

"Fat-fucking-chance," Repeat Ditto commented on the optimistic visions of the coxswain. "Those Japs have ears like sonar," he explained his doubt to Zoro Agilar.

" 'Japs?' " Agilar asked.

"Yeah. That's what everyone was callin' them when we first got here. Some things just stick."

If Chad Ditto had anything else to say on the subject, it got drowned out in the chug of the Honeywell in the hands of Doc Welby. Followed shortly on the first three chugs by the roar of exploding 40mm grenades low in the jungle underbrush. Screams followed. The PBR came to full throttle. An abbreviated rooster tail rose at the stern.

"Well, there goes any chance of sneaking by," Tonto Waters observed to no one in particular as he manned one of the previously idle M60s along the starboard rail.

They ran out of range in less than a minute. No casualties and only a couple of bright streaks on the freeboard of the hull indicated that any of the Cong had returned fire.

When the PBR arrived at the SEALs' AO, they surprised a number of sampan owners. Since they were out in broad daylight, the Vietnamese were judged to be friendly. Sharp questioning by one of the Provisional Recon Unit (PRU) scouts brought along as interpreter and guide established this to be correct. The PRUs had been formed in ARVN and were made up entirely of former VC who had come over. Knowing that they faced immediate execution as traitors if captured, they fought with even greater ferocity than the Vietnamese regulars or the enemy. More than once, Doc Welby reflected, they had proven their worth to the SEALs. Pope Marino stepped forward with an idea.

"Why don't we conscript these sampans and their owners? We can ride in the covered portion of the deckhouse and observe all around."

That proposition was put to the scout, who relayed it to the boatmen. A lot of agitated jabber followed. When his exasperation level reached its limit, the scout barked them into silence and pointed meaningfully to the weapons of the SEALs and indicated their relative size to the little brown men. Frowns appeared at first, followed by a tentative smile, then more as the Vietnamese grasped the implication of having their craft taken by force.

One fist on his hip, the other holding his AR-15 casually, Pope Marino grinned back. "Fine, then, we understand one another. Let's start loading up."

General Hoi Pac had returned to the lavish, French colonial villa that he used as his headquarters in Vinh province of North Vietnam. Charged with establishing total control over the Delta region for the government of the North, recent events greatly disturbed him. In particular the recent humiliating loss of supplies and the initiative they represented for a planned major offensive. He had lost uncountable face to those accursed US Navy SEALs.

In fact, his superiors had given him only one more opportunity to redeem himself. Failure would result in the ultimate humiliation. He would be stripped of rank, sent to a self re-examination camp and made to labor like a coolie. Utter disgrace. However, he experienced equal revulsion at having to distastefully grovel before that Russian *quai'lo* pig, Kovietski. Upon his arrival at his headquarters, a message had been waiting him. He was to handle the overall coordination of General Giap's visit to the Delta. NVA troops were to be used as a security force to protect the talented and unexpendable interrogation specialist.

The hell of it was, Gen. Vinh Toy Giap was already on his way, with a stopover in Cambodia on route. Hoi would have to scramble to assemble a company of regulars and dispatch them in the general's wake. At least, Kovietski knew nothing of that. Thinking about it gave him a tremendous headache. He badly needed some special soothing. With practiced familiarity his hand reached for the small silver bell on one corner of his huge desk. He raised it and had tinkled it only twice when an orderly appeared.

"Bring me a bottle of Chinese wine," Hoi commanded. "And, oh, yes, bring—aah—Soon An this time."

General Hoi's wine arrived a moment before a slightly built, painfully young, Vietnamese girl entered the room, escorted by the orderly. She was barefoot and wore only a sheer cotton shift that hung from her narrow shoulders, down her boyish body, to end at mid-thigh. She could not have seen her fifteenth birthday. The timid light in her large, doelike, ebon eyes grew brighter when General Hoi looked at her with intensity and smiled lewdly.

"Come here, child. I am in need of your curative talents," Hoi purred invitingly.

Soon An knew full well what that implied. She desperately fought back the scalding tears of shame that flooded her eyes. She hated doing *that thing* to this evil old man! Far from lacking in intelligence, Soon An knew that she had no other choice. She had been purchased from her parents—confiscated actually—for exactly this sort of activity. Resigned to her fate, Soon An took a hesitant step forward. General Hoi sat, sprawled in a large, high, curved-back rattan chair, a wine cup in one hand, the open bottle in the other. Soon An approached with mounting dread.

"Come, come, do not dawdle, child. You know how very good you can make me feel."

Vision mercifully blurred by tears, Soon An crossed the remaining distance and knelt between Hoi's outstretched legs. Loathing what she knew she must do, she reached out reluctantly with one hand and took hold of the zipper of Hoi's trousers.

The SEALs of First Squad spent a day learning that a waterborne survey was fruitless. They had seen a lot of jungle and a lot of the tributaries of the Mekong River. They had seen no Viet Cong or any sign of them. They certainly had not located anything that resembled a POW compound. With enough daylight left to locate their RON (Rest Over Night) site, Lt. Carl Marino called a halt to the exercise.

"We'll wait here until Bravo links up," Pope Marino whispered to his men after gathering them close.

"Good enough with me, Pope," Tonto Waters opined. "Ridin' in that sampan made my joints stiff."

Unable to resist a jibe at his friend, or a pun, Archie Golden quipped, "Hey, Tonto, I was ridin' in the same sampan. I didn't see any female that could have caused that.''

''I said *'joints'* plural, Numb-nuts. Like knees, an' elbows, and such.''

''Oh. There's a lesson to be learned there, Randy Andy,'' he turned to Andrew Holt to declare.

''What's that, Archie?'' Holt asked, playing into Golden's hand.

''That the older one gets, the harder it is to do some things. Say, did you hear about the two nuns riding on a bus through a rough neighborhood? One turns to the other and says, 'It's hard to be good these days.' An' the other one says, 'It's got to—' ''

''Yeah, I heard it about a dozen times,'' Lt. Marino interrupted in a growl. Raised a good Catholic, although sliding somewhat, after all he had been through in combat, he still didn't care for such jokes. ''Batten down that lip of yours, Archie and let's keep a sharp eye for Charlie.''

Second Squad arrived ten minutes later. The Vietnamese boatmen were glad to be rid of their unwanted guests. They poled and paddled their way out of sight with more energy than any among them had exhibited in years. They well knew what would happen to them if the VC saw them in the presence of these fearsome Men with Green Faces. With his force intact, Marino put Tonto Waters on point and they set out to cross overland to the RON site.

Tonto Waters heard the metallic clatter of dried bamboo poles behind him and knew at once what it meant. Spiderhole trap! Damned if these Cong weren't getting smarter, he thought as he spun back toward the staggered column of SEALs behind him. They had figured out not to fire on the point man any more from their cleverly concealed shooting stations. That way they caught the CO of whatever unit tried to pass through VC country on that particular trail.

Gazing over his sights, Tonto saw why the enemy had become smarter. The pith helmet and gray-green uniform shirt of an NVA soldier came into the field of fire. The North Vietnamese aimed an AK-47 at the center of the chest of Pope Marino. Tonto took it in short of a half second and loosed a round.

Number 4 buckshot from his Ithaca sprayed in a horizontal fan that struck the back of the NVA soldier's head. It disintegrated the pith helmet and most of the enemy's skull. The AK discharged into the ground six feet in front of him, and he jerked backward from a 7.62mm round popped off by Randy Andy from an oblique angle. Instantly the SEALs faded into the jungle. Hell sat down for breakfast in the next instant as what Tonto Waters estimated to be a platoon-strength unit opened up on the clearing he had just passed through.

"Bugger this," he heard Archie Golden grouse.

An M-26 grenade arced through the air. It was followed by the soft bloop of two M-79 tubes. The one was in the form of an XM148 grenade launcher under the barrel of Chad Ditto's AR-15. They exploded in a rolling crescendo that brought a momentary lull in hostile fire. Archie tried a Willie Peter (White Phosphorous) grenade next.

Its white plume of chemical smoke and glowing alabaster blobs of phosphorous elicited a satisfying number of screams. Randy Andy concentrated on the area around the shrieking VC and chopped up a lot of vegetation and human flesh with the M60. Doc Welby hunkered down behind the stump of a long-ago logged-out mahogany tree and squinted to pick out targets.

Full-auto fire might soothe shattered nerves, he reasoned, but aimed fire ensured a high body count. It also kept enemy heads down, which lessened the chance of buying the farm. The name of the game in Charlie country was not to die for one's country, but to make the other bastard die for his. Was this a random patrol? Doc wondered. Or did it mean they were much closer to the suspected POW camp than they expected? Either way, he didn't much like it.

It wasn't that YO/1C Kent Welby did not carry his load. He fought as hard and as well as any SEAL. Only Doc didn't believe it. After nearly two months in combat, Doc harbored the uneasy suspicion that he would turn yellow, chicken out, let his buddies down. Nothing so far had lent credence to that nearly incapacitating thought. Not even when he had been ignominiously shot in the ass.

It hadn't been that serious a wound, the slug had barely penetrated the skin and embedded in the muscle that Fil Nicholson, the platoon medic, called the *gluteus maximus*. But the tepid water that drained from his canteen and saturated the entire area of his buttocks had scared the hell out of him. Doc believed for a short while that he would bleed to death. That hadn't happened, and Fil had removed the slug, patched him up and gone on to tend other wounded. Doc had come in for a lot of ribbing, though, from the other SEALs of the platoon. In the end, and no pun intended, his pride had been hurt much more than his tail end. Unfortunately the incident had done nothing to dispel his lurking belief that he might yet prove himself a coward. A VC came at him out of the bush and ended that line of speculation.

Doc Welby opened up with his secondary weapon, a Stoner 5.56mm snorter. He ticked off one- and two-round bursts that found home in the chest of the Charlie who threatened him. The target went rubber-legged and fell with a crash. Already Doc was on the move to another position. Good thing that he did, too.

Enfilading fire slashed into his former position and chopped the top of the tree stump to sawdust. Doc located the shooter and longed for his primary weapon, the big 700 Remington sniper rifle. His sandy blond hair stood out from the camo headband, made more vivid by each wash of adrenaline that whitened his face even further. Steady on, he told himself. Before he could take aim, Repeat Ditto solved the problem for Doc.

A 40mm round from Repeat's XM148 gave a flash and roar overhead and slashed into the body of the exposed Cong. It ripped him to pieces. What was left fell from his cleverly concealed tree platform. That gave further concern to Kent Welby that they had stumbled upon the prisoner compound. Archie tossed a couple more grenades, which made angry bellows. Then, with the sudden, silent finality of all firefights, the battle ended. In that overwhelming minute after two sides disengage, single rounds are often not heard. A few pops and cracks continued while the SEALs cautiously surveyed the damage they had wrought.

"Awesome," Randy Andy breathed out in a hushed whisper. "How many were there?"

"I'd say a platoon," Tonto Waters offered. "For you newlies, that's twenty-four."

"We know that," Randy Andy complained in an offended tone. "That means we were outnumbered better than three to one."

"No. I'd say it was them who were outnumbered," Archie Golden offered.

"How's that?" Zoro Agilar asked, his Latino face alight with the afterglow of combat.

"Because we're SEALs, that's why. And we didn't even have to call on Bravo for help."

Zoro shot Archie the thumbs-up sign. "*Oye, muy macho, de veras!*"

"Hooyaa, indeed, my tamale-slurpin' friend," Archie returned, using a popular SEAL phrase.

"What do we do now?" Randy Andy asked.

"Keep movin', of course. What did you want, for Pope to call for extraction?"

"No, no, we got a job to do," Randy Andy accepted.

Before they left the area, the SEALs made a thorough search of the bodies. Doc Welby discovered the reason for the carefully planned ambush positions. A real first-class bunker and tunnel system had been laid out and amply supplied. Much lament went among them that they did not have any satchel charges along.

"What the hell do you think those Russkie grenades are good for?" Archie Golden advised. "Lemme rig them up to a long trip wire, and we'll blow this cage from a nice, safe distance. Say fifty feet from the entry."

"You gotta be kidding, Archie," Tonto Waters chided. "With all the ordnance down here, this place will go sky-high."

Archie assumed a far-off, worshipful expression. "Yeah. Ain't it nice?"

It took less than half an hour for Archie to satisfy himself as to the ability of the explosives on hand to destroy the tunnel system. He carefully carried the wire outside, made sure everyone was clear by at least a hundred meters, then gave a stout yank.

Nothing happened of course. At least not for four seconds. Then the ground erupted in a huge, swollen mound, as though ejecting a malignant tumor, the belly of the earth bulged, fumed and smoked, while ominous rumbles came from inside. When it suddenly subsided without fanfare, the SEALs felt it had been an anticlimax.

They made it three hundred meters farther along when Tonto Waters, again on point, made contact with a random patrol he quickly recognized as NVA regulars. The tough North Vietnamese didn't have time to open fire first. Tonto cut down two of them with a single round of buckshot. He dived aside, off the trail and heard the squad scatter behind.

We must be getting close, he thought, for there to be so many damned NVA around, and in daylight at that. Then he stopped thinking about it as four of Charlie's finest rushed directly at him.

CHAPTER 8 _____

FROM HIS right rear, Tonto heard the heavy cough of the M60 MG in what was proving to be the very capable hands of Randy Andy Holt. He trashed two of the bad guys facing Tonto in less time than Waters would have credited possible. That left a pair for him to deal with.

Tonto obliged himself. A slightly sharper recoil informed him that he had discharged a round. The nasty little hardened buckshot sprayed outward from the duck-bill shot disburser. Two of them impacted the wooden butt-stock of an AK-47. The trio traveling with them embedded in the gut of the NVA trooper who carried the 7.62mm weapon.

Waters watched a moment as the man dropped his rifle and clawed at his savaged belly. By the time Tonto had cycled in a fresh round, he had already cut his eyes to the other likely target. Charlie had charged forward, leaped over the writhing body of his comrade and kept on in his suicidal attempt to end the life of Chief Tom Waters. He might as well not have bothered.

An AR-15 spoke twice from the opposite side of the trail, and the NVA soldier did a brief death dance before he pitched into the awaiting spiked end branches of a shattered strangler fig. "Thanks, Pope, I owe you one," Tonto called out, as he stuffed three fresh rounds into the magazine tube of the Ithaca.

"Just keep that shotgun talkin'," Pope Marino called back.

From where he crouched in the knees of an ancient mangrove, Kent Welby felt the familiar coldness grow in his belly. Fleeting shadows flickered through the swampy jungle, the NVA in an attempt to flank the squad. Doc swallowed his uncertainty and thumbed the selector to full-auto. The next movement by the Cong brought an instant response.

Two of Poppa Ho's little boys went off to that big Central Committee in the Sky in a hail of 5.56mm jacketed bullets and their own screams. Instantly, Doc Welby forced himself to move. He dived and rolled away from the mangrove while an incoming cargo of Chinese Communist lead cracked by overhead. *Too damned close!* Doc held that thought while he wormed his way through the damp mulch that made up the jungle floor.

This heads-up, balls-to-the-wall sort of thing wasn't what they had become accustomed to. Usually they went out, hunted down the enemy, then got ahead of them and laid an ambush. Even Tonto Waters's favorite parakeet operations relied on elements of misdirection and surprise. No denying it had been Tonto who had been surprised by that VC ambush farther back on the trail. Hell, Tonto had barely time to get a shot off when he made contact with this bunch. Doc saw another furtive rustling in the brush and sprayed the vegetation.

These guys fight like NVA regulars, Doc continued his summary of their action. Those had been regulars back at the ambush. Suddenly this had ceased to be business as usual. The enemy rarely utilized NVA troops on routine patrols in the Delta, Doc recalled. Their own operations and those of Marvin the ARVN had battened down the hatch on the whole area. Something real important had to be close by for there to be so many regulars employed. The thought did little to lighten Doc's mood.

* * *

Corporal Qaun Sat of the Army of the Socialist Republic of Vietnam had heard of the ferocity of these Men with Green Faces from the day he first arrived. As a professional, he scornfully discounted the stories of their strength. After all, what could peasants, only recently converted into partisan fighting men, know about accurately evaluating the military prowess of the enemy?

Now, he found his confidence severely shaken. Counting muzzle flashes, as he had been taught in training, told Corporal Sat that his patrol faced a mere seven men. Yet, fully a third of his comrades had been cut down in less than three minutes. Unfortunately, that included Lieutenant Binh and Sergeant Van. That left him in command of the remaining eleven men. Corporal Sat had always tried to excel, to strive for political correctness and military skill, in order to win promotion. Only last week, Lieutenant Binh had told him that his name would appear on the next promotion list.

Sat's chest had swollen in pride at this, though he kept his spoken response suitably humble and self-depreciatory. He had muttered some politically correct party slogans and expressed his gratitude, then saluted with precision and left the stilt-supported hooch that served as office and living quarters for Lieutenant Binh. Yet, he now found himself in command, still unpromoted, and the lieutenant who had forwarded his name dead. If he failed to be successful in this engagement, any hope for advancement would be ended. He might as well be dead.

A sharp *burrr* of automatic weapons fire brought Sat from his grim reverie. Liana vines and air plants to his left exploded into shreds of green and white and fluttered to the ground. The deadly stream of copper-jacketed lead worked its way steadily toward him. Cpl. Quan Sat wanted very badly to move. In fact, the entire patrol should fall back to regroup and hit these green-faced de-mons when least expected. To that end, he raised his brass whistle to his lips and sucked in breath with which to blow.

The first sharp notes of the whistle drew decidedly un-wanted attention. Fire from several points concentrated on Corporal Sat. The shrilling ceased. Sat hunkered low while bullets cracked overhead and to either side. He did not hear the shot that sent five No. 4 buckshot pellets to smash into his chest and still his heart.

When the whistling failed to resume after the SEALs ceased fire, Tonto Waters observed, "We found out who's in charge over there."

"I'd say you're right, Tonto," Pope Marino opined. To Archie Golden, "Lob a couple of grenades their way, Archie."

"Aye, Pope."

Two M-26 frag grenades sailed into the air, two sec-onds apart. They burst accordingly and elicited only si-lence in answer. The NVA had properly assayed the meaning of the chirping whistle and moved out. Only, being suddenly leaderless, they had kept on going.

Pope put words to Kent Welby's speculation. "Damn, looks like we stepped into the middle of something big. When we reach our RON site, we had better dig in and let the area cool off a little. We have rations for two more days. What we need is to keep out of sight until they think the patrol has been pulled out." He paused, thoughtfully. "I'll work on something to make the illusion more real-istic. Check the bodies, if there are any, and we'll move on."

Kent Welby's stomach churned when he came upon a corpse that had been badly chewed by a close-up grenade blast. Enough was left to identify him as an NVA regular.

Beyond the man Doc found something that sent him to make silent hand signals to Pope Marino.

"Look at this, sir," Doc spoke softly when Pope joined him.

Lieutenant Marino gazed down on the sprawled body. His features pinched as he realized the importance of what he saw. "A regular officer. I'm positive now that we're not far from a major operation of some sort. If there is a POW camp, I'd say we've come close, right enough. What I said earlier stands. We lie low and divert their attention. Damn, I'm sorry we had these firefights. Charlie is goosie enough, these NVA types will go bat-shit over being caught way down here. We'll be lucky if they don't fold their action and boogie off somewhere far away."

Eloise Daladier stepped off the last step of the boarding ramp of the Air France flight from Singapore to Saigon. Every male eye in the civilian terminal at Tan Son Nhut turned her way. From her trim, well-turned ankles to her classic waist and firm, though feminine shoulders, Eloise left no doubt that she was every inch female. A fact which her mannish-cut, white-linen suit attempted to belie. It failed, though, much to every man's delight.

At twenty-six, Eloise was the youngest, and one of the first, female correspondents for the prestigious French international newspaper, *Le Monde*. She had worked hard to achieve that notoriety, something that did not go unnoticed among her male colleagues. That she was the daughter of a former Foreign Legion officer, with a Vietnamese mother, born in the country and totally fluent in her native language, as well as French, German, and English, made her a natural to head the Vietnamese desk of *Le Monde*.

That qualification elicited numerous growls and grumbles among the more experienced male correspondents at the magazine. Many resented being passed over for the choice plum of reporting a war. Some, the more chauvaninistic among *Le Monde*'s masculine journalists, went so far as to call it being "trampled over." None of which fazed Eloise in the least. She was good. Damned good, and she knew it. With camera and typewriter, she could produce volumes of hard-hitting material on a par with any Pulitzer winner. That she had so far not been tapped for that coveted prize she did not ascribe to her gender. Far from it. She accepted the reality of the situation.

Right now, war stories were not on the front burner of the Pulitzer committee. Particularly ones like she wrote, which put the American forces and their allies in a favorable light. She was definitely not a propagandist. Yet, Eloise had enough acumen to be aware that her even-handed treatment of American involvement in Vietnam gave her *entrée* to the offices of more generals, and a few admirals, than the display of any other attitude might possibly have. Her return to Saigon, following three weeks in Paris, had come as welcome news.

Her roundabout itinerary had tired her—long hours in the air, followed by equally boring ones in the international lounge of four airports—and she looked forward to a long soak and her soft bed in her suite at the Hotel International. The quarters had been arranged long before the initial escalation of American involvement. *Le Monde* paid for it, one of the perks for their Saigon bureau chief. Although fiercely proud of her heritage, Eloise had to admit that anyone stationed here deserved all of the perks she or he could promote.

After recovering her luggage, eagerly carried by a thoroughly infatuated teenage Vietnamese boy, Eloise avoided the kamakazi automobile taxis in favor of a pedicab. She would ride into town in its stately quiet and blessedly slower speed. A smiling, white-haired man, with wispy strands of matching beard on his age-wrinkled chin, swept his hat from his head in old worldly fashion and bowed low as Eloise approached the rank of pedicabs.

"Welcome back to Saigon, *Mademoiselle* Daladier."

"*Merci beaucoup,* Etian. I am glad to be here.," Eloise
answered sweetly.

She thought she must be a sight. Her long, black hair,
gathered into a rough ponytail, hung limply down her
back. Her clothes were wrinkled from over twenty hours
of travel. Etian Vahng was an institution among the cab-
bies at Tan Son Nhut. Raised by the Sisters of Charity,
in their Saigon orphanage, he had acquired European
courtly manners, along with a command of the French
language far superior to most Vietnamese. He must be
scandalized at her appearance. No, she readjusted her
concerned thoughts, Etian was accustomed to greeting
travelers. And, Saigon was a long way from nearly everywhere. He would understand.

Her worry over offending the old man's sensitivities
amused her. Long and leggy, she climbed into the wicker-
basket passenger compartment. Her luggage was strapped
to the rear. She tipped the porter, who gulped and swallowed with difficulty before thanking her. *Poor boy,* Eloise mused, *he is still suffering in the throes of adolescent
lovesickness.*

Eloise did not form that opinion from arrogance or
smugness, or from conceit. She had long ago become accustomed to the admiring gaze of most nearly every male
close by. Since her own teenage years, she had always
been able to tell which men were *poufs* by their obvious
lack of response to her looks.

"Hotel International," Eloise instructed Etian.

"*Naturellement, mademoiselle.*" The pedicab whisked
Eloise away at its own elegant, languorous pace.

As expected, her room awaited her. The desk clerk
fawned over her. Heads turned among the American journalists in the lobby and at the sunken conversation area
outside the entranceway to the Carousel Lounge. Several
hoisted glasses in informal, familiar greeting. Eloise gave

them the benefit of her sunny smile and followed the bell-boy to the elevator.

The ancient, creaky platform rose to the third floor and disgorged her on the oft-traveled carpet. She took the key from her large, leather travel purse and opened the door. The floor concierge had been ahead of her and turned on the ceiling fans. Humid air wafted slowly around the living room of her suite.

"Thank you so much," Eloise told the bellboy after he deposited her luggage in the bedroom. She tipped him generously and he departed.

Eloise went to the small refrigerator under the counter in her wet bar and extracted a bottle of Perrier. From the tiny freezer, she took a bottle of Stolichnaya vodka and a tulip glass. She poured a generous portion, opened the mineral water and emptied half into another glass, added ice and drank contentedly.

And that quickly, her thoughts turned back to what had occupied her all the way back to Saigon. A certain tousel-haired sailor with burled-walnut-colored eyes and a smile as warm and generous as any she had ever seen. Chief Tom Waters, Tonto to his friends. The rugged American SEAL who, for some reason, thrilled Eloise like no other had ever done.

"Oh, Tom, Tom, I do hope you are safe," Eloise spoke aloud, in almost a groan.

At their RON site, Doc Welby came upon Archie Golden seated alone, staring out from behind the camouflage netting that hid the entrance to a small cave that had been located a year earlier by SEALs from Team 1. It did not appear on any local maps, and seemed to be known only to the SEALs. Archie had a troubled look on his face.

"Something biting your ass, Archie?" Doc asked off-handedly.

Richard Golden did not answer right away. He continued to stare, then moved slightly, sighed and grunted, then turned to face his friend. "Yeah, swim buddy, I got something biting me. But it's . . . nothin' you guys in the Team can work out."

"Try me. You know what's going on with Betty and me. It ain't exactly that I have no experience with problems from The World."

"Sure. Yeah, you're right, Doc. This thing has me really in a stew. It's part family and part—ah—religious. Fact is, I'm damned worried about what's going on at home. My wife wrote me, I got the letter last mail call. Our youngest, David, is only a month short of turning thirteen."

"So? Is it sex rearing its ugly head?" Doc asked lightly, hoping to dispel some of Archie's gloom.

"Naw. Nothin' like that, kid. That's where the religious part comes in. Davey has now decided he does not want a *bar mitzvah*. In our faith, a boy takes on the responsibilities of a grown man at age thirteen. It's old—old, traditional. Of course, in modern times, the government's got laws that decide when a boy becomes a man. But, to Jews, there is still this tradition. I don't know if you know anything about it, but when the time comes, the boy stands up in front of the congregation in Temple and reads a passage he has chosen from the Torah and then recites the ritual words, 'Today I am a man.' Then there's a big party and lots of gifts after. Well, Davey doesn't want his."

"Why not?" a surprised Doc Welby asked bluntly.

"He says he has decided he wants to wait until I come home."

Archie's dilemma struck such a deep, responsive chord in Doc's psyche that his misery welled up so compellingly that he found himself unable to advise, or even suggest any solution. He groped with words a moment, then offered lamely, "Maybe you ought to talk it over with Tonto."

"Uh, yeah. Could be." Archie returned to his miles-long stare until Doc wandered off to find a sterno rig to heat a can of C-rations. Then, slowly, Archie Golden roused himself and sought out Tonto Waters.

"Tonto, I've got this problem." Archie went on to explain as he had done for Doc. When he had finished, Tonto mused over the seeming impasse for a long, quiet minute, cleared his throat, and put a hand on his friend's shoulder. "Archie, I think the answer is rather simple. Write the kid and advise him to go on, have his *bar mitzvah*. Does he have to have you there as his sponsor, or somethin'?"

"No. Not exactly. That's why it bothers me so much."

"Hell, then, can't the kid have his godfather stand in?"

Archie gave Tonto an odd look. "Tonto, old buddy, whether you know it or not, Jews don't have godfathers."

Undaunted, Tonto came back at once. "How about an uncle?"

A transformation came over Archie Golden. Considerably brightened, he spoke softly, with wonder in his voice. "Yeah. That's the ticket. His Uncle Morris, my kid brother, would love doing it. You're a gem, Tonto. Not bad for an Episcopalian. Too bad you weren't born into the Golden family."

"Uh—thanks, Arch."

In the gathering gloom of the brief tropical twilight, Maxim Maximovich Yoriko slipped unseen off the pathway along which he and some twenty Vietnamese peasants had been walking. They had spent the day unloading a large motorized junk that had moored along the river near the big compound. Maxim's shoulders ached from the chaffing and strain of the wooden yoke which he had carried over his shoulder. The thirty-five-liter, Soviet-made jerrycans, suspended from the yoke by raw hemp rope attached at the four corners of the square containers, had held rice for the most part. A whole day of trudging along, engaged in coolie work. It angered the KGB agent. Yet, it satisfied him greatly.

His ruse had allowed him to gain access to the interior of the large, well-concealed compound and ferret out every one of its secrets. Major Rudinov (aka Sr. Lt. Alexi Kovietski) would be highly pleased with his success. He would also be extremely angry. How clever of these Oriental *narodniki* to have designed and hidden so well such a large complex, Maxim thought, completely ignoring his own Oriental lineage, albeit his was Tartar blood from Khabarovsk, Kamchatka.

It was this that allowed him so easily to infiltrate the press-gang of local peasants dragooned into unloading the ship. She had brought more than rice and dried peppers. There had been ammunition aboard and several crates of AK-47s, or at least the Chinese copy, the Type 56. Most interesting. Major Rudinov would be astounded to learn that these weapons had found their way to the Delta completely unknown to him. Yes, he would have to make it to his extraction point quickly. Balong Doang, his Cambodian guide, would be waiting with the sampan.

"So, Major Rudinov, you are in for quite a surprise when I make my report," he whispered smugly to himself.

At midmorning the next day, the AN/PRC 25 radio set on the back of Chad Ditto softly announced an incoming call. The subtle vibration ended when Chad pressed the "Talk" switch on the handset. "This is Alpha. Over."

"This is Bravo. Lemme talk to Eagle One. Over."

"Second Squad on the horn, L-T," Repeat Ditto whispered to Pope Marino.

"Hope they have something," Pope muttered to himself. "Eagle One, Bravo. What's goin' down?"

"I think we've come upon something, Eagle One. There's a wide, well-used trail cutting through our sector. It has a lot of traffic on it. Over."

"What are your coordinates, Bravo? Over."

Pope Marino listened intently as Anchor Head Sturgis read off their location. "Uh—Roger, Eagle One. We are in Hotel-Juliet, at 10579 by 08965. Give or take half a klick. Over."

Silence crackled in the radio speaker while Lieutenant Marino found the coordinates on his map. He didn't like the imprecision of five hundred meters one way or the other, but he could live with it. Wouldn't do for calling in an air strike or artillery, let alone a hot extraction by a slick. Looked to him like another session of map drill was in order. He pressed the talk butterfly.

"Okay, gotcha. Hold what you've got; we'll be there in a short. ETA of two hours. Over."

"Copy two hours, Eagle One. Bravo out."

A thoughtful expression furrowed Pope Marino's brow. "Bravo says they think they've found the main trail to this POW camp. We'll have to move across country to link up. We have two hours to do it. Tonto, take point."

Francie Song set the soda can on the table in the Base Exchange (BX). Several off-duty personnel took their ease at similar tables, grouped in front of the self-serve snack counter. A few wilted sandwiches, in ordinary sandwich bags, remained on one serving tray, in the open front shelves, along with half a dozen disposable bowls of tapioca pudding, a scattering of limp salad, and some drying buns. A bored young Vietnamese woman sat behind the cash register. The lunch crowd had long since gone back to work.

It was coffee break, an American ritual that Francie

found fascinating, if a terrible waste of work time. Why could they not take tea, like the British, or an *aperitif* like the French, in late afternoon, after work hours? Francie dismissed it with a slight, negative shake of her head and charged the quaint tradition off to the American difference. She looked across the table at the Marine Corps sergeant seated there. He flashed her a wide smile, made brighter by his fair complexion and ruff of red, crew-cut hair.

"You're fitting in over at ops just fine, Francie," he praised her in a broad, Texas drawl.

Francie blushed. "Why, thank you, Sergeant Yates."

"Please, call me El. It's short for Elmore." He waggled head and hands in depreciation. "Though why my Momma chose to call me that, I'll never know."

"Perhaps it is an old family name, Elmore? A custom, no?"

Yates clapped one large palm on his left thigh. "Dang if you didn't hit on it right off. That's why, of course. Her grandpappy was named Elmore. My paw wanted to name me Cyrus, after his father, but Momma said no. So, here I am; Elmore NMI Yates."

" 'NMI'? What is that?" Francie asked, clearly puzzled.

"No middle initial. Military stuff. Speakin' of military stuff, you been followin' this very hush-hush operation the SEALs have got themselves into?" Grammar was not a strong point with Elmore Yates.

Francie lowered her gaze to study the uneven surface of the table. "No. I try to avoid the hush-hush as you put it."

Yates brushed it aside. "You oughten't to. That's where the excitement comes in what we do. Gettin' to know what all is goin' on all around us. Tell you what. You look at some of the orders and after-action reports that are comin' in an' tell me it doesn't get your old juices flowin'.''

"I—I think that would not be right, to mix myself into the affairs of your military."

"Naw, honey. I guarantee if you do it, you'll get yer body all excited, if you know what I mean? Jist knowin' there's all that danger out there can work you up right quick." Yates took on a sly, insinuating expression. "See, the way I figger it, what with that boyfriend of yours off on this special operation, you must be gettin' mighty lonely. Stands to reason you could use some—ah—companionship. Know what I mean?" He added a salacious wink.

Francie's face became closed, distant, forbidding. "I am sorry, *Sergeant Yates*," she said icily. "I haven't the least idea what you mean. But, I am sure you can find someone who shares your interest in official secrets to get 'the old juices flowing.' Thank you for the soda, Sergeant," she concluded in a tone of dismissal.

Elmore Yates would have liked to press his case further, but he correctly read the face of Francie Song and cut off his planned second approach. They had to work together, were elbow-close every day, and the bitch knew it. Some day he would get his share of that honey-amber quim. Of that he was certain.

CHAPTER 9 _____

POPE MARINO slid in beside Anchor Head Sturgis. "What have we got out there?" he asked in a soft whisper, with a nod toward the wide, spacious trail.

"Pope, we've got us a regular Viet Cong freeway. We've got Charlie and the NVA comin' and goin' all the time. Hell, it's an interstate highway. So much traffic a feller can't even move out of position to take a leak. True story," Dan Sturgis protested with a raised hand. "Two of my boys have had to piss in their drawers. Last night it wasn't so bad. But since daylight, we've had to hold tight." He paused, listening intently.

"Uh-oh, more comin' our way. Lieutenant, we ain't got enough Riverine boats on the fuckin' Mekong, you ask me," Sturgis offered. Whenever he sought to exercise what every NCO knew, that it was the chiefs and the other petty officers who really ran the Navy, Anchor Head became strictly formal in his manner of address to officers. For all their closeness as SEALs, he did not make an exception for Lt. Carl Marino.

"No, sir," he went on. "Gawdamned gooks been comin' an' goin' all mornin'. Sure, you expect that, come night. But this is just bra—brazer . . ."

"Brazen?" Pope supplied.

"Aye, that's it, sir."

103

"For all this heavy traffic you have observed, can you give me a headcount?"

Sturgis failed to detect the note of mild sarcasm in Marino's tone. "Right at forty, sir. Some fifteen of 'em came back out, along with three I'd not seen go in. Right, sir," he cautioned. "Here comes Charlie now."

Led by their point man, seven small brown men in black pajamas trudged along the trail. Their conical, woven palm-frond hats bobbed rhythmically to the movement of their sandals over the hard-packed ground. Directly behind the point, three VC and an obvious NVA clustered around a figure which towered over them. An Occidental; his size as well as his light brown hair revealed this.

His face showed the results of a savage beating. Welts and cuts abounded. Most remained red and raw, not yet showing the purple and yellow of age. He wore a stained flight suit, and one arm hung limply, at an odd angle, although it had been indifferently lashed to a bamboo pole that ran across his back. When the party of VC drew nearer, Tonto Waters, from his vantage point could make out the design of the pilot's wings. A jarhead. No doubt one from a Marine Corps squadron on one of the carriers off the coast. He tried to recall which one that would be. VMF-217, he supposed.

Sympathy for the pilot rose hot in Tonto's chest. The Marine pilots were the absolute best at flying close air support. Now here was one, hurting for sure. If they needed verification that a POW camp existed nearby, this was it, he thought. Something else occurred to him. It would have to wait until the enemy had gone out of sight and hearing, though.

"Keep moving, fascist American pig!" the NVA patrol leader barked as he gave the pilot a vicious shove.

With his ankles fastened together by a two-foot strip of vine, and a bamboo pole shoved down his trousers to the crotch, fastened to the crosspiece, and tied at waist, chest, and neck, the Marine went off-balance at once and fell heavily on his face. He stifled all but a small bit of a cry of pain. Two of the VC began to kick him. They did it slowly, methodically, clearly in no hurry to force their prisoner to his feet. Feebly the Marine tried to rise, only to be struck down by the butt-stock of a Type 56 assault rifle.

"Why don't we just waste these fuckers now and set that guy loose?" Anchor Head muttered close to Marino's ear.

"We wouldn't get half a klick, Anchor Head, you know that."

Sturgis sighed heavily. "Yeah. I do. But . . . *God* . . . *damn* . . . *it*, sir . . ." He let it hang.

Roughly dragged to his feet, the Marine pilot stumbled along, shoved repeatedly by the VC, until they went around a bend and out of sight of the SEALs. "Besides," Pope Marino explained in a louder voice, "this might prove useful to us."

"Just my thoughts, sir," Tonto Waters announced as he slid into place close by Marino and the Bravo Squad leader. "What say I take Zoro and three others from Alpha and go see where those dorks are headed?"

"Exactly, Tonto. You got it. Pick your men and head out."

In the living room of her parents' home in Chattanooga, Tennessee, Betty Welby angrily snapped off the television set. The network news was filled with stories of how badly the Americans were doing in Vietnam. Scenes of men badly wounded, with medics hovering over them, IV bags in hand, lines running to shattered bodies, haunted her. The scenes of stacked body bags, all purported to be American casualties, made her ache. Every night it was like this, and every night she continued to torture herself by watching.

It could be Kent in one of those zippered black plastic bags. After much self-examination and painful hours of doubt, her decision had been made. Or had it? *Damn all those small boys in grown men's bodies who wanted to play soldier!* The thought burst forth in her mind, unbidden. She didn't want to be a widow at the age of twenty-four. Why had Kent been so cruel? Why had he insisted on going to Vietnam in the first place?

He could say all he wanted about not letting the Team down, of it being what a SEAL did. *Break things and kill people*. She had heard it laughingly referred to that way by Kent's friends in the platoon on more than one Sunday afternoon in the backyard of their enlisted, married quarters in Virginia, at Little Creek Amphibious Base. High and haughty on the hill overlooking them to the east was the quarters for officers, married. Betty Welby imagined it to be more likely *looking down* on them.

Betty hated the officers' wives. A snooty clique, she considered them, always peering down their noses at the enlisted wives. And she despised the officers. It was they who gave the orders that sent her husband off onto dangerous training missions. And sometimes, like this transfer to Vietnam, on missions that weren't for training. Imagine, they called it a *tour*, as though Kent and all the rest had been sent to some luxurious resort.

Likewise, she resented the fact that Kent had refused to take the test and attend OCS. He could have *been* an officer. But probably not a SEAL officer, he had complained, if he took OCS before completing their silly UDT/R school. For several days now, Betty had felt increasingly wretched. From, in fact, the moment she had mailed the letter telling Kent that she had changed her mind about a divorce. Yet, she cringed at the thought of being widowed.

She couldn't change her mind again, could she? Kent would think her a featherhead. Yet, it continued to taunt her. Would she answer the door one day soon to find two members of Team 2 and the chaplain? Oh, she knew the routine. The SEALs kept such matters closely guarded within the Teams alone. No telegram, no visit by someone from the Department of the Navy, only a "friendly visit" by a couple of SEALs and their wives, with the padre along, of course. Betty stifled a sob and flung herself from the cloying grasp of the deep wing chair.

Without hesitation, she went to the small, fold-down secretary desk that her mother so cherished in the alcove off the reception rotunda that gave onto the wide flight of stairs that climbed to the second floor. Quickly, before she could change her mind, she took up pen and put it to paper.

Sure enough, the VC led them to what had to be a hidden POW compound. From the cover of the trees, Tonto Waters stared at it, stunned by its size. It certainly was a much bigger complex than anticipated by Jason Slater. Huge trees had been undercut and stout, coconut log huts constructed under them. They were small, more coffin size than a hootch. Cells, no doubt. Camouflage nets had been draped to further break up the regular shape of the structures.

The VC and their North Vietnamese supervisors had left enough foliage on the widespread limbs to provide a "normal" IR signature. Tonto reasoned that this would make the camp invisible to satellite and surveillance overflights. No wonder the Agency had come up with zip on their survey of the entire Delta. Tonto eased the small camera he carried in a cargo pocket of his BDU trousers. A Zeiss, a German make, ancient by present standards, the compact 35mm took clear, sharp pictures. Carefully he began to photograph the outer fence, then the inner.

He paid particular notice to the guard towers, then moved on to document the cells and the barracks for the guards and staff.

They would have to come back, Tonto knew, to make a more thorough survey that would provide what they needed to construct a mock-up and conduct rehearsals for the actual raid. And there was going to be one, Tonto knew when he saw the new arrival being subjected to a sadistic beating by a man he estimated to be the commandant. He wore an NVA uniform and carried himself with all the arrogance of the northern communist hierarchy. Tonto photographed that, too. Tonto knew that Archie Golden had a camera and was working away at another angle. He could see Zoro Agilar snapping frame after frame off to his right. Half an hour of this and they would be ready to move out and rejoin the rest of the squad.

Although in command of this patrol from Alpha Squad, Tonto Waters stuck to his preferred position on point. He wormed his way through the jungle, opening a new route to where the rest of the squad waited. He eschewed the trail, on the very valid likelihood that more VC or NVA regulars would be using it. Even so, it surprised him slightly when he suddenly rounded the bole of a mahogany tree and came face-to-face with a Viet Cong in his late teens. The boy's eyes went wide, and he opened his mouth to scream.

He didn't get the job done. Tonto Waters lashed out with the butt of his Ithaca shotgun and smashed it into the young Cong's jaw. The boy dropped, and Tonto followed him, his K-Bar knife in the lead. He drove it into the heaving body, below the diaphragm, slanted upward, so that it pierced that tough muscle and stabbed into the lower ventricle of the VC's heart.

Tonto's gorge rose as he felt the death spasms of the

youthful enemy under his knee. He thrashed and shuddered, then went still. Tonto pulled his knife from the wound and wiped it on the black jacket worn by the VC. Only then did he break his total concentration to look around.

Four more VC, in various positions of repose stared at him. The kill had taken less than thirty seconds. Now they seemed galvanized by the death of their comrade. Every one made a dive for a weapon.

"Ooooh, shiiiit!" Tonto yelped as he clawed for his shotgun.

All around him the jungle erupted in a roar of gunfire. Reflexes flung bodies of the dying VC in every direction. Over the fusillade, Tonto heard the voice of Zoro Agilar. *"¡Viva Zapata! ¡Viva Pancho Villa! ¡Arriba—arriba!"*

Jesus! The kid had gone nuts. It had the desired effect on the surviving VC, though. They froze in position long enough to die at the hands of the SEALs. The firefight, one-sided as it had been, lasted only another half minute. Even the howl of disturbed monkeys and screech of rudely awakened birds died out, to leave an eerie silence, more intense to Tonto's keyed-up senses than ever in a shoot-out before. After checking the bodies, Tonto went to Zoro.

"What the hell was that you let go with, kid?"

Zoro Aguilar blushed. "It is something I learned from my Tio Hernando. He is a very old man. He rode with Pancho Villa in the big revolution, you know, the one in 1916?"

"It turned those muthas to stone. You've got balls, Zoro. How come you were so close?"

"I saw you dive past that tree, an' I knew you were in some deep stuff. Archie did, too. So we come along to help out."

"You saved my ass, kid. But, don't ever tell any of the rest. I'll deny it if you do."

Zoro grinned. "You're shittin' me, right, Chief?"

"Right, Zoro. That's what SEALs are all about. We cover one another's ass all the time."

"Yeah. I got ya. One for all and all for one. Like the Musketeers, *¿de veras?*"

Archie Golden gave Zoro Agilar an odd look. "You talkin' about that kid TV show, Zoro?"

"Naw, man. Not the *Mouse*kateers, *The Three Musketeers*. I read the book. It was cool." To Tonto, "We gonna leave them?"

"I don't see we have any choice. They are bound to have heard this back at that POW camp. Be a carload of NVA spilling out anytime now. Everybody into your VC Jesus boots, see if we can confuse the scene and make them think it was Marvin the ARVN who jumped their buddies."

"Either way, we're in some deep shit, Tonto," Pope Marino opined when the patrol rejoined First Squad. "We stir up their little nest, likely the NVA honcho will move those Agency people out of there in a hot tick. It was smart wearing native sandals and leaving plenty of prints. Depends on who they send out to check the area. We'd better get back to Bravo and see about playing shepherd."

Randy Andy Holt wore a confused expression. "What?"

"Playing shepherd. Getting the flock out of here," Pope explained with a chuckle.

"Oh, yeah. Now I see . . . I think."

Archie Golden elbowed Repeat Ditto in the ribs. "I'll bet ol' Randy Andy here asked the Peter Four question."

Grinning, Repeat joined the badinage. "Yeah—yeah, I'll bet he did."

Seriously aggrieved, Randy Andy protested, "Awh, c'mon, guys. I was never dumb enough to fall for that."

"Enough," Pope Marino halted the exchange. "You

dork-tops are going to be caught out here with your butts hangin' out if you don't get a move on.''

Tonto took point and the squad moved out. An hour of painfully slow movement through virgin jungle went by without incident. Following Tonto's example, Pope had instructed the point man to lead them wide of the trail to avoid any further encounter with the enemy.

They were within half a klick of Bravo's position along the riverbank when Tonto dropped suddenly and held in place. Then, slowly, he raised a hand to signal Enemy in Sight. The Viet Cong detachment came on, thrashing frantically through the bush, apparently intent on catching up to whomever had trashed the patrol halted for its siesta. Instead of the citizen soldiers of ARVN they expected to find, they found seven highly motivated SEALs.

Instinct and superb training allowed the SEALs to quickly form an L-shaped ambush without revealing their presence to the oncoming enemy. They used it to great advantage. Randy Andy opened up with the M60, chopping into the center of the VC formation, downing three men like tenpins. Repeat Ditto let fly a 40mm grenade from the XM148 that showered another pair with a lethal dose of shrapnel.

Tonto Waters took out their point man with a blast from his shotgun. The VC died with an expression of surprise and regret on his face. ''Goes with the job, fellah,'' Tonto told him quietly. He pivoted and dived away from his previous cover to a preselected spot, from which he played scythe with the horizontal wave of buckshot he rapid-fired from the Ithaca.

At the moment it appeared that the VC were more interested in getting away from the torrent of lead and whirring metal shards, Lt. Carl Marino came to his feet. ''To hell with this. Let's go take them!''

Although it flew in the face of all previous doctrine, the charge proved overwhelmingly effective. Caught by surprise, the Cong gaped at the huge figures who rose out of the sawgrass and from behind fallen tree trunks, their faces indistinguishable from the jungle background. The enemy paused a fateful moment too long.

Those left standing died swiftly as the SEALs closed on them, weapons aflicker with muzzle bloom, lead spitting in steady streams. Bowled over, the VC went down while bloody bits of cloth and flesh flew from their bodies. The stench of death clung in the nostrils of the SEALs of First Squad as they continued their fast trot away from the scene. They linked up with Bravo in three short minutes.

"Gawdamn, Pope, you sure put the pork to those turkeys," Anchor Head Sturgis greeted warmly.

"You could see us?" an incredulous Marino asked.

"Hell, yes."

"Why didn't you join in?"

Sturgis pulled a face. "Well, I sort of figured you'd pull some crazy stunt like playin' Custer at the Little Bighorn, so I told everyone to keep their heads down."

"How did you know I wouldn't wind up like Custer?" Pope accused.

A new grin was born on Anchor Head's face. "Well, damnit, Lieutenant, that's simple. You done forgot more about jungle fighting than that dude ever knew."

Acid dripped from Pope's words. "Thank you for your profound confidence, Chief." He reached a hand out, and automatically Repeat Ditto filled it with the radio handset. "Eagle One to White Horse. Eagle One to White Horse. Do you copy? Over."

The airwaves to Tre Noc crackled a long moment. "This is White Horse, Eagle One, we copy. What do you need?"

"Out of here. We'd like immediate extraction from . . ." Lieutenant Marino gave the coordinates. "Suggest you send some slicks. Over."

"Roger that. Be on the way in a short. Call sign will be Trigger. Do you copy?"

"Roger Trigger. What's the ETA?"

"Humm. Say half an hour?"

"Too long. We're up to our asses in alligators out here. Over."

"Them's crocodiles, Eagle One. Over."

"These alligators are wearing black pajamas. Speed it up. Eagle One, out."

Belatedly, the Signals station keeper at Tre Noc responded, "Oh, shit. Why didn' you say that?"

Perspiration ran in rivers down his body. Kent Welby reached up and wiped at one track behind his left ear. From a short distance away, Archie Golden studied him. Fifteen minutes had gone by since Lieutenant Marino had contacted their base for a helicopter extraction. So far, the frantically searching enemy had not discovered them. It didn't help matters that the SEALs could *hear* the NVA and VC troops crashing through the bush in search of their small detail. Doc Welby reached for the sweat trail again.

"Pucker factor is gettin' to be a bitch, huh, Doc?" Archie whispered.

"I could slice a dozen washers right now, Archie."

"*!Por dios!* I could cut two dozen," Porfirio Agilar gasped softly.

Archie chuckled lightly. "Hang in there, kid."

Brush crackled fifty meters from their position. *Awh, Christ, don't let those choppers come now,* Tonto Waters thought.

They wanted a fair chance of confusing the enemy as to whom they sought. Appearance of American helicopters would dispel all doubt. And no doubt, sign the death warrants of the spooks in the POW camp they had seen.

The top of a cabbage palm waved frantically. Pope Marino had an idea. He edged over to the PRU scout who had come along. "Can you convince them you are one of them and that there is nothing over here?"

Grinning, the young ex-VC gave Pope the thumbs-up sign. "Sure, no sweat, *dahwi*." He sucked in air and called out in rapid-fire Vietnamese, "Who is there? Identify yourselves." A reply came, and the scout whispered in Pope's ear. "A corporal." Then aloud, "This is Lieutenant Min. My platoon has searched along the river. There is no sign, Corporal. Take your men and check your back trail. They may have doubled on you."

Marino's ruse worked so well that the rattle in the bush ceased to be heard within two minutes. Five minutes later, a pair of UH-1-D Huey slicks whuffled into view along one of the mail routes. When they neared the Mekong River, they veered suddenly and went into a steep descent. Noses down, tail rotors whining in a near-vertical position, they screamed in and hovered over a small clearing right on the riverbank. Skids less than a foot off the ground, they made stable platforms for the SEALs to ascend to the crew compartment with ease.

Pope Marino had his two squads on the move even before the choppers settled in. Alpha had the privilege of going first, since they had been the ones to track the enemy to the camp, Doc Welby figured. The Second Squad faced the direction of the bad guys and stood fast, ready to pump out withering fire if the extraction was compromised.

Everything went with textbook smoothness. Second Squad boarded and both birds crabbed across the sky, well away from the North Vietnamese soldiers and VC guerrillas without detection. So long as they only heard the helicopters, Pope Marino reasoned, and didn't really see them, the enemy would hopefully assume them to be ARVN, on loan from the Americans.

Totally unaware of the American presence, the enemy

continued to search for targets that no longer existed. The ride back to Tre Noc, in fact, became boring.

But, Doc Welby reminded himself, another visit to that chilling compound would happen all too soon.

CHAPTER 10 _____

LCDR LAILEY grudgingly offered congratulations for the success of the mission. His words had the ring of genuine insincerity until he reached his conclusion. "But," he warned Lieutenant Marino darkly, "you are not off the hook as yet. We still have to go out there and save the lives of those men. I am sure the Marine Air Wing and the Agency will be most grateful to m—er—you for your efforts on their behalf. Until that is accomplished, I shall continue to view your conduct with a jaundiced eye."

"Oh, I'm certain of that, sir," Pope Marino responded in a chipper tone. "I would expect nothing less, sir."

Lailey's eyes narrowed. "Hummph! I'll chose to overlook the sarcasm, *Lieutenant*, but the way you use that word, 'sir,' is dangerously close to insubordination. If I get the least sufficient impression you are attempting to be insubordinate, I shall have you up before an Officer Review Board so fast your ass will suck wind for a week. Do I make myself clear?"

"Crystal, *sir*." There was even more sneer in the word this time.

Lailey chose to ignore it. "Return to Tre Noc and have your men ready to go to work on the mock-up we're having built." He paused to fight back the powerful mental image of rising bile at the prospect of praising that arrogant prick, Waters, whom he considered another one like Marino. "By the way, that Chief of yours is a damn good photographer. We had his film quick-developed. It's been decided the photographs and measurements he provided will be sufficient to reproduce the POW compound for training purposes. Those taken by others in the squad served to verify his results. This is a big one, *Lieutenant*, so try not to screw it up, like you did in Nicaragua. Dismissed."

Marino stifled his sudden burst of fury, did a perfect about-face, and left the office. He joined First Squad in the new CPO mess. "We go back and practice on a mock-up, then do the raid. Right now, I opt for another parakeet. It's got the most shock value, and we can sure as hell use the fire from as many gunships as we can kumshaw."

"Right on, oh prescient one," Archie Golden chortled. "When's all this start?"

"Soon as they build the damn thing," Pope told him.

"You know, sir, we're overdue for the monsoon to begin," Tonto Waters reminded his CO.

"Yeah. Any bets it hits about the time we have to carry out this op?" Pope Marino had no takers.

YO/1C Kent Welby showed up at the Riverine Plans and Operations office in a stiffly starched set of camouflage BDUs. The toes of his rarely used jungle boots retained a carefully nurtured shine, and he carried a bouquet of flowers he had obtained through Rose Throh. Several of the female locals working in the office cast jealous glances at Francie Song when Doc crossed the room with purposeful strides and presented his token of apology with all the flourish and élan of a knight of old entrusting his lady with his banner.

"Oh, Kent Welby, they are so beautiful," Francie enthused. Then she produced a mock pout. "But I am still angry with you."

"I had so hoped not. You know that I'm not to blame for being sent off on missions like that."

"Yes, of course. Only, I sometimes feel as though our lives are constantly circumscribed by what is happening in this terrible war." Francie forced brightness into her face and voice. "Your mission? It came out all right?"

"Yes. You'll probably be processing the results to-morrow. I—ah—I didn't come by to talk about that." Fighting back his reservations about still being a married man, Doc rushed on. "I wanted to take you to Phon Bai tonight to make up for your birthday."

Oblivious to their surroundings, Francie came to her feet and hugged Doc fiercely. "Oh, Kent Welby, you are so wonderful. We will have the best of everything and eat until we burst, and drink white wine." She stopped sud-denly and a light of mischief glowed in her ebon eyes. "Oh, phoof, you can drink your wretched beer if you prefer."

"That's my girl," Doc Welby unconsciously patron-ized her.

His thoughts fled again to the knowledge that he should not, by rights, even be here. Betty had yet to make it clear about the divorce. A growing discomfort rose in Kent Welby as he perfidiously warmed to Francie's tight em-brace. Even so, he could not deny his growing desire and burning need for this Asian beauty. Suddenly conscious of the nature of his remark, he hastened to correct the impression it must have made.

"You're too good to me. I do admit I like my beer. But, lately I've come to discover that I enjoy some of that wine you push off on me."

They laughed together, then Doc told her, "You're off duty in half an hour. I'll meet you here."

Francie got an expression of consternation. "No! Oh, no. I have to go to my apartment, take a bath, fix up, so I look lovely for you. Go to My Flower with your friends.

Come for me at—how you say?—eighteen hundred hours?''

Doc Welby laughed again. "You're learning, I'll say that. What else have you picked up while we've been gone?''

Francie rolled her eyes. "Oh, lots of things. Before long I will be Numba One GI." She ended in a giggle. "Go on, now, Kent Welby. Drink beer, tell raunchy stories, and share some time with your friends. I see you eighteen hours at my place."

She set about arranging the flowers on her desk as Kent Welby departed. Outside, he found the late afternoon still warm and muggy. What had he expected? The five-ton air-conditioning unit kept the Riverine offices barely habitable, though they did squeeze most of the humidity out of the air. That helped a lot. Before he could soak his uniform to sogginess in perspiration, he headed for the main gate.

Doc made a perfunctory wave of his liberty card to the guard and passed through onto the widening, rutted road to the Vietnamese village of Tre Noc, which had not existed a year earlier when the first SEALs came here. It had, naturally enough, taken its name from the Naval base.

With a light step, he turned into Doc Tri Alley. Halfway down the second block, steam and smoke rose from the wood-fired boiler that served the laundry operated by the enterprising Rose Throh. There had been half a dozen fishermen's hootches gathered around the Chinese-run grocery and her laundry when the Americans came. Also some loggers lived with their families in this clearing along the Bassiac. Rose Throh saw riches to be had from the American trade she hoped to drum up. She put in a small bar in the front of her laundry, served local and black-market beer, saki, and white, Chinese wine to thirsty sailors.

When Francie Song and her little boy, Thran, came to the burgeoning village, Rose discovered the young woman had a lovely singing voice. She hired Francie to entertain when the Americans came after their duty hours and on restricted liberty. During the long daytime hours, while Francie worked for the herbalist who owned the building that housed her apartment, and sought to get work in the Navy compound, Rose attended to two-year-old Thran. She did not charge for this service. Her kindly heart went out to the struggling, single mother. She had been more than willing to organize and carry out the plans of Kent Welby for Francie's birthday party. Doc Welby smiled warmly when he thought of it.

Doc made his feelings known the moment he entered the laundry. "You're the most beautiful woman in the world, Mammasan!" he exclaimed.

Rose Throh feigned shock. "What would Francie say?" she jibed.

"When she knows what you've done to help make her happy, she'll say the same."

"Oh, you are a rascal, Kent Welby. Come, come, I show you what we have ready."

She led Doc out the back way to a mean and narrow street that twisted and turned like a snake until it joined the main drag. They were a block away from Phon Bai. Rose Throh beckoned urgently, seeking more speed from the long-striding Doc Welby. "Come-come. It is lovely. You see."

They entered through the recessed front door. Doc's eyes widened and he gaped in awed appreciation. More Chinese lanterns had been strung across the room. They glowed softly with inner candlelight. A large table occupied the center of the room. It had been decorated in accord with the Vietnamese tradition of birthday celebrations. A pagoda of fresh fruit formed the centerpiece, surrounded by floating lotus-blossom candles in stone bowls. They had as yet not been lighted. Place settings rested on slit bamboo mats, with party favors of confetti, streamers, and small strings of firecrackers.

Rose presented it with the consummate flourish of a French maître d'. "You like, yes?"

"Oh, yes. Double yes, in fact. Numba One, Mammasan. No one could have done this but you," Doc Welby praised.

Rose Throh blushed, adding new dimension to the creases of her age. "Oh, you making fun of me, Kent Welby. I just . . . fix nice, like you say. You friends? They all know? They come what time?"

"I told them nineteen hundred—ah—nineteen hours. I wanted some time alone with Francie before the party started."

Rose pulled a wise face. "Oh-ho, I know what you got in mind. This woman may be old, but she not forget what young lovers need."

"Don't be naughty, Rose," Doc chided in mock seriousness.

"It's hokey-dokey, *Oang* Welby. I keep you secret, though it not so much a secret, I think."

"This is one thing that has to be kept secret. It's supposed to be a surprise party for Francie. She thinks we are only coming here for a dinner together. So, if you see her, please don't say anything."

"I tell nothing. Not even to that big guy, Chief Waters. He come asking around right before you. That's why I take you out back way. He was in honey room. Not want him to know."

Pleased by her conspiratorial air, Doc smiled. "Good. I'll go on to Francie's and you go back to My Flower. That way no one will be the wiser."

"Except you an' me, huh?"

"You're one crafty lady, Mammasan. We will be here at nineteen hours."

*   *   *

Doc's surprise party for Francie went even better than he had anticipated. Her reaction had been captured on film by the Zeiss camera of Tonto Waters. Her eyes had gone wide and round; her mouth flew open and genuine tears of great happiness had streamed down her lightly rouged cheeks when Doc Welby had escorted her through the door of Phon Bai. She turned suddenly and hugged Doc with a fervor that promised much for the future. Even if he felt like hell for thinking the things he imagined would be.

Yet he found himself in Francie's apartment following the happy, noisy dinner, and rounds of drinks that followed. Doc had arranged to be out overnight and Francie led him across the floor of her living room by one hand. They stopped at a tiny, fragile table, where a small fruit soufflé rested on a plate edged in gold, red, and green figures. A single candle rose from its mounded middle.

"This is for our American celebration. I hope you like it," Francie said shyly.

"I know I will." Doc lighted the candle.

Francie served them slices and a sweet-tart Japanese plum wine. They ate in silence, sipped the last from their stemmed glasses, and set the dishes aside. Doc felt a tightness in his throat as he looked deeply into Francie's eyes. Little fires danced there, reflections from the oil lamps in wall sconces. They spoke of her desire. Slowly, provocatively, she began to undress.

Telling himself he did so against his will, Doc unbuttoned the jacket of his cammo outfit. He let the starched garment drop to the floor. Next, he pulled free his green undershirt and removed it. Francie sighed and cupped her bare breasts in small hands. Doc stifled a moan and reached out for her. They embraced, naked to the waist, and Doc felt the familiar electric tingling that accompanied each such touching.

Francie fumbled with the sliding bar of his military belt, freed it, and began to open his trousers. With fingers that grew more eager with each passing moment, Doc set clumsy fingers to undoing the buttons of Francie's skirt. It fell away with a faint rustle. His skivvies followed shortly after.

With his manhood freed to her loving touch, Doc could no longer contain himself with the admonishment that he was a married man. The last of his good intentions got trashed when Francie leaned in to him and nibbled his earlobe.

"Oh, Kent, Kent, make love to me. Make this the happiest birthday of all."

He lifted her and carried the most desirable woman he had ever known to her bedroom. Their joining came in a haze of euphoria. Both partners worked at prolonging the atmosphere of ecstasy to the ultimate.

All through morning PT, their run, breakfast and Quarters, YO/1C Kent Welby suffered under a heavy burden of old-fashioned guilt. He mentally heaped dung on his conduct of the night before. *Although, God, hadn't it been good!* a part of his mind kept taunting him. Now, at mail call, he looked upon himself as the lowest of lowlifes. When Tonto Waters called out his name, he didn't immediately respond.

"Doc, you got a letter. Air mail and special delivery. C'mon up," Tonto called out again.

Grudgingly, Doc went forward to take his mail. Two letters, long-delayed, from his parents. A light, airy postcard from one of his wacko friends from college. The beach at Daytona. Great. Just what he needed. Then his gaze settled on the large envelope with the green special-delivery sticker on the face. It was dated three weeks earlier, and the return address was the home of Betty's parents. It had been opened, so he knew that someone in

S-2 knew the answer waiting him. Cold dread filled him. Doc went off by himself to open it.

Under one of the few remaining trees in the compound, he slit the flap with his knife. What he took out astonished him. "Well, I'll be goddamned," he muttered slowly as he read the letter.

No hurt, this time, no sense of loss and abandonment. He read the tormented words of Betty Welby and felt only . . . cold numbness. The other shoe had finally dropped.

Kent,

I regret taking so long to write these words. I have thought, and agonized over it, for a long time. This seems the only right way to do things. For a long while now, I have seriously believed we could put it all together again. Forgive me for appearing to vacillate, but I just couldn't cope with the specter of you in one of those body bags they show on the television every night. I love you, but I hate what you are doing. Yet, I cannot give you up. Forgive me for the delay, my darling, but my mind is now clear. For the sake of my own sanity, I have decided not to file the divorce papers.

"*Oh . . . my . . . God!*" Kent bellowed.

"What's gotten into you?" Tonto Waters asked, coming over after finishing mail call.

"I ain't gonna be a free man after all," Doc Welby told him glumly. "Betty has written to say she is not going to file for divorce."

"Are you kidding? I thought you'd like that. What's the catch?" a dubious Tonto asked.

"Uh—outside of Francie and what it means to us, I don't know. Nothing, I guess."

"Have you read the whole letter?" Tonto prompted.

"No—no, I haven't." Doc read on in silence. The last sentence in the letter stunned him.

My attorney will send you a bill for the costs so far involved.

"Shit! I'll be in debt for the rest of my life. She expects *me* to pay for *her* divorce, that she isn't getting."

"Of course. They always do." Tonto spoke from experience, having had an early and rocky marriage prior to his entry into the SEALs.

"Tonto, what do I do?"

Waters chuckled low in his throat. "You pay, buddy. You pay through the ass."

"You seem as smug as the comrade with the samovar concession, Maxim Maximovich," Senior Lieutenant Kovietski declared after admitting the junior of his two Soviet operatives to his private office.

"With good cause, Comrade Rudinov."

Kovietski frowned. "You are not to use that name. There is no telling when one of our Cambodian comrades will overhear."

Yoriko shrugged. "What is the difference. To them we all look alike. With all the cover names we have used, they probably think names are interchangeable for us Soviets."

"Some of them may be in the pay of General Hoi. It would not do for him to suspect our true identities. What is it you have?"

"I've found out what it is that interests the Navy SEALs *and* General Hoi so greatly. And I suspect the Americans are as totally unaware of its location as we have been."

"Yes?"

"A prisoner-of-war compound, Comrade Lieutenant, deep in the Delta. I was there, walked all through it. It's big. A whole lot bigger than anything one would think would be built there.''

''*Pobbchnoe detyaehn!*'' Kovietski barked, then repeated, ''Those bastards! That's why the SEALs have been more active than usual. They at least knew about it, something we did not . . . until now. Yes, I see it clearly. They would like nothing more than to uncover a POW compound and free the inmates. What splendid propaganda it would provide for the Americans. Do you have any idea who is incarcerated there?''

''Eight Americans that I could verify. Three are pilots. The other five are civilians.''

A bright twinkly starburst appeared in Kovietski's blue eyes. ''CIA. I'll wager my next promotion on it. We have in our hands, or virtually so, five agents of the American Central Intelligence Agency, and we're not going to let these Asiatic *raevrattsat* keep them away from us. Eh, Comrade?''

''As you say, Comrade *Mayor*.''

''You have done exceptionally well, Maxim. I am proud of you. Here, have a vodka.''

''*Spasibo, Tovarish Mayor*'' He took the frosted tulip, held it up in salute and toasted, ''*Za vashe nostrovia!*''

Kovietski drank deep and chuckled. ''It's *our* good health you have ensured with this discovery. We will make plans to depart for this camp at once.''

Yoriko congratulated himself on making the right decision. The major always moved quickly and decisively when confronted with a problem. He had been correct to take this to him, rather than going around his superior and trying to build his own stairway to recognition, favor, and privilege. He would gain all that through his grateful patron, Major Rudinov.

Lieutenant Carl Marino, Lt. (jg) Cyrus Rhodes, and Ensigns Peter Brooks and Wallace Ott stood around a hastily fashioned sand table with Chief Tom Waters and the men who had gone with him to track the VC officer and his prisoner. The photographs they had made had been duplicated, and prints hung on the wall. The sand table had a cluster of small, crudely made models of buildings, of the general description of those they had seen and photographed.

"All right, those eight go right here," Waters directed to models of the narrow coconut log cells. Each appeared entirely portable, complete with occupant. Photos taken from varying angles revealed that none had any windows, except for a tiny square grid in the upper portion of the door. More appeared under construction.

"Yeah. Now that long, boxy thing, that's the barracks wing. Put it along here." He turned to Chad Ditto. "That look right to you?"

"Sure does."

"Good, then we go on."

Tonto directed the placement of each of the structures inside the compound, including the spacious quarters and office he believed belonged to the commandant. Each he placed with meticulous attention to a ruler so that the POW camp model would be in precise scale. Last came the inner cyclone-fence barrier, with its guard towers.

A crosshatch of thin wooden strips, painted silver, served for that. Beyond, the outer wall of concertina barbed wire was put in place. Once secured, Tonto gave the entire model a long once-over. "It'll do. Perfect as we can make it without surveyor's tools. It would be better if we made another trip to the compound."

"That would risk blowing the whole thing," Pope Marino reminded his platoon chief. "The construction crew should be able to do the training mock-up easy with this and the photos."

"First we need drawings of the buildings to know how to build them," Dusty Rhodes injected.

"Why can't they just rig 'em up and cover with plywood, then paint it?" Tonto queried.

"We need to get the effect of every shot, explosive charge, and the like. That's why you were asked how thick you thought the walls to be," Pope Marino explained. "Same for the doors."

Waters shrugged. "Well, hell, Pope, it stands to reason that they wouldn't make cardboard houses for the prisoners. The guards and staff barracks looked the usual cheap jungle construction. You know, hurry up and forget the nails?"

That brought a chuckle. "Okay, we've got your estimates. The CBs will get on it soon as they arrive from Binh Thuy. That wraps it up here. Tonto, I want you to do a class this afternoon on the crew-served weapons you saw, the standard arms of the guards, and how the staff are armed."

"Gotcha, Pope."

"From here on, then, we're at the mercy of the construction crew."

"They better be fast," Tonto opined. "You've got me convinced that place ain't gonna be there long."

CHAPTER 11 ───────────────

CONSTRUCTION BEGAN the next day. Navy Construction Battalion 56 moved on to the train-fire range and began to assemble a mock-up of the POW compound measured and photographed by Tonto Waters, Chad Ditto, and Archie Golden. Bulldozers, painted with jungle camouflage pattern, leveled hammocks and filled in depressions to create a replica of the sinister establishment. They even cut a ramp down to the Bassiac River like the one on which the commandant had tormented the injured Marine pilot.

When Tonto saw that, he ground his teeth in outrage. The memory was so fresh. Still bound to his bamboo poles, the pilot had been struck in the face and knocked to the slippery mud of the ramp on the Mekong. Then the NVA officer in charge had kicked him in the chest, stomach, and crotch. Two of the VC in the prisoner detail yanked him painfully to his feet. The NVA colonel backhanded the bleeding man until the pilot's eyes puffed shut. Then he was dragged off, bloody and muddy, to be released from his restraints and shoved roughly into one of the coffin-sized cells.

As though reading Tonto's mind, Pope Marino came beside him and quoted the famous lines from *Bridge on the River Kwai*. " 'Welcome to Camp Ten. I am the com-

129

mandant, Colonel Sieto. Our motto is, Let us be happy in our work!' ''

"Awh, hell, Pope, that's eerie. How'd you know I was thinkin' about that poor slob jarhead pilot?''

"You don't grind your jaws like that unless you're thoroughly pissed off at something, Chief. I naturally figured it would be the pilot. You took enough photos of him being beaten. By the way, S-Two got me on the horn. They were able to blow up one of your frames enough to make his name. It's Captain Perry, USMC.''

Tonto looked decidedly relieved. "Now I know who it is that I intend to personally break out of that hellhole. Thanks, Pope. I owe you one for that.''

"The one to thank is . . .'' Pope winced. "Commander Lailey. He put the pressure on the lab boys to get a name.''

"That must give you the ass to be obliged to Barry Lailey.''

"Yeah, Tonto, like the elephant, and he's got tons of it.''

"We just have to live with it. Though I'd be happy to pay him back for his favor,'' Tonto concluded with a wink.

"Be nice now, Tonto. Given enough time, Lailey's mouth is going to dig his own grave.'' Lieutenant Marino turned away to watch the construction johnnies begin to lay the foundation for the staff barracks. "These CBs sure aren't union construction types. They'd have stopped for at least two coffee breaks by now if they were.''

"The sooner they're done, the sooner we get to play with our new toys,'' Tonto suggested.

"Right, you are, and I can hardly wait.''

Maxim Yoriko returned to the Delta. With him came Feodor Dudov, the other Soviet operative at the KGB Cambodian station. Even with the aid of the most fanciful makeup artist, Dudov could not masquerade as an Oriental. A big, woolly bear of a man, his broad, flat, Slavic face and cup-handle ears betrayed his origins inescapably. To Yoriko's darting ferret, Dudov played a plodding donkey.

Not that he was mentally slow. He had graduated head of his class since grammar school in Sverolovsk in the Ural Mountains. It was not his fault he had been born to the *narodniki*, rather than the *vlasti*, the ruling elite of the *nomenklatura*—the communist aristocracy. Had he been so, he would have been sent to officer's training, like Major Rudinov, and perhaps would now wear the shoulder boards of a major, or even a colonel.

Rather than resent being the son of a peasant, Feodor Dudov relished his position in the KGB. Although only a senior sergeant, he often wore officer's rank, impersonating for the purpose of discovering hidden secrets. He was methodical and patient, two attributes that stood him well with his superiors. It never occurred to Feodor why he had been picked for this plum of an assignment. He had no idea that Major Rudinov had asked for him personally. Maj. Pyotr Rudinov had his own agenda, one which required promotion out of the ranks for Sr. Sgt. Feodor Dudov. For now, Dudov satisfied himself with covert surveillance of the POW compound.

He identified by photograph each of the prisoners when they were brought out individually for their daily hour of exercise. The civilians puzzled him at first, then he recalled Major Rudinov's mentioning agents of the CIA. Here he was, watching his American counterparts in captivity. It gave Feodor a powerful surge of elation. When they had documented this secret camp sufficiently, these selfsame CIA agents would be prisoners of the Soviet Union. Feodor felt confident enough of his major to be assured of that.

Yoriko daily went in among the Vietnamese. Fluent in

their language, he mixed with work crews, gossiped with the guards. After twilight, he would rendezvous with Dudov at a different site each night. He came now to where Dudov awaited him.

"There have been some probes by ARVN troops near to here. The commandant was overheard by two guards I befriended as saying he wanted to request an immediate move of the prisoners. It is said that General Hoi refused."

"We must tell Major Rudinov at once. He does not want to lose a chance of obtaining those prisoners."

"It will have to wait until tomorrow night for us to leave," Yoriko informed his partner. "Rumor has it that an important officer from the North is arriving tomorrow morning. We must find out who he is and report on that, also."

Dudov considered, his dark brows knit together over his flat, peasant nose. "Yes. That must be done. Then we take our findings to the major."

LCDR Barry Lailey turned in his swivel chair away from the operations order that lay on his desk, waiting the Intelligence Annex. The S-3 had worked it out rather well, Lailey thought. Then this thorn came up to prick him in the side. He looked with level, beady eyes at Jason Slater, who sat across the desk from him.

"You actually want us to snatch this General Giap?"

"That's the idea," Slater drawled. "He's their head honcho for brainwashing and interrogation—uh—we call it chemical debriefing."

Lailey made a prissy face of distaste. "Literary euphemisms don't hide its ugliness," he criticized. "As I understand it, what is done is to disorient and distort the mind of the subject through the use of chemicals. Deprive him of any sensory input, confuse his time sense to the point he can't even count heartbeats to gain some idea of how much time has passed between questioning sessions, am I right?''

"Essentially so. We usually take it slow. No need to rush the process, unless there is some external urgency. I've read of subjects who have been toyed with for a full week before any questioning went on. They sang like canaries. You see, the toughest character simply can't stand not knowing who, where, or *when* he is. The longer sensory deprivation and chemical blackouts can be drawn out, the greater the impact.''

Lailey made no bones about his opinion. "It's all a nasty business. And Giap is the NVA top dog at this sort of thing?''

"Right. That's why we want him out so badly. What do you say?''

Barry Lailey remained silent for a long while. His mind continued at full speed, however. How could he manage to pull off the snatch of General Giap and still put Carl Marino in a bad light? That was a given of every mission handed out to first Platoon. Marino was getting far too big for his britches. Far bigger than Barry Lailey liked. This just might be the time.

"All right. I'll list what you gave me about Giap in my Annex. Along with it will be a recommendation that General Giap be captured and extracted along with our people.''

Jason Slater produced his cat-with-canary-pudding smile. "Fine. I knew you'd see it my way.''

Archie Golden didn't win his bet about the monsoon starting the day they ran the parakeet op to free the prisoners. The monsoon began the next morning. Pope Marino, accompanied by Dusty Rhodes, Ensigns Peter Brooks, and Wally Ott, and the lead petty officers of the platoon set out to make a follow-up visit to the work in progress. Their jeeps had made it halfway down the road to the train-fire range when the sky opened up and sent a deluge of water cascading down upon them.

Warm and sticky, it was a typical monsoon rain. "Now don't this just beat the stuffin' outta everything?" Tonto Waters complained.

They all had taken much worse in BUDS and UDT/R school. SEALs were not strangers to wetness. Some surface sailors often speculated that they had webbed feet. It was just that there was something depressing about the tropical monsoon. It tended to grind a fellow down. When the sky became a world of swirling gray, every leaf and vine dripping steadily, with clouds below the treetops, a man got downright moody. And it rained every goddamned day until the season ended. Every one knew right then that this operation would be the pits.

"Don't forget," Dusty Rhodes quipped, "inform the men. Swim fins and trunks for this operation."

"Go back and chase Kaffirs around your station, Mr. Rhodes," Archie Golden bantered back.

"They're Kaffirs in South Africa. In Rhodesia, they're Zulus, and you'd best never forget that." An ornery twinkle lit his eyes as he ran a big hand through his sandy hair. "And they're called 'stations' in Australia, at home we call them farms. Or if big enough kraals."

"Thanks for the lesson in geography an' all, Dusty," Archie joked. "Don't know what I'd have done without it."

Reduced to a crawl by the heavy downpour, the jeeps slithered along a suddenly slippery track. The SEALs reached the range in about the time they would have on foot. They soon learned that the construction crews were no strangers to rain. Already they had the barracks buildings framed and were siding one of them. Coconut logs had been lashed together and formed into the cells. A pit, now half-filled with water, indicated where the punishment cages would be erected.

"Damn, it looks all too real," Tonto Waters declared when he took in the scene.

Pope Marino looked over the area, highly satisfied. "Not much left but the fence and guard towers. We should be able to begin training in three days. For now it's back to the classroom to talk our way through the actual hit."

Fat raindrops thundered on the roof of the cinder-block building where the photos and sand table had been set up. Pope Marino listened as each SEAL ran through his assigned duties during the raid on the camp. Each time they got it a little better, and usually added some fine details they had figured out on their own.

"So, two passes by the Cobras should have those little fuckers paralyzed," Tonto Waters explained his role in the break-out. "We go in on the slicks, down the ropes, and split up to take our targets. The Cobras remain overhead flying cover. Bravo will suppress anyone left in the towers, then lay bangalore torpedos to blow the wire. That's a nice thought, a diversion that will leave whoever comes by a puzzle to work out. I go to the last cell in line, on my right. Take out Captain Perry, secure the area around my target and make it to the pick-up point in the center of the compound. If Perry is in any kind of good condition, he gets my Browning. We suppress any hostile fire. Time from in to out, three minutes, thirty seconds max."

"Right. Good thought to arm the pilot, Tonto. But his mental condition should be more on your list than physical. If he's conscious and rational, and can hold a gun, he's okay. Archie, go," Pope Marino commanded.

"We go in, like Tonto said, I head for the barracks buildings with satchel charges. Randy Andy comes along to suppress enemy fire. I place the charges and set them, then we head for the pick-up point. Back-to-back with

Tonto to suppress fire. When the slicks come in, we go out. Uh—can we use one of those quick-extraction lines?''

Pope Marino considered it a moment. ''The squads can. But, remember, those freed prisoners are going to be in bad shape. They can't hold on long enough even if threaded through a loop. They have to be loaded aboard the Huey.''

''Roger that,'' Tonto Waters put in.

For the next half hour the squad went through their individual actions in what would be a three-and-a-half-minute strike. Finally, Pope Marino verbally went through his assigned task. ''When we hit the ground, Wally Ott and Zoro Agilar will come with me. We are to take out General Giap. If it appears he is about to escape, he is to be terminated. There's no need to allow that kind to run around alive. He will no doubt be in the commandant's quarters, here . . .'' He pointed to the photo and then the model on the sand table. By then everyone else should be in the center of the compound. Giap won't be cooperating, so we'll be last to reach that point. Repeat, be sure you have contact with the slicks by the time you see us headed your way.''

''Roger, L-T. I'll have my target freed and join Tonto within the first minute. I'll be on the horn from then on.''

''All right, I think we have it. We'll shake out the bugs on the mock-up and then go through it until we can do it in our sleep. So far, we've never blown a parakeet op. This is no time to make it a first.''

Francie Song sat at her desk, a stack of papers meant for filing forgotten under her fingertips. Rain beat down on the roof of the Riverine Force Special Operations office, and that only served to make her feel worse. Her Kent Welby acted so strange now. So what if his wife had not sent the divorce papers? What difference did that make?

There was no love between the two of them. Francie knew that for certain. Kent loved *her*, not some pale-skinned *quai'lo* woman half a world away. She had proven her love time and again. And so had he. Was it her worry over possibly losing Kent Welby, combined with the stress of her job, that caused that awful uneasiness every morning? No, she had been through all that before.

Already she had felt that certain quickening of life within her. She had suffered terrible morning sickness with Thran. She had lost seven pounds because of her condition. Now it was happening again. She was carrying Kent Welby's baby. She had been with no other man since she had fallen in love with the handsome, sandy-haired young American. But, oh! If he rejected her for his wife . . . ?

She would keep it a secret. Kent Welby must never know. At least until he decided what he would do about this Betty. Francie hated her without ever meeting the woman. She didn't even know what Betty Welby looked like. It was enough that this wife might still have a demand on the future of her own beloved. For that alone, Francie hated her.

How could she go on, though? In two or three months she would start to show. There would be no hiding it then. What would Kent do when he found out? Francie felt the touch of a heavy hand on her shoulder and stiffened. She knew to whom it belonged.

"What say we get together for a little drink after work?"

"No thank you, Sergeant Yates," Francie replied icily. "I am meeting someone, and we have other plans."

"If it's that web-footed SEAL, forget him. I can give you a lot more and a lot better than he can." His fingers slid insinuatingly along her shoulder and up her neck toward her ear.

Francie fought to contain her disgust and keep her voice low. "Take your hand off me, Sergeant Yates, or I will be forced to complain to Commander Farmer."

.Yates chuckled throatily and shook his mane of red hair. "You wouldn't do that, sweet thing. Lieutenant Commander Farmer would like nothin' more than to get you alone in his office. Just look at him. He wants to jump your bones every bit as much as I do. Only he can't make you as happy as I can."

Francie bit off her words through clenched teeth. "You disgust me, Sergeant Yates. Do you have as little respect for white women?" She thought about that for a moment. "I suppose so, considering your obvious lack of proper upbringing."

"My upbringing was just fine and dandy, little lady." Yates eyes narrowed and his face turned mean. "You write it down, so's you don't forget. The day will come when you come begging to me. Count on it."

He gave her a vicious squeeze on the neck, spun on one heel, and stalked away. Francie wanted to put her head in her hands and weep out her angry frustration. She knew she couldn't, though. Every eye in the place was fixed on her. *Oh, Kent—Kent, you could make this all go away*, she pleaded inwardly.

"You know, this sucks," Archie Golden grumbled as the squad ran through the attack on the mock-up of the POW camp.

Drenching monsoon rain poured down on the SEALs as they made their third rehearsal assault on the buildings behind the wire. Doc Welby, who fired his 700 Remington at the paper targets in the guard towers, lowered the scoped rifle from his shoulder to nod in agreement.

"You got that right, Archie. Usually even Charlie shuts

down in the monsoon. But, here we are, slogging through this greasy mud, up to our knees in crap.''

"All the better to catch our little slope friends unaware," Tonto Waters told them cheerfully.

"Yeah, get 'em with their pants down, like that one you jumped during our sweep of the arms caches."

Tonto recalled the surprised look on the face of the VC who had been squatting in the bush, his trousers around his ankles, relieving himself. He died with that shocked expression.

"That happens only once in a lifetime. C'mon, we've got work to do."

"Pope want us to go through this again?" Archie complained.

"Yep. And again, and again. You know the drill. Every move we make has to be automatic. I'd guess we'll be gettin' wet out here for at least a week." Groans answered him.

They started all over again. A tower had been rigged to simulate the helicopter they would be using. The sodden SEALs climbed to the platform and used the quick-slide lines to make a rapid descent to the muddy ground below. Brown goo oozed around their sneakers and boots as they struck the jungle floor.

Tonto fired at two simulated NVA guards, blasting the dummies into doll rags with loads of buckshot. Then he turned sharply left and right, verified that the area was secure and started for the model cell that would contain Captain Perry. He smashed the wooden locking mechanism with the barrel of his Ithaca and swung the door outward. Inside, another dummy lay on a pile of coconut fronds. Tonto jacked another round into the pistol-grip shotgun and picked up "Perry" in a fireman's carry. He was out the door and to the center of the compound in two seconds over one minute.

He set down the practice prisoner and fired a round

into a window of the staff barracks. Chambering another, he spun at the flicker of movement to one end of the wooden structure. A target had appeared, and Tonto plastered it with a load of No. 4. Archie Golden darted around the side of the second barrack, and a moment later an M-80 artillery simulator went off, indicating what in the real thing would be a forty-pound satchel charge.

Repeat Ditto had the handset of the AN/PRC 25 to his mouth, talking to the simulated Huey pilot. Zoro Agilar trotted up, another dummy over his shoulder. This one wore civilian clothing. He, too, turned his fire on the buildings that would house the staff and off-duty guards. One by one the squad assembled. Three more simulators went off, signaling the blowing of the wire. Anchor Head Sturgis double-timed his squad to the pick-up point. They were all ready for the extraction.

Pope Marino squeezed the button on his stopwatch. "Excellent. Exactly three minutes, thirty seconds. We'll take five while the stage is reset, then go at it again. Smoke if you've got 'em."

"Hell, mine are so wet, I got brown stains on my shirt pocket," Randy Andy Holt complained.

"To match the ones in your skivvies, huh, kid?" Archie Golden taunted.

"Watch it, Archie. Someday someone is going to take offense at what you say."

"Naw, Randy Andy, I'm just a harmless, lovable, little fuzzball."

"Save it for your wife, Archie. Maybe she'll believe you," Tonto Waters quipped. Sighing, he turned away to find what shelter he could for his brief rest.

Already the construction guys were at work on resetting the mock-up. Tomorrow, Pope Marino had promised everyone, they would do it live, with choppers and all. Not surprisingly, the new guys looked forward to that.

CHAPTER 12 ⎯⎯⎯⎯⎯⎯⎯⎯

ELOISE DALADIER handed her travel permit to the SP on duty at the headquarters in Binh Thuy. He glanced at it and her French passport and initialed the appropriate box, then handed them back.

"Everything is in order, Miss Daladier." He pronounced her name like Day-ladder. "Have a safe journey south."

"Thank you, I shall, I'm sure. Maybe when I'm through in Tre Noc, I'll do an article on the Shore Patrol here at Binh Thuy."

"Really? That'd be cool. I'm MA First Class Grogan, miss. You'll let me know if you do, so I can help out, take you around and all that?"

"I'd be delighted, Grogan. And I will keep you in mind." Smiling sweetly, Eloise left the office and walked to the helicopter landing pad. Without a backward look, she passed through the cyclone fence gate onto the helipad for her trip to Tre Noc.

Francie Song continued to worry about Sergeant Yates, the redheaded Marine. She saw some hope in the party she planned for the SEALs of First Platoon at the My Flower. It was to boost the morale of her favorite Americans. The monsoon made her gloomy also, but not as

141

much as the Westerners, who had not grown up with the wet season. She chatted happily with Rose Throh as they set out small items of decoration, then brought platters of finger foods from the small open-air café down the way.

When the first of the SEALs arrived, Francie flirted with them outrageously. She sang several songs, danced with all of the young men, and kept an eye on the doorway, expecting Kent Welby at any moment. The SEALs laughed and talked and drank beer. They gulped down the small, shrimp puffs, Imperial Rolls, and other hors d'oeuvres with gusto. Francie really began to worry when she saw the familiar mop of red hair in the doorway. Elmore Yates had come looking for her.

Momma Troh came to the rescue. "You go now," she scolded, waggling a finger in the face of Yates. "We closed. Big party today. *Priiivate party.*"

"Hey," Yates protested. "This place is open to everybody, ain't it?"

"Not today. Not today. You go away, please."

Yates cast a meaningful glance toward Francie. "If I do, I'll be takin' her with me."

"I think not," came a low growl Francie had never heard before. Kent Welby stood behind Elmore Yates, his face clouded with fury. "She doesn't want to go anywhere with you. And the lady said she was closed. Time to move on, jarhead."

Yates turned, a disarmingly cordial expression on his face, while he balled his fists for a sucker punch.

He never landed it. Doc Welby surprised even himself by launching a short, hard right that decked the Marine with seemingly no effort. Yates shook his head to clear the groggy sensation that swam behind his eyes, then bounced up. He swung a looping left that Doc took on the point of one shoulder, while his fists pistoned, working on the mid-section of the belligerent Yates.

Yates grunted and back pedaled. He popped a right to

Doc's cheek, then bounced off the doorframe as Doc mashed Yates's lips with a solid left. Blood flew and Yates hunched down, intent on going in for the kill. He barreled into Doc and drove him against the bar. Bottles rattled and two fell noisily to the floor. The tatami matting cushioned the drop and neither broke. Doc used an *aikido* windmill to free himself and drove a closed fist down on the top of Yates's head. The Marine tottered away. Doc followed.

Yates threw a kick at Doc's crotch, which Welby deflected. Then Doc pivoted and cocked his torso to his left and unleashed a snap kick that connected with the meaty inner portion of Yates's thigh. The Marine sergeant went to one knee. Doc closed on him, grabbed Yates by the collar and the back of his web GI belt and gave him the bum's rush to the door.

Doc's voice sounded light, almost jubilant. "It's a private party, friend. Stay the hell out."

Archie Golden was filled with surprise. "Hey, Doc, I ain't never seen you fight like that before. You can really kick ass an' take names."

"I—ah—I don't know what got into me." Doc's face flared with scarlet embarrassment. "That's only the—the sixth fistfight I've ever been in."

"You couldn't tell that by the moves you made," Archie praised. "That dork was way out of line. He got what he was askin' for."

"Thanks, Archie." Doc turned to Francie. "I've never seen him in here before."

Francie averted her gaze, to study the matting on the floor. "He works in the operations office. He has . . . been trying to see me."

"I'll convince him otherwise if he keeps on." A sharp stab of guilt pricked Doc's conscience. With Betty wanting to get back together, he had no rightful claim on Francie.

She came to him, as though reading his mind. "Oh, please, Kent Welby, let us be happy tonight. That little fight shouldn't end our party. Mamma Rose and I worked so hard." She pirouette like a ballerina. "Come on, everybody. Have a drink while Kent dances with me."

She hurried to the phonograph and put on a slow, mellow French orchestral number and faced back to Doc. She raised her arms and spoke coyly. "Well, aren't we going to dance?"

The arrival of someone else in the doorway put a worried look on Francie's face. Doc noticed it at once. "What's wrong? Did that jarhead come back?" he asked, turning.

Standing in the opening, in a rain-spattered, rumpled bush jacket and safari shorts, was a sight to delight the heart of Tonto Waters. Eloise Daladier had arrived on the late-afternoon mail run from Binh Thuy. Doc's scowl vanished, and Tonto let out a whoop.

"Ellie! I thought you were stuck off in Pakistan or somewhere, doing something about the troubles in Afghanistan."

"I finished that story a week ago. It took me this long to get back to Saigon and get a travel permit to come here," Eloise Daladier explained as she hurriedly crossed the room and let her scuffed accessories bag drop so she could embrace Tonto Waters.

"It's good to see you again, kid," Tonto murmured into her lilac-scented hair.

"I could hardly wait, Tom. I wanted to be here the day after I got back. But the assignments had piled up on my desk. I had to call every reporter we had in to cover them."

"When the cat's away," Tonto jested.

"So, I'm catty now. Is that what my absence has done to you?"

"Not in the least. Come on, sit down. Let me get you a drink."

Eloise looked around the room. "What is the occasion?"

"Ask Francie. I suspect she's got it in mind to cheer us up some."

"Why do you need cheering?" Eloise let Waters steer her to a chair and she sat.

"You might say it's the monsoon. It's our first and we're kind of out of sorts. Also, there's this big hush-hush operation making ready. We're on it. Tell you about it some other time."

A frown creased the brow of Eloise Daladier. "Tom, you don't have to tell me what it is you are doing."

Tonto grinned. "I know that. Now, what brings you here?"

"I got word that your CIA has an embarrassing situation on their hands. Rumor is that something big is building up at Tre Noc."

"Ummm. Best you keep those rumors to yourself, El-lic. Wouldn't do to have any talk like that coming from someone outside the family, so to speak."

Eloise's eyes went wide. "It's true, isn't it? That's the big operation you are talking about."

"Bite your tongue," Tonto suggested. "I'm sorry I said anything at all. Officially, you know nothing, and I've said nothing, am I right?"

Eloise nodded solemnly. "I hate it in my journalist's heart to sit on a story, but I'll keep quiet if you want me to."

"Good. Now, what say we blow this place and have dinner at Phon Bai? And then . . ."

Mischief and a certain sauciness shone in Eloise's eyes. "Then we can watch the midnight submarine races from the window of my room in the hotel, *mais non*?"

Grinning, Tonto patted Eloise on the shoulder.

"Wouldn't miss 'em for anything in the world." It pleased him that she had remembered the SEAL euphemism for an amorous encounter. And he seriously looked forward to it.

Tonto Waters lay on his back, resting the footed base of the champagne glass on his hairy chest. Eloise Daladier poured from the foaming bottle of Dom Pérignon and Tonto listened to the bursting of the bubbles.

"Damn, it's nice they can still get this good stuff in Saigon," he remarked about the bubbly.

"I bought this in the free port store in Singapore. I wanted us to share something special."

"I thought we just did," Tonto replied with a mock pout.

"Oh, that."

" '*That*' what? Didn't the earth move a bit for you?"

"Of course, you ninny. But, it's not the first time we've made love. After a while, it becomes—old hat."

"Where'd you pick up that expression?" Tonto wondered.

"From a charming American Army colonel whom I met up on the Pakistani/Afghanistan border. He was wearing civilian clothes and trying very hard to pretend he was not in the Army. You know, at some time in the near future, I think the Soviets are going to invade Afghanistan."

Tonto looked incredulous. "You have to be kidding. What the hell would they want that place for? Nothing but boulders and mountains and sand. And the meanest bunch of raghead mountain bandits anyone has ever seen."

Eloise laughed lightly. "That is what everyone says. I think you are all underestimating the situation up there. Afghanistan would give the Soviet empire another back door to the Middle East, as well as access to India and

Southeast Asia. It wouldn't take much pressure from the Russian Bear to shove the Shah out of Iran. Iraq would fall easily, and the Soviets would be sitting on the doorstep of Saudi Arabia. And there, my friend, goes Western Europe's oil, not to mention seaports for the Soviet Navy."

It was Tonto's turn to laugh. "You sound like a military analyst or a journalist."

"*I am* a journalist."

"Caught me on that one. But, Ellie, there are other things I think are more compelling right now than an analysis of Soviet expansion into Asia."

"Such as?" Tonto drained his champagne and set the glass aside. He touched her in a special, sensitive place. "Oh—oooh, yes, I see. You are right, *mon amour*, some things do take precedence. Ummmm—oooh—yes-yes-yes," Eloise sighed out as Tonto brought her to full arousal.

Their night was a long and happy reunion.

"Damn these Oriental bastards!" Sr. Lt. Alexi Kovietski bellowed when he heard the report of *Starshii Serzhant* and Junior Sergeant Yoriko. "They have to be more paranoid than the entire Central Committee." He clapped a hand to his cheek. "Forget I ever said that. Now, where was I? I have become irritated about this matter. Their prisoner-of-war camp is a flagrant invitation to have the American Navy SEALs become more active. As *Resendentura* for southern Cambodia and the Delta I should have been informed of this. Maxim Maximovich, through your contacts with the Northern party elite, I want you to find out every detail of this place.

"I have had a meeting with the American sergeant," Alexi changed the subject. "He has informed me that some sort of rehearsal for a high-level raid is going on. It involves the SEALs." He smiled pleasantly. "His red hair reminds me of your father Feodor Viktorovich. Perhaps you should be the one to serve as his control, eh?''

"I would be honored, Comrade Maj—er—Lieutenant.''

"*Dobro—dobro.*'' Then he repeated, "That is good. See to it, will you? And tell him to devise a means by which he can access the operations orders and order of battle for this anticipated action, *da*? You have done well, Comrades. Your photographs will allow me to know everything in advance, when I make my little visit to this compound.''

Surprise illuminated Dudov's Slavic features. "You are going there in person, Comrade?''

"Yes. Now that I know the infamous General Giap is there, it will be soon.''

Early in the morning, after the party given by Francie Song, Pope Marino presented First and Second squads a surprise. "The rehearsals are canceled indefinitely. Local assets have come upon a number of VC who are observing our activity on the range. Two of them are going to guide Alpha to where they last saw Charlie. Then we hunt them down and waste every one of them.''

"That's hard, sir, real hard,'' Randy Andy let pop out before he could guard his tongue.

"It's what we have to do. None of them can get back to pass the word on what we're doing,'' Lieutenant Marino emphasized.

"What about prisoners?'' Archie Golden asked hopefully.

Pope Marino produced a grim quirk of one corner of his mouth. "Not this time. Too much chance they could pass the scoop along. Chow down, draw your weapons, and make ready to move out.''

After breakfast, Archie Golden tentatively fingered the M-203 he had selected. His pockets bulged with the greasy-feeling plastic casings of the 40mm grenade rounds he had stuffed into them. The originals had been brass, but the latest ammo resupply contained these new jobbies, made of high-impact plastic. They had a golden brass color. *The whole fucking world is turning to plastic*, Archie thought grumpily.

Doc Welby walked up to Archie Golden. "I don't much like it, either, Arch. I don't mind killing in the heat of battle, but what if some poor dork surrenders? What am I supposed to do?"

"Blow him away, like the old man said," Archie growled.

This new order, added to the gloom of the monsoon, brought morale to an all-time low. No one had a doubt that it would get worse when the plan was put to practice. Pope Marino showed up ten minutes later to check everyone's weapons and equipment. He didn't look any too pleased either, Doc Welby noted.

After the last man had been cleared, the squad moved out on foot. They made a wide circle of the train-fire range. The musical chatter of the local fishermen who led them faded out as they went deeper into the jungle. Kent Welby noticed that, and the tightness in his gut increased appreciably.

These men knew the enemy waited out there. They had seen them and, being loyal to the Saigon regime, had reported them to the Riverine headquarters. The price they would pay would be terrible, provided the VC found out their identity. Doc did not envy them their position in this topsy-turvy world. Though he had enough to worry about on his own. Small comfort to him that two heavily armed PBRs ghosted up the Bassiac to provide support. If Charlie had found clever hiding places, they could all be dead before the PBR sailors even knew a firefight had occurred.

Stop it! Doc mentally lashed himself. That kind of outlook was part of the past. He'd gotten over it the previous night when he'd kicked hell out of that Marine sergeant. Or had he? his mind mocked. Up ahead, Tonto Waters halted abruptly and shot a fist into the air.

Everyone took cover, eyes intent on the point man. Tonto crouched low, moved forward a half dozen paces, stopped again. Then he turned and raised his weapon in the signal for Enemy in Sight.

Tonto Waters heard an incautious exchange in Vietnamese less than twenty-five meters ahead. He signaled at once to halt, then eeled his way through the close growth of air plants and lianas. Wet from the monsoon's incessant rain, the vines clung to him. He crossed half the distance to where the sound seemed to have emanated from. He paused again and looked around the bole of a fat mahogany tree.

Seven of them, waiting for the rehearsals to begin. Beyond them Tonto could see the remains of the tower that had simulated a helicopter before they began to work with the real thing. Slowly, avoiding any contact with the brush, he turned back to face the squad. He raised his Ithaca above his head, one-handed. With the other, he ticked off the count of enemy soldiers.

If all went well, Tonto opined, they would have eliminated the problem within less than five minutes.

With the SEALs otherwise occupied, in rehearsals Eloise Daladier believed, she returned to Binh Thuy on the early chopper run. She reached there in time to get access to a battered IBM electric typewriter in the spartan pressroom, maladroitly misnamed the information office. There, she began to piece together from what she had heard and what she had not heard a compelling story.

Everyone outside Vietnam expressed great concern for those listed as missing in action or confirmed as prisoners of war. What she believe would soon happen was a raid on a POW camp, to free the prisoners. Eloise had put most of that together from what Chief Tom Waters had skirted around, rather than anything he told her directly. She had picked up tantalizing snippets from casual conversation among the Riverine sailors.

Such as—''That place is damn big from what I saw out there. Must hold a whole hell of a lot of guys.'' And— ''Those SEALs are gonna play hell gettin' anyone out of that setup.''

Eloise remembered a poster her father had told her about, one that dated all the way back to World War II. ''Loose Lips Sink Ships!'' it had read. Well, these loose lips were giving her an inside on what might prove to be the biggest story to come out of Vietnam to date. It could even lead to the Pulitzer. If only she could get clearance to go along, she mused as she struggled for the proper words to put her suspicions and speculations on paper.

She finished at two-thirty and left the information office. Eloise did not feel that she had accomplished a lot. Yet, she did believe she had put enough down to arouse the interest of the editors in Paris and get a go-ahead to pursue the article she had in mind. Dutifully, she took a copy of her dispatch to the S-2 office of NAVSPECWARV. She filed it there with a yeoman and departed, determined to return to Tre Noc and dig out anything else she might, also to try to wheedle an invitation to accompany whatever units of the SEALs went on the operation.

She left Binh Thuy promptly at 1600 hours, while LCDR Barry Lailey routinely went over any dispatches filed by visiting journalists. He read the first three with mounting boredom. Why the hell he should approve this blatant negativism, he had no idea. One would think the brass would be eager to weed out these misleading, skewed, and blatantly lying accounts of American operations. On that, at least, he had to grudgingly admit he was in full agreement with Lt. Carl Marino. If one be-

lieved the goddamned press, the American forces were
losing the war big-time.

When he got to the fourth, he read only half of the
first paragraph when his face suffused with red. Outrage
steamed inside his portly figure. Not from the disinfor-
mation unfolding, rather from the painfully accurate sur-
mise outlined in the communique. A planned raid on a
POW camp! How in hell had that leaked? He looked at
the top for the by-line.

Eloise Daladier. That French bitch who had been nosing around the SEAL compound at Tre Noc. Goddamnit,
he had to get to her fast and put a muzzle on any more
speculation. Of course, this article could not go forward
to her paper—no, magazine. She wrote for *Le Monde*, he
recalled. She knew too damned much.

Although the involvement of the SEALs was not mentioned, such a leak like this could of itself be a bigger
disaster than he could account for. He reached for the
handset of the telephone on his battered field desk.

"Get me the OIC. No, get me General Belem's office,
Combined SPECWAR-MACV in Saigon." When the ad-
jutant came on the line, LCDR Lailey all but barked into
the mouthpiece. "We've got a hell of a leak. Some
woman reporter," he feigned unfamiliarity with Eloise,
"name of Daladier, that's French, Daladier, has gotten
hold of information on Operation Zipper . . . What? No.
Nothing's been filed that I know of. What I want of your
office is to pull her access to the Delta. Shut her down."

From the other end came the trying question. "Do you
know her whereabouts at this time?"

"Uh—no. Not exactly. She arrived here this morning,
went to work on this piece I'm looking at, and filed it
half an hour ago. I just came across it."

"Well, keep her there until we can arrange to pull her
access."

LCDR Lailey drew a deep breath. "Aye, sir. I'll do that sure enough."

When he had hung up, he decided this was too important to leave to some subordinate. He went himself to the transient civilian quarters and asked the young clerk there for Miss Daladier's room.

"She's not there, sir," the youthful sailor informed him. "She checked out at fifteen-forty hours."

An icy premonition gripped Barry Lailey. "Do you happen to know where she was headed? Back to Saigon, I suppose?"

"No, sir. She said something about the last flight to Tre Noc."

LCDR Lailey had the presence of mind to get out of hearing of the enlisted man before he groaned out his reaction. "Oooh, shiiiit!"

CHAPTER 13 ———————————

TONTO WATERS eased his way back to the squad. Silently he directed them by hand signals to spread around the hidden observers. He knew full well that they could let none of the Cong survive. He didn't have to like it, but it had to be that way. Tonto watched his friends and teammates disappear into the bush. As always in such moments, he wondered if he would see all or any of them when it was over.

He banished such speculation and slowly worked his way to the mahogany tree where he had sighted the enemy. Lieutenant Marino accompanied him. When the SEALs had time to get into position, he would signal for the skirmish to begin. The grim expression on his face told Tonto that Pope didn't like what they must do any more than he did. Whatever way it went, it would soon be over.

In preparation for that, Tonto snaked the barrel of his Ithaca around the trunk of the sturdy hardwood tree and pointed to the nearest VC. His breathing came easily and his heart no longer pounded in his chest. Only that odd tingling itch in his nose, that made him want to scratch the back of his head, reminded him that they were on the knife edge of combat. That and, as usual, he had to take a leak.

* * *

LCDR Barry Lailey rounded up a shore patrol CMA (Chief Master at Arms) and headed for the helipad at Binh Thuy. He was, by God, not going to let this Frenchwoman make a fool of him. Further, if he could somehow make life uncomfortable for Carl Marino in the process, he damn sure would.

His trip was delayed longer by having to fill out a requisition form for a chopper. The last flight of the day to Tre Noc had already left. Fuming, Lailey accepted that, his mind occupied with what he might do to turn the tables on Marino. Suddenly he had it. No doubt the woman was a spy. An agent of the North Vietnam intelligence service. And all chummy with Marino's SEALs. How cute. He could parlay that into one hell of a smelly situation. If he could somehow connect her to Marino, he might get the man up on charges. Damn fine idea. He could hardly contain himself when the flight crew showed up and began to preflight the Huey slick.

Face smeared green and black, Lt. Pope Marino peered through the screening fronds at the Viet Cong who waited at the end of their lives. The senior one seemed agitated that the Americans they expected to see had not as yet arrived. His concern would not last long enough to become suspicion, Pope thought as he sighted in on the man's head.

At such close range, a kid could make a head shot. The perfunctory small-arms training given in a boot camp had stressed aiming for the center of the target, the bull's-eye, or center of mass in a silhouette. The SEALs had been trained by expert marksmen, the best the Marines and Army had, to make consistent head shots as far out as two hundred meters. All except Tonto Waters, who freely admitted he was no supershot like Kent Welby.

"Hell, I ain't no Annie Oakley," he frequently said. "I ain't even a chick."

He made up for it with his shotgun, though. Also in close with a "hushpuppy," one of the suppressed S&W .38 Supers or 9mm Brownings. Carl Marino had come to count on Tom Waters for a lot more than keen eyes on point. The SEAL lieutenant made a check of his diver's watch. Enough time had elapsed. He nodded to Archie Golden, who fired a flare from his XM-148.

An instant after it popped open above the surprised VC, Randy Andy opened up with his M60. In a crash of exploding gunpowder, the ambush erupted around the hapless Cong. No slouches at pulling off, or being caught in, surprise attacks, Charlie soon got off some serious return fire.

Steel-jacketed slugs cracked and buzzed overhead, shredding deciduous leaves and palm fronds, to make emerald-and-chartreuse confetti. Three of the most steady gained control over their aim and brought their grazing fire uncomfortably close to the invisible SEALs. The grenade-launcher tubes belched softly. Detonation of the projectiles sent spinning shards of crimped wire shrapnel whizzing through the vulnerable flesh of the enemy in black pajamas.

At its low cyclic rate of 550 rounds per minute, Randy Andy found it disarmingly simple to tick off three to five round bursts, and even single shots, from the M-60. He chopped down one wide-eyed VC with a three-holer to the chest. The legs went out from under another when a single round from the 7.62mm MG popped through both kneecaps. He went to the ground to flop and squall, while Andy Holt sought another target. It was then he saw the result of Tonto's first round.

Tonto had decapitated the chunky VC who held a Soviet-made AT-53 backpack radio. His second load trashed the transmitter. Archie Golden got off another

40mm grenade and the last of the seven Cong went down. Silence fell over the clearing near the training site, interrupted by the occasional moans of the wounded man, who clutched his bloodied legs.

That condition lasted only until the monkeys recovered from their shock enough to give voice to howls of protest. Outraged birds joined in. Lieutenant Marino and Tonto Waters emerged from their green background. They walked over to the wounded man. He stared up at them with frightened eyes. Tonto exchanged glances with Pope. The eyes of the wounded enemy grew larger and filled with tears when he read the meaning of that exchange. Tonto unlimbered his Browning hushpuppy and shot the Cong between the eyes.

Take no prisoners can be hard on the minds of those who must do the killing. All through the sweep that verified the enemy to be clear of the training site, Tonto Waters brooded over the wounded Charlie he had shot. It hung with him even when they returned to Tre Noc, cleaned and put up their weapons, showered and put on fresh uniforms. Remorse still clung when he received a note from the platoon yeoman that Eloise Daladier had returned to Tre Noc and waited at the hotel.

His boots felt as heavy as his heart with each step he took. His spirits hadn't risen much by the time he reached the hotel in the village. Eloise Daladier was in the tearoom off the postage-stamp lobby. She took one look at the troubled expression Tonto wore and hurried to him.

"Oh, Tom. Something awful has happened. Come to my room. We can talk about it there."

"I don't want to talk about it. I—can't. Classified stuff. But, you're right, it's . . . something shitty."

They went to her room, where she produced a bottle of Johnny Walker Black. Tom tried to beg off, in favor of beer. Eloise insisted. He drank the scotch, made a face, and drank more.

"This would go a hell of a lot better with some water and ice," he grumbled.

"There, you're getting better already. I can tell by how you complain." A lightness danced in the words Eloise spoke. "We can send for ice." She crossed to the door and went into the hall to speak to the concierge. When she returned, she pulled a long face.

"I'm afraid I've been a bad girl."

"Oh? How's that?"

"A dispatch I filed today to my office in Paris. I know you said nothing directly, but I added up some stray innuendos and a few stray facts. There's something going on about a POW camp, isn't there?"

Tonto went blank. "I can't say anything about anything."

"I know you can't, *mon cher amour*, but even your denials have meaning to a journalist." She made a face. "And no! Decidedly no, I am not using you."

"I believe you, Ellie. It's only . . . today was a bitch. We did something that I never thought I'd have to do. It isn't nice, and I won't look at myself as being very damn nice either. Not right now. I want to get piss-your-pants, falling-down dead drunk and forget all about it."

Eloise cupped his haggard cheeks in her soft, warm palms. "Thomas Waters, you are truly a gentle-man in all meanings of the word. This war, it is all crazy. It is not for you."

"Yes it is," Tonto hastened to contradict. "It's why I joined the Navy. Why I became a SEAL. Like my uncle, who joined the army in the Second World War, I owe something to my country for having been born and raised there. I owe my best."

Mock exasperation filled Eloise's voice. "You men! In each of you is buried an idealistic little boy. Some of you, as in your case, the burial is not very deep. I cannot understand this, but I do love you. I realized while I was away exactly how much I love you. You should not let this torture you. Get it off your chest. Even if you have to tell it only to your mirror.''

Tonto smiled for the first time since he had shot the kneecapped VC. "Well, hell, I suppose it isn't any worse than what a lot of others have had to do. And I was following orders." He looked sheepish. "That's what those guys at Nuremberg said, isn't it?"

"Not a comforting thought," Eloise hastened to say. "Forget about that aspect. We will order dinner in from Phon Bai, the best on the menu, and then we will make love."

Dinner had ended half an hour earlier. Tonto and Eloise sipped tea and relaxed naked against the pillows of her bed, when the rest of their plans for the night evaporated in a harsh knock at the door. Tom Waters rose to answer, and slid into skivvies before he opened up to reveal an agitated LCDR Barry Lailey and an unfamiliar CMA in shore patrol helmet and arm band.

"What the hell is this . . . sir?" Waters asked belligerently, belatedly adding the term of respect.

"We have come to arrest a spy by the name of Eloise Daladier. I am informed that she is in this room," Lailey announced pompously.

Tonto Waters blinked, his disbelief written on his craggy face. Lailey and the SP Chief pushed past him and stopped in the middle of the room. Lailey stared gapemouthed at Eloise Daladier, who hugged the sheet to her shoulders to cover her nakedness. It took several noisy gulps to get his voice working again.

"Are you Eloise Daladier?"

"I am. And may I ask what the hell you are doing in my room, Commander Lailey?"

"I'm here to arrest you for espionage, Miss Daladier.''

Surprise registered on Eloise's face. "Why, that's absurd. For whom am I supposed to be spying?"

"The North Vietnamese, no doubt. Now, I haven't time for idle chitchat. Get out of that bed and get some clothes on."

Fury flared on the face of Tom Waters. "Sir, I suggest you get out of this room while she does."

Lailey turned on Waters in a rage. "I'll do nothing of the sort!" A sudden idea broke through the self-induced outrage. He developed it, relishing its implications, as he spoke. "You know, I think I've discovered her source of classified information. Chief, put the cuffs on this sorry excuse of a sailor."

Tonto Waters shook his head in disbelief. How could this be happening? The burly chief came up behind him and roughly grabbed one arm. He wrenched it behind Tonto's back and snapped a handcuff in place. Quickly he grabbed the other arm and bent it behind Waters's back. Cold, hard steel circled Tonto's wrist. It was only then that he belatedly remembered he wore only undershorts.

"What's the charge, you—sir?" Tonto growled.

"Espionage against the United States. Same as her. It's obvious you have been providing her with sensitive information." A lascivious expression twisted Lailey's features. "She been paying you in Swiss francs, or just with nookie?"

Had he not been securely handcuffed, Chief Tom Waters would have committed a serious breach of military courtesy. It didn't prevent him from visualizing the satisfying feeling of tom-turkey tromping the shit out of LCDR Barry Lailey. Lailey spun back toward the bed.

"Get out of there now and put on your clothes."

Barry's beady, evil little eyes never left the shapely form of Eloise Daladier as she climbed from the bed. Sheathed in humiliation and indignation, Eloise dressed in an outward appearance of sensual abandon. To the amazement of Tonto Waters, she openly flaunted her lovely body in the face of her accuser. Tonto's rage cooled somewhat when he saw the effect it had on Lailey.

Beads of oily sweat popped out on the portly lieutenant commander's forehead, and he repeatedly licked suddenly dry lips. Tonto figured that Lailey probably hadn't had a woman in a good six months, maybe even for years. His anger flared again when Lailey handcuffed Eloise. Lailey deliberately brushed the back of one hand over her left breast, lingered there for several seconds, then painfully yanked her arm behind her.

Fighting back his fury, Tonto angrily grated, "This is all a crock, Ellie. We'll out of it in no time, trust me on that."

Lailey cocked an eyebrow and twisted his lips into a nasty grimace. "So, it's Ellie, eh? And, I wouldn't count on getting out of anything for a long time. Spying during time of war is a hanging offense, Waters."

Senior Lieutenant Kovietski had ample reason to be furious. In fact, he had two good reasons. First off, an inquiry to the headquarters of Gen. Hoi Pac had elicited a flat denial of any POW compound in the Delta. Worse yet, he had only minutes ago received word that the Vietnamese he had spying on the activities of the SEALs at Tre Noc had been wiped out to the man. To compound that disaster, they had not been able to report anything before being ambushed by those selfsame SEALs. He bridled his anger before he turned back to Feodor Dudov.

"We will have to rely upon what we can get from our operatives inside the Riverine compound. The sergeant is a responsible man and clever in how he relays information. Fortunately, our top female agent is well placed and able to uncover operations orders and other hard intelligence. Get word to the sergeant that he is to operate the girl. She will work with him.''

"Excuse me, Comrade, but how are we going to ensure that they have unobserved access to such sensitive material?''

A wicked smile creased the thin lips of Kovietski/Rudinov. "I have something in mind that should prove effective. Now, to this other matter. General Hoi lied. We know that. I will draft another demand for information, and you arrange to have it sent by courier, along with copies of the photographs you took. Then we'll see what that wily, Oriental son of a bitch has to say about that.''

To make matters more difficult, LCDR Lailey withheld information on the arrest of Chief Tom Waters from Lt. Carl Marino until morning quarters the next day. When Marino heard the preposterous charge, he erupted in a sulfurous string of profanity that questioned the parentage of Barry Lailey, his sexual proclivities, and the origins of all his ancestors. Dogs and pigs got prominent play in Marino's tirade. When he cooled down, he took a second look at Lailey's ploy and saw it for what it was.

"He's out to smear my ass, Dusty," Pope Marino told his AOIC (Assistant Officer In Charge) Cyrus Rhodes. "You take them through the drill this morning. I'm headed for Binh Thuy. You can reach me at the brig.''

" 'At' or in the brig, Skipper?''

Lieutenant Marino produced a rueful grin. "That remains to be seen. If Lailey pisses me off enough, it may well be in it.''

Surprisingly, or perhaps not so, considering what Pope Marino suspected lay behind this ridiculous charge of espionage, he had no difficulty gaining access to Chief Tom Waters. They were even allowed the privacy of one of the two small interrogation rooms. Bugged no doubt, Marino suspected.

When a shore patrolman ushered Waters in, Marino made a gesture to the walls and his ear. Tonto understood at once. He nodded and took his chair.

"What the hell is going on here, Chief?" Marino broke the silence.

"It's Commander Lailey's doing, sir. He's trumped up charges against me and . . ." Tonto glanced significantly toward the suspected listening devices. "Miss Daladier," he concluded, confident that having his formal manner of address on record might prove helpful in the event of a court-martial.

"I was told that you had been arrested for spying. Who were you supposed to be spying on?"

"On us, sir. Ain't that a crock of shit? Lailey claims he has evidence that proves El—er—Miss Daladier is an agent for the North Vietnamese."

"I agree this is all a crock. At least where you're concerned. But, truth to tell, what do we know about Miss Daladier?"

"Awh, come on, Skipper," Tonto protested. Pope Marino raised a hand to silence him.

"I mean, really. She says her father was a French Foreign Legion officer, her mother Vietnamese. You told me that much before."

"That's right, sir. She also went down to Tre Noc to cover us SEALs. That's where we all met her."

"Yes," Pope went on. "And that's when weird things began to happen. Like the arrests in Saigon."

"Awh, that was that prissy, stuffed-shirt major. Ground-pounders can't be trusted, you know that. They all suck."

"Maybe so, but Eloise Daladier seemed to know a great deal more about it than she should be expected to know. You said so yourself, Chief."

"True," Tonto unwillingly admitted.

Lieutenant Marino gave Chief Waters a hard look in

the eyes. "Then she showed up right when we were going on that search and destroy mission. Now, she comes nosing around when we're getting ready for another big op. Think about it, Tom. What does it sound like to you? Given, of course, that it was someone other than Eloise Daladier."

Slowly, like a kid on the way to the dentist, Tonto responded with the obvious. "I'd have to say that person could be a spy."

"I agree. Only I don't believe she works for the North Vietnamese."

"Who then, sir?"

Lieutenant Marino leaned close to whisper in Chief Waters's ear. "She and Jason Slater have seemed more than a little chummy the times I've seen them together."

Tonto brightened. "You think then . . . ?"

"I doubt it," Marino hastened to dispel the false hope. "But it's something to consider." He bent toward Waters again and spoke softly. "And it's something to drive Lailey nuts trying to figure out what we came up with."

"I like that! I really do," Tonto Waters chortled.

"I'll see what I can do about getting you out of here, in my custody, so training can keep on. Only don't get your hopes up too high."

"There's going to be a general court-martial," LCDR Lailey growled half an hour later.

Pope Marino sat across the desk from the S-2, uncomfortable in the hard, straight-backed chair, fuming for an excuse to punch the lights out for this arrogant sack of garbage. He had been compelled to sit and listen to Lailey's litany of innuendo, fabrications, and wild speculations for endless minutes, before he could request the return to the unit of his platoon chief.

Lailey went on in his pompous way. "So, in light of that, he don't get out, paroled to you or anybody else. I have already sent forward the statement of charges and specifications. I'm making arrangements this afternoon with Admiral Collins and General Belem, who is the SPECWAR convening authority, to have a general court panel assembled. I want to get this distasteful matter behind us as soon as possible.''

Marino responded icily. "I'm sure you do.'' His eyes narrowed. "Have you made any effort to verify anything they might have told you? Especially Chief Waters?''

Lailey shrugged. "Why bother? She's a foreign national and a spy, plain and simple. As for Waters, white-hat sailors all lie. Particularly in order to get out of trouble. I'm satisfied, and you ought to be, too. I'd suggest you keep your nose out of this.''

"I'm not satisfied, and I intend to put my nose very deep in this farce of yours. In fact, I intend to defend Waters if it goes as far as a court-martial.''

"I think I can see to it you wish you hadn't,'' LCDR Lailey warned ominously as he made a dismissing gesture.

CHAPTER 14 _____

TWILIGHT SWEPT over the jungle surrounding Tre Noc with the usual speed. It went unnoticed behind the monsoon clouds, which only faded to black. Everyone expected the nightly mortar harassment. Instead, without any advance warning, a large, determined force of Viet Cong swept up the banks of the Bassiac and out of the jungle to the north. Mortar rounds began to fall then, and in serious number. Charlie advanced, yelling and screaming, and firing their weapons indiscriminately.

"What's this all about?" Archie Golden shouted above the tumult. "They've never pulled a stunt like this before."

Enemy fire concentrated on the guard towers. The heavy rumble of 12.7mm machine guns came from inside the screen of trees. One of the tower guards screamed and pitched over the railing of No. 3 tower. Kent Welby had already scrambled for one of the Stoners in the armory. He charged it as he answered Archie.

"Probably found out Tonto was gone."

"I hate a wise-ass," Archie quipped. He inserted a round in an M-79 and let fly.

Charged with the security of the base at Tre Noc, the SEALs had reacted instantly to the surprise attack. None too soon. The VC ran across the open ground, two out of

166

every eight lugged ladders. These they flung over the concertinas. Trip wires pulled the pins of M-26 frag grenades and white phosphorous. Just as the battle-crazed enemy began to scale the barriers, these went off with a flash and roar.

Blobs of burning, sticky white chemical splattered their faces and clothing. Horrible screams followed as the Willie Peter began to eat into flesh and set fire to black pajamas. Snippets of wire whizzed through the air, raining more death and dismemberment. Fully turned out, the SEALs of First Platoon kept up a steady stream of hot lead. Copper-jacketed rounds and forty mike-mike grenades wrought havoc with Charlie.

Determined, and high on speed, the furious warriors of Poppa Ho threw themselves at the concertinas of barbed wire fearlessly. *My God, there's hundreds of them out there*, Doc Welby thought, his mind cleared of all but the need to survive and to repulse the enemy. He had never seen so many VC concentrated in one place before or since the mission to destroy their arms caches.

"Get a case of grenades up here," Archie Golden bellowed from Doc Welby's right.

An M60 cut a long, burring burst that swept five VC off their feet. Archie began to lob grenades right into the fence line. Doc heard a PBR fire up and the low rumble of its engine as it headed out into the stream. Moments later, the steady chug of 40mm Honeywells reached his ears. From somewhere behind him, someone got a .50 caliber Browning going. Huge chunks began to be blasted from the bodies of the advancing Cong.

Suddenly a wide section of the barbed wire erupted in smoke and flame and the broken ends flew skyward. The little brown men swarmed into the base.

While the battle raged, no lights came on in the Riverine Force offices. Inside, the redheaded sergeant in the employ of Kovietski/Rudinov made a methodical search of the desk drawers in the Plans and Operations section. With him was a silent, grim-faced Vietnamese woman. She was young, attractive and decidedly unwilling to commit this invasion of the American's secrets. Yet, when the sergeant had come to her after work that day and said the words she had been told to expect, she knew she had no choice.

Perhaps they would find nothing, she equivocated. For her own part, she had kept silent all along about the documents she had seen and interpreted as to their significance. But that alone would not do. She was, in effect, a hostage. Her life and that of an aged father were held in the grasp of the big, suave, soft-talking Russian. Quickly she rifled the last drawer.

"There's nothing here," she informed the redhead.

"I found nothing, either." He looked around the darkened office. "They must have put everything important in the safe."

"I don't know the combination."

"Neither do I," he grumbled. "I suppose we had better get out of here before we get caught."

"Yes. I want to leave."

"You did all right, babe. Was I ever surprised when I was told who I was to contact. Never thought you had it in you."

"I . . . don't want to talk about it. Let's go now."

"Whatever you say. Only now, you owe me a little something, huh?"

"No!" she jolted abruptly. "I owe you nothing. I was only following orders."

"Think about it, and you'll come around," the sergeant said confidently as he tilted up her chin and kissed her with mounting urgency.

*   *   *

Repeat Ditto stood his ground, facing a pair of screaming VC. They fired their weapons wildly, far overhead, eyes glassy, as they charged directly at him. How had they gotten inside so fast? Repeat asked himself as he leveled his AR-15 and put three rounds in the chest of one. He recalled the loud explosion of only seconds ago. They had blown the wire. He pumped two slugs into the face of the second Cong and quickly swung right, then left to find another target.

One swiftly obliged. Chad Ditto could feel his heart pounding in his chest as he shot the Charlie in the gut. These suckers had launched a major attack against the base. Everyone was fighting for his life. He saw Archie hurling grenades dangerously close to friendly forces, in an attempt to stem the flow of black-clad bodies through a huge gap in the wire. An instant later, muzzle flashes were not the only illumination. A generator coughed to life and huge floodlights flared from their poles.

For a moment it paralyzed the VC. Stunned by the intensity and suddenness, they froze. Not so the SEALs. They chopped and blasted their way through the ranks of the Cong. Grenade rounds flung bodies and parts thereof into the air. The coppery odor of huge quantities of blood tingled in every nose, along with the tang of burnt powder. Kent Welby inserted another belt in the Stoner and slashed a staggered line across four ardent VC. To his right, another Charlie raised a Soviet-made stick grenade and made ready to throw it. Kent gulped and emptied five cartridge casings as he cut the enemy from crotch to eyeballs.

The grenade fell among the dead Cong's comrades and blasted two of them to perdition. Ruptured intestines added their own peculiar aroma to the medley of death around the young SEAL. Face powder-grimed, Kent checked his drum magazine and saw to his amazement he had shot off nearly half of the rounds it contained. Conditioned by SEAL training, he kept careful count and expended his remaining ammunition judiciously.

Suddenly, whistles began to shrill among the VC inside the compound. Above the ear-numbing cacophony of battle, shrill voices barked commands. Charlie had nearly overrun the compound. Some of them continued a fight of desperation, trapped in among light rivercraft up on shore for repair. Implacably, the SEALs hunted them down and killed them. Fewer of them, it appeared to Kent Welby, remained inside. The night had begun to swallow the enemy.

Not enough, he decided, when he saw one of Anchor Head Sturgis's squad go down with a blood-spouting shoulder wound. A million-dollar wound, Doc thought. That guy would be shipped back to Okinawa, or perhaps to the Olangapo Naval Hospital in the Philippines. What a place to recuperate. He'd screw himself cross-eyed with all those dusky Filipino girls.

What was he thinking about sex for at a time like this? Doc admonished himself as he removed the nearly spent magazine from his Stoner and fed in a fresh one. Last one in the pouch he had grabbed up, he reminded himself. He turned to find a terrified, teenage Charlie rushing at him, wielding a machete. Damn, he hated shooting a kid. But he wasn't going to lose his head over it. The Stoner bucked in his grip and the youthful communist insurgent jolted to a stop.

He wavered, a look of disbelief on his face, then he died. With abrupt finality, the firing ceased all around. Doc wanted to be sick over the needless death of the young Cong. *But why bother*, he chided himself. *Him or me, right? Yeah. Right.* Jesus, he had been scared. Enough so to make him regret nothing that had happened, as he looked back on it with a calmer mien.

Archie Golden soon got a body count. The Riverine sailors lost three KIA in the machine-gun towers. Five wounded among the squads. And, he was surprised to discover, they had a dozen prisoners, all wounded. They would be choppered out to Binh Thuy in the morning. That accomplished, Archie swaggered up to Doc, the wild light slowly dying in his eyes.

"You done good work, Doc. You can play that Stoner like a piano. We'd best find some of those River Rats and get them to fixin' the wire."

"Sure. All in a day's work, huh, Archie?"

"Yeah, Doc. But, there's days and then there are days."

Alerted at the Transient Barracks, Pope Marino met the helicopter when it brought the prisoners to Binh Thuy. He complimented Ensign Wally Ott on a job well-done and then headed to the headquarters of NAVSPECWARV. There he obtained use of a secure line and put through a call to the Special Forces compound in Saigon, at Tan Son Nhut airport.

"Captain Andrews, please," he spoke to the clerk who answered.

"He's out in the field, sir. They're due back later today."

"I'll call back. Thanks."

Disappointed, Pope headed for the brig. He had papers filled out appointing himself unit legal officer, which he presented to the first-class at the desk. Again, he and Waters had an interrogation room to themselves.

"How's it going?" Lieutenant Marino asked the moment Tonto entered.

"How do you expect? Funny thing, so far no one has questioned me."

That puzzled Pope Marino. "I expected that you would have been interrogated by now. ONI or the CID should have been around first thing."

"That's what I thought. Me, I ain't too smart on military law, but this thing smells even more, considering. Like they have their minds made up and don't want to hear anything from anybody.''

Pope Marino considered that. ''You might be right. Did anyone advise you of your rights? Did you sign a DN 3881?'' Tonto shrugged a no. ''Or they could be on such thin ice they don't want to get in any deeper,'' he added, oblivious to the mixed metaphor.

''Hell, Pope, I figured Lailey would have been here trying to beat a confession out of me long before this.''

Marino pulled a face. ''It could happen yet. Tre Noc got hit last night. One hell of a big firefight. Charlie got inside the wire. Brooks and Ott distinguished themselves leading the defense. I'm thinking of putting them in for something.''

Waters smiled. ''They're good kids, Pope. I wish I had been there.''

''For once they did without you,'' Marino said with a laugh.

''I don't know how,'' Waters muttered. ''Say, what are you doing about getting me out of here?''

''I'm working on it. I figure to talk to this blanket-head.''

Puzzled, Tonto made a face. ''What for?''

''I'll tell you later, once I find out what I want to know.''

''That's nice.''

''Yeah, I thought so, Tonto. Well, got to get crackin'. See you tomorrow. Oh, by the way, it's official. I am the unit legal officer. We're all set if it comes to a trial.''

Tonto's face turned glum. ''Don't say that word. I've got a bad feeling about it.''

This time when Pope Marino called the Special Forces base, he got his party. ''This is Andrews, sir,'' Capt. Bill Andrews responded when summoned to the phone.

"Carl Marino here, Blankethead."

"Why, howdy, Webfoot. You in Saigon?"

"Nope. Binh Thuy. I've got a problem."

"You always do. What's the skinny?"

Pope Marino went on to explain the situation involving Tonto Waters and Eloise Daladier. When he concluded, he cautiously broached the subject of his call. "Bill, I'd like to ask you to look up someone in the French embassy for me. It'll most likely be an undersecretary or an attaché," Pope suggested.

A soft chuckle came over the line from the Saigon end. "Oh, you mean a spook."

"Uh—yeah, I suppose I do," Marino responded, then made his request.

Bill Andrews accepted at once. "Sure, glad to. Where can I reach you when I get back on this?"

"At Tre Noc, or here, I suppose. If Lailey gets his way, the court-martial will be rushed through, and I'll be in Saigon. Whatever, I'll let you know."

After he hung up, another possibility occurred. Using the same secure line, he rang up Jason Slater. Like Captain Andrews, the CIA station chief readily agreed and said he would get back to Lieutenant Marino. It left Pope Marino feeling considerably relieved.

When the turnkey came for Tonto Waters, the chief thought that Pope Marino had returned. He found out differently when ushered into the interrogation room. LCDR Barry Lailey waited for him. A stub of foul-smelling cigar distorted the officer's thick lips and made his sneer lopsided.

"Well, Waters, what do you have to say for yourself?" Lailey began the interrogation.

"Nothing, sir."

"You will have before we're through. How long have you been selling information to the enemy?"

Tonto said nothing.

"You will answer me, if I have to beat it out of you," Lailey threatened.

"With all due respect, sir, you're not man enough," Tonto challenged.

Lailey's face reddened. "Goddamn you, Waters. I know you are in collusion with that French bitch. All you have to do is come clean, and I'll see the court goes easy on you. Again; how long have you been selling information to the enemy?"

"Would it matter if I told you that I have never sold or given information to the enemy and never could?"

"Drop that sanctimonious pretense, you bilge rat," Lailey snapped. "You are guilty as sin. Before we're through, I'll have your confession."

"You will like hell . . . *sir.*"

Barry Lailey came close to losing it then. He shot out of his chair and stormed around the table that separated him from Tom Watson. Shoulders hunched, he balled his fists and raised the right one to deliver a hard jab, then regained control, if only barely.

With a silent, inner struggle, he regained his composure. "Consider this. You are going to be tried separately. If you provide me with details of how she enlisted your help, how she transmits her information, other than through the articles she has published, I can get you off lightly." Lailey deliberately omitted any reference to immunity for being a government witness.

"There is nothing I have to say to you. Miss Daladier and I are friends. Nothing more. And I could no more betray my country than I could gnaw my way out of this brig. So, please leave me the fuck alone, sir."

"I've had enough of you. I think I'll turn you over to Chief Toomey. I'm sure the five-time fleet heavyweight champ might jar the truth out of you. What do you say to that?"

Tonto Waters grinned nastily. "The cuts and bruises will look great before the court-martial panel."

Consumed with frustration and rage, LCDR Lailey stomped out of the room.

Early the next morning, after an overnight trip to Tre Noc, Lt. Carl Marino returned to the brig to bring Chief Tom Waters up-to-date. He found Tonto in unusually low spirits.

"Lailey finally paid a visit. It was mostly bluster and bullshit. One thing got to me, though. He wanted me to invent testimony that would be damaging to Ellie. He's determined to get her executed as a foreign spy, or at least put away for a long time. What's he got against her?"

Marino considered it frowningly. "The scuttlebutt is that she made him look the fool over that little incident in Saigon, when Archie and True Blue were arrested for assaulting those poor jarheads."

That brightened Tonto some. "Couldn't happen to a more deserving guy." Then he grew serious again. "Only now it looks like he's come back to get in a few innings."

"Well, that might not be so easy. It takes time to convene a general court. Then there's all of the pretrial paperwork, investigation, that sort of stuff."

Tonto frowned. "This is during time of conflict, sir. They can speed things up because of it."

Marino paused, considered that. Then leaned to Tonto and whispered news of his efforts to find something to bring an end to this farce.

It seemed to do little good. "I don't see how that will help. The chance of finding out anything are slim. Chances of learning what you want to are none, I'd say. What I need right now is a good three-day drunk. I remember the one Archie Golden and I went on right after graduation from UDT/R school . . ."

. . . It began as usual at Vesuvio's. Tom and Richie

Golden downed two frosty mugs of beer each, then consumed a pair of the thick, half-pound, handmade hamburgers the place was famous for. That called for more beer, so they finished another pitcher.

"Let's go to the Palm Garden," Richie suggested.

"Naw, too ritzy for my taste. I say we hit the Bayside," Tom disagreed.

"They've got half-price drinks and pitchers at the Palm Garden from sixteen hundred to twenty hundred. You ain't goin' home to New Jersey an' Iris took the kids to her mother's at the beach, so I can't start my liberty at home for a couple of days. So, why not?"

Tom considered it. "Okay. But just for a couple of pitchers."

Their "couple of pitchers" grew to be six, whereupon five other graduates entered the Palm Garden and pulled up chairs. Sea stories about the rigors of their schooling flew thick and fast around the table. The newcomers bought a couple of pitchers, then all agreed to adjourn to the Bayside Inn.

There they found the remainder of the class. The party lasted to closing and was carried on after that at a secluded beach on Chesapeake Bay. Along about 0200, Tom Waters swaggered up to Richie Golden grinning like a ninny. "You know who you look like? Archie Andrews, that's who. Yeah, that red crew cut and the freckles make you a dead ringer." Several others heard it and from that day the name stuck.

Their party went on the next day, after a hangover cure swim in the chill water of the bay. No one actually became sober. They merely coasted. Archie, a moderate drinker by nature, outdid himself. Tom Waters held his own throughout that day and the following night.

"Some of the guys are pullin' out," Tom confided to Archie about midday the third morning of their spectacular drunk. "You gonna head north?"

"Yep. Iris will be back by evening. I want to be well on my way."

"You're too drunk."

"No, I'm not. I've been sippin' a single beer the last hour. It tastes skunky warm."

"I know that. Let's go in to Vesuvio's and have some burgers, then I'll pour you on the train."

"Okay, only no more beer for me."

"I'll look out for you, buddy. You know I will."

They always had and they always would . . .

. . . Tonto Waters lost the faraway look in his eyes as he finished relating the monumental event to Pope Marino. "That was before you came on board as skipper. What a hell of a time."

"We'll throw another one after this nonsense is taken care of, count on it, Tonto."

"Sure, Skipper, sure." Only Tonto Waters did not sound convinced.

CHAPTER 15 ————————————

FRANCIE SONG was determined to find out why Kent Welby had distanced himself from her. She did not believe that his wife had as much influence as she seemed to have over the somewhat shy, self-effacing young sailor. When he failed to meet her after she finished work that day, she sought him out.

She found him in the platoon bar. The place had the look of transiency about it. It had been set up in one of the rooms of the cinder-block barracks. A single lightbulb hung from the ceiling, a shade fashioned from empty beer cans had recently been added. Tables had been made from packing crates and the stools around them from grenade cases. Planks, raw and stained, formed a small bar, behind which a refrigerator, that had magically appeared from among the stores of the Riverine Force, stood in solitary splendor. It contained sodas and beer, purchased on the honor system by hash marks on a slip of paper taped to the door. C-Ration cans served for ashtrays. Smoke hung heavily in the room when Francie entered. She saw Kent at once and crossed to him.

"Kent Welby," Francie began in that oddly formal manner she had. "We have to talk."

"Can you say it here?"

Francie looked around. None of the SEALs seemed to

be paying them any great attention, yet she felt reluctant to air the difficulty between them in the presence of others. "I would rather go elsewhere, please?"

"You say where."

"We can go for a walk outside to compound, yes?"

Doc Welby shrugged. "Sure. Why not? See you alcoholics later," he tossed off to his teammates.

Before leaving the compound, Francie retrieved her bicycle. Kent walked at her side, guiding the vehicle by its handlebars. Now that she had him alone, Francie seemed unaccountably shy about bringing up the subject that plagued her. They made idle chatter as they progressed along the road to town. Across the bridge that spanned a shallow stream which fed into the Bassiac, she at last girded herself and spoke in a serious manner.

"I need to know what you are doing about your wife. When is she sending the divorce papers?"

Her question put a knife in the heart of Kent Welby. He swallowed hard, avoided her gaze, and stared off into the jungle. At last he could conceal the truth no longer, could not keep up a pretense of nothing being wrong. He felt something akin to relief when he made his decision.

"Francie—Francie, I've had a letter. It . . . just came. Betty—Betty wrote me to say that she has decided not to divorce me."

Horror made a mask of Francie's face. She blinked in incomprehension. "What are you saying? Do I hear you right? She—this Betty Welby is not divorcing you?"

"I'm afraid so. I'm sorry, Francie. I would have said something sooner, but I just didn't know how to explain it to you."

"You are not explaining it well, now. What about us? What happens to you and me?"

"That's another thing that's been bothering me. I feel guilty as hell about—about keeping on, like we've been."

"Well, I don't. You said yourself the love between you

two is dead. Why don't—why don't you get the divorce?''

"I—uh—well, you see, I can't. It just wouldn't be right," Doc finished lamely.

"Not . . . right!" Francie shrieked. Stricken, her thoughts on the baby that grew within her, she yanked the handlebars from Doc's grasp, straddled her bicycle, and pedaled furiously away, tears streaming down her face that Doc did not see, and would not have understood.

LCDR Barry Lailey sat behind his desk. He appeared deep in thought as he reviewed the orders establishing the court called to try Chief Thomas Waters. He paused in his reading to sigh and look up at the framed photograph of himself with Admiral Gates and General Yarburogh. That had been taken when he had first arrived and been posted to the S-2 slot in NAVSPECWARV. High old times, indeed. He went back to the orders.

It pleased him to note that an old friend would be prosecuting. "Erwin Quade will be handling the prosecution," he announced to his assistant S-2.

"You know Commander Quade?"

"We were at the Academy together. He was a year behind me," Lailey recalled with a note of sadness. Quade was a full commander. "We got a break on the military judge; Captain Arthur Benson. Not too bad. Neither of them has much use for white-hat sailors."

"Who is on the panel?" Lt. Jensen inquired.

"Captain William Spence, Captain Burke Travis, Captain Charles Dawson, and Commander Loren Kirkpatrick. Then there are three master chiefs. Dawson and Travis are all right. They were classmates of mine." Again the twinge self-pity colored his voice.

Lieutenant Jensen gave him a curious look. Like every office in NAVSPECWARV, he had heard of Lailey being passed over for promotion. It happened. A solid tour in a combat zone should have cured that by now, yet Lailey had been here two tours and still no promotion to commander. Was it an attitude problem? he asked himself.

"Well, we should look forward to success, I suppose," Jensen offered to cover his silence.

"You can put that in the bank." He smiled happily as he put away orders. "Now, if I can get in touch with Erwin and Art Benson and arrange to have the trial date set up, all will be well."

"You have preserved the decor superbly, Hoi Pac," the visitor to the general's headquarters complimented.

"General Giap, I am pleased you like it. Your previous visit was so hurried you hardly had a chance to appreciate it."

"Yes. A pity. The French . . . did have a flare for interior decoration. You are aware that I am due again in the Delta in a matter of days?"

"Yes. I received orders to detail you a company of troops to go along. Unfortunately on your last journey to the camp, they came belatedly, and I sent them off with dispatch."

"And they never caught up," Giap reminded Hoi with a tone of censure. "Not to criticize you, my dear Pac. It's those bureaucrats in Hanoi. They are forever quibbling over who has jurisdiction. It is something to keep them busy, I suppose."

General Hoi nodded. "Yes. It would be nice, though, if they were kept busy at their work, and sent out orders in time for us in the field to fulfill them."

Vinh Toy Giap raised a hand in mock warning. "We must not criticize . . ."

"Lest we be criticized," Hoi Pac concluded. "I am aware of that. I do wish that you were not headed to the Delta. The American forces have been most active of late. It could be hazardous."

"Not in the least," Giap dismissed.

"Will you be in contact with any of them?"

"I will, no doubt, be interrogating some of the Americans before the week is out."

That interested General Hoi no end. He leaned forward in his eagerness to learn more. "I have recently learned the name of the American field commander of the SEALs, who recently foiled my planned offensive. Col. Tre Fon Lok of our esteemed Army provided it to me. I have intended for a long while to send a special team to capture this man. I done so and will turn him over to you for the full treatment. What marvelous irony," Hoi gloated.

"It will be remarkable to turn this Lieutenant Carl Marino into a hidden bomb to use against his own men!"

Yeoman Henning looked up from his desk to see a worried Kent Welby. "No, Miss Song did not report for work this morning," he informed Doc. "And she has not passed the word or called."

"She must be ill," Doc suggested, covering for her.

"Could be. Well, we don't require a note from Mommy, so I suppose we'll find out when she returns."

Doc Welby could not take it so lightly. He thought about it all through the morning run-through at the range. Considering the conditions under which they parted the evening before, he began to heap up a heavy load of guilt. At noon chow, it decided him. He did not even change out of field gear, but took his liberty pass and headed off base.

Doc found Francie in her apartment. She hesitated only briefly before stepping back and letting him into the room. Thran lay on his tatami mat and futon, tossing restlessly. He wore nothing at all and his small, bronze body was slickly wet with a sheen of perspiration.

"It's Thran," she said, well aware from the concerned look on Doc's face the reason for the midday visit. "He has a temperature of thirty-eight-point-nine.''

Doc made the conversion to Fahrenheit. "That's a hundred and four. My God, Francie, he's burning up. Get some cold compresses and wipe him with them. Ice water if you've got it.''

Doc knew how woefully lacking the local medical facilities were. One look told him Francie was frantic. He knelt by the boy and put a hand to his swollen abdomen. He was no medic, but he was willing to bet the boy had dysentery.

"Look, there isn't much I can do. Just keep him cool, and pour the liquids down him. Boil the water first if that's all you have. Same for milk. I'll do what I can to get help and be back later.''

Francie wore a distraught face. "Oh, Kent Welby, I should have known I could trust you. Hurry back now, and I will see you this evening.''

The afternoon run-through was pure hell. In the absence of Tonto Waters, Archie Golden took point. Lieutenant Marino harried every member of the two squads, demanded greater and greater speed and precision. When they had finished, he called the squads together.

"You're good. But not good enough. We're going to do it again. This time I want no more than one minute, ten seconds between hitting the deck and opening the cells. We want to be out of this fuckin' place in no more than two minutes, forty-five seconds.'' Several groans rose from the ranks. "I'm serious. This is a big compound with lots of guards. They're regulars, not Charlie. But, Charlie is going to hear the noise we make and come on the run. There aren't enough of us to sustain a pitched battle. We have to scoot out of there as fast as we scoot in. So, let's do it one more time.''

They did, and to their astonishment, they pulled it off in the time frame Pope Marino had demanded. Grinning, he faced the semicircle of SEALs. "All right. Four more run-throughs tomorrow, then this place is torn down. Provided you keep it within that two and three-quarter minutes."

Shortly after nightfall, a special team of NVA intelligence types materialized out of the jungle. They were met buy a ranking cadre from the local VC infrastructure, who represented the tactical units around Tre Noc, the Naval Base being only half a klick away.

"I am Major Li Son Thao. Welcome to the Delta."

"You may address me as Comrade Bok," the leader said sardonically. "As you know, we have come to capture a certain American officer in the Naval compound at Tre Noc. You have preparations made for this mission?"

"Oh, yes. The tunnel is this way, Comrades," the VC major instructed.

"You are most kind to meet us, Comrade Thao. I will see that General Hoi is made aware of your full cooperation," the leader replied.

On the way to the site, Li Son Thao spoke amiably, and with pride, of this VC unit's accomplishment. "It is a rather complex tunnel arrangement. The men have worked on it for two years. When the Americans came and set up their base, a branch was excavated in their direction at once. We have only a few meters to dig through to bring us out inside the compound."

"Excellent," Nguyen Bok responded. All this chatter made him nervous.

"We had intended it for the major offensive that . . . did not come. The local unit, The Peasant Heroes Liberation Front, hoped to attack the Americans. Of course, they are proud and pleased to sacrifice that opportunity to further such a worthy endeavor as yours, Comrade Bok."

"As you say, Comrade Major." *Would the man never shut up?*

"They are working now. The tunnel should be done by the middle of the night." Thao paused then, a look of caution on his face as he added, "We are growing very close to the enemy now. We must remain quiet. They have listening devices that are quite sensitive."

About time, Bok thought hotly. If his mission failed, it would be disastrous for him.

Kent Welby skipped evening chow, so concerned had he become over young Thran Song. He appeared on the threshold of Francie's apartment with Hospital Corpsman First Class Filmore Nicholson. Fil bore an uneasy expression and carried his abbreviated medical kit.

"I brought Fil to see what could be done," Doc Welby explained.

"I am grateful," Francie murmured, eyes downcast.

"I shouldn't be here." He said it more to Doc than Francie.

Regardless, he went to where Thran lie and knelt by the pallet. He took the boy's temperature and blood pressure, shaking his head in concern over the results. From his bag, he extracted a vial of antibiotic solution and a syringe. He drew three cc's of air and plunged the needle through the membrane to squirt the air inside. Then he drew a like amount of the drug and injected the boy.

"It's dysentery, all right," he diagnosed. "I've given him an antibiotic." Fil reached into his bag again and took out a small vial of tablets. "Give him one of these every four hours until they are all gone." Fil made a wry face. "I could get myself busted down to seaman for this. But what the heck, the little tyke has become somewhat of a mascot to us. I'm glad to do anything to help. Besides, what the hey. Some of the blankethead corpsmen I trained with at Fort Sam Houston Army Medical Center often treated the children of Mexican illegals who wandered onto the military base. They never got in trouble."

"Yeah," Doc Welby remarked. "Win their hearts and minds. That's what those guys are supposed to be good at. I owe you, Fil. Big-time."

"Just keep Charlie off my six and we'll call it square," the young medic responded. "Now, we'd better get back. I want some chow before it's all gone."

"I'll stay a while, eat here."

Fil cocked an eyebrow. "Oh. Yeah. I guess you can." With a laconic grin, he departed.

LCDR Barry Lailey spoke obsequiously into the telephone. "Good morning, Captain Benson. I'm the S-Two for NAVSPE . . ."

"I know who you are," Benson growled, cutting Lailey off abruptly. "What are you calling me about so early?"

Lailey had a sudden, cold intuition that their old friendship had cooled appreciatively. He tried to force warmth into his words. "Well, sir, I have this major operation laid on. Unfortunately time is of the essence with it, and the officer leading it is the defense counsel for that general court for which you'll be judge. I've already discussed a change of trial date with Commander Quade, sir, and he says he can be ready anytime. I was wondering if your schedule would permit it, sir, to move the trial ahead to say . . . next week?"

Arthur Benson considered that in silence. So far as he knew, there had not been any investigation, either by ONI or the CID, to work up a case. They hadn't even interviewed the accused. Yet, if counsel for the government felt confident to proceed in that short a time, it wouldn't hurt. Such nasty cases as this should be squared away fast as possible.

"Hell, Lailey, if you're in need of the man so desperately, we can move it up to next week if you want."

Pleased and surprised, Barry Lailey could not have hoped for such an advantage. That would give Marino even less time to prepare a defense. "Why, that would be excellent, Art."

"Then let's pencil it in for next Thursday. From what has come forward so far, it shouldn't take more than two days."

"Yes, sir. That will be just fine, Art. Thank you. And, good day to you, sir."

A serenely happy LCDR Lailey returned the handset to its cradle, then looked up sharply when a rap came on the door to his office. "Come," he barked crisply.

An instant frown wiped away his good humor when Lt. Carl Marino entered. "Good morning, Commander," the young SEAL officer greeted. "I brought along all the properly filled out paperwork on the trial. I would like copies of the charges and specifications. I intend to stay over here tonight and study them."

"You have a mission to train for," Lailey grumbled. "I would suggest you put that foremost in your priorities."

"I have. The men are ready. Another run-through tomorrow and we're through. We'll be ready to go soon as I have Chief Waters out of jeopardy."

Lailey fought down an angry retort. He wanted to tell Marino about the change in trial date, but refrained. Let the cocky bastard learn it through channels. "I doubt you'll have that spy along for this operation. The prosecutor has assured me of a conviction."

"Yes, sir," Marino returned. He didn't sound at all convinced. "Now, where may I pick up the charges sheet?"

"At the provost marshal's office in Saigon, or wait for them to come down through channels." Lailey's icy tone left no doubt which he preferred.

"Thank you, Commander. I think I will go on to Saigon."

With that, Pope Marino exited the office. Behind him he heard a harsh grunt of annoyance. It put a smile on his face.

CHAPTER 16 _____

AT THE direction of Comrade Bok, the VC sappers waited until 0300 before they dug through the last two feet of dirt. The tunnel opened up behind a low machine shed on the naval base at Tre Noc. Silently, the black-clad figures oozed up out of the hole and melted from shadow to shadow.

They walked on the balls of their feet, heels never touching the ground. They knew the enemy had vibration sensors that would detect their movement. Capt. Nguyen Bok of the NVA had been superbly trained for the type of covert operation he now ventured upon. Part of that training had been conducted at the notorious Black House in the People's Republic of China. His "graduate course" as he thought of it, had been given in the Soviet Union. Bok soon learned that his superior skills acquired in China were like child's play compared to the abilities of his Soviet instructors. Captain Bok benefited from this, driving himself until he was graduated second in his class, above even most of the Russian students.

It made him an ideal adjunct to his nation's intelligence service. When assigned to the service of the suave, sophisticated Col. Nguyen Dak, he saw it as an opportunity for major career advancement. He had been highly honored by being given command of this mission. He had every intention of making a success of it.

They had acquired excellent intelligence on this operation. Local Viet Cong cadres had given the precise location of the quarters assigned to the SEAL personnel. They knew to within a meter where the officers could be found. Two rows of low, concrete-block buildings had been roofed over jointly to form an interior hallway. The men sent by General Hoi even had a description of the layout of the interior of the officers' quarters.

With practiced stealth, they entered a hall door. The corridor gave internal access to the rooms of the platoon officers. They padded silently along the plank floor to the proper concrete block cubical said to be occupied by their target, one Lt. Carl Marino. Bok had even brought along a tube of powdered graphite, an old KGB trick. This he sprayed into the latch mechanism before trying the knob.

It gave easily, and without a sound. Dim light through a window that gave onto the parade ground revealed the room to be as described. Two men shared it. Only one occupied it at the time. He lay on his side, deep in sleep. Captain Bok motioned for two of his men to advance on the enemy officer. By the time they had reached position, Bok had removed a syringe and vial from his jacket pocked. Then he, too, made his slow, silent way to the bed.

Once there, he filled the syringe and removed the protective cap from the needle. At a nod from Bok, one of the NVA intelligence agents clapped a hand over the mouth and nose of the sleeping man while the other pinioned his arms by laying across the supine body and grabbing the wrists. Captain Bok jabbed the needle into an exposed shoulder and shoved on the plunger.

Violent struggles began the moment the SEAL officer had been touched. They continued, steadily abated, as the powerful sedative did its work on his system. When he went slack, the burly NVA soldiers rolled the body in a damp, green sheet and bundled him out of the room. Captain Bok smiled to himself in satisfaction.

With a precision for which they would be highly praised at the far end of the tunnel complex, the NVA operatives hustled their burden out of the building and across the open corner of the parade ground. They froze in a long shadow when a light came on in one of the barracks. Bok urged them on.

"There has been no difficulty and no movement, Comrade Captain," one of the men left to guard the mouth of the tunnel reported.

"Excellent. We will leave now," Bok whispered back.

Inside the tunnel, the trip became much less hazardous. With justifiably pride, Capt. Nguyen Bok looked back on their exercise as an unqualified success. Only one flaw afflicted his plan. He would not learn of it for some time.

Early in the morning, the phone in the hallway of the Transient BOQ at Binh Thuy rang stridently until answered by one of the Vietnamese staff. He listened, asked the party to wait, and searched through the roster of those residing in the building. He then went to the proper room and knocked diffidently.

"Sorry, please, Lieutenant. You are wanted on the telephone."

Grumbling, Lt. Carl Marino crawled from bed, pulled on canvas shorts over his skivvies, and headed to the telephone. The identity of the caller surprised him.

"This is Marino, sir."

"This is Lieutenant Commander Jorgensen. We were hit last night from a tunnel," said the Riverine Force CO.

Visions of badly wounded SEALs filled Marino's mind. "How bad did my people get it?"

"No one was KIA or wounded. There wasn't even a firefight. But we don't know about your Jay-Gee, Rhodes. He is missing."

"He's what!"

"Missing, Carl. No sign of blood in the room or on the bed, nothing disturbed. He plain isn't here anymore."

"What's being done about finding Dusty?"

"Your ensigns are organizing a search party. I have my boats out, and all local assets have been put on watch for a party of VC."

"I'll get what I'm working on squared away and come back. I want to lead that search."

"I'll be looking for you. And—I'm sorry about what happened. Rhodes was a good officer, and a good man."

Pope Marino's voice turned grim and hard. "Dusty isn't dead yet. I won't let myself believe that."

Lieutenant Marino hung up and returned to his room. He dressed quickly and went to the NAVSPECWARV headquarters. "I need transportation to Tre Noc," he announced to the yeoman behind the travel office desk.

"I'm sorry, sir, I have other orders already cut and here on my desk for you. You and Chief Waters are to be flown to Saigon. There's to be a pretrial inquiry, sir. The court-martial date has been advanced to a week from Thursday."

He would have less than two days to prepare for that! Pope Marino bit off a harsh expletive. "I'll take my copy of the orders and the full set for Chief Waters. I'm headed to the brig now."

"Not necessary, sir. Chief Waters is on his way, under guard. You are cleared to depart in half an hour."

In Saigon, Lieutenant Marino and Chief Waters were met by a pudgy, balding man Pope immediately pegged as a smug, smirking, supercilious desk sailor. "Lieutenant Marino, I'm Erwin Quade. I'll be prosecuting the case."

"May I ask who is on the court?" Pope prompted.

"I have it in this file. Now, I would like to ask the chief a few questions," Quade demanded.

"Not without my being present."

Quade showed an expression of disapproval. "That's hardly necessary. After all, Lucky and I are old friends. He's told me all about the case."

Who the hell is Lucky? Pope Marino blinked. When CDR Quade saw the blank expression, he explained, "Lucky and I go all the way back. We were classmates at the Academy."

Fuckin' Barry Lailey. Marino let the commander know his displeasure. "All the more reason for me to be there."

"You—ah—disagree with Commander Lailey's findings in this case?" Quade asked as though astonished anyone could hold a contrary opinion.

"Absolutely. He has trumped up this entire farce out of strictly personal animosity."

Quade pursed pink, pouting lips. "Against whom is this animosity directed, Lieutenant?"

"Obviously Chief Waters. But that isn't entirely accurate. For the time being, I think I'll keep that information to myself."

"Whatever turns you on," Quade responded in a show of indifference. He prided himself on keeping up with the slang of the youthful sailors, while distrusting and despising them for being lesser than he. He patted idly at his bald spot, as though in search of the hair that had once occupied that space.

"Pretrial inquiry is set for tomorrow morning. You'll meet the members of the court panel then."

"Isn't this sort of rushing things?" Marino inquired.

Quade gave him a pale blue, watery gaze through thick spectacle lenses. "There's a war going on, or haven't you noticed? This is a serious matter; we'd like to get it cleared up quickly so as not to create a backlog."

Pope Marino shot his sleeve to reveal the puckered, pink gouge from a round out of a Type 53 assault rifle that was healing nicely on his left forearm. "I am fully aware of the military situation, sir," he growled, then cut it off before getting himself into serious trouble. "My concern is that I understand this could be a capital offense."

Quade considered that a moment and again pursed his lips. "I had not previously considered trying this as a capital matter. I could, perhaps, be persuaded to change my mind on that."

Marino cooled the head of steam he was building. "Does this file contain the discovery material regarding what evidence you will be presenting?"

CDR Quade shrugged that off. "You will be provided that tomorrow."

"Will Chief Waters be billeted in the CPO quarters?"

"I think the brig is more appropriate."

"Commander, need I remind you there's nowhere in hell he can go to escape in Saigon?"

"I happen to think otherwise. Now, will there be anything else, Lieutenant?"

"If I am to accomplish anything at all for the defendant, it would help to at least know the names of the court-martial board." Marino kept quiet about the fact he already knew.

Quade sighed impatiently. "Very well. Captain Arthur Benson will be military judge. On the panel are: Captains William Spence, Burke Travis, and Charles Dawson. Commander Loren Kirkpatrick, and Master Chiefs Owens, Dunop, and Fowler."

Pope Marino swallowed hard at this confirmation of what he had heard before. "That's some heavy guns. If you don't mind, I'd like some time alone with Chief Waters before he's taken to the brig."

Petulantly, Quade replied, "Very well."

After the officious legal officer had departed, Tonto Waters looked at the troubled face of his commanding officer. "I'm in some deep shit, ain't I, Pope?"

"You got that right. As of this moment, your chances are somewhere between slim and none. But I still have my ace in the hole. Provided it turns out an ace and not a joker."

Dusty Rhodes rested himself as well as he could against the gunwale of the sampan. He had his arms bound to a stout bamboo pole threaded under his armpits and behind his back. He had only regained consciousness early in the daylight hours. He had no idea of where he was or what had happened.

He did know he was a prisoner. The faces surrounding him were all Oriental, the language Vietnamese. The chattering ceased abruptly and a hard, cruel face swam into Dusty's view, an unthethered balloon.

"You are awake, Lieutenant Marino. So nice to have you with us." The English was heavily accented.

It came clear to Dusty in that second. Somehow these gooks had grabbed him, mistaking him for Pope Marino. He spoke slowly, his tongue thick from the residual drug in his system. "I . . . am . . . not . . . Lieutenant Marino."

Sudden and unsuspected, the slap startled Dusty Rhodes. "Do you think me a child? I came into your compound, I entered your room, and I took you away without raising the least alarm. I know who you are, and your pretense fools no one."

"I . . . tell . . . you, I am not Lieutenant Marino. I am Rhodes, Cyrus, Lieutenant junior grade, service number three-four-seven-two-one-six-eight-five-zero."

Another slap resounded solidly. "You are Lieutenant Marino. Answer me properly."

"I am Cyrus Rhodes, goddamnit. Look at my dog tags."

That elicited a smug smile. "A not-so-clever ruse, no doubt, designed to confuse us as to whom we capture. I am from the army of the People's Republic. I am not some peasant lout, doing his six months service with the Liberation Front. Where you are going, you will be made to reveal all of your most intimate secrets. Not just military secrets, but the dark, private things you would prefer no one ever knew about.''

''Where are you taking me?'' Dusty asked, though he suspected he knew their destination exactly.

That brought another blow to his face. ''*I* ask the questions. You answer.''

The crude interrogation, intended to be intimidating, went on for an hour. By then, the sampan had been paddled out of the Bassiac into the Mekong. It only served to verify their destination for Dusty. Next stop, the POW camp that First Platoon even now trained to raid. No matter what happened to him, Dusty swore to himself, he would reveal nothing about that.

Fat chance, the calculating side of his mind mocked him. *Every man has his breaking point*. The trick was to hold on until he first felt himself slipping, then tell them unimportant things, undone operations, long-ago abandoned, the laundry list, anything to lull them into believing you have come over. Holding on to that thought, Dusty Rhodes let the gray-black fog of numbness swallow him as the hard fists of Captain Bok pounded him into unconsciousness.

Lt. Alexi Kovietski climbed from the GAZ-69 that had brought him to the riverbank. Painted in jungle camouflage pattern, the 4 × 4, half-ton standard field vehicle resembled the American jeep. Feodor Dudov had radioed ahead that he had important information. He wondered what that might be. The sampans bearing his Soviet comrades arrived twenty minutes late.

''American river patrol,'' Dudov explained. ''We had to hide in a tributary while the boat went by. I was surprised to see them this close to the Cambodian border.''

Kovietski/Rudinov spoke through his anger at that situation. "They have stepped up activity everywhere. Now, Comrade Senior Sergeant, tell me this vital news of yours."

"From what I observed, and Yoriko here learned inside, the commandant, Col. Xieng Van Gnduc, is cleaning up the compound and putting some polish on his staff and troops. General Vinh Toy Giap is due to return within a few days. He is expected to handle the interrogation of the Americans."

Kovietski thought a moment. "This *Komandira* Gnduc, Feodor, he is a regular?"

"Yes, Comrade, they all are. This is no undertaking of the Viet Cong."

"Then he will think and act like a soldier. Which makes sense that he would prepare as for an inspection to welcome General Giap. What we must not allow is for Giap to work on the prisoners. Did you verify that some are CIA operatives?"

"Absolutely, Comrade Major. Five are in civilian clothes." Dudov took on a sly look. "They have devised a means of communicating that baffles the guards. They are nearly as good as our agents of the *Komitet*."

Kovietski/Rudinov smiled condescendingly. "You flatter them, or grossly overestimate. No one is as good as our people."

For a moment, Dudov looked stricken, then he recognized the dry humor of his superior. "You are right, of course."

"I must update my plans for going to this marvelous camp of yours. Those duplicitous Oriental allies of ours have kept it secret long enough. I wish to be taken there within the next week. We will return to our station and make preparations."

*   *   *

Inordinately proud of his accomplishment, Capt. Nguyen Bok arrived at the Rising Truth Confinement Camp with his prisoner in tow. Col. Xieng Van Gnduc, as usual, met with each new detainee.

"I am Commandant Gnduc. You will remain with us until you become enlightened."

Dusty Rhodes, despite his pain, raised his head and stared defiantly at the commandant. "You're talking brainwashing here, am I right?"

Gnduc struck Dusty a vicious blow in the stomach that, because of his pole bindings, put him on his knees. "You will speak only to answer questions, Lieutenant Marino."

Usually mention of the prisoner's name by someone who should not have known it damaged his confidence. This one did not seem so affected. In fact, winded though he was, this one was laughing.

"There's where you're wrong. Your stooge here fucked up. I'm Lieutenant jay-gee, Cyrus Rhodes. Lieutenant Marino was not on the base the night Bok-baby showed up."

Gnduc's eyes narrowed. "What is this you are saying?"

"I am not Lieutenant Marino. I tried to tell Bok that, but he would not listen. Take a look at my dog tags. That'll show you."

Xeing Gnduc took a step forward and groped inside the now-ragged, green skivvy shirt Dusty wore. He extracted the metal wafers and scrutinized them carefully. "This name, *Rhodes*, it is not Italian?"

"No, it is English. I am a citizen of Rhodesia, a nation named for my great-great-great grandfather, Cyrus Rhodes."

"What are you doing in the American Navy?"

"Earning my citizenship in their country. You see, I am the third son and will not inherit from my father, so the military it was for me," Dusty rattled on. "I didn't take kindly to Sandhurst, or anything much in England, so I applied to the United States Navy and was accepted at one grade lower rank, an ensign in fact. I've been promoted since.''

''You are remarkably cooperative for an American officer,'' Gnduc opined.

''I've been encouraged by your stooge, Bok, to hold nothing back. Also, I am eager to clear up this matter and be returned to my unit.''

Colonel Gnduc's sardonic smile disposed of that possibility. ''What unit is that?''

''I'm sorry, I don't think I can tell you that.''

This time, Gnduc backhanded Dusty; a sharp, one-two motion that split both corners of the young SEAL's mouth. ''Then I predict that it will be a very long time before you ever see this unnamed unit, Lieutenant Rhodes.'' He nodded to the two burly NVA guards who flanked him.

Methodically they went to work on Dusty. For an agonizingly long quarter hour, they punched, kicked, and pummeled him in a savage beating. Mercifully unconscious at last, Dusty received a pair of well-aimed kicks to the kidney region and was dragged off to be dumped in a cell.

CHAPTER 17 _____

LIEUTENANT CARL Marino had not yet heard from Capt. Bill Andrews or Jason Slater. He arrived at the pretrial inquiry session considerably out of sorts. The courtroom had been set up in the ballroom of an old French colonial mansion off the cathedral square. Facing the dividing bar, Lieutenant Marino saw beyond it a large, raised dais, which supported a spacious table, its front and sides skirted with navy blue cloth. To the right, a smaller table had been placed for the recorder. In front of it, at a right angle to the judge's bench was the witness stand. Two folding-leg tables had been erected, facing each other in the middle space, beyond the swinging gates. Those, Pope knew, were for the opposing counsels.

To the left of that, arranged theater-style, were two long, skirted tables with chairs for seven occupants. The court panel. The US flag and that of the Navy had been put in the proper places. Marino appeared to be the first to arrive. He crossed to the table nearest the bar and took a seat. Captain Benson popped his head in and saw that no one else was present, then returned to his chambers. Within five minutes of the appointed time, two SPs brought Tonto Waters. Then Quade and another lawyer for the government showed up. Lastly, Captain Benson entered. The bailiff called for all to rise. The military judge strode briskly to his elevated bench and took his seat.

"Everyone be seated." He turned then to those attendant on the court. "This is a formality. In a minute I will ask for the panel to join us and introduce them. After that they will be excused and we can get on with the inquiry." He didn't wait for a reply. "Bailiff, will you invite the court panel to join us?"

A first-class, wearing a Shore Patrol armband, went to a door and knocked smartly five times. A moment later it opened. "All rise," he commanded.

When all had been seated, the Judge went on. After introducing the panel and then dismissing them, Captain Benson asked upon what Marino intended to base his defense. Marino considered that out of order, but replied politely.

"All things considered, Your Honor, I haven't had access to the charges and specifications until right now. Since I am unaware of what the Government alleges to prove, I have no idea, other than the innocence of the accused, how I'll go about defending him."

"Hummm. Well said, Lieutenant." He turned to CDR Erwin Quade. "Can you tell me why it is defense counsel has not been given access to the C and S documents?"

Quade cast a hot frown on Marino. "Sir, it was my understanding that Lieutenant Marino came here to Saigon and obtained copies of them."

His little ploy had fallen flat. Maybe a little help was needed. "It's true I came here, Your Honor. But I was told that the charges and specifications could not be released without permission from Commander Quade. So all I got was a brief read-through."

Captain Benson glowered at both parties. "Well, it appears we have little progress for today. Is the Government ready to proceed with the inquiry?"

"Ready, Your Honor."

Judge Benson nodded to CDR Quade. Quade lifted a sheet of paper from the table and began to read from it. "Be it known that Thomas James Waters, Chief Quartermaster, United States Navy, Service Number RN28947703, is by competent authority charged with violations of the Uniform Code of Military Justice, to wit: Article 104, Aiding the Enemy; Article 106, Spying; and Article 106a, Espionage. Conspiracy to commit the above-mentioned violations. And Article 107, Making False Official Statements." Then he went on to read the specifications.

Throughout it, Lt. Carl Marino tried to maintain a facade of calm deliberation. Only a small tic that developed at the corner of his left eye betrayed his growing outrage. Of course he had seen it, but reading it on paper robbed it of its emotional impact. When Quade finished, Pope Marino found he had been gripping a pencil so tightly it had snapped in two. For the first time since the lawyer had begun to read, Marino looked at Quade, who in turn peered expectantly at the Judge.

"Are there any motions, Commander Quade?"

"I move we proceed directly to trial."

"I object, Your Honor. That would not allow me even twenty-four hours to study the charges and do my casework. Let alone to summon witnesses."

"Motion is overruled. This court-martial will convene as directed on next Thursday. Does the Government have any other motions?"

"I move that any witnesses be excluded from the audience and that they be admonished not to discuss their testimony among themselves."

"Yes—yes, of course. Only please do so at the proper time, Counselor," the Judge ordered testily. "Once the court is convened will be suitable. More?"

"No, Your Honor."

"Defense, Lieutenant—ah—Marino?"

"I move for a dismissal, on the grounds of a complete lack of evidence."

"Your honor, these are serious charges. We cannot simply lie down and forget it because the Government hasn't two dozen witnesses to parade before the Court."

Captain Benson leaned forward over the long table sat on the dais. "I gather that is an objection?"

"It is, Your Honor."

"Sustained." To Marino, he went on, "I must assume that your brief reading was most thorough. Even so, it is the opinion of this court that sufficient cause exists to try the accused under the authority of a general court-martial. Motion to dismiss denied." He rose, and Quade sprang to his feet. Marino was already standing. "If there's nothing else, we'll dismiss until trial date."

"All rise!" the bailiff belatedly barked.

Biting back an angry protest, Pope Marino remained silent until the Military Judge walked from the room. He watched in white-faced anger and embarrassment as the Bailiff took Tonto Waters into custody and left as well. Outside he headed to the officers' club at the Special Forces compound at Tan Son Nhut.

When Lieutenant Marino had settled down in the small reading room, off the bar, he spread the documents provided to him out on the long, folding-leg table and began to put them in sequence. He read for the third time the charge of espionage and the specifications that indicated:

- In that Chief Quartermaster Thomas J. Waters, assigned First Squad, First Platoon, Team 2, SEAL program, stationed at Tre Noc, Republic of Vietnam, did at a hotel in said Vietnamese village of Tre Noc, on or about 17 February 1968 with intent to convey classified material to wit: details of an impending combat operation to a foreign national by the name of Eloise Daladier, a citizen of France and the Republic of Vietnam. And further that:

- Said information was of a sensitive, and classified nature, pertaining to Top Secret operations of the United States Navy. And that:
- At times and places, herein unspecified, the said Thomas Waters had conveyed other classified information to the aforesaid Eloise Daladier in exchange for money and other services. And that:
- Upon his arrest, the aforesaid Thomas Waters made false statements, to wit: that neither he nor Eloise Daladier were spies in the meaning of Article 106 of the UCMJ. And further:
- At the time of such arrest, that Thomas Waters did resist such arrest.

Taken all in all, quite an accusation, Pope Marino considered. He worked in total absorption for the next three hours, rereading each of the specifications and looking up case notes of similar situations in other court-martial proceedings.

To his disappointment, he found Erwin Quade to be meticulous and accurate, if somewhat indifferent to the facts as he, Marino, knew them. He was about to give up on it for now and have lunch when he recalled that he had promised to visit Tonto in the brig. He closed his books, gathered them, and stowed them on a sideboard. Looking up from that, he found one of the replacements, Andy Holt, standing in the doorway.

"I was told I could find you here, Lieutenant."

"Yes, Holt. What is it?"

"Sir, I went to the intelligence school—it's in my two-oh-one—and served with ONI before going to BUDS. I wanted to help the chief, so I did a little digging on the background of the members of the court."

Pope Marino cocked an eyebrow. "That's highly irregular, Holt.'' Then he flashed a grin. ''But, now you're here, what is it you learned?''

''From the top, sir, Captain Benson has a low regard for enlisted personnel. He is also a moderate drinker, sir. Favors the single-malt scotches. He has served as military judge on close to a hundred courts-martial. Although he is considered cordial and friendly outside the court, he absolutely terrorizes everyone in the court. Especially young, inexperienced lawyers. In every case heard, he has upheld the maximum penalty, if the offender was a petty officer or EM. He is known to the JAG office as 'Hang 'em High Benson.' ''

Lt. Carl Marino did not like the sound of that. ''Go on,'' he urged.

''Captain William Spence is considered an even-handed man when serving on a board. Even when he held captain's mast for his own command, he was known to go easy on his men, sir. He is a golfer, has a wife and four children. His eldest, Norbert, is XO on a missile cruiser of the Fourth Fleet, serving in the Med. His daughter, Mildred, is a nurse, serving with Sixth Fleet, stationed at the Naval Hospital, San Diego, California. The younger two are still in school. Bobby in high school, Nicholas in the sixth grade. Captain Spence has never been known to tolerate sloppy work by the prosecution.''

''Sounds like a good man. I think I know to whom I make my pitch. What else do you have?''

''Commander Kirkpatrick has never served on a general court before. He does not have any legal experience, short of what he got in Academy classes, and captain's mast, of course. He has put in two tours in-country. This is his third. I've heard that he doesn't think much of Special Warfare types. He considers us to be an embarrassment, like intelligence types, 'too unconventional' is the way he puts it.''

''Well, hell, we're *supposed* to be unconventional,''

Pope Marino barked. "Still, if he can be even-handed, we shouldn't have much to worry about."

"He's also a golfer. Plays a weekly round with Captain Spence."

"Humm. All the more reason to work on Spence. Okay," Marino changed pace. "Give me the bad news."

"And, that's what it is, Lieutenant. Captain Burke Travis. He and the prosecutor, Commander Erwin Quade, were at Annapolis together with—"

Marino interrupted him to say, "Our beloved Lieutenant Commander Barry Lailey. Yes, I know that. What else?"

"Captain Travis has been visited four times in the last week by Commander Lailey. They are considered best of friends. On two of those occasions, Commander Quade was present."

That brought a scowl to the forehead of Pope Marino. "I would sell my soul for photographs of that. Lailey is about the only witness the prosecution has, and here he is hobnobbing with one of the panel members. Can your source be made available for the trial?"

Holt thought about that. "I'm not sure, sir. He's from Binh Thuy and wasn't exactly authorized liberty in Saigon. He's on a chopper crew, the one that took Commander Lailey to Tan Son Nhut each time. He told me he knows the chief well and wanted to help, so he faked his way off the air base and followed Lailey. It could cost him his Crow if it comes out."

"If he's that willing to help Tonto, then he'll take a bust if necessary. We'll hold him in reserve in any case. Might be able to impeach Barry Lailey's testimony with him." Lieutenant Marino glanced at his watch. "I was about to break for chow. Let's go over to the NCO club. They've got better food. Then, I've got to visit Waters."

"I'd like to go along, sir."

"Might as well. You've earned it. Oh, by the way, how did you get liberty to Saigon?"

Randy Andy Holt produced a guilty grin. "Same way my informant did. I faked it."

Chief Tom Waters greeted his visitors with a big, warm smile, something Pope Marino had not seen in several days. "Hey, Randy Andy, what brought you here?"

"Oh, nothin', Chief. Just wanted to sneak you in a carton of smokes with a file in it."

"I'd be happier if you'd made it a case of beer. Bein' in this brig makes a man thirsty. Where do we go from here, Lieutenant?"

"Trial is still set for next week," he said, more for Holt's benefit.

"What have you found out about Ellie?" Tonto asked anxiously.

"She is supposed to be in civilian custody. I assume that means Jason Slater. Only I haven't been able to get ahold of him so far," Pope Marino answered. "Whatever, it will be a federal trial, probably back in the States."

"What's the court-martial panel goin' to be like?" Tonto prodded. "I don't know any of them by face or reputation."

Marino gave him a level gaze. He did not want to raise false hopes. "Tough as a rhino's hide. But, I'm working on something for that. Meanwhile, you try to dig out every detail of where and when you met with Eloise. Make notes. Also the names of everyone you know who saw you together. Commander Quade may know of some of them, but we can use all the rest to bring out the true nature of your relationship."

For once, given the circumstances, Tonto looked uneasy. "Does that include—ah—er—*intimate* details?"

"Use your judgment on that. I'm serious, Tonto. Right now, they have you by the balls. Your accuser is a senior officer in the Navy, those sitting in judgment are also, not to mention one of flag rank. Most of them give short shrift to petty officers and enlisted men.''

''Then they don't know fuck-all about how the Navy's run, do they, sir?'' Tonto challenged.

''I'm glad to see you in a fighting mood, Chief. But, that isn't at issue here. Our job, and I'll admit it's an uphill one, is to sway them from their convictions. You have to be believed, instead of Barry Lailey.''

Tonto scowled. ''You should have left that fuck behind in Central America.''

Amused by Tonto's vehement partisanship, Pope shook his head. ''Wouldn't work, Tonto. There's never been a SEAL left behind. And if I had brought him out at room temperature, there would have been an investigation. Case closed. Now, I'm going from here to see what I can about Eloise. You take care and keep making notes.''

''Yes, sir. If you think it will help. Good to see ya, Randy Andy,'' Tonto offered to Holt. With that, he left the room. When he thought he was well out of sight, Tonto's shoulders slumped.

''You will open this gate at once, *soldat*. I demand to speak with the *komandira* immediately!'' Sr. Lt. Alexi Kovietski bellowed into the face of the startled NVA guard at the gate to the POW compound. ''Send for him.''

The soldier overcame his fear of seeming authority enough to remark to his subordinate at the sentry post. ''This arrogant *quai'lo* bastard demands to see the commandant. Take the message to Comrade Gnduc, and we can watch the destruction of this foreign devil.''

Without delay, the younger trooper took off at a shuffling pace. He returned in five minutes, fighting to hide the smirk on his lips. ''Comrade Gnduc replies that he will see you at his pleasure in his office, later on," he added meaningfully.

"Tell him," Kovietski began in Vietnamese, "that Major Pyotr Rudinov of the," and he switched smoothly to Russian, "*Komitet Gosudarstvennoi Bezopasnosti* will see him here, at once!"

A blank look came from the young guard. "I cannot pronounce those stupid foreign words," he responded in newfound defiance. "And I don't know what they mean."

Kovietski/Rudinov's voice changed to a menacing purr. "You have heard of the KGB, have you not?" he asked, using the English equivalent for the acronym of his service.

Paling, the soldier nodded dumbly. "I will go at once, Comrade Major," he responded in his native language.

When Col. Xieng Van Gnduc arrived at the gate, he had worked himself into a fine mood of outrage. How dared this *quai'lo* presume to give orders to him. Then he saw Kovietski, and he knew who he was. The self-righteous anger flowed away like the tidal bore in the Mekong. He was all but washing his hands in an obsequious gesture when he stopped inside the gate. Even a lowly sergeant in the KGB outranked him, and he knew it.

"What are you standing there for, you idiots? Open the gate for the good major," he demanded of his guards. Then he turned to Rudinov. "My apologies, Comrade Major. I have, of course, known of you, but not by your right name and rank. It is my pleasure to welcome you to our camp. The Rising Truth Confinement Camp is a pilot project, designed to make way for many similar camps, to hold and interrogate the massive numbers of Americans we anticipate capturing when the major fighting resumes after monsoon. Please to come in and observe as you wish."

"You are most kind, Comrade Colonel." Kovietski/

Rudinov strode through the opening gate and waved a careless gesture toward the cluster of cells. "I am curious. Why is it you have so few confinement cells?"

"At present, we build them as we need them. For every prisoner brought here, we build two. It keeps us ahead."

"Then you must have—aah—" Rudinov made a quick count. "Eleven inmates at present, yes?"

"Actually twelve. One was brought in early this morning. We begin two new cells tomorrow."

"And who might that be?"

Proudly, Gnduc told him. "An American Navy SEAL officer. It was intended to be the commanding officer, but it is another officer of lesser rank."

"Really? I would be most interested in seeing him," Rudinov purred.

"I am afraid—I am afraid, Comrade Major, that it is impossible. He is being prepared for interrogation by . . ." Gnduc abruptly cut off his babble.

"General Giap. I am aware of his impending arrival. He has been here before, has he not?"

"Why, yes, Comrade. H-How did you know?"

Rudinov merely stared at the hapless Vietnamese. He was KGB, how else would he know, his hard gaze said. "Colonel, I would like the identity of all of your other prisoners."

"The military are easy. There is Lieutenant Rhodes, whom I mentioned, a Captain Perry, a Marine pilot, another pilot, Lieutenant Carstairs of the American Air Force. An ARVN colonel named Dahk and three ARVN enlisted. The remaining five, I do not have names for. They are civilians, but they are far from decadent or soft as we have been told Americans are."

That news verified what Dudov had told him, and excited real interest in the camp. Rudinov listened closely as Colonel Gnduc rambled on. "General Giap is most interested in them. He expressed his intention to interrogate them immediately upon his return. Accordingly, we have begun a regimen of sensory deprivation that he prescribed."

"Ah—Comrade, I am also most interested in these civilian prisoners. Where were they captured?"

"Two south of Da Nang, in the Chaine Annamitique, among the Montagnards. One along the supply trail inside Khmer territory. The other two were captured in a covert station northwest of Lac-giao." He stopped to snicker. "They told us that they were there to do geological surveys. For an oil company of all things."

This was news to Rudinov. "In the *highlands*?" he demanded.

"Exactly. No foreign civilians have been allowed in those areas for the past eight years."

Rudinov decided to test the man. "Then who do you think they might be?"

"The CIA, of course. Exactly as you do, Comrade. Am I right?"

"You are. Your superior, General Hoi, has twice lied to me about the existence of this compound. Am I to infer from that the possibility that it is his government's intention not to share this find of yours with your ally, the Soviet Union?"

"I do not speak for the government. Speaking for myself, it is definitely not my intention to deny you information on this subject."

"Excellent. However the requirements of your Soviet partners are farther reaching than that. First off, why was I not notified of this camp?"

Colonel Gnduc made an elaborate gesture and sought to dissemble. "I do not understand, Comrade Major. As far as I know, the proper notification was sent."

"Nothing sent has ever failed to reach me before. I find it hard to believe that this is the first time. Something of this importance would have been hand-delivered, yes?"

"Of course, Comrade Major."

"And you are not missing any of your men?"

"No. But then, I was ordered not to communicate with you. The notice would have been sent from General Hoi's headquarters."

"Which it obviously was not. Now then, what about the momentous news of five CIA agents captured and held here? Why was I not advised of that?"

Gnduc shrugged. "Again, I was ordered not to contact you."

Rudinov held back his growing rage. "That will suffice for now. The second part of our requirements is this. I will inspect each of the prisoners, determine their physical and mental condition. Then I will leave this camp. When I return, I will require of you to fulfill the last part of your obligation to your Soviet partners. You will turn over every single one of these prisoners to me. Is that clear?"

Col. Xieng Gnduc paled and swallowed hard. His lower lip quivered as he made weak reply. "Entirely clear, Comrade Major. I will so inform General Hoi."

Thunder rumbled in the voice of Major Rudinov. "You will do no such thing. Any attempt to contact the general will be considered as an act of treason against the Soviet Union and you will be treated accordingly. *Vepolananee*. It is a good Russian word. Look it up some time."

Colonel Gnduc, having been educated in Siberia for his post as a prison commandant did not need to look it up. He already knew that the Cyrillic characters which sounded as *vepolananee*, meant **execution**. It stood out in bold letters in his brain.

CHAPTER 18 _____

WITH A rap of his gavel, Military Judge Arthur Benson seated those in attendance upon the court-martial of Chief Thomas J. Waters. Then he proceeded directly to the matter of oaths.

"Let the record show that in accordance with Articles Forty-two-a and 136-a-six of the Uniform Code of Military Justice I have taken written oath before an officer qualified to administer such oaths. The Government's counsel, Commander Quade, has likewise taken the required oath on Department of the Army Form 3497-R. It is now the duty of the Government's counsel to administer the oaths to the general court-martial members, assistant trial counsel, defense counsel, and recorder. Commander Quade."

Quade rose and faced the bench. "For the sake of expediency, I will ask that LCDR Olsen and Lieutenant Marino rise together and take the oath. Gentlemen?" They rose and faced Quade. Then CDR Quade took a sheet of paper from the table in front of him and began to read.

" 'You, Lieutenant Commander David Sven Olsen and Lieutenant Carl Richard Marino do swear or affirm that you will faithfully perform the duties of assistant trial counsel and defense counsel in the case now in hearing. So help you God.' "

Pope liked that last part. He knew from his study of AR27-10, which now guided courts-martial for all services, that it was optional. That Benson had most likely instructed Quade to include it gave Marino some hope. "I do," he answered in unison with Olsen.

CDR Quade then turned to the members of the panel. " 'You,' " and he read off each of their names and ranks, " 'each of you do swear or affirm that you will answer truthfully the questions concerning whether you should serve as a member of this court-martial; that you will faithfully and impartially try, according to the evidence, your conscience, and the laws applicable to trials by court-martial, the case of the accused now before this court; and that you will not disclose or discover the vote or opinion of any particular member of the court upon the findings or sentence unless required to do so in due course of law. So help you God.' "

After their answer in the affirmative, he turned to the recorder. " 'You, Chief Yeoman Barbara Willis,' " he began and read her oath. When she answered in the positive, Quade resumed his seat.

Silence held for a while, Judge Benson staring off at the ceiling. Cherubs had been carved and painted there and may have accounted for his interest. At last he leaned forward and began the examination of the panel members. With that concluded, he again examined the ceiling in silence for a long minute before he spoke earnestly, although in an offhand manner.

"I realize this is a bit irregular, but bear with me. I have found in the past that courts-martial can often be prevented from being conducted if we can reach agreement without it. So, I would ask counsel for the Government, and counsel for the defense if there is any means of resolving the issue without a general court-martial."

Without hesitation, CDR Erwin Quade rose from his chair. "There is none for the Government's case, sir."

"Does the defense have anything?"

"Yes, Your Honor, members of the panel, I believe there exists ample reason for, and means of, resolving this issue without a trial. As a matter of course, you were all provided with copies of Chief Waters's two-oh-one file. I have taken the initiative of making copies of certain specific notations therein. First, which I'll hand to you, is the complete wording of the Unit Citation, which Chief Waters earned along with First Platoon, Team Two SEALs. The second, which I give you now, is the specification for his award of a Bronze Star for bravery in the face of the enemy. The last is his citation of the Purple Heart. I would ask you to read these carefully and then tell me if you can find it even remotely probable that such a man, such an exemplary sailor, could have engaged in espionage against his country."

At once, Quade came to his feet again. "Oh, Your Honor, the defense is making his closing argument at the beginning. I must object."

Captain Benson pursed his lips in a moment of deliberation. At the same time, Captain Spence raised a hand to indicate he had a question. Judge Benson acknowledged him and he left his place to approach the bench. There he leaned toward Judge Benson and whispered urgently. The judge listened, nodded, then ruled. "You may be right. But I think we'll hear this. Proceed, Lieutenant Marino."

"I would point out, Your Honor, gentlemen of the panel, that were this case to be tried before any civilian criminal court, with no more evidence than what I have obtained through my discovery motion, it would be laughed out of court. The charges and specifications are supported by nothing more than the unsubstantiated statements of a single individual. Only military law gives credence to such evidence, and that is being changed almost as we speak."

Judge Benson leaned forward to interrupt Lieutenant Marino. "Now you are straying into summation, young man. Could you please tie this up?"

"Yes, Your Honor. It is very simple. Chief Thomas Waters is too brave, dedicated, and loyal to be a spy for any enemy of our country. We have little in the way of hard evidence. I feel that in these circumstances, the Government's counsel and I should join in asking for a dismissal of charges at this time. Or if you and this panel finds it necessary, that further, more thorough investigation be undertaken. Thank you."

Marino sat down beside Tonto and gave him a hopefully confident look. "Round One," he mouthed silently. Captain Benson looked across the room at the officers and petty officers serving on the panel. Spence nodded in the affirmative, Dawson and Kirkpatrick shrugged, and Travis shook his head vehemently in the negative. The master chiefs all agreed with Marino's proposition.

"Very well, Counsel. We shall take this under advisement." Pope Marino rose when the judge stopped talking.

"One more thing, Your Honor. I would ask that Chief Waters be released from the brig into my custody, pending your decision, and if necessary, throughout the trial."

That met with general approval. CDR Quade rose to object, but Judge Benson put him in his chair with a stern nod. "Agreed. Let's recess for two hours."

Outside the large ballroom of the former colonial mansion, where the court-martial was being held, Tonto Waters turned an admiring gaze on Pope Marino. "That easy? Son of a bitch. Looks like you took Round One."

"I didn't win it by a knockout, but we may win the whole match by a TKO. Best we can consider is I won that round on points. We'll see how good a job I did when we come back. Now, let's get something to eat."

"I'm for a beer. I've almost forgotten what it tastes like."

Lieutenant Marino laid a hand on Tonto Waters's shoulder. "I wouldn't if I were you. Not when you will be sitting close enough for the panel to smell it on your breath."

That gave Tonto pause. "Humm. I hadn't thought of that. Do you think we can be out of this by sometime this afternoon?"

"Maybe. Maybe not. Right now I'd say we have Captain Spence solidly in our camp. The Judge has an attitude problem with enlisted men, but he is known to be fair. He'll decide based on the facts. Burke Travis is entirely prejudiced against us. That leaves it up to the other five. They could jump either way."

A deep frown had returned to Tonto's clear, high brow. "You make it sound pretty shaky."

"I meant to," Pope Marino answered him seriously.

Blinding sunlight pierced the retinas of Dusty Rhodes's eyes. With equal suddenness, a shadow filled the open doorway of his cell. A high-pitched Vietnamese voice spoke in broken English. "You come now."

Dusty had named this guard Squeaker because of his high, shrill tone when he spoke. He climbed lethargically off his bunk and faced Squeaker. "What is it this time?"

"No talk! I search you now."

Immediately angry and wary, Dusty barked, "What the hell could I have possibly found to hide in this rathole?"

Squeaker enjoyed searching the prisoners. Especially he liked to pay particular attention to their crotches, where a lot of heavy groping went on. It disgusted and infuriated Dusty Rhodes and the others no end.

"You come out. I search. You go see Gnduc."

Dusty shuffled from his cell. He endured the hundredth fondling of his private parts and let the little NVA pogue guard herd him toward the commandant's quarters. There he was made to stand in the sun for an hour, before Xieng Van Gnduc made an appearance. The scowl told Rhodes that the commandant was not a happy camper. His first, harsh words confirmed it.

"You are a disgraceful prisoner. I do not tolerate such sloth and slovenliness in my camp. For your punishment, you will clean the latrines. You will *lick* them clean. Do you understand?"

Fury boiled inside Dusty Rhodes. "I understand this. I am a prisoner of war, and an officer in my country's navy. I cannot be compelled to perform such degrading and health-endangering tasks. I refuse."

Squeaker smashed Dusty in the right kidney with the butt-stock of his Type 53 rifle. Dusty went to his knees. Instantly, Colonel Gnduc was upon him.

"Up—up! Stand up at once! You will not go to sleep in my presence. Get up, American pig."

"Oink, fucking oink, you slope bastard," Dusty grated out through clenched teeth.

That got him another buttstroke to the opposite kidney. The breath wheezed out of him and he flopped facefirst in the cleared, packed earth of the pint-sized parade ground. Dusty rolled onto one side and curled up in a fetal position, hugging his pain to himself. He would be damned if he showed them how much he hurt. Colonel Gnduc came down the steps, highly polished brown boots a clatter on the bamboo steps. He towered over the supine SEAL officer and worked his thin lips in a rhythmic circle. Then he spat on Dusty's upturned cheek.

"Three days in punishment cell. You will learn to obey."

That delivered, he ascended the steps to the veranda that enclosed three sides of the quarters. He watched impassively as Squeaker and another guard hustled Dusty off to the subterranean cell at the center of the compound.

A hatch in the bamboo-pole cage swung open and Dusty was dumped unceremoniously inside. He hit heavily on the earthen bottom of the cell, and darkness blissfully washed over him.

Tonto Waters had his own ordeal to face that afternoon. After a short delay, the Military Judge entered and called the court to order. He then summoned the panel, who filed back into the converted ballroom at 1310 hours. After the room had come to order, Judge Benson read from a closely written sheet of typescript.

"We have concluded that the evidence presented is woefully lacking in sufficiency to merit consideration at this time. We further concluded that the Government's counsel acted with unseemly haste in setting trial date. We also agree that there is sufficient cause to believe that the trial should go forward. It is our decision then, that this matter be continued for not less than two weeks, during which time the Government's counsel is encouraged to develop further evidence to support the charge and its specifications. The defendant is remanded to the custody of Lt. Carl Marino until the final disposition of this court. We will entertain no motions at this time. As for now, this court stands adjourned."

Tonto Waters could not believe what he just heard. Stripped of all its legal mumbo jumbo, it sounded like the judge had just cut him loose. With a tug on his elbow by Pope Marino, he let the SEAL lieutenant lead him out of the courtroom.

They descended the stairway with Tonto in a fog. Out on the street, he cut his gaze to Pope's impassive face. "Does that mean we got the TKO?"

"Sort of, Tonto. Quade and the panel still want this to come to trial. Perhaps they are waiting to see the outcome of the trial Eloise faces."

"But, this only gives them more time to cook up some shit against me," Tonto protested.

"It also gives us the time to get together what we need to knock this clear out of the ring."

"What do we do now?"

"First we go back to Tre Noc and prepare to yank some birds from their cages. We're going to take that POW camp apart. Any way you look at it, you being a part of that is going to count in your favor with the court-martial panel."

Francie Song hated what she knew she must do. If she could contrive any way to avoid this meeting with the disgusting Marine sergeant, Elmore Yates, she would. Yet, she had no escape from the realities of her life. At least she had managed to win the point over their meeting place. They would meet off base. She hurried to the location, a small, out-of-the-way Buddhist shrine, her heart pounding in agitation.

To make matters worse, she discovered, Yates had not preceded her. She had to wait. Half an hour passed without sign of him. Francie became agitated, and filled with doubt and fear. What had gone wrong? At last she heard footsteps crunch on the walkway and the tall redhead came into view around a bend in the white-gravel trail.

Everything at the shrine was like that pathway. Meticulously tended by dedicated monks, the carp pool shined with clear, fresh water, the golden, white-and-pink, and black fish swam serenely among the lily pads. During her wait, Francie had longed for even a small share of their equanimity. Now the image of Yates was reflected on the surface, robbing it of its allure.

"You're early. Do you have anything for me?" he asked urgently.

"No, not really. I've . . . been troubled lately."

Yates snorted in ugly amusement. "Oh? With what?"

"My son is only now recovering from a case of dysentery. If it had not been for Kent Welby, he would have died. I owe him so much."

"Forget that frog-footed slob. He's nothing."

"Oh, but he is. He's wonderful, so kind, so . . . but he'll never be mine." Francie lowered her eyes, her fingers twisted into torturous patterns in her lap.

Alerted by this, Yates pounced. "What have we here? Unrest in the love nest?"

"You insult me," Francie flared. But her misery outweighed her caution.

Gradually, admittedly against her will, she unraveled the entire story of her relationship with Kent Welby. She left out only the intimate details of their love life. Even so, she sensed that this despicable Elmore Yates could read both sides of the paper. When she poured out her misery over Betty Welby's recent decision not to complete the divorce, tears ran down her face. She felt wretched and abandoned, and she didn't care that this evil man was her sole confidant.

Her purging left a burning sensation of illness in her stomach. Dare she reveal her physical condition to Yates? No! Her basic common sense warned against that. When the Marine sergeant responded, his words revealed his utter lack of compassion.

"A sad story, but hardly why we met here. What information do you have on a highly secret operation being laid on about now?"

"Nothing. I have seen none of that material. Although I did see a most interesting operations order just this morning." In the awful moment that followed, Francie wished her tongue had been cut out.

"What was it about?"

"I cannot tell you," Francie evaded.

"You had by-God better," Yates growled.

"I will not. I don't know what it refers to. It would only be a wild guess."

Yates grew angrier with each of her words. "Then guess, goddamnit!"

Francie thrust to her feet and ran away from him, past the carp pool and down the white gravel pathway. She left Elmore Yates behind, furious with her for withholding information he was certain he needed to know.

Tonto Waters returned with Pope Marino to Tre Noc. The pilot of the Huey had radioed ahead with the news, and the entire platoon had turned out to welcome the threatened SEAL home. When he managed to quiet the shrill whistles, yells, and catcalls, Tonto raised his arms over his head like a victorious boxer, which elicited another round of whoops and applause.

"Hey, you guys, listen up. I ain't out of the woods yet. The real poop is that there will be a trial." Boos drowned out his next words, so he had to repeat himself. "That ain't any problem, the Pope here tells me. The Judge said he didn't see enough evidence to make a case, and they can't get any more because there isn't anything to get. But the panel voted to have a trial. So, when this finally does come to trial, chances are it will be thrown out for lack of evidence."

"Keep a twenty in your sock, Tonto," Archie, wise in the way of court-martial and time in the brig, cautioned. "Now, how about a beer?"

Tonto finished the night, until curfew, in the platoon bar. Morning came entirely too soon. Nearly a week of inactivity in the brig had softened the burly CPO. He ached in every part of his body after only a single run-through of the POW camp problem.

"Can you believe they wouldn't let me do my daily dozen in the brig?" he asked Pope Marino during the break.

"Yes, I can. They wanted to break your morale and weaken you physically. Then you wouldn't make a good appearance before the court-martial panel."

Tonto found that interesting. It excited his imagination. "Yeah. If I looked like I was beaten, it would be easier to get those captains and the admiral to believe the lies Lailey was going to pump them full of."

Lt. Carl Marino winced at the mangled grammar. Even though he had come up through the ranks, a Mustang officer if ever they had been one, he frequently wondered if the ragged and dangling parts of speech in the spoken words of enlisted men and petty officers were deliberate. He couldn't accept that they had never been taught to speak better than they often did. He abandoned that; Waters needed recognition for figuring out what he had meant.

"You've got it, Tonto. Now, stretch those legs and let's get at it again."

"I ain't finished my cigarette yet, Skipper."

Lieutenant Marino answered that with a sorrowful look, then spoke low to Tonto's ears only. "Are you sure it was only a week you were in the brig, Tonto?"

Hell, Tonto knew he wouldn't even get a smoke from the time the op began until they were back at Tre Noc. So, why the bellyaching?

Their second rehearsal went far better. Tonto found the kinks working out, his movements smoothing. By the third go-around, after noon chow, he even managed to maintain the 2:45 time frame the rest of the squad had achieved in his absence. In fact, he was even looking forward to a visit to My Flower.

Rap! . . . *Rap-rap* . . . *Rap-thunk-rap-rap-raaap!* In the misery of his hole in the ground, Dusty Rhodes groggily listened to the tapping out of the jailhouse code as it passed from one cell to another. It was not Morse code.

It was a unique combination of sounds and pulses devised by a couple of the spooks held captive there. Before his term in solitary began, Dusty had contributed a couple of improvements himself. Now, in the middle of the night, the guards far from alert, communication was easier. Dusty suddenly realized the message was for him.

"Gnduc is a sadist. He feeds on hurting people. You're not the first to get his attention," the raps and thuds conveyed. "He regularly abuses and humiliates us." Dusty figured the author meant all the prisoners.

It fit, his slowly clearing mind allowed. He had daily watched the commandant brutally kick and punch the three captive pilots. "There isn't much chance of our getting out of here," the communicator relayed. Dusty knew better, but he had sworn to himself not to reveal to any of the prisoners that a grab-and-snatch operation was already laid on.

He consoled himself that he would sleep better for that knowledge. But, it would have to be soon. Very soon.

Early the next morning, Dusty Rhodes had his high hopes swiftly shattered. General Vinh Toy Giap returned to the camp, complete with a company of NVA regulars, all armed to the teeth, accompanied by two OT-62s—Czech modifications of the Soviet BTR-50, Amphibious Tracked APC. Both had what appeared to Dusty Rhodes in his punishment cell to be 12.7 DShK 43 heavy machine guns. And one of them, he could swear had been retrofitted with a side-firing AGS-17, a 30mm automatic grenade launcher. A cold shaft of ice slid along Dusty's spine while dust roiled up around his open place of confinement.

Those gooks up north had sure pulled out all the stops, he thought glumly. Dusty watched helplessly while the fresh troops formed up on the parade ground. There would soon be work details for the local peasants and the prisoners, obliterating all traces of their presence here. Colonel Gnduc bustled down from his office in his quarters, his face alight at the prospect of a larger force to command for the security of his command. He obviously had some very happy thoughts, Dusty grudgingly realized.

Let the Russian try to take my prisoners now! Colonel Gnduc thought triumphantly as he gazed over the ranks of the regulars who had appeared so magically out of the jungle. Or at least so it seemed. He had known that General Giap would return, with an escort. But an entire company. Marvelous. And armored personnel carriers, too. He could stand off the KGB and the American SEALs. Let them come. He hurried down the steps and greeted General Giap when he dismounted from a four-wheel-drive GAZ-69.

"General, I am honored and so pleased to greet you again. Welcome to our Rising Truth Confinement Camp."

"Thank you, Colonel. I am eager to begin my work. I want to start on one of them tomorrow morning. I think one of the pilots. It is my considered opinion that they are the easiest to break. They are, after all, so far removed from the actual brutality of any killing they must do."

Colonel Gnduc privately agreed and had to stifle a snicker. "It sounds a reasonable assumption, General. I suggest you begin with Lieutenant David Allen of the American Air Force. He has only recently been released from confinement in the punishment cell. He is nicely softened-up as a result."

"Fine. Have my orderly shown to my quarters and I will join you in a cup of tea on the veranda. Tomorrow you will witness the most scientific of interrogation techniques."

CHAPTER 19 _____

A STRANGE voice crackled over the radio. "Eagle One, this is Sierra-Tango Two-Niner-Four. Do you copy, Eagle One? Over."

"Who the hell is this?" Repeat Ditto barked into the mouthpiece.

They were operating on low power and an obscure frequency for this, the next-to-last practice run. No one from outside should be in the net. Static crackled in Ditto's ear as the voice spoke again.

"This is your little eye in the sky, put me on to Eagle One, over."

Chad Ditto passed the handset to Lt. Carl Marino. "This is Eagle One, over."

"Eagle One, this is Sierra-Tango Two-Niner-Four. You can call me Lighthorse. I have visual on some unfriendlies on your three. They are taking a big interest in everything you're doing. Over."

"Are you hot, Lighthorse?"

"Negative, Eagle One. I'm a glorified Cessna. A one-seventy-two with a hot engine. All I can do is keep an eye on the unfriendlies and vector someone in to take them out. Over."

That meant an Army L-19, retrofitted with wing slots and an overpowered engine for heavy cargo STOL (Short

Takeoff and Landing) operations, Pope Marino reflected. Which got him to wondering what the Army flyboy was doing in the Delta. "Good enough. We'll send someone around to check their membership cards. Can't have the common trash invading the country club. Keep us advised, over."

"Roger that, Eagle One. Do you want me to mark them with smoke?"

"Negative. Say, what are you doing out our way anyway? Over."

"VIP tour of your present activity. Very VIP. Lighthorse, out."

That made it clear enough. Someone from COM-SPECWAR-MACV (Combined Special Warfare-Military Assistance Command Vietnam), maybe even General Belem himself, was checking them out prior to the parakeet operation. Pope Marino dismissed speculation on that to deal with the immediate.

Charlie had infiltrated the area again and had them under observation. On their three would correspond roughly to due east. That left out using the PBRs. A little tributary of the Bassiac ran through there, Lieutenant Marino recalled from the map. Might get a chance to use our STABs (Seal Team Assault Boats) after all. Pope Marino reached out and turned the channel knob on the radio backpack worn by Repeat Ditto.

"Charlie One, this is Eagle One," he spoke into the mouthpiece, summoning Ensign Peter Brooks, who had taken the missing Dusty Rhodes's position as AOIC, and commanded the reserve element.

"Roger, Eagle One. What's up? Over."

"We have visitors." Pope went on to quickly describe the situation. Then he added, with a note of regret that he would be denied to opportunity of leading the assault-boat attack, "Ready the STABs. I'll send Tonto to act as your point and get back with the coordinates, then you head out. Take lots of firepower. Eagle One, out.''

Lieutenant Marino told Chad Ditto to pass the word quietly of what was going down to the rest of the squads and the young RTO hurried off to comply. Ten minutes later, Marino had the exact coordinates of the VC observers from the L-19 pilot. He gave them to an audibly excited Peter Brooks. ''I copy that, Eagle One. Tonto just arrived. We will depart in five. Charlie One, out.''

The hardest thing would be to keep on with business as usual at the camp mock-up. Pope Marino would give anything to be leading that surprise attack on Charlie.

It took only two minutes for Tonto Waters to recall that riding in a STAB got a lot wetter than in a PBR. The little twin-hull craft, with their quiet-running engines, purred up the Bassiac to the mouth of the narrow stream that joined at a point half a klick from where the army pilot had indicated the VC watched the rehearsals. It felt good to be going in on this one.

His inactivity in the brig had given him a real thirst for battle. How better to work off his anger and frustration? Charlie might be the worse for it, but then, Tonto reasoned, someone had to lose. Mr. Brooks had seemed competent in preparing for the surprise raid on the spies, and capable of leading the small force. Waters slid his gaze to the boat following his.

Seated on the amidships thwart, Peter Brooks presented a placid appearance under his smear of camouflage paint. His jaw jutted, lips closed and at rest. The crucible for the young ensign had come in the search and destroy mission that had netted so much enemy equipment destroyed. Brooks had ceased to be a kid fresh out of UDT/R school. Now he exhibited a confidence and familiarity around weapons and explosives, which extended over into the manner in which he related to the enlisted SEALs.

Yeah, Pete Brooks would do, Chief Waters allowed.

One damn fine sailor, even if he was an officer. Traditionally the Navy fought at sea. At least until WW II came along and changed all that. Oh, there had been the occasional shore party since the time of John Paul Jones, but nothing like the demands of the Second World War. Airpower came first. Then the need for silent, invisible warriors who could slip in among the enemy's landing obstacles and rig them for destruction. The UDT was born out of that need.

Yet, the emphasis of a seagoing Navy persisted on through Korea. The Korean conflict made wider use of UDT personnel on shore missions. Their role extended beyond clearing of hedgehogs, dragons' teeth, and other hazards to landing craft. For the first time, teams of frogmen went inland to wreak havoc among the enemy.

They blew up bridges, blasted huge holes in dams, cut telephone lines, and even carried off the disruption of the communist chain of command by selective terminations. In language less prissy, they assassinated several ranking North Korean officers. Tonto was aware of all this. It had been drummed into him and all the other SEAL candidates during the classroom sessions of their training. Right up until the early sixties, this had been the accepted doctrine of employing Underwater Demolition Teams. Only now, here in Vietnam, they were writing a whole new book on the function of SEAL and UDT units.

John F. Kennedy had gotten it started. He had called on all the armed services to produce what he visualized as the warriors of the future. Nuclear power, the president had come to accept, had made warfare by massive armies and huge flotillas of battleships and cruisers obsolete. And Jack Kennedy had reason enough for believing it. He had served his country in WW II as captain of a PT boat. He had had one of them, the 109 Boat, shot out from under him by fire from a Japanese destroyer.

At his direction, the army had received the most in

equipment and training for their new Special Forces units, organized under President Dwight Eisenhower in the late fifties. No longer the poor cousins of the airborne divisions, Special Forces received a huge area of Fort Bragg, North Carolina, in which to train and hone their skills. With the patronage of John Kennedy, they received so much that they had named their training center for the young president, following his assassination in 1963.

Chief Tom Waters had taken airborne training at Bragg, and gone on to highly specialized classes at the Kennedy Special Warfare Center. The blanketheads were good, Tonto Waters would always be first to acknowledge that. But not nearly as good or highly trained as the SEALs. The SEAL program had been John Kennedy's gift to the Navy.

And the Navy had taken it and ran with it. While going through BUDS (Basic Underwater Demolitions School), Tonto and his classmates had heard of how difficult it had been to outfit the earliest SEAL Teams. They had to beg, borrow, and steal everything they got for training. The only things that were not stinted on was ammunition and explosives. They developed a superior knowledge and skill with foreign-made weapons, because of a more readily available supply of these than those of US manufacture. Many of them survived into this later day in Vietnam, such as the German MP-40 *Sweedish K*, frequently carried by Repeat Ditto. One of the best of the scroungers to supply the early SEALs had been then CGM Carl Marino.

Things had not been the same when Chief Gunner's Mate Marino had gone off to Officer Candidate School, then the Basic Officer's Course, before rejoining the Teams at Little Creek, as a jg in Team 2. It was only then that Tom Waters had met the legendary ''Thief of Baghdad,'' the one and only Pope Marino. Not a thing had changed in Marino. There was nothing he wouldn't do for his men. And there wasn't anything Tonto Waters would refuse to do for the Pope. A swelling of pride grew within him at having been chosen to act as point on this cleanup mission. It meant the Pope trusted him implicitly. And that was good enough for Tonto Waters. A light tap on one shoulder from the coxswain alerted Tonto to the present.

Ahead lay the jump off. Charlie had about thirty minutes left to live.

At first, Cpl. Thihn Anguyn had not liked the assignment to accompany these lowly partisans to spy out what the Americans were doing in this secretive area of their base on the Bassiac. Whatever importance it might have in regard to their cleverly hidden compound along the banks of the Mekong River he could not fathom. It did not take long to discover why Captain Quahc had detailed that one of his regulars go along.

To his consternation, what he looked down upon seemed to be an exact duplicate of their prisoner camp. Incredibly, the Americans must have discovered them in secret. Yet, how could that be so? When the American forces discovered any installations constructed by the Viet Cong or the People's Republic, they acted swiftly and overwhelmingly to destroy them. He had learned that at the NCO academy. The Americans were terrible barbarians who would rather destroy perfectly good tunnel systems and bunkers, rather than occupy them for their own use.

That was wasteful. It grated on his frugal soul. Thihn knew that many in his company thought of him as a counter of rice grains. It didn't matter. If he was careful with his kit, it only served to last him longer, and saved the loss of face, not to mention the expense, of replacing some missing or damaged item. If he laundered his uniforms and underclothes, instead of paying some peasant woman to do it, that kept the copper coins in his pocket longer. His mother, a thrifty person herself, had taught him that. And in tribute to her, he sent back half of his pay each second month on payday. He sighed as he thought again of the profligacy of the Americans. Then he stiffened and blinked.

Thihn had caught a hint of movement in the corner of one eye. He slowly turned his head and stared in that direction. Nothing. No, wait. There was something after all. Vaguely he made out the shape of a man. Yet, that could not be. He seemed to have no face. No more activity followed, and Thihn dismissed it. He did open his mouth, though, to alert the less-security-conscious Freedom Fighters who had accompanied him. They had gathered to chatter softly and drink cold tea.

Corporal Anguyn had barely formed the first word of his admonition when he heard the thunderous roar of an American light machine gun. Then a soft *chunk*!

The 40mm grenade detonated directly over the heads of the three VC who squatted under the lower limbs of a large, gnarled mangrove. Its shrapnel slashed them to ribbons. The American light machine gun continued to fire. Then the faceless figure moved.

Thihn Anguyn could see him clearly now. Hands smeared with green and brown, he competently held a shotgun that belched flame and a spray of buckshot. Corporal Anguyn had already opened up with his Type 56 assault rifle.

It had been easier than he had expected. Tonto Waters had oriented himself and the objective on the small map and established the correct compass bearing. Then he had set out on point, the squad following, toward the enemy.

When he made contact, he actually felt some disappointment. Only six of them. Child's play. No, there were seven. The last one an NVA regular. No doubt the man in charge. He signaled the squad and they melted from sight. Then Tonto crouched low and watched for a long, sweaty ten minutes, made careful note of the position of each of the Cong. Beyond them he could see the train-fire range and his own squad hunkered down to eat noon chow.

When their inactivity prompted laxness in the VC, Tonto watched while three of them left their positions and gathered under a mangrove to BS and drink from water bottles that no doubt contained tea. Perfect. He eased away from his vantage point and returned to the squad.

Tonto did a dumb show to describe the positions of the enemy. To him it seemed like being in his parents' home as a kid, playing charades. Only the gestures he made now had a far more grim intention behind them. One of the replacement kids in Charlie Squad raised a finger to signal he had a question. Tonto slithered close to him and put an ear to his lips.

"What if one gets away?"

Tonto shook his head in a forceful negative gesture and drew an index finger across his throat in a sign that they would take no prisoners and hunt down any who escaped the initial onslaught. Everyone understood clearly. Then he raised his right hand to shoulder height, palm outward and fingers spread. He squeezed a fist two times to indicate they would have fifteen minutes to get into position.

Silently he led them to the killing ground. Mr. Brooks patted Tonto on one shoulder to show his approval of the layout of their ambush. Then he, too, faded into the bush. When the fifteen minuets had passed, the squad automatic weapon opened up with a roar and the soft bloop of an XM148 tube followed.

Full-jacketed rounds cracked through the air as two of the three tea drinkers screamed and writhed on the ground. Tonto Waters pushed forward out of the screen of low undergrowth and saw at once that only two of the enemy had reacted with alacrity. He popped a round from the Ithaca toward one of those and watched puffs of dust, mangled cloth, and flesh explode on the chest of black pajamas. Another Charlie whirled about from where he watched the training session below and blazed away with his Type 56.

Only to be cut down by Will Dawson's M60 machine gun. That left only the NVA noncom who still blasted wildly away well above Tonto's head. The Ithaca in Tonto's hands moved his way. At such short range, the charge of buckshot lifted the slightly built NVA corporal off his feet. Chest and gut riddled with No. 4 .24 caliber holes, the soldier was flung aside like an unwanted rag doll.

Almost before it began, the battle ended. Or at least the SEALs thought so until they began to take fire from their left flank. "Jeez, there's more of them!" Will Dawson broke silence to announce.

From their hiding places under the trees, two squads of NVA regulars streamed out to engage the SEALs. Col. Xieng Van Gnduc had not been so dense as to trust such a difficult mission to his Viet Cong allies without protection. Especially when all of those sent out before had failed to return. In their initial charge, the NVA soldiers put down two of Charlie Squad, one with a minor, the other a serious wound. Then the remarkable prowess of the SEALs began to tell.

In a rapid, disciplined move, they swung their skirmish line around to face the attackers. One Northerner took a 40mm round in the gut from extreme close range. The explosive force of the detonated grenade spread him thinly over his comrades and splattered the shooter as well.

"Awh, shit," Buck Thompson grunted as he wiped at a red smear on his forehead.

He quickly reloaded his M-79 and blooped off another

charge. Less than fifty meters separated the SEALs from the NVA. The volume of fire swelled to deafening crescendo, than began to ebb. Inexorably the distance closed. Buck Thompson drew his K-Bar and readied the blade for immediate action. The dark saffron face of an NVA enemy loomed larger in his line of sight. No time to reload the blooper.

His opponent had apparently expended all his ammunition. He flailed at Buck with the barrel, the small, folding bayonet glittering in the gray brightness of the monsoon cloud cover. To hell with this, Buck thought. He laid his M-79 aside as the NVA soldier came within dangerous distance. Quickly he filled that hand with the butt of a Browning Hi-Power and pumped two 9mm pills into the raging enemy.

The NVA private took the medicine with ease, only the dosage killed the patient. To his right, Buck saw Tonto Waters smash the barrel of his Ithaca into the side of the head of a too-close NVA regular. The man went rubber-legged, and Tonto buried the blade of a wide K-Bar to the hilt in the exposed chest.

Without retrieving his knife, Tonto began to shove fresh rounds through the loading gate of the Ithaca. He had managed four when a brawny trooper leaped onto his side. It sent the shotgun flying. Tonto dipped and flexed his knees in a violent upward thrust. It failed to dislodge his assailant and he found himself in a desperate effort to dodge the deadly kukri-style blade with which his opponent flailed at him.

Although slippery with sweat, Tonto managed to get both hands on the wrist of the knife hand. He gave a ferocious yank and spilled the lighter-weight NVA trooper onto the ground. A solid kick to the ribs was followed by a powerful stomp to the exposed throat above a heaving chest. Tonto ground his arch into the gagging man's windpipe until the little brown enemy ceased to struggle and went slack.

Tonto heaved a deep breath into his own chest and looked around to find that the hummock had gone quiet. Not a man moved anywhere. The enemy dead lay in heaps. One had fallen to drape himself across a wounded SEAL, who struggled feebly to cast off the unwanted company. Tonto tottered over the assist him.

"Jesus, Mary, and Joseph, Chief," Ensign Brooks gasped to Tonto Waters. "For a minute there I thought we were goners."

That echoed the sentiments of Tonto Waters exactly, though he forced a lopsided grin and spoke low, with vibrant confidence. "Not a chance, Mr. Brooks, not a chance." He turned to stare downhill to the camp mock-up, where Alpha and Bravo Squads remained in the frozen postures they had assumed when the firefight broke out. "Now, if you don't mind, sir, I'll just choggie over there and join my people, and you can handle the cleanup."

Peter Brooks swallowed his amazement. "Go . . . right ahead . . . chief."

Jason Slater arrived at Tre Noc at 1420 that afternoon. His deep worry over the integrity of the mission tele-graphed from the furrows on his brow. He had his Stetson pushed back and the beginnings of a widow's peak showed clearly. Without preamble, he closeted himself with LCDR Jorgensen of the Riverine Force and Lt. Carl Marino.

"You are certain that at least three Viet Cong got away?"

"Yes," Pope Marino answered glumly. "Only at least two of them were NVA."

Slater shot a look of displeasure. "How far will they have to go to get word to the camp?" Slater pressed.

"Hard telling. We don't know, for that matter, if they saw what we were doing. None of those in direct observation survived. That much we know."

Slater eyed Marino a long, silent moment. "I say we can't wait and take the chance. Can you lay this on yet today?"

Incredulous, Marino's face went slack. "You have to be kidding."

"No. I'm serious. There's no waiting now. We can't take it on trust that none of those in the final firefight saw the mock-up and figured out what it was. How soon?" the CIA station chief insisted.

"Maybe by . . ." Pope figured rapidly in his head. "Maybe by dawn tomorrow."

"Then do it."

"I'd like to add another element. It is sort of superfluous, but it might buy us some surprise factor. Tim—er—Commander Jorgensen, can you free up two PBRs to transport Charlie and Delta Squads of Second Platoon to the Mekong? An all-night run if necessary. I want them in place to enter the camp and make their exfiltration through the jungle, along with the ARVN prisoners, to create a diversion.

"If this goes right, if we hit them entirely unexpected, there won't be anyone around to witness our extraction by slick." Pope Marino paused and looked pleased for the first time since the attack. "It will be just one more little mystery, courtesy of the SEALs. We're playing in the big leagues with whoever is out there. This General Giap, no doubt."

Jason Slater nodded. Pope continued. "Here's how we work it. Everything is to look normal until after evening chow. Then we gather for the briefing, draw weapons and head out. The slicks can come in here at say zero-two-hundred. From there, it's by the numbers."

Everyone listened intently as he went on to detail his hastily assembled plan. They had good reason to. In less than twelve hours they would be laying their lives on the line, based on Pope Marino's reading of the situation.

CHAPTER 20 ———————————

FRANCIE SONG knew that the highly secret operation had begun when Kent Welby did not meet her outside the plans and operations building after work. Something must have happened suddenly to alter the timetable. She also knew what she now had to do. Fearing the encounter, she turned reluctant footsteps in the proper direction and walked toward a meeting she wished could be avoided.

With each stride, her mental turmoil became more agitated. She recalled the old man who had raised an orphaned child like his own. "Do that which you know to be right with an easy heart. Only evil brings one regret."

He had repeated that lesson in various examples from a time when she had been barely able to understand the meaning behind the words. Now it came back to haunt her.

She could not endure the idea of any harm coming to that dear old soul. He had treated her like a father would his daughter. Francie still envisioned him as her parent. The only one she ever knew. And there was Thran. His recent illness had pointed so clearly to how utterly vulnerable the boy was. She could not willfully place him in jeopardy.

But what about Kent Welby? The question echoed inside her head as though everything else had been removed. If she did her duty, would she not be sending Kent Welby into clear and certain harm's way? A mocking spirit voice told her that the life of this American, of all the Americans, was not worth the loss she would suffer for disobedience.

Yet, there had been much more peace and safety *since* the Americans had come. If she had Kent Welby near to her and Thran and old Phan Vu, surely no harm could come to them. Nothing had actually been said; nor had she seen anything in writing involving the operation. This was pure speculation, her determined self rationalized. It would be easily believable to say she had no idea that the time for the operation had been moved up. Who could prove otherwise?

Slowly her footsteps faltered. Francie slowed her pace to a standstill, then resumed. Her destination altered, she headed directly for the security she knew could be found with Mamma Rose, in the warm, steamy atmosphere of the My Flower laundry.

Two slicks dropped out of the black, lead-bellied sky shortly before 0215 the next morning. Heavily laden with their choice of weapons and supply of ammunition, the SEALs of First and Second Squads filed out of the darkened hangar where they had waited, and boarded. Charlie and Delta Squads had departed at 1930 the previous night. They would have a long run down the Bassiac and then into the Mekong.

Tonto Waters did not envy them their ride. They did not have to be in position until the Cobras opened up on the camp. A half-klick walk through the night jungle awaited them upon reaching their IP (Initial Point). Tonto was last to board the Huey carrying his squad. He sat on the lip of the deck and looked across the dimly lighted space to the second chopper and into the face of Anchor Head Sturgis. They exchanged nerve-tautened grins and thumbs-ups. Then the eggbeaters over their heads began to wind up, and they had to swing their legs aboard and fasten up.

A change in the vibrations through the outer bulkhead told Tonto when the bird lifted off the helipad. In spite of the crammed-full Alice pack the steady thrum of the helicopter gave him an overall back massage. Tonto's dislike of swimming did not carry over into any prejudice against flying. He felt at home in any kind of aircraft. That reflection brought a smile as an image of Kent Welby filled his mind. Doc Welby had an aversion to flying, Tonto recalled, landings in particular. Every one was a white-knuckle job for Doc. Tonto looked forward along the line of strapped-in SEALs to where Doc sat.

Sure enough, Doc had that tight-lipped frozen expression he wore whenever he realized that he was truly airborne and would eventually have to land. *Well, at least not this time*, Tonto amended. They would be going in by way of the new "fast ropes." That terminology played hell with Navy tradition, Tonto believed. There simply never had been any *ropes* in this man's Navy. There were lines or hawsers. Damn straight. That still left Doc Welby with the unpleasant journey ahead of him.

Abruptly, Doc turned his head stiffly, as though sensing Tonto's eyes upon him. He produced a sickly smile and a weak thumbs-up. Tonto grinned wider and shot his thumb outward from a tight fist. The vehemence of it forced a more natural upcurve of Doc's lips. Doc pointed to the deck, indicating the enemy ground below, and made a questioning gesture. *What about the bad guys*? he asked.

Tonto responded by thrusting his fist and forearm upward, while slapping his biceps with the other palm, an Italian gesture he had quickly learned the meaning of as a kid in his neighborhood in New Jersey. *Yeah, fuck you and the horse you rode in on, too*. That brought a wild light to Doc's eyes. Uptight about aircraft or not, Tonto knew Doc would be all right on the ground.

Waters knew more about Welby's self-induced lack of self-confidence than the young SEAL might have suspected. He also knew that Doc fought like a Viking in combat. He knew no fear and literally carried the battle to the enemy. Why Kent Welby refused to recognize this in himself, Tom Waters could not figure out. So long as the kid kept on as usual, no one had anything to worry about. His thoughts slid off to Hawsehole Wilkerson.

Charlie and Delta would about be at their IP by this time, Tonto calculated. He lowered his diver's watch and tried to visualize their approach through the jungle.

Jim Wilkerson represented the stereotypical "swabby." He was compact and built low to the ground, a hint of bow-leggedness apparent whenever he wore his Class A uniform. His forearms and biceps bulged, as did his thighs, and tattoos of dragons, serpents and a solitary seal, writhed in lifelike animation above and below his elbows whenever he moved his arms. When not asleep or at a meal, he constantly chewed on the stub of a cigar.

No one in the Teams could recall ever seeing him light up a stogie, yet the stub of one forever protruded from one corner of his mouth. Hawsehole Wilkerson was indeed a sailor's sailor. He gave a sign to his men as his keen vision defined the darker black of a riverbank from the stygian background. The coxswain cut the throttles and the PBR drifted broadside to the shore until an overside fender rubbed against the muddy slope.

Quickly, and with only a minimum of sound, the SEALs went over the side and gained the land. With the water jets barely making a ripple on the surface of the Mekong River, the PBR slid away into invisibility. They would, Wilkerson and his men had been assured at the briefing, be going out by helicopter. That is, had they been landed at the right place, and Charlie cooperated. Huge, warm raindrops began to patter down, delayed in their contact with the SEALS by the dense forestation above. Some danced on the muddy brown surface of the river, and made silver streaks in the all-but-nonexistent light.

Landmarks could not be reliably spotted at night, and especially during monsoon. All Hawsehole could do would be to keep on his compass bearing and orient himself when it grew light enough. Wilkerson made three hundred meters when he suddenly discovered that something was definitely brewing in this neck of the woods.

"Who goes there?" came a whispered challenge in Vietnamese.

Mule Carlson, point man for Hawsehole's squad, went to ground instantly. For all his ability to learn a foreign language, Mule had no ear for accent of inflection, so when he responded in Vietnamese that he was only a fisherman caught out late by a storm, he was answered with a hail of steel-jacketed slugs.

"Well, shit, that pulled the plug," Hawsehole grumbled as he unlimbered his AR-15.

He cut out half a magazine in single shots, then switched the fire-selection lever to full-auto. From staggered positions to his left and right, muzzle flashes illuminated the undergrowth as the squad opened up. Answering fire popped and snapped holes in low-growing palm fronds and air plants. A thick liana fell across Hawsehole's legs, heavy and snakelike, it writhed for a moment and went still. He fired a three-round burst and rolled to one side.

A mistake! He felt a hard gouge to his ribs. He should have gone right. No time to check for damage. He sighted in on a bright flicker of yellow-orange and squeezed off another trio of full metal jackets. A scream rewarded his marksmanship. He heard the chunk of an M-79 and smiled. His demo man was taking no chances with Charlie.

An earsplitting crack marked the 40mm grenade's detonation. More screams and thrashing in the bush. How many of them could there be out there? For answer, Hawsehole Wilkerson got only silence. Must have been a damn small patrol, he mused. He saw faint motion as Mule Carlson edged forward to check out the situation. A moment later the all clear came.

Silently, the SEALs moved out. *Don't let there be a whole hell of a lot more* of *them out here*, Hawsehole thought almost prayerfully.

"Sure weren't nobody listenin'," Hawsehole whispered in the ear of his point man when Mule came back to report a dozen VC staked out around a clearing that the trail crossed through. "Find a way to lead us around them," the squad leader ordered.

Carlson faded out of sight. Twenty minutes later he returned and signaled the squad to follow. The SEALs vanished into the night. After ten minutes of silent walking, hearing only the jungle noises and the beating of their hearts, the SEALs came close enough to the ambush to hear a couple of less-security-conscious VC chattering away softly in their musical language.

Is this trip necessary? Hawsehole wondered to himself. Up ahead, he had been assured, a whole nest of nasties waited for them. NVA regulars at that. No reason to flirt with discovery like this. Then he saw why.

Trip wires had been uncovered by Mule Carlson and the traps disarmed. Put out in concentric circles, they would have the effect of forcing any unwanted visitors directly into the ambush site. The risk of going farther away from the enemy outweighed that of breathing down his neck. At least this time, Hawsehole reminded himself.

Ten long minutes went by while the SEALs moved beyond hearing range of the VC. They walked on the balls of their feet, barely lifting them, feeling for fallen branches or other noisemakers. At last Hawsehole and his RTO came to where Mule waited for them.

"They'll never know we were around," Mule crowed quietly.

"Let's hope not. I wonder if they set this up after that first firefight? Naw," he reconsidered. "That's a regular ambush site. No time to rig those booby traps. That tells me we're getting close. Most of those monkeys don't know the big picture. They're just told to do something and be somewhere and they do it. This POW camp's supposed to be run by regulars. You won't find them out riskin' their asses in the jungle. I doubt those dorks know what it is they are protectin'. "

"If they don't, they'll probably think we're just a routine patrol," Mule opined.

"Let's hope they do. Get your compass bearing and let's start out again, here come the others."

Time dragged by. Hawsehole's softly glowing watch face indicated the hour to be 0310. First Platoon would be on the way by now. He lowered his arm in time to see the signal from Carlson. Enemy in Sight. How many this time? After the squad had melted into the underbrush, Hawsehole edged forward to his point man.

"Where," he mouthed silently.

Mule Carlson pointed. He leaned to his squad leader, and whispered. "A motorized unit from the sounds of it."

"Naw. In the jungle," Wilkerson rejected.

Carlson beckoned Wilkerson forward. The last fifty meters they covered on elbow and knee. The point man gestured and Hawsehole parted the fronds of a cabbage palm.

Three VC sat around a low table in the dim light that emanated from the open rear door of what looked like a BTR-50PK. At least that's what it looked most like. Only it had twin cupolas at the front of the glacis. From one of them protruded the barrel of a Soviet DShK heavy machine gun.

Hawsehole studied the enemy to his content. He came to the conclusion that they were on roving patrol. Only the NVA had equipment like that. He signed to Carlson he wanted to go back. Nothing but bad news out there.

At the place where he had left the squad, Hawsehole spoke with silenced urgency. "We're getting in among the NVA now." He described what he had seen. "We can't be far away. And only three hours to daylight. Mule, find us a way around that bunch and let's *di-di* the hell out of here. We want to be within three hundred meters when the Cobras open up. An' be careful, Mule. Keep a good eye out."

Mule Carlson slid between the trees and vines like an eel on the bottom of the Thames. He barely left a trailing liana swaying in his passage. It earned him his most gut-grabbing experience to date. The NVA trooper was there before Mule saw him. He stepped out from the black shadow of a tree trunk and right into the big SEAL's face.

Knowing it would be folly to fire a shot, Mule grabbed for the first thing he could reach. It was his entrenching tool. He swung it like a tomahawk. The cloth-covered edge of the steel blade made a soft, meaty sound when it contacted flesh. A soft gasp came from the soldier, and he went slack. Mule Carlson eased him to the ground, then used his Randall combat knife to slit the exposed throat. One less to worry about.

Mule guided the squad out around the corpse and on into the bush. So far he had held tight to his proper heading. Only he and Hawsehole would be using their compasses. The others had enough to do. With an icy shock, Mule Carlson realized that the man he had killed had been wearing an NVA uniform. They were for sure in the deep stuff now. He glided on through the jungle.

Gradually his ears began to pick out unnatural sounds for the jungle. Man-made noises, he concluded a moment later. A faint, diffuse glow began to pervade the rain-distorted distance. Huge drops fell on his shoulders and the cammo bandanna over his unruly auburn hair. The irregular clicks and clangs that reached him told that somewhere up ahead someone was working on a vehicle. In another ten minutes he could smell the acrid odor of cigarette smoke.

Mule Carlson had learned from unfortunate personal experience that everywhere in the Orient people smoked such shitty cigarettes. Strong enough to stagger an elephant, the coarse, black tobacco gave off an odor that would gag a maggot. He was smelling it now. Time to hold back. He turned to face the squad.

He signaled the halt, then signed to spread out. They would hold here and be well out of the way of any over-rounds from the deadly AH-1G Cobra gunships.

Hawsehole Wilkerson thought of the Cobras also. He had been impressed with the importance of this operation when he heard that six of the speedy, murderous Hughes killers had been laid on. *All that firepower could level any stinkin' thing the gooks could build in this jungle,* he thought confidently. His thoughts jumped ahead to the extraction site.

A clearing had been chosen, some three klicks away from the POW camp. They were to go in, and through the compound and back out where the wire had been blown by Bravo Squad. *A piece of cake, that spook, Slater, had told them at the briefing. Fat chance*, Hawsehole Wilkerson thought as he settled in to wait for the arrival of Hell.

At first, the faint, high-pitched, insect hum blended with its natural counterpart. Then it grew louder, a more droning, insistent burr. The sound divided into six distinct deep-voiced roars shortly before sunrise. Already the overcast sky had lightened from horizon to horizon, only a hint of purple-black to the west. Then the source of the sound swam into sight in the sky.

Spindly tails crabbing as the AH-1G Huey Cobras lined up on their targets ahead and below, the insect similitude became more pronounced. The bug-eyed windscreens reflected back the green-blackness of the jungle in a glassy, bug stare. Then the noses tilted downward and the black canisters on the starboard hardpoints began to revolve.

"Woooooonnnnnk! Wooooooonnnnk!" A thousand rounds spat from each 30mm minigun.

Geysers of detritus and soil erupted in streams through the jungle, tracking unerringly to their targets. Two guard towers became thick showers of splinters, shredded flesh mixed in with the shattered bamboo. A ready room under the overhang of boughs exploded and spilled corpses onto the ground. With a seething hiss, two missiles whooshed from the portside hardpoints of a pair of Cobras.

Yellow mushrooms appeared where a camouflaged BRT-50PK APC had been before. The crew, sleeping between the treads, never knew what killed them. A hellhound bellow announced the opening bars of the .50 caliber chain-gun symphony of death. Then, with a roar and clatter of rotors, the Cobras swept over the compound, whirled and realigned on a bearing ninety degrees from the initial attack path. Grimly they surged in again.

Beneath their feet, the SEALs in Second Platoon felt the earth tremble to the terrible power of the gunships. A vast variety of murderous ordnance pummeled the enemy camp, always careful to avoid hits on the upright coffin-like cells that housed the American prisoners. At the end of this run, the Cobras spun about and poured a torrent of projectiles into the barracks of the staff and guards.

Fires broke out in the upper stories of the bamboo and

matting buildings. Men, their clothing aflame, leaped from windows and holes forced through the wall material. Few of them arose when they struck the ground. Inexorably, the AH-1Gs swept across the compound in a fury of death and destruction. At the end of their run, they swerved to make a pass back in the direction of their initial attack.

They battered more buildings, ripping gaps in the fence and shredding the surrounding jungle. Fortunately for them, the SEALs of Second Platoon were on the opposite side of the camp, well dug in behind and under huge old tree trunks that littered the ground. They knew only too well that the men behind this friendly fire hadn't the slightest idea where they were located.

Full dawn had come by the end of this fourth pass. The Cobras gained slight altitude and began an ominous circle around the area, deadly Indians circling the battered wagon train. It was then that the Huey slicks darted in. They came to a hover thirty feet above the stunned compound and large, thick lines snaked down. The fast ropes were soon festooned with human fruit, that slid rapidly toward the ground.

Right according to plan, the first man to touch ground was Tonto Waters. He blasted a groggy NVA soldier into oblivion with his 12 gauge Ithaca and turned left, then right, cut off the life of another guard, and spoke sharply to the SEALs he knew would be at his sides and forming behind.

"Clear," he repeated with each turn.

"Clear," echoed Zoro Agilar.

"Clear," Archie Golden assured his teammates.

Shotgun at the ready, Tonto moved out toward the cell on the far right. He would soon see the face of Captain Perry, USMC. He had already worked out his first words; "Sorry we took so long."

A blur of movement on his left drew Tonto out of his invisioned meeting with the pilot he had sworn to rescue.

He swung the muzzle of the shotgun in that direction and blew away a determined NVA sergeant. Thirty feet to cover. Waters reached into his ammo pouch and pulled free three rounds to replace those expended. Then he checked himself and reached for a double aught buck round in his shoulder harness bandolier. He added it last, so it would be first in the chamber.

Half a second later he cleared the chambered round into the face and shoulders of an NVA trooper laying prone on top of a maintenance shed. The dying soldier fired a long string into the air from his AK-47 before he left the world of the living. Tonto Waters chambered the double aught and stepped to the door of the cell.

"Stand clear!" he shouted, then gave a long five count and fired into the wooden locking mechanism.

CHAPTER 21 _____

BUCKSHOT SHATTERED the latch and part of the doorjamb. Tonto had it open in less than a second. Inside, crouched in the far corner, was a wretched figure. Unshaven, dirty, his flight suit torn and stained, the Marine Corps pilot looked more the castaway than one of the Corps' "few good men." He looked up with large, worried eyes.

"Sorry we took so long," Tonto said in a voice choked with emotion.

"Thank God you're here," Perry croaked.

"Can you walk?" At Perry's nod, Tonto Waters made an impatient gesture. "Then let's get out of here."

"Th-the others?"

"Sure. Now move out, jarhead—ah—sir."

Frank Perry cracked his first smile in two weeks. Tonto looped an arm around Perry's shoulder to support the pilot, and they left the tiny confinement space. It soon became obvious that hunger and inactivity had taken a powerful toll. Frank Perry reeled and would have walked in circles except for the support of Tonto Waters.

They made it to the extraction point with fifteen seconds to spare. Tonto handed the still slightly dazed Marine officer a Browning Hi-Power and told him to keep his eyes out for any enemy.

A soft, wistful smile spread on Perry's face. "I'd like that. Yes, I'd like that very much."

Tonto Waters blew out a second-floor window of the guards' barracks and knocked a North Vietnamese soldier off his feet. He fired again. A shrill scream answered him. There would be more, Tonto knew.

Kent Welby followed Lt. Carl Marino and Porfirio Agilar. They headed directly toward the building designated in the mock-up as the commandant's quarters. He saw movement to one shadowed side of the rush-mat structure and fired instinctively. A crashing of bamboo poles and a sharp cry told Doc that he had scored. To his right, Zoro Agilar put down a pair of NVA troopers with a trio of three-round bursts from his Swedish K. A quick glance at his watch revealed to Doc that it was 0531 hours. They had been on the ground a full minute.

During that time, he had emptied the magazine of his 700 Remington and eliminated the only survivors in the guard towers. The first had been easy.

Dazed by the hellacious fire from the Cobras, the wounded NVA guard had levered himself upright in the relative silence that followed the windstorm of lethal metal. When the slicks arrived, he had presence of mind to attempt to get the DShK-38 heavy machine gun into play. Already on the ground, Doc Welby had seen the movement and quickly sighted in.

He fixed the post and crosshairs of the 10X Redfield scope on the soldier's forehead and gently squeezed the trigger. Solid recoil from the .30-06 cartridge slammed familiarity into Doc's shoulder, and he rode it smoothly, which allowed him to see his target's head explode from the impact of the soft-nosed, hollow-point round he had fired.

Immediately he sought out another. In a tower sheltered by a large mangrove, he sensed movement. A splash of red revealed a man on hands and knees, behind the badly shattered matting wall. Doc took aim and fired again. The partly seen soldier slammed away from the bite of the slug under his left armpit. Incredibly, Doc saw him place hands over the railing and drag himself upward.

Another shot from the Remington smashed him back into the pedestal of the 12.7mm machine gun, and smashed the life from his body. Doc gave himself a curt nod of approval and surveyed the remaining towers through the scope. It gave a dizzy aspect to the terrain that whirled past so suddenly. In the fourth tower he inspected, he found a triangle of face, with a single eye staring back at him.

"Give me a little more target," Doc muttered to himself.

Obligingly, the NVA sentry inched along the side of the tower to where an opening had been blasted by one of the Cobras. His forehead came into view in the torn spot, then his eyes and nose; lastly, he shoved outward until his upper chest also became exposed. More than good, Doc thought as he lined up his shot.

Cracking along at better than twenty-four hundred feet per second, the bullet took less than a quarter second to cross the small distance separating the target from Doc Welby. Numbed and terrified by the fury of the gunship attack, the NVA regular stared blind and unfocused while the slug took him in the small notch at the bottom of his throat. His head snapped backward with enough violence to unhinge the skull from his spinal column.

Gouts of flesh, blood and bone flew from the back of his truncated neck. A second slug, already on its way, thudded into his arched chest, though he never felt it. Doc cursed himself for wasting a round, then admitted that training had reflexively taken over, and that it really was better to be safe than sorry.

And in that reflection, Doc recognized his old, grim companion, self-doubt. When assailed by his nemesis, he thought and spoke in clichés. Archie Golden made bad puns, and Tonto Waters longed painfully for a beer when the nervous side of combat got ahold of him. Every SEAL had his own way of handling it. Yet it was the discovery that each man suffered from it to one degree or another that had lifted Doc out of his doldrums and made him the first-class fighting machine he had become in so few, short months. A rattle of gunfire to Doc's left ended that train of thought.

He lowered his 700 and swung the compact Smith & Wesson M-59 into place. The bolt already positioned on a round, he had only to slip the safety and trigger a five-round burst into an incautious NVA staffer who darted into the open with his AK-47 on full rock and roll. Doc swung left and right to clear the area and joined Pope Marino and Zoro Agilar in his primary assignment.

Contact by his sneaker sole to the bamboo stair treads brought Doc Welby back to reality. Damn, it had been only a minute, and he had wasted five men. A loud rattle from above, on the veranda alerted Doc, who had time to shout and duck.

''Grenade!''

Pope Marino and Zoro Agilar went to ground along with Doc Welby and the hand grenade exploded harmlessly above them. When the shrapnel had whizzed past, Doc took the steps two at a time and fired short, quick bursts from the S&W M-59 into the thick matting that formed the sidewalls of the building. A body thudded to the floor. Two NVA guards fired blindly back from inside.

Doc and Zoro tracked them by the noise they made. The K subgun in Zoro's hands bucked and chattered at six hundred rounds per minute, spitting 9mm slugs through the fragile walls and into the body of one NVA soldier. It staggered him, and he crashed into several pieces of furniture on the way down. Doc Welby blasted a hole with his S&W that revealed another NVA trooper staring unbelievingly at the twin holes in his chest. He toppled forward while Doc and Zoro made for the door.

General Vihn Toy Giap had been sleeping soundly at 0500 hours. He dreamed, as usual in Technicolor, one of his favorite dreams. The great People's Hall in Hanoi had filled to capacity and beyond. Hundreds of the party elite filled the front rows, in full dress uniform. Their white-gloved hands made soft patters as they applauded politely. Ranked behind them came the lesser party members, the military, also in full dress, and then those of the people who could crowd into the rear, the alcoves and side rooms of the great hall.

All clapped their hands in the Western manner of showing approval, eyes fixed on the stately procession that advanced along the red carpet that ran from the high, double front doors to the low stage at the far end. The accolades increased in volume as General Giap, escorted by Ho Chi Minh himself, proceeded to the tall-backed gilt chair with its crimson-velvet upholstery. The party secretary, president of the presidium, President Minh, and the rest of the most powerful figures in all Vietnam ascended to the platform and took their places.

At a signal from the chief of protocol, they sat as one. Ho Chi Minh was introduced by the party secretary. He came forward, bowed by age, his face lined and seamed, a thin shock of white hair clinging tenaciously to the crown of his large head. When he spoke, his voice was low and quavery. Though those words rang loudly in the ears of Vinh Toy Giap.

''Comrades, the time has come for me to seek my well-deserved rest. The reins of our reunited country should be turned over to one younger and more able to serve the Party and the people. What more fitting person should that be than the man responsible for the glorious victory against the capitalist American enemy and the traitors of the South? Comrades, I give you my successor as president for life of the People's Republic of Vietnam . . . General Vinh . . .''

By then the clock read 0525 and General Giap's wake-up call came in the thunderous roar of miniguns, chain guns, and exploding missiles. The first detonations propelled the young general out of bed, eyes wide and staring, face contorted in pain at the murderous deluge of sound. A 3.75" rocket exploded against the rooftree of the commandant's quarters and blew away most of the conical roof thatch. Shards of its fins joined the shrapnel and wood splinters that ripped through the rooms below.

Cut in a dozen places and bleeding, as well as stunned to dumbness by the ferocious explosion, General Giap nevertheless had wits about him enough to draw on trousers and a uniform tunic, and thrust his long, narrow feet into black, knee-high boots. Outside, the world continued to come to an end.

A moment later, the door to his room flew open to reveal the commandant, Col. Xieng Van Gnduc, entirely naked, his face alive with writhing terror. Blood ran in ribbons from the cuts on his face and torso. "What is it? What is happening, Comrade General?" the frightened man demanded.

"I would gather the Americans are paying us a visit," Giap responded, his own fear conquered. "Strange, but I do not hear any return fire from the tower guards. I would see to that at once, if I were you." His tone of dismissal cut through the panic of Colonel Gnduc.

Still in an unseemly state of nakedness, Gnduc rushed for the rear entrance to the quarters. The attack sounded to come from the opposite side. With what aplomb he could muster, Colonel Gnduc burst out of his rear door and waved frantically at the soldiers in the nearest tower.

They stood dumbstruck, unable to comprehend what had descended upon them from the peaceful dawn sky.

Neither trooper saw the camp commander's attempt to gain their attention. Only belatedly did the senior one spring to the receiver of the 12.7mm machine gun, charge it, and swing the barrel in the direction of a Hughes Cobra that bore directly down on them. Pale yellow flame winked at them as he took aim. A blur of orange-white announced a salvo by the 30mm minigun. The NVA soldier even managed to get off three rounds before the entire tower platform disintegrated in a hail of exploding 30mm and .50 caliber rounds.

Like puffs of dust, the building materials of the tower formed a cloud around the central core. Flames began to flicker in the thatch of the roof. The Cobra flew on past. Piles of tattered clothing remained, to cover two emptied-out skin bags. Twin, thick streams of scarlet dripped through the shattered floor.

Like most sadists, Colonel Gnduc was a coward at heart. Stunned to immobility by the tumultuous destruction of the guard tower, he froze in place. Unbelievably, the six helicopters spun around and made a pass in another direction. Large portions of the barracks roofs disintegrated. Fires broke out behind the onslaught. One Cobra veered slightly and lined up directly on Colonel Gnduc. It suddenly gave him new life and movement.

Scampering like a hairless monkey, the camp commandant made a hasty, if undignified, retreat. He cleared the kill zone of the Cobra before the first rounds crashed into the ground. Through the bare soles of his feet, he felt the deadly ripple of their detonation and felt the heat of the bursts on his skin. He literally dived through one of the overhead shutters, which had been lowered for nighttime, and crashed on the floor of his living room.

Only then, out of the fearsome sight of the American helicopters, did his ears mark the slow, heavy chug of the DShK-38s returning fire. Raising his head from the rush matting, he saw a stream of green tracers arch through the sky. The broken edges of the shutter fanned vigorously in the stiff downdraft of the Cobras' main rotors. Billows of dust joined the smoke from fires and explosives. Dimly he could hear the hopeless screaming of the wounded, the burned, and the dying.

Then, as quickly as it had begun, the appalling violation of their peace ended. Flames crackled dully, soon to be drowned out by the roar and whine of four UH-ID (Model 205 Bell Huey) Rolls-Royce Gnome, coupled turboshaft engines. Staggered by the enormity of what he witnessed, Colonel Gnduc stared through the opening as six streams of men slid down ropes to the center of the compound from each of the hovering birds.

They hit the ground shooting. Quickly they took out the survivors in the guard towers and eliminated all resistance from the guards who had rallied in their ready room. With that accomplished, they spread out as though directed by a choreographer, every movement graceful and flowing, synchronized with those of the others, so that no potential danger spot remained uncovered. Only at the last moment did Colonel Gnduc realize that three of them made directly for his office and quarters.

A quick glance around located four soldiers cowering under pieces of furniture and a heavy counter along one inner wall. Anger replaced the horror Colonel Gnduc had been experiencing. He fairly bellowed at the quailing men. "Do something! Make yourselves useful. Defend this place!"

Laggardly, they sprang to life. Two of them shuffled to the ruined shutter and poked their weapons outside. The staccato roar of a submachine gun and bark of an M-15 came to life beyond the wall. The soldiers went down screaming. By then, Colonel Gnduc had rushed into the sleeping quarters once more. There he looked around in confusion until he recalled his naked state.

He quickly threw on mustard green uniform shorts and

a pair of boots. He planted his bill cap on his head and grabbed up his pistol belt. A hand grenade exploded with an ear-zinging blast. Then footsteps pounded on the veranda. At that moment, Colonel Gnduc had his first cogent, useful thought since the attack began. He had to get out of there.

Major Pyotr Rudinov knew that he had let his fiery temper interfere with his good judgment in regard to the commandant at the People's Republic POW camp. He should never have revealed his identity. For bad or worse, it was done. *Nekta ne prerotovlyat borsht co repa*, he dismissed his concern philosophically with a favorite saying of his dear, long-dead mother. *One cannot make borsht with turnips.*

If fortune smiled on him, he would be back in time to whisk the prisoners out of there and have them off to the *Rodina* before the SEALs located the camp or General Hoi and his minion, Colonel Gnduc, could do anything to prevent it. Only fifty miles to go. Slow miles because of the almost total lack of roadways. Fortunately the last ten kilometers of trail had been widened, and kept concealed, to allow for vehicular travel. He would be there before 0600 hours. Ample time to catch Gnduc by surprise and make off with the prize.

Armed with that pleasant thought, Kovietski/Rudinov leaned back to catch what sleep his could as the GAZ-69 ground and bumped its way toward the camp.

Tonto Waters continued to fire into the second floor of the staff barracks. The enemy there might be paper-shufflers, but they knew how to load and fire a weapon same as any soldier. Another thirty seconds had gone by, during which three dazed civilians and two men in pilots' flight suits had been brought to the extraction point. Tonto held them together with harsh commands.

"Get down," he would order each new arrival. "If you can use it, take a weapon from the man who brought you out. Fire on anything that moves in those barracks."

For a couple of those captive the longest he had to repeat his instructions. Randy Andy Holt showed up with a worried expression. Tonto noticed at once that Andy did not have his second rescue with him. Holt gave a negative shake of his head.

"I can't find one of the pilots. Who have we accounted for so far?"

"Captain Perry, USMC, Colonel Vhang of ARVN, and Commander Nash, USN."

"That leaves an Air Force lieutenant—uh—Dave Allen. But all of the cells are empty," Andy Holt declared.

There was one other possibility. Tonto turned a worried frown to the officers. "Where were you taken to be interrogated?"

"Over there," Perry stated. "That little, low building without windows." The others agreed.

"There you go, Randy Andy. Why not check it out?"

Holt hurried off to do that. What he found after he forced the lock nearly made him lose the breakfast he had not eaten. Inside the walls had been painted a flat black. A naked figure lay strapped to a rubber flotation device of some sort. When gray, morning light spilled in, Lt. David Allen cringed as much as his bonds would allow. Andy Holt hurried to his side.

"It's going to be all right, we're here to get you out." Then he noticed the plugs sealing the pilot's ears, the tape over his mouth. IV bottles hung above the platform, their lines extended to veins in Allen's forearms. Allen moved feebly, like a frightened child or a sick, old man.

Andy tugged at the tape, wincing in sympathy when it came noisily away from tender, reddened skin. Then he removed the ear stopples. All through it, Dave Allen kept his eyes tightly shut. The first sound he made was a pitiful, whining cry. Then the words spilled out in a broken babble.

"I—tol—tole—yu—ever'thing. Ple'se let me sleep."

"Hang in there, Lieutenant. I'm here to help," Holt continued to urge while he released the unfortunate victim of Gen. Giap's talents.

What a rotten bunch of bastards, he thought. It was obvious this one could not walk or do anything on his own. Andy Holt lifted the softly sobbing pilot over his shoulder and started for the door. Right then he wanted nothing more than to get his hands on this General Giap. When he got through, Jason Slater and his spooks wouldn't have much to work with. Outside the interrogation room, Lieutenant Allen cried out in pain from the brightness. It took all of Randy Andy's stamina to get them to the center of the compound.

There, Fil Nicholson peeled out of his BDU jacket and covered part of Allen's nakedness. He shot a look at Randy Andy.

"They were pumping him full of all kinds of shit. I didn't see what. But his mind is all messed up. It's like he's been whipped, but not a mark on him."

Fil's lips formed a grim line. "I don't dare give him morphine until I know what they've dosed him with and how much."

Tonto Waters fired off a load of buckshot at a pair of NVA troopers who rounded one corner of the staff barracks, then bent over the tortured officer. "Better do something fast, he's in rotten shape."

Archie Golden and the demolitions man from Second Squad went forward under covering fire from Bravo. Each carried two forty-pound satchel charges, which they would plant in the barracks. They separated at the staff building. Archie took the farther structure. The moment he exposed his head around the corner of the nearer barrack, a hail of fire came from the windows of the second. He popped back as slugs cracked into the wooden walls.

"Hell of a note," he grumbled.

An AR-15 hung around his neck, fitted with an XM148 tube. He released his hold on the explosives and swung the weapon into place, then inserted a 40mm grenade. Back around the corner and he fired it toward an open window. The projectile barely had time to arm itself before it disappeared inside. A sharp crack followed, accompanied by screams. Another round should do, he figured.

Archie's second grenade silenced opposition long enough for him to run to the side of the barrack. He set the timer on one charge and hurled it through a ground-floor window. The second he carried to the far end and repeated the procedure. Then he got the hell out of there.

He and his counterpart from Bravo Squad had barely cleared the barracks by thirty yards when the buildings went up with a tremendous roar and hot flash of detonating TNT. The shock wave hurtled them off their feet and they spilled, rolling, onto the ground near the extraction point. Jagged splinters hummed through the air, along with chunks of wall studs and bits of human flesh. Archie scrambled on hands and knees to where Tonto and the others lay, covering any enemy action.

"Overdid that a bit, didn't you Arch?" Tonto asked dryly.

"Wanted to make sure. What's up now?"

"We're into our second minute and still no sign of Pope with that NVA general."

A sudden burst of fire came from the commandant's quarters, followed by screams.

CHAPTER 22 _____

Doc Welby kicked in the door to the commandant's quarters and sprayed the room with his S&W M-59. Two NVA soldiers, one already wounded, tumbled into grotesque postures of death. Doc went in low, after lobbing a grenade ahead to clear a path if necessary. Pope Marino followed, with Zoro Agilar bringing up the rear.

"Clear!" Doc called out.

"Clear left," Pope responded.

"Clear right," Zoro added.

They had entered by way of the office. A desk showed scarring from the shrapnel. Splinters still smoldered. Another NVA trooper lay dead beside a filing cabinet, his face and chest shredded by fragments from the grenade. Nothing and no one moved. Slowly, Zoro Agilar crossed the room to an open doorway, the portal ripped free at the top and sagging drunkenly. He signaled a hallway beyond. Pope nodded and gestured for him to proceed.

Weapon held nearly vertical, Zoro rolled around the doorjamb and into the hall. At once the muzzle of his Swedish K swept the length and paused on the door at the far end. On tiptoes, he advanced. Kent Welby came behind him. At a door jutting off to the left, Zoro paused, then bent low and spun into the room behind it. His Swedish K barked a three-round burst, followed by the clatter of a falling body. Zoro's hand and forearm came out into the hall.

He signaled the all clear, then came out himself. By that time, Doc Welby had advanced on the next room. It had been an orderly room, accommodating quarters and work space for the commandant's orderly, before a 3.75-inch rocket from a Cobra had trashed it. Doc swallowed hard to drive down the gorge that began to rise when he saw the bits of the orderly strewn around the room.

"It's clear," he croaked in a low tone.

Doc Welby could read the expression of puzzlement on the face of Pope Marino. He, too, had expected greater resistance. Where was everyone? The commandant and General Giap, in particular? Two more doors gave off the hallway. The one at the far end bothered Doc especially.

He could almost sense some malevolent presence behind the closed portal. They would learn about it soon enough, he reasoned. On tiptoe, the three SEALs continued toward the ominous entry. A floorboard squeaked loudly right outside the last side door. Immediately a hail of fire cut through the thin panels and sprayed the opposite wall. Doc felt somethin akin to relief. He cranked the S&W 9mm subgun on the wall to the nearside of the opening and sent ten rounds through it. At once he dashed past the danger area and a moment later bullets zipped through the wall where he had formerly stood.

"Close, *hermano*," Zoro Agilar breathed out.

"You tell me," Doc answered.

They both turned their weapons on the walls and hosed down the room beyond. This time no answering fire came at them. Satisfied, Zoro gave a nod, stepped over and kicked open the riddled door. It swung partway and collided with a freshly made corpse. Zoro obligingly sprayed the interior once more for good measure. When the roar subsided in the enclosed area, he turned back to his teammates.

"Clear."

That left the room at the end of the hall. Butterflies sprang to life in Doc Welby's stomach. He felt light-headed and giddy. None of this was real. They were back at the train-fire range at Tre Noc. Just another exercise. Now, if he could just convince himself of that, he might come out of it without a nervous breakdown.

Bullshit! the combat-wise part of his mind contradicted. *Start thinking about this as another war game and it's a sure way to not come out of it alive. Keep alert.* That had been drummed into the head of every SEAL from the time he began as a neophyte in diver's school. Even when they had been out on their feet from fatigue and no sleep during Hell Week at UDT/R, the instructors continuously bellowed at them to stay alert. Well, he had sure as hell better be right here or else.

Doc Welby blinked his eyes to discover he had covered the remaining distance to that baleful final door. If anyone was behind it, it would be locked. No sense in trying the knob. Doc reared back and cocked his right leg. Smith 9mm submachine gun at the ready, he hauled off and kicked alongside the latch. The wood splintered and the door flew inward. Doc blazed away with his S&W then stopped in amazement. For a second he could only gape and point.

Kovietski/Rudinov tapped the shoulder of his driver and signed for him to shut down the jeeplike GAZ-69. For a moment he believed he heard a faint sound of gunfire in the distance, followed by the apocalyptic rumble of explosions. He could not distinguish from which direction it came. He strained his ears, listening for the noise again.

"Did you hear that?" he asked the young Russian corporal-driver.

"What, sir?"

"I thought I heard gunfire."

Seated beside their commander, Dudov and Yoriko exchanged puzzled glances. They had not heard any gunfire.

"I heard nothing, Comrade Major."

Rudinov listened a while longer. Slightly under twenty kilometers to go. There! His features enlivened. More gunfire. Where did it come from?

"Did you hear it that time?"

His driver wore a puzzled expression. "I'm not sure, Comrade Major."

His decision came quickly. "Get a move on, Sukin. I want to be to the camp before midmorning."

Two NVA soldiers writhed on the floor, blood pouring from their multiple wounds. Beyond them another door, one to the outside, stood open, a startled and infuriated Colonel Gnduc faced the muzzle of the AR-15 in the hands of Archie Golden.

"Thought I'd lend a hand," the redheaded Archie said laconically.

"Good you did," Pope Marino injected as he stepped into the room and covered General Giap with his AR-15. "General Vinh Toy Giap, I presume?"

"Filthy American, capitalist pig!" Giap spat in Vietnamese.

Lt. Carl Marino took a step closer and slammed the butt of his rifle into the chest of General Giap. "Where's Lieutenant Rhodes? I know you can understand English, you little fuck. Answer me."

General Giap squeezed his eyes tightly shut to contain the pain. Then he answered levelly. "I am an officer of the Army of the People's Republic of Vietnam. As such I am entitled to proper treatment as a prisoner of war."

Lt. Marino gave him a nasty smile. "You are in the hands of the United States Navy SEALs, and we'll do with you whatever we goddamned please. Now where is

Lieutenant Rhodes?'' Gen. Giap remained silent, enduring his pain, until Pope rapped him again. ''He is . . . being detained in a special cell. It is under this residence.'' A dry, bitter laugh emitted from the general's thin lips. ''You will find him quite close to the edge of madness. I have . . . been amusing myself with him.''

Pope Marino shot General Giap through the thigh. ''Our chief spook said he wanted you back alive. He didn't say what shape you had to be in. Now, both of you, drag your asses out of here.''

Archie Golden produced two tough plastic strips, a common commodity of late—riot cuffs. He quickly secured General Giap's wrists, arms above his head, and did the same to Colonel Gnduc. Then he and Zoro Agilar frog-marched them to where the two squads continued to suppress enemy fire. Pope Marino and Doc Welby located the trapdoor that led to the confinement cell below the floor.

Doc went first, his way lighted by a tape-wrapped flashlight. The sight that greeted him caused his stomach to churn. Dusty Rhodes crouched in one corner, entirely naked, chained to a steel post driven into the ground and butted against the subflooring above. The odor of human feces gagged Doc, and his eyes swam with the effluvium that hung thick in the air. All at once, Dusty jerked and slammed against the concrete block wall. The second time this happened, Doc saw the cause.

An alligator clip, with long electric lead, clung to Dusty's scrotum. A rotator switch turned on a shelf beside the twenty-four-volt aviation battery and booster coil to which the device of a depraved mind had been attached. When the contacts closed, a jolt of unknown strength ripped through Dusty. His hands bound behind him, unable to free himself, Dusty could only jerk and whimper, his throat long ago made sore beyond screaming.

"Pope, get down here," Doc barked stridently.

Doc rushed to the shelf and jerked the lead from the battery terminal. Dusty shuddered and moaned. From over his shoulder Doc heard Pope's reaction.

"Jesus Christ! What have they done to him?"

"Giap's fun and games," Doc said tightly. "We have to find a way to free him."

"Time's running out, Doc. I'll get on the horn."

Repeat Ditto had been on the radio continuously since the squads engaged the first of the enemy. When the handy-talkie hung on his belt squawked he put the pilot of the lead slick on hold and retrieved the handheld two-way. "Go, Eagle One."

"Search Giap. You should find a metal handcuff key in one of his pockets. Over."

Repeat grinned. "Roger that. Find that key. No doubt he'll have it, the other one ain't got a stitch on. Over."

They must have stripped the commandant, Pope surmised. "Send someone in here with it ASAP. Eagle One, out."

Pope had the key in twenty precious seconds. So what. His time frame was shot in the butt. But he knew, as he knelt to free Dusty's hands, that even the most brilliant plan, perfectly rehearsed, got shot to hell at the moment of first contact with the enemy. The initial scenario called for them to be on the ground for three minutes thirty seconds. Time to move, or that deadline would be passed, too.

Gently, Lieutenant Marino cradled his AOIC in his arms and lifted him from the stone flooring. Kent Welby took his CO's weapon and preceded him up the steps. The first shout of outrage came from Zoro Agilar, who had retrieved the key and waited by the hidden cell for news of what happened below.

"Those sons of bitches," Zoro blurted. *"¡Hijos de la chingada!"* he repeated furiously in Spanish.

"Help me with him," Pope commanded curtly.

Zoro sprang to assist the Old Man. Worried about Dusty's condition, Pope still took time to nod his thanks. They had been on the ground three minutes when he emerged from the building.

"Archie," he called out. "You got any more explosives?"

"Sure do, Pope."

"Then blow that place to fuckin' kindling wood."

"My pleasure."

"Bring 'em in! Bring 'em in!" Chad Ditto, the RTO shouted into the mike he held.

Rotor blades whopped the air close at hand and the turboshaft engines spooled up to full throttle. The slicks rose from behind a screen of trees and hovered briefly, aligning themselves, then dropped to inches off of the ground at the center of the ravaged compound, where the SEALs awaited them. They looked to the powder-begrimed men like Valkyries come down from Valhalla.

So far it had run like clockwork. Then Pope Marino found they had been on the ground too long. The SEALs on the perimeter of their LZ began to take fire from out in the jungle. They immediately responded. Repeat Ditto switched frequencies and Pope took the handset.

"Sierra-Tango-Five-Two-Eight, this is Eagle One, we're taking fire from our nine. Do you copy?"

"Roger, Eagle One. We copy that. Will be there in a short."

At once, above them, the Cobras snarled into action. They ended their orbits and vectored on the source of enemy fire. The miniguns opened up, their howl like a banshee out of Hades. Chunks of jungle flew upward. A heavy machine gun began to chug in the bush and the ugly prow of a BTR-50PK shoved aside a small tree.

Two 3.75-inch missiles belched flame and smoke along the side of the lead Cobra and sped to the target. One

struck at the base of the right-hand cupola. The hatch of
the gunner's cupola flew skyward, along with the DShK-
39 heavy machine gun. The second rocket blew off the
right-hand tread and killed the driver. Uncontrolled, the
APC lumbered into the compound in an awkward circle.
Another missile finished it off. Pope broke off watching
to check the loading.

With skids only inches from the ground, the captive
NVA officers were chucked aboard the slicks. Pope now
noted that the choppers had been loaded with the freed
prisoners. At a signal from him, the SEALs of Alpha and
Bravo Squads clambered aboard. Pope and Tonto waited,
checking each teammate into the birds. He noted several
of Anchor Head's Second Squad men had taken minor
wounds. He bit his lower lip, and thought of the men in
the Second Platoon, who had yet to make it to their extraction point. He wished them luck. A final look around
and he exchanged thumbs-up with Tonto and they
climbed aboard the last slick.

"A classic parakeet op," Lt. Carl Marino declared over
the boom mike in the crew chief's helmet while the choppers zipped over the treetops.

"Roger that, Pope," Tonto chirped back. "How's
Dusty?"

"He's still alive," Pope answered through a tight
throat. "For how long, I can't say."

"Is he . . . how's his mind?" Tonto queried hesitantly.

Pope gave him a bleak stare. "Only God knows that."

Jolted with astonishment, Coporal Sukin slammed on the
brakes without being told. He stared with his mouth agape
at the ruin of the POW camp. He recalled how it had
looked on their last visit. This smoldering ruin bore not
the least resemblance to the proud accomplishment of the
NVA soldiers who had built it.

"What happened, Comrade Major?" he asked, stricken.

Eyes bugged, face contorted and vermilion in his rage, Major Rudinov fought to regain his voice. Far off in the distance, climbing ungainfully into the sky, he marked the insect forms of eight helicopters dwindling rapidly. Deep in his gut he knew that he had been foiled again by the same damned SEAL lieutenant who had destroyed the major offensive planned by Gen. Hoi Pac.

In his fury, he also blamed the NVA general for keeping the POW camp secret from him. Now they had both lost the major trump card of the CIA agents. Slowly the words formed and came, quavering from his mouth.

"*Yeb vas*, Lieutenant Carl Marino," he gritted out. "Fuck you," he swore again. Silently, he vowed to get his revenge.

The pilot of the slick brought it in hot and fast. He knew of the condition of Lieutenant (jg) Rhodes and determined to spare the man every moment of pain he could prevent. A three-quarter-ton, 4×4 ambulance waited at the helipad. Its rear door flew open the moment the dust cloud from the rotor dissipated. Litter bearers and a medic rushed forward. They off-loaded the wounded prisoner first and started for the ambulance. Lieutenant Marino saw this and called to them.

"Oh, no, not him. Take my AOIC first."

The stretcher men looked perplexed. "But sir, he's obviously a ranking officer and a prisoner of war. We're required . . ."

"Not this time. He tortured my AOIC, while he was *their* prisoner. Let the little fucker walk."

Jason Slater, who had been contacted by radio from the helicopter, came forward. "I'll take charge of the prisoner, sailor," he informed the medic, who was also preparing a protest. "He belongs to us now." Then, to Pope

Marino and his SEALs, "Good job. Damn fine one, in fact. We're gonna have a lot of fun wringing this baby out. I owe you a dinner, and a couple of drinks, and maybe a week's R and R in Japan for this. And, oh, yeah, I gave your SF buddy what we had. He'll be in touch."

That suddenly brought back the court-martial looming over Chief Tom Waters. A disturbing change came over Lt. Carl Marino. The fatigue of combat and pride of accomplishment faded, to be replaced by a hard, cold visage. "Out there I completely forgot about that. Well, thanks in advance for whatever you could dig up," he added evasively, conscious of the need to keep any results absolutely secret. "And, I for one could sure use that R and R."

Laughing, Jason Slater clapped Marino on one shoulder. "You've got it. Just say when."

Pope Marino did not answer, his mind back on the troubling situation with Tonto Waters. The trial would resume in four days.

After the debriefing, which was held in high good humor due to the remarkably low loss in WIAs. In fact, only three SEALs of Second Platoon and four of first received any notable injuries. Porfirio Agilar did get a bullet scrape on the deltoid muscle of his left shoulder. It was treated with an antibiotic powder and field dressing. He looked disappointed about the whole affair. When asked about that during the debriefing, his answer came low, almost muttered.

"I always wanted my first scar to come from *un toro grande*, not some little brown gook with a Chinese rifle." Laughter from the others halted the question-and-answer period for a couple of minutes.

Freed from the interrogation, with praises aplenty and promises of a unit citation being awarded, the SEALs went on to clean weapons and then a long, hot, well-deserved shower. In the quarters he shared with Dusty

Rhodes, who was already on his way to the field hospital at Binh Thuy, Pope Marino began packing his ditty bag for the trip to Saigon. He already had his Class A suntans in a garment bag, hanging on an over-the-door clothes rod. His mood turned darker.

There was nothing he hated more having to do than what was about to happen. Even with the distinguished way Tonto had worked on the op, he realized it would matter little to surface fleet captains and desk sailors. The former viewed heroics in the scope of the Battle of the Coral Sea or the invasion of Inchon. The latter fostered too much contempt for Special Warfare types. Contempt born of jealousy, Carl Marino firmly believed. He heaved a sigh and wondered what Tonto would be up to now.

Tonto Waters sat on the end of his bunk, a dew-beaded can of Miller in one big fist. He drank from it slowly, staring at this Class A tunic, with the slim, single row of campaign ribbons just below his UDT badge. Headed by the Naval Commendation Medal, and Bronze Star, he also had a Purple Heart and the Vietnam theater ribbon, red and green vertical stripes on a yellow background. Trailing all of those, the Good Conduct Medal looked ridiculous.

Would he be wearing all of that for the last time before the general court? The prospect haunted him. Hell, he hadn't done anything wrong and already he was looking at himself like he was guilty. Portsmouth or a firing squad? Would he have a choice? He had been offered a way out, just rat on Eloise. Emotion surged through Tonto so violently his hand spasmed and crushed the beer can. Amber brew geysered toward the ceiling. This was getting him nowhere. *God damn* Barry Lailey.

YO/1C Kent Welby left the showers for his quarters in high spirits. He had worked like a killing machine out there. And had been the one to find Dusty Rhodes. The world went well for him right now. Then the mail clerk for the Riverine Force hailed him from the COs office.

"You're Welby, ain'tcha?"

"Yeah, that's me. Why?"

"Got a Special Delivery letter came in this morning. You guys were out, so we took it here."

Doc Welby crossed to the sailor and accepted the long, white envelope. Sure enough, Special Delivery green stickers festooned the front, although they were useless in any mail that went through an FPO (Fleet Post Office) address. He glanced at the return address. It was from Betty. His hands developed a slight quake as he opened the bulky envelope. When he drew out a thick document, his heart began to pound and he went deathly pale. The letter accompanying it was brief to the point of being brusque.

Kent, I have decided to go ahead with the divorce. I just can't handle the terrible news coming from where you are. I am sorry. And it was signed, *Betty*. He read the divorce papers with growing disbelief. "Irreconcilable differences," it read in one place. "Mental cruelty," in another. "Abandonment," in yet a third place.

What the hell. *She* left him, not the other way around. Then he got the real shocker. Betty had included another bill from her attorney. Gloomily, he stared blankly at the paper. What could he do now?

CHAPTER 23 ─────────────

LCDR BARRY Lailey wanted to throw the telephone which had delivered the news across the room. He very much wanted a dog to kick, or a face to punch. Not only had Marino's SEALs come back with General Giap in tow, they brought the camp commandant, leveled the place in the bargain, and got out all the prisoners, without losing a man. And Carl Marino had not even picked up a scratch.

Much worse, from the glowing praise heaped upon Marino by Jason Slater, the incompetent bastard was now the fair-haired boy of the CIA. Another thought pierced his cloud of anger. The upcoming court-martial would fix Marino's wagon, and that of that uppity chief, Tom Waters. At least that would be good news. He lifted the handset of his telephone and spoke crisply.

"Get me the office of Commander Quade, in the Staff Judge Advocate's office, Saigon." When the connection was made and Quade on the line, Barry Lailey spoke with all the unctuous smoothness of a snake-oil peddler. "Erwin, Barry Lailey here. How are things proceeding?"

"Not at all well," came the crisp, impatient reply.

"What's the matter? Didn't you interview the witnesses I sent up to you?"

"Yes, I did. And, outside of the SP chief, every one

of them is a goddamned liar. And it shows. I don't dare use a one of them. Don't you *have* any actual witnesses?"

Lailey brooded over that for a long silence. "This is—ah—a rather—ah—sensitive issue around here, Erwin. We cannot afford to compromise anyone from the intelligence community, don't you see?"

"I see my losing the case if we can't corroborate what you claim in the Statement of Charges."

"Pleeease, Erwin. Don't worry. It's just that I can't shop one of our people, or some Company spook, in order to get this case made. Not to worry. You know how Burke feels about this. I assure you I will have some credible witnesses."

"You had better. The trial is only a week away."

Barry Lailey hung up and looked at his watch. Only 1100 and he needed a drink in the worst way. He also needed something to eat to put an end to the burning in his stomach. The lieutenant commander pushed away from his desk. The drink first, then something to soothe his gut.

The victorious SEALs got liberty at 1200. Still in a turmoil, Doc Welby badly wanted to discuss the latest development with Francie Song. He hurried to the Riverine Force Special Operations office and met her on the way out to noon chow. Her reaction puzzled him. Perhaps she had been startled to see him back so soon.

"Let's go somewhere off base," he suggested.

"You can leave this time of day?"

"Yes, I'm on liberty for twenty-four hours. There's something we have to talk about."

Francie screwed up her face into an expression of pain. "I don't want to hear any more about how you have to remain loyal to a wife who does not love you."

Shocked by her vehemence, and not realizing that Francie could not know what he knew, Doc took her roughly by the arm. "It's not that at all. In fact it's . . ." He cut off what he was about to say. "I'll tell you later. We can go to Mr. Houang's place. He always has great prawns."

"All right, Kent Welby. Only, please, tell me what this is all about?"

"Later, at Houang's."

Cao Houang had his shop in what would be called a *palpa* in Mexico. The open-air snack bar had been covered over with a peaked thatch roof and low, circular walls of woven raffia palm leaves. Diners sat at small round tables or stood around circular shelves around the four main upright posts that supported the roof. In the center, under clouds of steam, three giant woks bubbled away on their charcoal-burning, brick stoves. A similar ovenlike fire pit rested alongside, with a grill for broiling fish and eels. Doc and Francie walked there in a matter of minutes.

A persistent patter of rain began the moment they entered. They greeted the proprietor and selected a stand-up place in the crowded eatery. Francie thought only a moment before she ordered. "I'll have a bowl of prawns and noodles, and a broiled eel."

Doc made a face. Eel was one item of Vietnamese cuisine he had not been able to handle thus far. "I'll have prawns and a grilled fish."

Francie placed their order and Houang came back with two chilled bottles of *Bahminbah* beer. He set them deftly on the table and departed. Francie took a long swallow and peered with jet eyes into Doc's clear, blue orbs. "Now, tell me what this is all about."

Doc sighed and returned her steady gaze. "I meant what I said. This is not at all about me having to stay faithful to Betty. Quite the opposite. I just received a letter with the divorce papers in it. She has changed her mind again. This time she went through with filing."

Francie, who had feared and worried about Doc finding out about her meeting with Sergeant Yates, brightened immediately. Great relief and joy washed over her. She clapped her hands excitedly, a little girl with a new dress. Then a shaft of greater horror stabbed her. It would be even worse now if Kent found out about Yates. Dare she tell him, make a complete confession? Would he love her then? She decided on silence about the subject.

"Why, that's marvelous, Kent Welby. I told you she had lost all feeling for you. This proves it."

"It also makes me a free man. Uh—when the divorce decree is final. Which brings up another problem. I—er—well, American service men cannot marry Vietnamese nationals. At least not so long as the conflict is ongoing."

Stunned, Francie could only gape. Did he mean what she thought he did? "Was that a proposal, Kent Welby?"

Doc blushed to the open V of his jungle cammo T-shirt. "A delayed one, let's call it."

"Oh, yes, yes, I will marry you."

"When we can. Maybe, by the time a year has gone by, the regulations will have changed."

Francie made a small moue. "So long?" Fear goaded her that surely within that time her Kent Welby would find out about Sergeant Yates. How could she explain herself?

Doc patted her hand consolingly. "It's not a terribly long time. Many couples back home are engaged for longer than that."

Their food arrived then, and they changed the subject. Doc breathed deeply of the ginger and chili-pepper seasoning on the prawns and licked his lips. "Delicious as ever," he told the beaming Mr. Houang in the Vietnamese Francie had so carefully coached him in speaking.

"How is your work?" he asked Francie, when it appeared the proprietor was not about to depart.

"The same. I shuffle papers, take some in for Lieuten-

ant Fuller to sign or stamp, file them and forget them."
She laughed. "That last is what the sailors working there
say."

"They are yeomen," Doc corrected.

"Like you?"

"Yes, only most are third class. Low man on the totem
pole."

Francie wrinkled her brow. "What is a totem pole?"

Doc explained and Francie made a face of rapt delight.
"They sound so wondrously barbaric. So wild and free.
To think, your Indians make these."

Mr. Houang's thirteen-year-old daughter called him
away before Kent continued. "They have for thousands
of years, I suppose. Ummm," he went on, biting into a
plump, tender shrimp. "These are really good today."

"It is your good news that has improved your appetite,
Kent Welby," Francie teased. "You have liberty for how
long?"

"Until tomorrow. Twenty-four-hour liberty."

"And I know just how we are going to spend it. Kent,
it is vastly better than what you call a Cinderella liberty.
You have never told me what that means."

"That I have to be back on base before midnight or I
get turned into a pumpkin," Doc told her with a straight
face.

Francie wrinkled her nose. "I do not believe that, Kent
Welby. How could you be turned into a pumpkin?"

Kent laughed. "*That* means that I'd get a captain's
mast for being AWOL."

"We do not want that to happen. But, oh, Kent Welby,
I do so much want you to make long, delicious love to
me."

"And I will. I promise you I will."

Kovietski/Rudinov had at last conquered his fury over being once more outsmarted and outmaneuvered by Lt.

Carl Marino of the American Navy's SEALs. He worked off his fury by devoting himself to the thick pile of reports and documents that had accumulated in his absence on his trips to the POW camp. Most of his work was routine, until he came upon a report from the sergeant.

Any other time, he would have considered it to be a normal, less-than-stimulating, communique. But the name of his nemesis stood out in bold print to his eyes. **Lt. Carl Richard Marino** had been assigned as legal officer and defense counsel in the general court-martial of a petty officer named Thomas Waters. From the report of his agent, Rudinov surmised that the Government had a weak case at best. It had been duly noted by the redheaded sergeant that the Government lacked any witnesses to alleged acts of espionage. Major Rudinov pursed his lips and thought long and hard on that.

Finally he purred aloud over steepled fingers. "A chink in Marino's armor. It might be that I can get to Marino through this chief petty officer. The least I can do is provide the American government with a suitable witness."

He had only one problem. Whom could he safely sacrifice to achieve that result?

Lt. Carl Marino would find it disconcerting to know he shared anything in common with LCDR Barry Lailey. The fact was, he did. Becoming the apple of the CIA's eye pissed him off every bit as much as it did Lailey. Granted for a different reason. Since those operations in Central America, Pope Marino had little use for spooks of any stripe. What galled him even more was that Jason Slater seemed, for all his Western affectations, to be a highly competent operative.

Which would no doubt negate a longtime career with the Central Intelligence Agency, Marino thought cynically. The truly capable did not last long in an atmosphere where the successful fed on a diet of bureaucracy and bullshit. No, Langley was too close to Washington, DC, for Carl Marino to trust most of its minions. So why was it he was sitting here in the Phon Bai drinking with Slater's deputy station chief?

"Jase had to get back to Saigon with Giap and that other turkey. So, here I am, buying you that drink and dinner he promised. So what will you have?"

Pope eyed him askance. "They have some excellent black-market scotch. Johnny Black, even some single malt Glenfiddich."

"I'll go for the single malt," Rick Eiler declared.

"Me too."

"What about chow?"

A big grin spread on Marino's face. "The works, naturally. Giant prawns with mushrooms and lemongrass, a whole roast suckling pig, wok-fried vegetables. Everything is first-class here, so relax and enjoy, Rick."

Rick Eiler looked slightly ill. "This is going to be costly," he proposed hesitantly.

Pope laughed sharply. "What the hell? Your boss is picking up the tab, right? Actually it won't be so bad. About a hundred piasters a shot for the scotch, but the whole meal for both of us won't go over five hundred piasters." Pope found he was enjoying himself.

He liked seeing an uptight spook worry over money. Though, truth to tell, he sort of liked Eiler, who seemed an all-right dude. Did Slater have any say in personnel decisions? Never mind. He might as well kick back and make the most of this. Already he found himself not to be so entirely pissed off.

Four days later, Lieutenant Marino and Chief Waters took the morning mail chopper to Saigon, being as they were on the tail end of the route at Tre Noc. As a morale builder for Tonto, Pope eschewed free lodging at the Special Forces base and opted for the Hotel International.

They would wear civvies and mingle with the journalists. They could change into uniform in an anteroom off the huge hall where the court would be convened.

That arrangement suited Tonto well enough. At least until he recalled the fantastic times he had enjoyed there with Eloise Daladier. It prompted him to ask again about her whereabouts and condition. Pope had little to offer.

"From what I get, she's supposed to be in the custody of the 'civilian authorities,' whatever that means."

Tonto frowned into his beer. "If it's Thieu's stinkin' corrupt cops, she's in some deep stuff. Be a wonder if she's not killed. Goddamnit, Pope, we gotta do something about getting her out of there."

"Having you acquitted will go a long way toward that, I'm sure," Marino answered mildly. He sought to change the subject by gesturing across the Carousel Lounge to a cluster of journalists surrounding a young, black-haired, crew-cut reporter in the usual bush jacket and open-collar shirt. "Look over there. That's Tom Brokaw. They say he has actually gone out in the bush with the blanket-heads, the jarheads and the ground-pounders, instead of hanging around here inventing defeats for our troops."

Tonto glanced that direction and a scowl deepened on his forehead. "No shit?" he growled. "If he has, I'll bet he's the only fuckin' one."

"You got that close to right, Tonto. Now, first off, I want you to relax in this joint. You need to practice keeping that surly expression off your face. No kidding. What you look like will play a lot on how the court-martial panel will perceive you. I want you to be cool, confident, and avoid any appearance of distrust."

"That's a tall damn order, Pope. Especially since I *don't* trust four captains and a commander sitting in judgment on my life."

Marino raised a hand in dismissal. "Military justice ain't the best system, but it's the only one we've got for this case. Cool out and be ready to go in there with a beaming smile on your face three days from now.''

''God, it's that soon?''

''You knew that.''

Tonto looked even more ill at ease. ''Yeah. Only I was tryin' to ignore it.''

Acceptance of the proximity of the trial generated a long silence. Tonto finished his beer and signaled the hovering waiter for another. Pope drank off the last of a San Miguel and raised the brown bottle for a refill. At last Tonto broke their protracted quiet with an observation.

''You know, I'll bet we're the only ones in here drinking beer.''

''Naw. The lowly cameramen on the television news crews can't afford single malt, even at these low prices.''

''Yeah, you've got a point. They're just like us. I wonder if they ever get disgusted at the bullshit those pretty faces spit out every day?''

Lieutenant Marino broke a grin. ''No doubt. That's why you won't see them much in here. They're all down on Truman Key.'' He suddenly put on a stricken expression. ''It just came to me. What if some of these scumbags get wind of the court-martial?''

Tonto groaned. ''You just made my day, Pope. That happens, an' we get fried in our own grease.''

Captain Bill Andrews left the French Consulate in Saigon with a broad grin on his face. It had taken him three weeks to get an interview with the slender, sardonic young bureaucrat whose office he had just left. Slippery as greased cat shit, the Special Forces officer mused. Never a straight answer to a direct question. But he had come away with something he hoped would be valuable to his SEAL friend, Marino. He headed for one of the better lounges on Rang Tre Street, which he knew to still have a working telephone.

Once he had paid for the privilege of using the instrument by ordering a double shot, he dialed the number of the BOQ at the Special Forces compound.

"BOQ, this is Sutton, sir," came after the third ring.

"Captain Andrews, Sutton. I want to leave a message for a Navy lieutenant, name of Marino."

"Uh—he's not staying here, sir. At least he's not signed in."

"Okay, thanks." Bill Andrews hung up with a frown.

He finished his drink and left the bar. He would have to go back on post to use the military communications in order to run down Marino. With an automatic gesture, he raised his arm to summon a cyclo cab. He told the driver to take him to the Special Forces compound.

Bill Andrews used the telephone in the Two Shed (S-2 Office) of his B Detachment. He tried Binh Thuy first. Again, no luck. One operator, at the Base Locator office, even claimed not to know of anyone by that name. By the time Andrews had his fourth negative, he began to wonder if military telephone operators knew anything about anything. He gave up on NAVSPECWARV headquarters.

His next call was to Tre Noc. "No, sir," he was told. "Lieutenant Marino and Chief Waters left here day before yesterday for Saigon."

"Thanks." Bill Andrews hung up and turned to stare out the window. "That means the trial is coming up soon," he told himself. "But they may have left, they sure didn't show up here."

He grabbed up the phone again and called the Military Arrivals desk at Tan Son Nhut. Somehow he had to connect with Marino and give him the news. The more Andrews thought of it, the more important it seemed to him.

Francie Song lay nestled in the crook of Kent Welby's elbow. She sighed contentedly and arched her back as his dexterous manipulations with his other hand brought a surge of rapture from her groin. They had made love twice, hungrily, eagerly, before settling down to a more domestic routine.

Francie cooked them dinner, never bothering to put on clothes. They ate it, equally naked, and then renewed ardor in her eyes had summoned them back to the bed. Their third coupling had been splendorous. No man before had ever treated her with such care and attention to her needs. She could get aroused merely thinking about it. And she worked harder, with more concentration, than ever before, to bring pleasure to her darling Kent Welby. Now, incredibly, he seemed ready for another amorous encounter.

"Oooh, yes—yess—yessss. Asian men do not find such activity to be to their liking. They have no interest in pleasuring the woman, only themselves," she criticized in a whisper.

"I find everything about you interesting," Doc Welby replied softly, exerting more pressure on his manipulations.

"I know you do. Or you would not spend so much time on doing such wonderful things to me. Oh, hurry, dearest. Fill me with your great American magic."

Gladly, Doc complied. They made full contact, melded, became one. The world whirled away as Doc thrust deeply within her. Every thought of Betty, and even his deep concern over the court-martial of Tonto Waters, fled in a world of heady passion.

CHAPTER 24 ──────────

COURT CAME to order at 0900 hours on Thursday of that week. After the usual beginning formalities, Judge Benson turned to CDR Quade. "Does the Government have an opening statement?"

"Yes, we certainly have, Your Honor."

"Proceed then."

Quade drew himself up and commenced without resorting to notes. "Your Honor, gentlemen of the court. We have here a situation old as mankind. An attractive, beguiling woman inveigles a man into doing her dirty work for her. Wasn't the first woman to elicit classified information reputed to be Eve? Remember Samson and Delilah. Didn't Cleopatra use her wiles to try to get information on the strength of Rome from Julius Caesar? And later from Mark Anthony? There is nothing new or original about the crime of espionage. Nor about the role women have frequently played in its commission.

"No, sadly, it is an old story." Quade paused and crossed to a position where he spoke from behind the accused, one elbow resting on the front counter of the witness box. "Fortunately, it has not been often that it has involved members of the United States Armed Forces," his voice cracked as he delivered this slight exaggeration. "No, gentlemen, *this* is enough a rarity as to be called special. You heard read the charges the accused faces. The Government is prepared to show how the accused's accomplice, the Frenchwoman, Eloise Daladier, used her articles in *Le Monde* to transmit classified information to her employers in North Vietnam. Further, the Government will show how Miss Daladier recruited and compromised the loyalty of Chief Waters, through gifts of sex and money, and enticed him to engage in espionage against the United States.'' Quade stopped for a moment, clasped his hands before his belt buckle, turned away from the defense table, and gave his profile to the panel.

"The Government will show, through witnesses, that the accused and his accomplice were arrested in a hotel room at Tre Noc, in the act of exchanging information and—ah—favors. You will also hear, from a witness previously unknown to counsel for the Government, that on other occasions, earlier, the accused passed classified documents and verbal information to Miss Daladier.''

Taken off guard, Tonto plucked at the sleeve of Pope's Class A tunic. Lieutenant Marino turned an astonished face toward him. He read the question in the face of Chief Waters that he had asked himself, *"Who the fuck is that?"* Confident that this had to be some last-minute contrivance of Quade's and Lailey's, Marino came to his feet.

"Your Honor, I have to protest this spur-of-the-moment surprise witness. Under the conditions of the discovery motion, I should have been advised of the existence of such a witness, provided with a name, and given the opportunity to investigate the . . .'' His voice cut off when Judge Benson raised an admonishing hand.

"Yes—yes, I understand. But this is best discussed out of the hearing of the panel.'' He turned to the court-martial panel. "Gentlemen, if you will withdraw for a few minutes, we will inquire into this unexpected development.''

"All rise,'' the bailiff intoned.

When the panel had filed out and the door closed behind him, Judge Benson folded his hands and leaned forward on the table that served him as a bench. "The defense has raised a valid question, Mr. Counsel. Even *I* did not know of this witness. Perhaps you could explain it in a way that will enlighten us and justify your inclusion of this witness?"

CDR Quade walked slowly to his table, chin down, his face a study of concentration. He hadn't expected this nonlawyer, inexperienced legal officer to catch on to that. For that matter, he had not been aware of the witness until early the previous morning.

LCDR Barry Lailey appeared in the doorway to the Saigon office of CDR Erwin Quade at 1040 hours on Wednesday, the day before the trial. He beamed broadly and literally rubbed palms together in anticipation of the news he would impart. Stepping over the threshold, he brought with him an obviously Oriental man somewhere in his late twenties, Quade judged.

"I found what you were looking for, Erwin. Hang Jung Minh. He is from Tre Noc, and he has seen Waters with Miss Daladier on several occasions."

CDR Quade showed his doubt and irritation. "The CID has produced several from here in Saigon, including Gaston, the maître d' at the Maison Dupris. All have seen the two together."

"But have any actually seen an exchange of information for any sort of reward?" Lailey glowed with the importance of his find. Perhaps, he had reasoned, listening to Minh's recounting, something was behind the charges he had invented after all.

Sudden interest flared on the face of Erwin Quade, who leaned forward abruptly, oblivious to the stack of case records that spilled across his desk when he bumped them. "Tell me more." A light of suspicion glowed in his gray-green eyes. "This isn't one of your inventions is it, Lucky?"

"No, not at all. Mr. Minh came to me."

"Why you?"

"I have seen him around Tre Noc when I visited the base, he saw me, naturally, knew of who I am. He traveled clear up to Binh Thuy to reveal what he knew."

"Why was that?" Quade directed his question to Minh, rather than Lailey.

Hang Jung Minh bobbed his head and pressed his palms together in the Buddhist gesture of peace and honesty. "Everyone know at Tre Noc of the Chief Waters's trouble. Most do not believe. But I know. I see him with lady. He take long, brown—how you say?—envelope from her, pass her papers."

"When was this?"

"Not long ago. Maybe two weeks. There other times, too."

"Tell me about them."

The man who called himself Minh had been carefully instructed on this aspect long and well by Major Rudinov. They had rehearsed it thoroughly. It didn't surprise Minh that the major seemed to know exactly, and in advance, the questions he would be asked. Now, he responded with the ease of absolute truthfulness.

"Three, four times. Before lady go away for long time."

CDR Quade knew of Eloise Daladier's assignment to Pakistan. This fitted too nicely to be another crude attempt by the bottom man in his class at Annapolis. He smiled, nodded. "Would you mind if someone took down what you have just said?"

"Excuse me, please?"

"I want to have a written statement. For that we need a recorder."

"Oh, yes, yes. That be good by me."

"Thank you, Mr. Minh." And Erwin Quade meant every word of gratitude he would deliver that long, informative morning.

It didn't bother CDR Quade in the least that he had not been given time to notify the defense. He maintained his calm as he answered Judge Benson's questions.

"The witness, one Hàng Jung Minh from Tre Noc, came forward only yesterday. He presented himself to another of the Government's witnesses, LCDR Lailey. He provided vital information to the Government's case."

"Did you take time to verify what he told you?"

"As much as possible, Your Honor. It was because of doing that I found myself unable to inform defense counsel of my new witness."

Judge Benson considered that for a long, silent minute. "It is irregular, and I don't like it. But since the burden of proof lies on the Government, you must be granted every leeway in obtaining that proof. I will allow the inclusion. Now, let's have the panel back in."

Chief Tom Waters leaned to Lt. Carl Marino and whispered urgently. "You mean the judge is going to let him get away with that?"

"That's how he ruled. Could make for good grounds on appeal."

Tonto's high, smooth brow furrowed. "Hell," he growled, "I don't fancy doin' life at Portsmouth or Leavenworth waitin' on an appeal."

Five sharp raps on the connecting door were followed by the usual, "All rise."

When the panel had resumed their seats, the Military Judge explained. "As you no doubt heard before recessing, the Government has uncovered a new witness who, I have determined, has vital information relating to the Government's case-in-chief. Therefore we will return to the opening statement of counsel for the Government."

"I have very little to say. This new witness will show that there was an ongoing relationship of spy and accomplice that resulted in the compromising of the tactical and strategic position of our Armed Forces in the Delta region of South Vietnam. We will satisfy the requirement that you be able to find, beyond any reasonable doubt, for the guilt of the accused. Thank you."

CDR Erwin Quade sat down and turned his head away from the Panel in order to hide the smug smile which he could not suppress. "Counsel for the accused?" Judge Benson prompted when Lieutenant Marino failed to rise at once.

"Yes, Your Honor. I have very little to say, beyond what I said the other day." He came forcefully to his feet. "This is all a sorry attempt to discredit a fine young Petty Officer, one of the best SEALs I have ever known. The able counsel for the Government cannot prove the Government's case because there is nothing truthful in it. Whoever this surprise witness turns out to be, his testimony will hold no more water than the thin tissue that supports the allegations of the Government's star witness, LCDR Barry Lailey. We will show their alleged evidence to be false and without merit, so that you, Gentlemen, will be compelled to exercise that critical element of any judgment, the concept of *Reasonable Doubt*, and find the accused not guilty. Thank you."

Lieutenant Marino took his seat and followed the judge's eyes to the large sweep second hand dial of the clock. It showed 1135 hours. CDR Benson touched fingers to his lips, darted his gaze to CDR Quade. "Is the Government ready to proceed with calling witnesses?"

"We are, Your Honor."

"How long do you anticipate the first one will require?"

"With cross and redirect, very likely three-quarters of an hour."

"Very well. It is close to the noon hour. This court will recess until thirteen hundred. Be ready at that time, gentlemen."

"All rise," the bailiff droned.

First the panel departed, then Judge Benson. Lieutenant Marino led Chief Waters from the courtroom. Both remained silent, lost in their private thoughts, until they found a small, doorway lunchroom. Then Lieutenant Marino laid out what strategy he had pieced together since the introduction of the mystery witness.

"*I don't want to meet you anymore!*" Francie Song blurted vehemently as she turned in anger away from Sgt. Elmore Yates.

Tightly, Yates reminded her of the ultimatum that lay between them. "You don't have any choice."

Francie looked across the otherwise-peaceful surroundings of the Buddhist shrine. Physically as well as mentally, she experienced such a turmoil she could hardly keep her attention on her work. To make matters worse, she had found that recently her dresses and black pajama trousers fit her tightly. Soon she would begin to show. That she remembered only too well from Thran. Would it be another boy, or a girl? No matter what gender, she had first to get this terrible person out of her life. Why had she ever agreed to—no! She rejected the word, forced its implications out of her consciousness.

"What I am doing is not right," she protested. "I should not have ever agreed to do this. I hate that awful man, as I hate you," she ended hotly.

Yates reached up insolently and cupped one of her breasts. With a cruel force he pinched the nipple between forefinger and thumb. "You are going to learn to like me a whole lot, before this is over. Believe that." His nasty, yellowish eyes flickered with inner amusement at her reaction. Unrestrained, unpleasant laughter rose to cross his full, sneering lips.

I could kill him, Francie thought in utter desperation. Only how? For all the cruelty she had witnessed in her homeland, she remained ignorant of the means of ending the life of someone and disposing of the remains. She would be caught, and what then of Thran and old Phan Vu? And, what of Kent Welby? She could never tell him the real reason. Still, she could not quell her revulsion to Yates.

"You have always disgusted me. You always will."

"Not true, my sweet piece. Now, you have something for me?"

A sickness totally unrelated to her pregnancy, rose in Francie's throat as she dug a hand into her purse and extracted an envelope. Without looking at it, she handed it over to Yates. He took it in his usual superior attitude. His lips curled into a sign of contempt.

"This time I have money for you," he informed Francie.

"I don't want it!"

Yates laughed at her, softly, deridingly. "Then I'll keep it for myself."

"Do so and be damned. You make me feel dirty."

He pinched her nipple again. "I'll make you feel something else . . . when the time is right." Abruptly he released his grip and turned away from her.

Yates left Francie standing alone, sobbing, beside the small, brass, potbellied statue of the Buddha.

Planting a false, corroborative witness on Lt. Carl Marino did not constitute the full extent of Kovietski/Rudinov's plans to exact his revenge. He had also learned from his redheaded contact at Tre Noc that Marino's AOIC (Assistant Officer in Charge) remained in hospital as a result of the tender ministrations of General Giap. If Marino were to lose his leading chief and his second-in-command at nearly the same time, he would be crippled in the field. He might well make mistakes. To that end, he appealed to two Cambodians, members of the Khymer Rouge, and agents of the KGB Wet Affairs.

"Your mission is simple, if risky. You are to travel by covert means to the field hospital at Binh Thuy, Vietnam. There you will find someone to assist you in your mission."

"Is it to be a trained operative, Comrade?"

"No," Rudinov replied. "Someone you recruit. Some credulous man or woman working in the hospital there to be your *obmanoote*. Your dupe," he added in Cambodian for clarification. "After you accomplish what you go there for, you will arrange that this person is found at the scene."

One of the Cambodians snickered. "Comrade Major, you are clever enough to be doing this yourself, no?" he asked in his native tongue.

Rudinov stiffened but prevented the flush he felt rising in his neck from betraying himself. "That is not your concern. Here, let me outline to you your route of approach. Remember every detail. You will not be permitted to take maps."

Both *Mokryee Della* agents bent over the map Rudinov spread on the table. He pointed out landmarks and places where the local Viet Cong establishment would assist them. When satisfied the pair had committed it to memory, he went over the actual mission.

"It would be advisable if it appeared a result of his previous injuries. Some subtle means of ensuring his death. Then you would not have to sacrifice your dupe." Rudinov shrugged expansively, indicating his utter indifference to this faceless, nameless accomplice. "The important thing is to make certain that this American officer, Cyrus Rhodes, is dead."

CHAPTER 25 ⎯⎯⎯⎯⎯⎯⎯⎯

Tonto Waters did not enjoy his meal. A bowl of noodles and broth, even one generously filled with slices of roasted duck breast, would never replace a big, juicy hamburger in his mind. It was a damn poor substitute for a steak, for that matter. Yet, that is not what put him off his feed. His mind refused to empty of worry over the trial, and this surprise witness in particular.

They had nothing to prove his innocence. Everything rested on how convincingly the Government put on its case. And Tonto knew from experience that Barry Lailey could be a convincing liar. He gave little hope to this undisclosed idea of Pope Marino. It simply would come up with a blank at best, or more bad news at worst. He walked in silence, to the left of Lieutenant Marino, back to the mansion which had been converted for use by the Staff Judge Advocate.

He had been surprised how many court-martials were held in that old ballroom. He did not recall that so many sailors and other troops broke the law so often before they came to Vietnam. The building literally swarmed with military lawyers, witnesses, accused enlisted and petty officers, and the regiment of clerks necessary to keep the legal boat afloat. One could easily tell the bright young men, most fresh from law school, who served as counsel for the Government.

Rosy-cheeked, hair closely cropped, newly arrived

from the World, they wore the jungle cammo uniforms seen everywhere. Only their black-against-green insignia of rank and branch indicated they were almost to a man the equivalent of lieutenants in the Navy. That made them captains in the Army. And all had the branch badge of a wreath backgrounding a quill and saber of the Judge Advocate General Corps. He saw it everywhere; in offices, in the halls, in the courtroom where his case was being heard, and on every collar of those he encountered there. Tonto fervently wished he had never seen it at all. Nothing for it, though. They had to go on with this thing.

First to be called for the afternoon session was the Shore Patrol Chief. At the request of Quade's assistant, the bailiff left the court for the witness room and summoned the Chief Master at Arms. When he entered, the assistant counsel rattled off the ritual with practised ease.

"Please come forward, Chief, pass through the bar and turn to your right. Step up on the witness stand and face the panel." When that had been complied with, he went on. "Raise your right hand. 'Do you swear, or affirm, that the evidence you are to give before this court be the truth, the whole truth and nothing but the truth?' "

"I do."

"Please sit down, Chief. State your full name, your rank, duty station, and service number."

"Toomey, Colin H., Chief Master at Arms. I am assigned to Seven-seventy-ninth Shore Patrol detachment, Bihn Thuy, Republic of Vietnam. My service number is RN34577803."

"Thank you, Chief Toomey. At the time in question, on or about . . ." He gave the date, time, and place. "Were you engaged in your regular duties at Binh Thuy?"

"Yes, I was, sir."

"And can you tell us what happened subsequent to that?"

"I received a request to report to the S-Two—uh—the Intelligence Officer, Lieutenant Commander Lailey, sir."

"For the record, is that Lieutenant Commander Barry Lailey?"

"Yes, it is, sir."

"Did he tell you for what purpose?"

"He said we was to go to Tre Noc to arrest a female spy."

Beyond a swiftly arched eyebrow, Pope Marino gave no outward sign of having even heard the answer. He did make a note on a yellow legal pad. LCDR Wayland was continuing with his witness.

"And you subsequently went to Tre Noc?"

"Yes, sir. By helicopter, sir."

"Who, if anyone, accompanied you?"

"Commander Lailey, sir."

Wayland rolled his eyes in a show of exasperation. "I mean any other Shore Patrolmen?"

"No, sir. It wasn't judged necessary, I imagine."

"Oh? Why is that?"

The burly Chief gave a superior smile. "To arrest a female, and a foreign national at that, sir?"

That brought involuntary smiles from some on the panel. Wayland looked appealingly at Judge Benson. "I think I can understand your confidence, Chief. I merely wanted to establish who all went along. Thank you."

"Will you proceed, Commander?"

"Yes, Your Honor. What did you do upon arrival in Tre Noc, Chief?"

"We learned from security—ah—the gate guard, sir, that Miss Daladier took a cyclo to the hotel in the na—ah—Vietnamese village, sir."

"You and Commander Lailey proceeded to the hotel?"

"Yes, sir."

"And what did you do when you got there?"

"We got the room number for Miss Daladier and went right up."

"Did the desk clerk announce you?"

"No, sir. I don't think there are any telephones in the rooms."

A snicker came from somewhere among the half dozen military trial buffs in the gallery. Judge Benson gave them a stony glare. "Please continue, Counsel," he rumbled over steepled fingers.

"So, Commander Lailey and you went to the room. What did you do and what did you find?"

"At the direction of Commander Lailey, I knocked on the door. It was opened by a man in a state of considerable undress."

"Objection, Your Honor. The degree of dress or undress is not germane to the charges and specifications as presented.

"Sustained. Please keep this train on the track, Counselor."

"Yes, Your Honor. The door was opened by a man. Did you know his identity?"

"No, sir. Not at the time. He was subsequently identified to me as Chief Petty Officer Waters, Thomas J., sir."

"And do you see the same CPO Waters in this court?"

"Yes, sir, right over there."

"Let the record show that Chief Toomey has pointed to the accused. Now, Chief, what happened next?"

"Commander Lailey pushed his way into the room."

"I beg your pardon?" Wayland interrupted.

"Commander Lailey demanded admission to the room."

"And was it granted?"

"Yes, sir."

"What happened after that?"

"We discovered a woman in the bed, buck naked, sir."

"Object! Goes to relevancy, Your Honor," Marino interrupted from his seat.

"Agreed. Objection sustained. Can we move this on, Counsel, without a peep show?"

Wayland flushed to the roots of his blond hair. "Yes, Your Honor."

No wonder Quade let him handle this examination, Pope Marino thought ruefully. *This way he don't take the flak. Smart feller.*

Wayland continued. "Were any statements made at that time?"

"Yes, sir." Chief Toomey went on to describe what Tonto Waters said, and what LCDR Lailey said. Also what was said by Eloise Daladier.

"And what happened after that?"

"Commander Lailey ordered me to place Chief Wat—er—the accused under arrest for espionage."

"Which you subsequently did. Was Miss Daladier likewise arrested?"

"Yes, sir."

"Then what did you do?"

"We allowed both of them to get dressed and took them into custody."

LCDR Wayland walked to the Government's desk and lifted a plastic evidence bag. "At the time of this arrest, was anything beside the persons named taken into custody?"

"Yes, sir. There was a notebook in the purse of Miss Daladier."

"Now, Chief, I show you this envelope and ask you to tell me if you recognize its content?"

Chief Toomey examined the contents of the bag through the clear side. "Yes, sir, it looks to be the same notebook I took from Miss Daladier's purse."

"Thank you, Chief. Is there anything by which you might make positive identification?"

"Yes, sir. If I may open it?" At a nod from the judge, he did so and then opened the cover of the notebook. "I placed my initials on the flyleaf, sir. And I see them there now."

"Very good. Now, can you tell us if you observed anything significant about that notebook that you recall?"

"Yes, sir, it appeared to have notes on military units and operations."

"Thank you, Chief." He turned to the bench. "I would ask that this be marked Government's number One for identification and entered into evidence."

Judge Benson nodded and Wayland approached, to hand the bag to the recorder, who placed a sticker on it, wrote a moment, and then returned to her stenograph machine. Wayland returned to the witness by way of Lieutenant Marino at the defense table, to whom he showed the notebook.

"Now, Chief, can you tell the court if any particular entry in that notebook stood out over all of the others?"

"Yes, sir. On the last page, there was only a single line written. It said SEALs, sir."

"Seals, as in the sea animal, flippers and balancing a ball?"

"Oh, no, sir. It was written all in capital letters, as in Navy SEALs, sir."

"I see. And there was nothing more written?"

"No, sir."

"Why do you suppose that was?" Wayland tried to sneak past.

"Objection! Calls for speculation by the witness," Pope Marino broke in without even rising.

"Sustained. Please avoid that sort of thing, Counsel."

"Yes, your honor." But the smug smile on the face of Erwin Quade indicated that he and his apparently inept cocounsel were pleased to get it in the hearing of the panel. "Moving right along then. What did you do after taking the accused and his accomplice into custody?"

"Objection!" This time Lieutenant Marino came rapidly to his feet. "Counsel is being argumentive and the phrase 'his accomplice' is prejudicial to the accused. Neither he nor Miss Daladier has as yet been convicted of anything."

Judge Benson hid a smile behind a large, hairy hand. "Quite right, Counsel. The objection is sustained. Be a little more attentive to the rules of taking testimony in the future, Commander."

LCDR Wayland tried to look contrite. "Yes, Your Honor. Now, what was done following the arrestees being dressed and searched?"

"They were escorted back to Binh Thuy."

"Was Miss Daladier detained there?"

"No, sir. She was sent forward, here to Saigon."

"And did you have anything further to do with this case?"

"No, sir. Except when I was called by your office to be interviewed by the CID."

"Thank you, Chief. That will be all."

"Does the defense wish to examine?"

"Yes, Your Honor." Pope Marino rose and walked up close to the witness and leaned familiarly on the counter before the Chief. All the while he ran though what manner and in which order he would put his questions.

His face held a musing expression. "Chief Toomey, as I recall, you were five times fleet heavyweight champion, is that correct?"

Chief Toomey beamed, pleased with the recognition. "Yes, sir."

"That's quite a record. I enjoyed watching film of you boxing."

Warmed by the flattery, Toomey relaxed. "Just good with my hands, sir, that's all."

With his subject placed at ease, Lt. Marino launched

into his line of questioning. "Chief Toomey, were you acquainted with the accused prior to the trip to Tre Noc with LCDR Lailey?"

"No, sir. Only by reputation."

"And would you say his reputation to be good . . . or bad?"

Chief Toomey shot a nervous, worried glance toward CDR Quade. "Uh—er—"

"I want your opinion of that, Chief, not that of the Government's counsel."

"Uh—very good, sir."

"Would you say even . . . excellent?"

"Well—ah—yes, sir."

"Now, Chief, on direct examination, you testified that you were told the trip to Tre Noc was to arrest a female spy. Is that correct?"

"Yes, sir."

"Any mention that she had an accomplice?"

Colin Toomey had been involved with enough courts-martial to understand the procedural error that had slipped by. His face went blank and white for an instant. "Uh—no—ah—sir."

"No mention of a sailor who was aiding her? No mention of Chief Waters?"

Toomey tried to fill the loophole. "Not at that time, sir."

Pope Marino's eyes narrowed. "When, then?"

"Af—after we was in the room."

"In other words, not until LCDR Lailey found someone convenient to pin the charge on?"

"Objection. This witness is put on for the purpose of establishing probable cause and to attest to the fact that an arrest of the accused was in fact accomplished. Counsel for the accused is also attempting to put words in the mouth of my—er—the Government's witness."

Amusement crinkled the well-tanned skin around the

eyes of Judge Benson. "I'll allow the first part of that. Sustained due to improper cross. You may proceed, Lieutenant Marino."

"Let me rephrase that. When you left Binh Thuy you had no idea that you were to arrest two or more persons, did you?"

"No, sir. But, we found him there," Toomey protested. "Caught him with his pants down."

That last brought smiles from several on the panel, the three MCPOs in particular. Lieutenant Marino produced a startled expression, as though he did not believe what he had just heard. "We'll move on. Now, this notebook, Government's number One for identification. Did you, or Commander Lailey produce a search warrant before searching the possessions? For that matter, what about the arrest warrant?"

"No, sir," Toomey admitted, looking miserable. "We didn't have either one. There wasn't time."

" 'Wasn't time,' " Marino repeated softly. Then he turned to the bench. "Your Honor, the defense moves to disallow the Government's number One because it was the product of an illegal search and seizure."

Judge Benson could no longer contain his amusement. " 'Fruit of a tainted vine,' eh? Yes, I think—"

Wayland interrupted. "There are precedents for that, Your Honor."

Benson considered. "Hummm. I'll hear them. Would the panel please retire while we mull this over?" They rose as one and filed from the room. When the door had closed firmly behind them, Judge Benson leaned forward and spoke over folded hands. "Lieutenant Marino, you are proving far more adroit than I had expected. I will hear the argument of the Government's counsel, but I admit I am inclined to rule in your favor."

His voice tight, as though he had to force the words through a constricted throat, LCDR Wayland cited three items of case law, all thoroughly obscure enough to convince the judge that the cocounsels had long ago anticipated this. And he believed they likewise considered the search to be illegal, if not the whole affair. When Wayland concluded, he leaned back and stared off at the cherubs on the ceiling.

At last he came back. "All right. I'm going to rule on this. The notebook is out. No—no, Counsel, I will not need any more of your arcane citations."

"Thank you, Your Honor," Pope Marino said with relief. "Now, as to the arrests themselves, I move for a dismissal on the grounds of no warrant pertaining in the cause cited."

"Well-done," Judge Benson praised. "But we have only heard from one witness. I think we need a little more before deciding on so drastic a course. Bring back the panel. And there will be no more mention of the notebook after I instruct them."

True to his word, Judge Benson informed the panel that they were to disregard any mention of or presence of a notebook, or what they had been told the contents might be. He concluded by a gentle comment to Lieutenant Marino. "You may continue, Counsel."

"No further questions."

"Does the Government wish redirect?"

"No, Your Honor."

"Then call your next witness."

"The Government calls Lieutenant Commander Barry Lailey."

CHAPTER 26 ⸻

LCDR LAILEY entered through the tall double doors with a regal stride that Carl Marino thought could be best described as pompous. The pear bulge of his waist robbed his entrance of dignity. He passed through the gate in the bar to the usual litany of instructions, took his place on the witness stand, and raised his hand.

He was duly sworn and seated. After stating his name, duty assignment, and service number, he waited silently for the questioning. Erwin Quade began lightly.

"Commander Lailey, it has been previously testified that you summoned Chief Toomey of the Shore Patrol and had him accompany you to Tre Noc. For what purpose was that?"

"To place one Eloise Daladier, and any accomplices that might be with her, under arrest."

Obviously he and Toomey had discussed this breach of procedure in violation of the court-imposed gag order, Lieutenant Mario thought, his mouth turned down in a grim line. If they continued to collaborate like that, he had damn little chance of a favorable verdict.

"And why was this?" Quade pressed on.

"Sir, I had reason to believe that Miss Daladier was engaged in espionage against the United States."

"What was that reason?"

"May I preface the reason with an explanation?" To Quade's spoken permission, he went on. "For some time we have been aware of a leak of vital information, much of it classified Secret and Top Secret, from some source inside the Naval forces in the Delta area. Recently I came upon another article relating to our SEAL detachment at Tre Noc that came close to breaching security. It was also written by Eloise Daladier, a French national. It occurred to me that this was a dandy way to transmit information. I knew Miss Dalidier to be extremely friendly with a chief petty officer highly placed in the SEAL detachment."

Lailey went on to tell of reading the copy of the latest story she had routinely filed. Then he added the damaging part. "I thought the information on our parakeet operation to free some captive servicemen to be classified Top Secret and wondered how she had acquired access to it. Although the article did not refer directly to that, it contained language I marked as pointing directly to that operation. Then I recalled that she had been present in the Delta some months back, during another operation to interdict large supplies of arms, munitions and medicine in the hands of the enemy. From nearly the day of her arrival, we began to have problems."

"Could you illustrate what sort of difficulty your forces encountered?"

"Yes, sir. Patrols were ambushed. Equipment breakdowns grew in number and frequency. Shortly after Miss Daladier left the area, things returned to normal."

Lieutenant Marino rose to his feet. "Move to strike all of this as irrelevant. What does it have to do with the accused?"

"I can connect it up, Your Honor," Erwin Quade hastened to insert.

Judge Benson gave him a fish eye. "You had better. I am inclined to agree with defense counsel."

"From your experience as an intelligence officer, did

you draw any conclusions from this recollection and the articles?''

"Yes, I did, sir. I decided that Miss Daladier was a spy.''

"And then what did you do?''

"I made arrangements to have her access to the Delta withdrawn, only to find out she had departed Binh Thuy for Tre Noc on the last flight of the day.''

"What did that cause you to do?''

"I believed the mission then currently under preparation was about to be further compromised. I called for a helicopter and summoned a Shore Patrolman to accompany me.''

"That would be Chief Master at Arms Toomey?''

"Yes, sir, the same.''

"You said earlier that you intended to apprehend Miss Daladier and any accomplices. Were you confident that a single SP Chief would be sufficient for the task?''

"Of course.'' Lailey looked across the room, directly at the panel. "She is a young woman, healthy and agile, but hardly a match for a strong man. Anyone caught in her presence, in the act of conveying secrets or receiving pay for such, would be too shocked to put up much resistance. Which proved to be the case.''

"Let's cut to the chase, Lieutenant Commander. When you arrived in Tre Noc, did you proceed directly to where you could find your suspect?''

"No, sir. I had to ask around until I learned that she was at the hotel in the village. The chief and I went there at once. From the room clerk, we learned which room she occupied and went upstairs to that room.''

"After gaining access to the room, what did you find?''

"We found the accused, dressed only in skivvies. Miss Daladier was in bed, unclothed.''

"Did you find any incriminating evidence?''

"I object to this line of questioning, Your Honor," Pope Marino interrupted. "It goes to your ruling on the Government's number One."

"I'm going to allow this for a moment," Judge Benson ruled. "Proceed."

"What did you find?"

"A notebook in Miss Daladier's purse."

"Same objection, Your Honor. And I would add that there has been no proper foundation laid as to the ownership of the purse."

"Sustained. Can we get past this notebook business, Counsel?"

"I apologize, Your Honor. Did you obtain an arrest warrant or search warrant prior to going to Tre Noc?"

"No, sir. In cases of espionage there is hardly ever time enough to observe the formalities. Spies rarely hang around waiting for judges to sign warrants. I acted based on my interpretation of what I had observed in the past and at that time."

"Very well." Erwin Quade went on with Barry Lailey's testimony. Lailey did not lie outright, but he did continue to shade the truth in such a way as to make it appear Tonto Waters was guilty. When Quade finished, he turned away.

Judge Benson glanced at the clock. "Do you anticipate a long cross-examination?"

"I have nothing on cross at this time, Your Honor. Although I reserve the right to recall the witness for cross-examination at a later date."

"You may." Judge Benson turned to LCDR Lailey. "You are admonished not to discuss this proceeding, or your testimony, with anyone other than the Government's counsel, the counsel for the defense, or the accused, if so wish to talk to him. Other than these four persons, if you are approached by anyone, you are to say that you cannot discuss anything that has been said or done. Do you understand?''

"Yes, Your Honor.''

"Very well, Lieutenant Commander Lailey. You are excused, subject to recall by defense counsel. I'm going to put you on a string. You are to leave a telephone number with the trial division office where you may be reached at all times, and be able to return upon notice within thirty minutes.''

"Yes, Your Honor.''

"You may step down. Now, the hour is getting late. Will your next witness for the Government take much time?''

"I don't expect it to, Your Honor,'' Quade responded.

"Then call the witness.''

"The Government calls Hang Jung Minh.''

Minh entered and was sworn. At first sight of him, Tonto Waters became agitated, wrote furiously on his notepad, and handed it to Pope Marino. "*I know this dork,*'' it read. Marino gave him an inquiring gaze. Tonto scribbled furiously while Minh took the oath.

"*He's a friggin' VC cadre.*''

"Would you state your name, occupation, and place of residence?''

"I am Hang Jung Minh, I am a cadre lieutenant for the Seventh Provisional Liberation Front, what you call the Viet Cong. I—ahaha—do not have a regular residence, you understand?''

"The guy's got balls,'' Pope Marino whispered to Waters.

"I'd like to kick 'em off him,'' Tonto growled.

"Now, Lieutenant Minh, have you been offered any inducement for being present here today?''

"No, sir. Ah—I have been granted immunity from capture as an enemy, and given a reward of ten thousand piasters.''

"Anything else?"

"Nothing else. Oh, I was offered an opportunity to join a provisional reconnaissance unit, or the Kit Carson Scouts. I have refused." His smug smirk told of his intent for the future.

"Do you recognize anyone in this courtroom?"

"Yes. The officer and—ah—Petty Officer?—seated at this table to my left."

"Let the record show that Lieutenant Minh has pointed out the accused and his counsel."

Tonto wrote furiously again. *Goddamn, is Lailey trying to cook your ass, too?* Marino shook his head slightly. CDR Quade continued.

"How is it that you know Lieutenant Marino?"

"I have fought against his Men with Green Faces. I have seen him at places in the Delta."

"And the accused?"

"I have seen him many times."

"In combat?"

"Yes. And other places."

"Could you tell us where these other places happened to be?"

"Yes. Three times here in Saigon. He was with a lady. Each time he gave her a large envelope and she handed him a smaller one, very fat. With money, I think."

"Object. Calls for a conclusion."

"Sustained. Instruct your witness, please, Counsel."

"In our courts, Lieutenant Minh, you cannot testify to what you think, only to what you saw and what you heard."

"Ah-yes. I understand."

"Then go on, please."

"I see them many times in Tre Noc."

"The same woman?"

"Yes."

"And what did you see and what, if anything did you hear?"

"He—the Petty Officer—give her small box one time. She give him envelope, not so fat as those in Saigon. Other times, they just talk."

"Did you hear what they said?"

"Only some. First time, he say, 'I di'nt find out anything.' They talk some more, then go to hotel. They not come out for three hours."

"I . . . see. On the other occasions, did you hear what was said?"

"Not much. One time, maybe month ago, he said, 'It's top secret. Good stuff.' " Minh looked directly at Tonto when he spoke that.

Tonto's pen was fast at work. *The lying son of a bitch! I never said anything like that to Eloise.*

Lieutenant Marino leaned toward him and whispered urgently, "Remember what I said about keeping cool. The guys on that panel may not appear to be noticing you, but you can be sure they're checking you out all the time. Don't let this little gook get to you."

Tonto grunted in reply and Minh spoke again. "Every time she give him package."

"Thank you, Lieutenant Minh. Is there anything else you can tell us?"

"No. Only that he is hell of a good soldier, fight like crazy."

"He's a sailor, but I know what you mean to say," Quade replied. "Nothing further, Your Honor.

"Cross?"

"I have nothing for this witness. I would request he be made available for recall if need be."

"Granted." Judge Benson launched into his usual admonishment of the witness and excused him. "We'll recess at this time until oh-eight-thirty tomorrow."

Once the panel had left the room, the face of Tonto

Waters dissolved into a mask of trepidation. Lieutenant Marino escorted him from the courtroom. What could he use against this enemy commander? And what could he find to challenge Barry Lailey?

Pope Marino had not yet heard from Capt. Bill Andrews. When he called the Special Forces compound, he got the familiar runaround that told him Andrews was in the field on an op. What shitty timing, he complained to himself. After a day in court, especially one with Barry Lailey present, Pope felt the need for a shower. He excused himself outside the door to Tonto Waters's room and went to take care of that.

Refreshed, he joined Tonto in the Carousel Lounge. Waters had two shot glasses and a beer lined up in front of him. "That don't look good," Marino greeted the chief.

"I don't feel good. Where did Lailey get that creep?"

"I wish I knew. If he is who he says he is, his testimony will be believed without a doubt. I'm not going to say we're going to find a way to compromise him. I . . . just don't know."

"You're a lot of fuckin' help . . . sir."

Marino struggled to put on a confident face. "Hey, what happened to Pope?"

Waters flushed. "I'd just insulted you, sir. That sort of canceled my right to be familiar, sir."

"Cut the crap, Chief. Let me relieve you of one of those shots. Believe me, I need it." Pope grabbed a glass quickly and downed it. Then he signaled for a beer and another bourbon. "I feel like getting shit-faced drunk. What about you?"

"If it would help any. Where do we go from here?"

"I don't know. I can't reach Andrews. I have no idea what he got from Slater, and Slater is gone from Saigon."

"We might as well get blown out of our minds. But

that would make a mess out of tomorrow, wouldn't it?''

"You got that right.''

"Then we'll down these and grab chow, okay, Pope?''

"Might as well.'' He could think of nothing better to do.

When the trial resumed the next morning, CDR Quade called a succession of CID agents who had interviewed Tom Waters, Hang Jung Minh, and a number of people who had seen Tonto in the presence of Eloise Daladier. Their testimony proved not to be damaging in and of it-self, but added credence to what the Viet Cong officer had said. Quade couched his questions in a manner to make the answers have a damning effect.

"Now, Agent Walker,'' he said at one point. "At any time during your interview with the accused did you ask him if he was guilty?''

"No, sir. It is our policy to try to build a rapport with the suspect, get him to feel we are on his side. Direct accusations tend to build a defensive posture.''

"Did you ever tell him that he was a liar?''

"No, sir. Again, it would tend to break down the intimacy between the suspect and the interviewer.''

"So at no time did he make an admission of guilt?''

"Not to me, sir. And the summary of other agents' interviews does not indicate that he made such a statement to any of them.''

"Is it easy to break down a seasoned combat veteran's resistance?''

"Not in my experience, sir.''

"You are familiar with the record of the accused?''

"Yes, sir. It's an impressive combat background.''

"He's a tough man, would you say?''

"Yes, sir. One of the toughest I've ever interviewed.''

"And he didn't once admit his guilt?''

"Object. Asked and answered.''

"I'll allow it." Judge Benson's impartiality had apparently been bent by this succession of testimony.

"No, sir. He never said he had done anything wrong. To the contrary, he constantly maintained his innocence."

"But there were inconsistences to his story?"

"Yes, sir. In my evaluation he proved evasive as to how many times and where he had met with Miss Daladier. In my estimation he seemed not too clear of what he was charged with."

"Thank you, Agent Walker. I have nothing more."

"Nothing for the defense," Lt. Marino responded. Tonto shot him a worried glance, and he added, "Subject to recall."

"Then I think we will take a short recess. Be back here in fifteen minutes."

Out in the crowded hallway, Lieutenant Marino saw a familiar head and set of shoulders covered by tiger-stripe camouflage fatigues. The head wore a green beret. Surprise and relief registered on his face as he surged forward and called out a name.

"Bill Andrews."

"Yeah. It's me. You're sure hard to get ahold of."

"*I'm hard to* . . . Hell, man, I've been burning up the phone line to your compound trying to get ahold of you. What do you have for me?"

"Something that will help, I hope." He handed Pope Marino a manila envelope. "Slater really came through."

They spoke inconsequentially while visiting the vending machines, where they gulped down bitter coffee. While he munched a stale Danish, Pope opened the flap and drew out the papers within the envelope. He read them with mounting excitement. For the first time since the court-martial began, Marino's face wore a smile.

"I think we've got something here. You did a four-oh job, Bill. I'll thank you properly later."

CHAPTER 27 _____

WHEN JUDGE Benson called the court to order, Lt. Carl Marino rose from his chair. Ignoring the brown envelope flat on the desk before him, he addressed the bench. "Your Honor, I'd like a sidebar."

"I hope this is important, Counsel."

"It is, sir. Permission to approach?"

"All right, Government's Counsel?"

When the three counsels huddled with the judge, Pope Marino pressed his case. "I wish at this time to recall Lieutenant Commander Lailey."

"I have another witness to call, Your Honor," Quade protested.

"I did reserve the right to recall for cross when I had the need. I do at this time, and I think it will clear up this entire farce. No disrespect to the court, Your Honor," he hastily added.

"I understand." Judge Benson raised his voice. "Bailiff, please summon Lieutenant Commander Lailey." Then to the panel. "We'll recess again, I'm afraid. For half an hour."

"What do you have up your sleeve, Marino?" Erwin Quade demanded.

Pope smiled and waggled a hand at shoulder height. "Hide and watch, Commander. I'm gonna bust your little bubble."

*   *   *

This time, frowns furrowed the brows of the panel when they filed in. They seated themselves, and two poured water from metal pitchers. When Judge Benson entered with his usual jaunty pace, he, too, was scowling. He rapped once with a gavel.

"Let's get on with this."

Lieutenant Marino rose. "I call Lieutenant Commander Lailey to the stand."

Lailey finally entered and took his place. The judge bent toward him. "I remind you, Lieutenant Commander, that you are still under oath."

"Yes, sir."

"Proceed, Counselor."

After questioning Lailey on his previous testimony, Lieutenant Marino came quickly to his point. "Now, I ask you this. Other than the questionable testimony given by one of the enemy, do you have any confirmation or physical evidence that either Chief Thomas Waters or Eloise Daladier are agents of the Viet Cong intelligence network, the intelligence service of North Vietnam, or of the KGB?"

LCDR Lailey looked pained. "No. I regret to say we do not. But it's obvious on the face of it that they were spying."

"Did you or anyone from ONI, the CID, or the CIA make any effort to discover if either Waters or Daladier have any connections whatsoever with any intelligence service, other than the enemy's?"

Lailey looked even more uncomfortable. "It was not deemed necessary to look into friendly or allied nations' intelligence operations, if that's what you are getting at."

"Your Honor, where is this going?" Quade interrupted to give his witness a chance to recover himself.

"I quite agree, Counsel. Where are you headed, Lieutenant?"

"I'll connect it right now, Your Honor." He walked to the table and picked up the envelope given him by Capt. Bill Andrews. "Permission to approach?"

"Come."

Lieutenant Marino walked to the bench. "Because of the sensitive nature of the material contained in this envelope, Your Honor, I feel it necessary to have its contents unrevealed to any others present, and reviewed by the court only."

"I have a right to see those," Quade blurted with indignation.

"Do you have a Top Secret clearance, Commander Quade?" Lieutenant Marino demanded.

"Uh—no. I don't."

"I do, and Chief Waters does, and during the recess I ascertained that the Judge does. Therefore, you have no need to know."

Judge Benson extended his hand and accepted the envelope. For a long four minutes, he perused the contents, his eyebrows rising higher with each sentence he read. At last, he sighed, returned the pages to the folder, and handed it to Marino. "Go ahead, if you wish."

"Thank you, Your Honor. Now, where were we? Oh, I had just asked if you had made any effort to determine if Miss Daladier or Chief Waters were connected to any friendly intelligence service. And you answered that you didn't deem it necessary. Well, Lieutenant Commander Lailey, too bad you did not. Because, if you had done so, you would have found out that Eloise Daladier is indeed a spy."

A gasp came from one of the panel and another was seized with a violent coughing fit. Pope Marino waited them out. "Yes, she is a spy. Or rather a more polite term would be an intelligence agent. She is an agent of the *Deuxième Bureau*—French Intelligence. Her assignment is confidential, though the French government and the

CIA have vouched for her. The documents the court just read assure us that she is not involved in espionage involving United States Armed Forces, in Vietnam or anywhere.'' He paused for a long, tension-fraught moment. ''I have no further questions of this witness.''

''Redirect?'' the judge asked through a fleeting smile.

''N-no, sir, Your Honor.''

''A motion from defense?''

''Not at this time, Your Honor. I know it is vexing to keep delaying this proceeding, but I do want to call one witness to corroborate what you have seen.''

''Who is that?''

''Jason Slater.''

Judge Benson sighed. ''Very well. Call your witness.''

''It may take a while, Your Honor. I left a message at his office to come here if he gets back to Saigon in time.''

''Then find out,'' the judge snapped.

Twenty minutes later, Jason Slater advised the bailiff of his presence. Hastily the court assembled. Marino called his witness and swore him in.

To the request for his name, occupation, and identity number Slater responded, ''I am Jason Edward Slater. I am station chief for the Central Intelligence Agency here in Saigon. I am not permitted to reveal my Agency identity number.''

''We understand, Mr. Slater,'' the Judge broke in to say. ''Go on.''

Quickly, Lieutenant Marino ran Slater through the information contained in only his written statement, carefully avoiding what the Second Bureau case officer at the French Consulate had written. He verified every detail of Eloise Daladier's status. Marino thanked him and turned him over to Quade.

''No questions.''

''*Now* I have a motion.''

''I'm sure I know what it is,'' Judge Benson replied.

"I move that all charges and specifications against my client and Miss Daladier be dismissed. In as much as she is not spying on us, then Chief Waters cannot be an accessory. He is only what he is—a SEAL, and a damned good one."

"I regret that it isn't so easy. This must be given to the panel to decide." After giving the necessary instructions and sending out the panel, he turned back to the legal officers awaiting him. "This court stands recessed until tomorrow morning."

"I thought it would be all over with that." Tonto Waters shook his head in confusion.

"So did I. It's this new system, I suppose. I still don't understand most of it. I'm sure I made procedural errors that the judge let slide. Hell, Tonto, I'm not a lawyer."

Jason Slater came up to them then. "Who is the little gook in the witness room?"

"A VC cadre named Hang Jung Minh. Why?"

"No, it's not. I thought I knew him. But only from photographs. His name is Maxim Maximovich Yoriko. He's KGB."

"What!" Pope exploded. "Why would they be mixing into this?"

"I don't know. What is even more puzzling to me is why would they take the risk of compromising one of their most effective agents? I don't like this at all. What did he pull anyway?"

Pope Marino told him. Slater whistled softly. "Well, this is going to have to be taken care of. I'll see the Judge tomorrow morning before court convenes."

"What for? It looks like they are going to cut Tonto loose."

Slater gave him a grim smile. "I want to inform the Judge of what the situation is, and that the false witness has been terminated with extreme prejudice."

Marino raised both eyebrows. "Jesus. You play that hard of ball?"

"With one like him, yes. Be seeing you at the victory party."

Early the next morning, when the panel filed into their seats and sat, Judge Benson turned to them. "Have you completed your deliberations?"

Captain Spence, the president of the court rose. "We have, Your Honor."

"Before you render your verdict, I must inform you that one of the witnesses called here was flying under false colors. The man identified as a Viet Cong cadre lieutenant was in fact a Soviet citizen and an agent of the Soviet KGB. His testimony must be considered as entirely false."

"Pardon me, Your Honor, you said 'was.' What does that mean?" CDR Quade asked.

"Comrade Yoriko of the KGB met with an unfortunate accident last night. He is quite dead."

Quade turned deathly pale. "I . . . see." *How much of this would smear off on him*? Quade wondered in desperation.

"That doesn't make any difference to us, Your Honor," Captain Spence declared.

"Then may we have your verdict?"

"We find the accused not guilty. By voice vote and separate secret ballot we have all put our hand to the finding of not guilty."

"I want to thank you and congratulate you for a job well-done. In my opinion you reached the proper and only possible verdict. The accused is discharged with prejudice."

Unable to contain himself longer in this sea of unknown terms, Tonto blurted out, "Huh? What's that mean?"

Judge Benson looked kindly at him. "It means that these charges can never be brought up against you again."

"About time, sir. Uh—thank you, sir."

Laughing, Judge Benson dismissed the court.

Barry Lailey put his fist through the wall of the BOQ at the MACV compound when he learned of the verdict. He wanted to howl, to roar, to get his hands on the neck of Chief Tom Waters and squeeze the life out of him. What really hurt most was the blistering reprimand he received from Commander Erwin Quade.

"Why?" he bleated when Quade calmed down. "You said you needed a reliable witness, and I got one for you. Remember, he came to me, not the other way around."

"Because he was KGB, you incompetent asshole!" Quade roared.

Barry Lailey went white at that. Now, with the stinging humiliation still fresh in his mind, he wanted nothing more than to get drunk. Rip-roaring drunk. He had to do something to calm the burning in his belly. He went to the phone in the hall and placed a call.

"Ralph," he barked into the mouthpiece when Major Ralph Harkness answered in the Provost Marshal's office in Saigon. "You able to get away? I want to get good and drunk, and I may need a friend in high places to cover my ass."

"What's wrong now?"

"That goddamned Marino got to me again. I had one of his SEALs up for a general court, maybe even to hang, and somehow the son of a bitch came out smelling like a rose. I'll be down there in twenty minutes, tell you all about it."

He rang off and changed into civilian clothes.

The victory party began in the Navy Bar on Truman Key and moved on to the Special Forces NCO club at the

SPECWARMACV compound at Tan Son Nhut. Jason Slater ordered a pitcher of beer each for himself, Carl Marino, Tom Waters, and Bill Andrews. After long, appreciative swallows, Marino rounded on the CIA station chief, his natural skepticism toward spooks rising to the fore.

"Why did you keep me in the dark for so long?"

"Buddy, they pulled the rug out from under me on this one. Changing the trial date did the worst. I wasn't even in town."

"Where were you?" Marino demanded.

Slater lowered his voice to a near-whisper. "I was up North."

"The DMZ?"

"No, North-North."

"Uh—guys as high up as you take that kind of risk?"

"Not by choice, believe me. I like running the store well enough, and when I want a little up close and personal action I know I can always count on you SEALs. But, sneakin' and peekin' in the enemy's homeland is not my idea of fun and games. Speaking of which, we've got wind of a little something that might be right up your alley."

Marino gave him a look of mock horror. "Save it. Right now, we're not in the least interested. What I'm gonna do is guzzle beer until I have a nice little glow, then buy you and Bill the biggest steaks in Saigon. Then we're headed back to Tre Noc."

"And I'll eat it, too," Slater chortled.

"What about Eloise?" Tonto asked. He had been asking since they left the court-martial chambers. "I thought she would be here."

"Obviously she's not," Slater answered blandly. "Since he handled that end of it, I'll let Bill here answer that."

"The French got her out of the hands of the MPs in

Saigon about a week ago. She's been at their consulate since then. I have no idea why she's not here. And, no, she's not been harmed in any way." He nodded to Tonto Waters and Pope Marino. "I believe you two are acquainted with a certain Major Ralph Harkness? I understand that he bellowed like a gored ox when she was taken from his clutches."

"How'd they manage to get her out without revealing who—or is it what?—she is?" Tonto asked.

Mischief alight in his eyes, Bill Andrews peered at Tonto Waters. "You mean you're a Chief Petty Officer and you haven't memorized the UCMJ?"

"I try to keep clear of Military Justice, if you please, sir. I've always considered it a contradiction in terms anyway. What's that got to do with gettin' Eloise sprung from the Military Police?"

"There's an article in the UCMJ regarding foreign nationals. They have the right to be detained by their embassy or consulate. That got her free of Harkness."

"Well, I'm glad. Only . . . where is she?"

Their laughter held no meanness.

A happy, smiling Eloise Daladier was on hand to greet the helicopter that returned Lieutenant Marino and Chief Waters to Tre Noc the next morning. She thanked Pope for saving her and promised to meet them later for drinks at Phon Bai. After checking in, Pope and Tonto headed directly for the hotel.

Once seated with their choice of beverage, Tonto noted a hint of sadness behind the cheery facade Eloise wore. He asked her about it.

"I am afraid our time together is going to be far too short. In fact, we won't be able to see each other for a long while after this weekend."

"Why is that?"

Eloise made a face. "Your Lieutenant Commander

Lailey's little fiasco has been too much of an embarrassment to my employers. They have decided to send me away for a while."

"You mean *Le Monde*?" Tonto asked with a wink.

Eloise stuck out her tongue, a most unladylike gesture. *"You know who I mean,"* she admonished him. Their reunion turned serious for everyone then. Tentatively, Tonto asked if he would ever see her again.

"Maybe. Though we do have a few days left before I have to go."

Tonto only nodded, cynically certain that if anything could happen to mess up their plans, it would.

Kovietski/Rudinov received two bits of bad news simultaneously. First off, the skilled team of *Mokryee Della* agents he had sent to deal with Lt. (jg) Cyrus Rhodes had so far been unable to recruit anyone in the hospital at Binh Thuy and had not penetrated the facility themselves. It would take time, they assured him. Sometimes he believed that those Wet Affairs people were entirely too cautious.

His second piece of misfortune struck closer to home. The Saigon *residentura* had messaged him that Maxim Yorkio's body had been found in an alley in a squalid section of Saigon, shot twice in the back of the head. That blow staggered him. One more, he cursed as he drank deeply of a glass of vodka. One more to hold Lt. Carl Marino accountable for.

Perhaps he should send the *Mokryee Della* after the SEAL officer? The prospect clung to him for two long days.

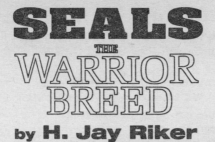